ALSO BY MICHEL HOUELLEBECQ

FICTION

Serotonin

Submission

The Map and the Territory

The Possibility of an Island

Platform

The Elementary Particles

Whatever

POETRY

Unreconciled: Poems 1991–2013

NONFICTION

Public Enemies: Dueling Writers Take On Each Other and the World (with Bernard-Henri Lévy)

H. P. Lovecraft: Against the World, Against Life

annihilation

annihilation

{A NOVEL}

Michel Houellebecq

TRANSLATED FROM THE FRENCH BY
SHAUN WHITESIDE

FARRAR, STRAUS AND GIROUX
NEW YORK

Farrar, Straus and Giroux
120 Broadway, New York 10271

The quotations on pages 182–184 and 483 are from *Wicca:*
A Guide for the Solitary Practitioner
by Scott Cunningham, Llewellyn Publications, 1989.

Library of Congress Cataloging-in-Publication Data
Names: Houellebecq, Michel, author. | Whiteside, Shaun, translator.
Title: Annihilation : a novel / Michel Houellebecq ; translated from the French by
Shaun Whiteside.
Other titles: Anéantir. English
Description: First American edition. | New York : Farrar, Straus and Giroux, 2024.
Identifiers: LCCN 2024024692 | ISBN 9780374608422 (hardcover)
Subjects: LCSH: Presidents—France—Election—History—21st century—Fiction. |
Cyberterrorism—Fiction. | LCGFT: Political fiction. | Thrillers (Fiction) | Novels.
Classification: LCC PQ2668.O77 A8313 2024 | DDC 843/.914—dc23/eng/20240610
LC record available at https://lccn.loc.gov/2024024692

www.fsgbooks.com
Follow us on social media at @fsgbooks

1   3   5   7   9   10   8   6   4   2

annihilation

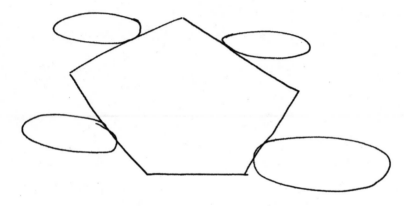

one

1

Particularly if you're single, some Mondays in late November or early December make you feel as if you're in death's waiting room. The summer holidays are a distant memory, the new year still far in the future: the proximity of nothingness is unfamiliar.

On Monday 23 November, Bastien Doutremont decided to take the metro to work. Alighting at Porte de Clichy, he found himself facing the inscription that some colleagues had been talking about over the previous few days. It was just after ten o'clock in the morning; the platform was deserted.

He'd been interested in the graffiti on the Paris metro since he was a teenager. He often took pictures of it with his ancient iPhone – by now they must have been up to generation 23, but he had stopped at 11. He classified the photographs by stations and lines; he had plenty of files on his computer devoted to them. It was a hobby, one might say, but he preferred the term *pastime*, which sounded gentler but was in essence more brutal. Moreover, one of his favourite bits of graffiti, in precise, italic letters, which he had discovered in the middle of a long white corridor at Place d'Italie, energetically proclaimed, 'Time will not pass!'

The posters of the 'RATP Poetry' initiative, with their display of witless nonsense that for a time swamped every Paris station, even spreading by capillary action to certain carriages, had prompted many reactions of deranged fury among passengers. Thus he had

3

been able to collect, at Victor Hugo station: 'I claim the honorific title of King of Israel. I cannot do otherwise.' At Voltaire, the graffiti was more brutal and more consumed with anxiety: 'Definitive message to all telepaths, to all Stéphanes who tried to disturb my life: the answer is NO!'

The inscription at Porte de Clichy wasn't a piece of graffiti in the strict sense of the term: in huge fat letters, two metres high, written in black paint, it stretched the full length of the platform for trains heading towards Gabriel Péri-Asnières-Gennevilliers. Even by moving to the opposite platform he had been unable to get the whole thing in the frame, but he had managed to work out the text in its entirety: 'Survival of monopolies/In the heart of the metropolis'. There was nothing very troubling, or even very explicit, about it; and yet it was the kind of thing that might arouse the interest of the DGSI – the General Directorate of Internal Security – like all the mysterious and obscurely threatening communications that had been filling the public space for some years, which could not be attributed to any clearly identifiable political groupuscule, and of which the internet messages that it was his job to interpret right now were both the most spectacular and the most alarming example.

He found the report from the lexicology lab on his desk; it had arrived with the morning's first mail delivery. The lab's examination of the messages that had been accepted as genuine had allowed him to isolate fifty-three letters – alphabetic characters, not ideograms; the spacing had allowed them to divide the letters into words. Then they had set about establishing a one-to-one correspondence with an existing alphabet, and had made their first attempt with French. Unexpectedly, it appeared to correspond: if one added to the twenty-six basic letters the accented characters and the ones with a hyphen or a cedilla, you ended up with forty-two signs.

4

Traditionally, one then added eleven punctuation marks, which provided a total of fifty-three signs. They were therefore confronted with a problem of classical decoding, which consisted of establishing a biunivocal correspondence between the characters in the messages and those of the French alphabet in the broadest sense. Unfortunately, after two weeks of effort, they had found themselves confronted by a total impasse: it had not proved possible to establish a correspondence using any known coding system; it was the first time this had happened since the laboratory had been established. Distributing messages on the internet that no one could read was plainly an absurd undertaking; they were obviously intended for someone, but for whom?

He got up, made himself an espresso and walked to the bay window holding his cup. A blinding light shimmered on the walls of the High Court. He had never found any particular aesthetic merit in that unstructured juxtaposition of gigantic glass-and-steel polyhedrons dominating a bleak and muddy landscape. In any case, the goal pursued by its designers was not beauty, or even really harmony, but rather the display of a certain technical skill – as if the most important thing in the end was to ensure that it was visible to any notional extra-terrestrials. Bastien had not known the historic buildings at 36 Quai des Orfèvres, and did not in consequence feel any nostalgia for them, unlike his older colleagues. But it had to be acknowledged that this district of the 'new Clichy' was moving day by day towards an urban disaster pure and simple; the shopping centre, the cafés, the restaurants set out in the original plans had never come into existence, and relaxing outside of the work context during the day had, in this new site, become almost impossible; on the other hand there was no problem with parking.

About fifty metres below, an Aston Martin DB11 drove into the visitors' car park; Fred had arrived. It was a curious trait that a geek like Fred, whom one might have expected to own a Tesla, should have remained loyal to the outmoded charms of the combustion engine – sometimes he spent whole minutes daydreaming as he basked in the murmur of his V12. At last he got out, slamming the door behind him. Allowing for the security procedures at reception, he would get there in ten minutes. He hoped that Fred might have some news; in fact it was his last hope that he might find out about any kind of progress at their next meeting.

Seven years ago, when they had been taken on as contract workers by the DGSI – on a salary that was more than comfortable for a pair of young men without so much as a degree or any professional experience to their names – their interview had been merely a demonstration of their ability to penetrate different websites. In front of fifteen agents from BEFTI, the Brigade d'enquêtes sur les fraudes aux technologies de l'information, the police cybercrime department and other technical services of the Ministry of the Interior who had come together for the occasion, they had explained how, once they had got into the RNIPP, the National Register for the Identification of Individuals, they could, with a simple click, deactivate or reactivate a health insurance card; they had explained what they would do in order to get inside the government taxation site, and from there, very simply, find out the total sum of declared revenue. They had even shown them how – the procedure was more cumbersome, because the codes were changed regularly – once they'd made their way into FNAEG (Fichier national automatisé des empreintes génétiques), the national DNA database, they could modify or destroy a DNA profile, even in the case of an individual who had already been sentenced. The only thing they had thought it wise to pass over in silence was their incursion into the site of Chooz nuclear power station. They had taken control of the system for forty-eight hours, and could have launched an emergency stoppage procedure in the reactor – depriving several French *départements* of electricity. They would not, however, have been able to provoke a major nuclear incident – to enter the core of the reactor they still needed a 4096-bit decryption key that they hadn't yet cracked. Fred had a new piece of decoding software that he'd tried to launch; but by common accord they had decided they might have gone too far that day; they had come back out, erasing all trace of their intrusion, and had never mentioned it again – not to anybody, not even between themselves. That night, Bastien had had a nightmare in which he was being chased by monstrous figures consisting of assemblages of decomposing new-born babies; at the end of his dream, the core of the reactor had appeared to him. They had allowed several days to pass before seeing each other again, they hadn't even spoken on the phone, and it was probably from that moment that they had first imagined putting themselves at the service of the state. As teenagers their heroes had been Julian Assange and Edward Snowden; collaborating with the authorities hadn't been the obvious next choice of career but the context of the mid-2010s was quite an unusual one. After a number of Islamist atrocities, the population of France had begun to support, and even to feel a certain affection for, its police and army.

Fred, however, had not renewed his contract with the DGSI at the end of the first year; instead he had gone off to set up Distorted Visions, a company specializing in digital special effects and synthetic imaging systems. Basically Fred, unlike Bastien, had never really been a hacker; he had never really experienced the pleasure, not unlike that of slalom skiing, which Bastien felt when he managed to negotiate his way around a sequence of firewalls, or the megalomaniac sense of intoxication that filled him when he launched an attack by brute force, mobilizing thousands of zombie computers to break a particularly cunning code. Fred, like his teacher Julian Assange, was above all a born programmer, capable of mastering within a few days the most sophisticated languages that were constantly appearing on the market, and he had used that aptitude to devise thoroughly innovative form- and texture-generation algorithms. Much is made of France's excellence in the field of space or aeronautics, but less credit is given to special digital effects. Fred's company's most regular clients were the big Hollywood blockbusters; within five or six years of its establishment, it was ranked third in the world.

When he got to his office before slumping on the sofa, Doutremont knew at once that it was going to be bad news.

'Actually, Bastien, I don't have anything very encouraging to tell you,' Fred confirmed straight away. 'OK, let me talk to you about the first message. I know it's not the one you're interested in; but still, the video's a strange one.'

The DGSI hadn't spotted the first pop-up window; it had essentially borrowed from airline ticket and hotel reservation websites. Like the next two, it consisted of a juxtaposition of pentagons, circles and lines of text in an indecipherable alphabet. When you clicked anywhere inside the window, the sequence was set off. The view was filmed from an overhang or a static balloon; it was a static shot about ten minutes long. A vast meadow of tall grass stretched to the horizon, and the sky was perfectly clear – the landscape was suggestive of certain states of the American West. The wind formed huge straight lines on the surface of the grass; then they came together to form triangles and polygons. Everything calmed down and the surface relaxed again, as far as the eye could see; then the wind blew again and the polygons reappeared, slowly marking out the plain into infinity. It was beautiful, but it wasn't particularly troubling: the sound of the wind hadn't been recorded, and the geometry of the whole developed in total silence.

'Recently we've made a fair number of scenes of storms at sea for war films,' Fred said. 'You can model a grass surface of that size pretty much the same way as you would model an area of water of equivalent size – not the ocean, something more like a big lake. And what I can tell you with certainty is that the geometric figures that form in this video are impossible. You would need to imagine that the wind was blowing in three different directions at the same time – and sometimes in four. So I have no doubt: it's a synthetic image. But what really intrigues me is that you can enlarge the image as much as you want, and the synthetic blades of grass still look like real blades of grass; and normally that's impossible to do. No two blades of grass are identical in nature; they all have irregularities, little flaws, a specific genetic signature. We've enlarged a thousand of them, choosing them at random within the image: they're all different. I'm willing to bet that the millions of blades of grass that appear in the video are all different; it's extraordinary, it's a crazy piece of work; we might be able to do it at Distorted, but for a sequence of that length it would take us months of calculation.'

2

In the second video, Bruno Juge, Minister of the Economy and Finance – who, since the beginning of the five-year term, was also Budget Minister – was standing, hands tied behind his back, in the middle of a moderate-sized garden that must have been to the rear of a mansion. The hilly surrounding countryside suggested the landscape of the Suisse Normande and must have been verdant in springtime, but at this time of year the trees were bare, so it was probably late autumn or early winter. The minister was dressed in a pair of dark suit trousers and a short-sleeved white shirt, worn without a tie and too light for the season – he had goose bumps.

In the next shot he was wearing a long black robe and a conical hat, also black, which made him look like one of the penitents on Holy Week in Seville; the same type of headgear had also been worn as a sign of public humiliation by those sentenced to death under the Inquisition. Two men dressed the same way – except that their hoods had holes at eye level – were gripping him under the arms to drag him away.

Once they had reached the end of the garden, they violently ripped the pointed hood from the head of the minister, who blinked several times to become accustomed to the light. They were at the end of a little grassy hillock with a guillotine on its summit. Bruno Juge's face at the sight of the instrument showed no hint of fear, just slight surprise.

While one of the two men made him kneel, positioning his head in the lunette and applying the lock mechanism, the second fitted the blade in the mouton, the heavy cast-iron weight designed to stabilize the fall. With a rope passed through a pulley the two men raised the device consisting of the mouton and the blade to the crossbar. Gradually, Bruno Juge seemed afflicted by great sadness, but a sadness more general in nature.

After several seconds during which the minister was seen briefly closing his eyes, then opening them again, one of the men activated the release mechanism. The blade came down in two or three seconds, the head was severed with one blow, and a stream of blood flowed into the basin as the head rolled down the grassy slope before coming to a standstill right in front of the camera, a few inches from the lens. The minister's eyes, wide open, now showed enormous surprise.

The pop-up window and the video linked to it had appeared on administrative information sites such as *www.impots.gouv.fr* and *www.servicepublic.fr*. Bruno Juge had spoken about it first of all to his colleague in the Ministry of the Interior, and it was he who had alerted the DGSI. Then they had informed the prime minister, and the case had gone all the way to the president. No official statement had been given to the press. So far, all attempts to delete the video had been in vain – the window reappeared, posted from a different IP address, after several hours, sometimes several minutes.

'I can tell you,' said Fred, 'that we have watched this video for hours, we have enlarged it as far as we possibly can, particularly the shot of the decapitated torso, at the moment when the blood poured from the carotid artery. Normally, if you enlarge something enough you start to see geometrical regularities appearing, artificial micro-figures – most of the time you can even guess the equation the guy used. Here there's nothing at all: you can enlarge it all you like, it remains chaotic and irregular, exactly like a real cut. I was

11

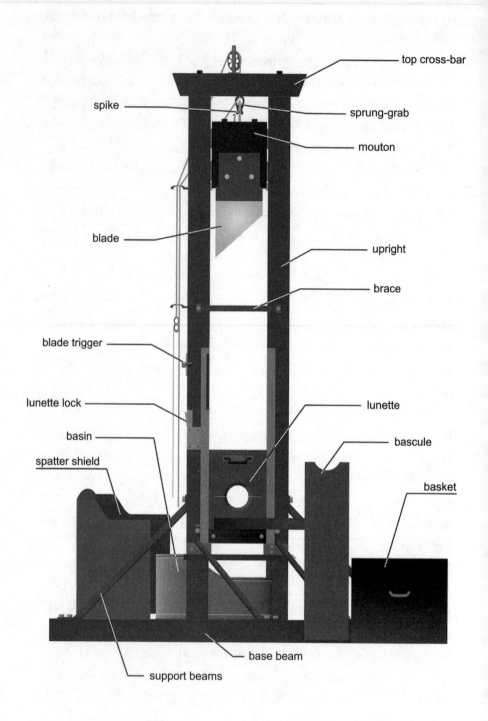

top cross-bar

spike

sprung-grab

mouton

blade

upright

brace

blade trigger

lunette lock

lunette

basin

bascule

spatter shield

basket

base beam

support beams

so intrigued by it that I talked to Bustamante, the boss of Digital Commando.'

'But they're your competitors, aren't they?' Doutremont said.

'Yes, we're competitors if you like, but we get on, and we've even worked on films together. We don't exactly excel in the same fields: we're better than them in terms of imaginary buildings, generating virtual crowds and so on. But when it comes to gory special effects, organic monsters, mutilation, decapitation, they're better than we are. And Bustamante was as staggered as I was: he hadn't a clue how it could have been done. If we'd had to give a statement under oath in a court of law, and of course if it hadn't been a minister but a man in the street, I think we'd have sworn that it was a real decapitation . . .'

There was a silence. Bastien looked at the bay window, and let his eye wander over the huge planes of glass and steel. The building was definitely impressive, even frightening in good weather; but it was probably necessary, for a high court, to inspire fear in the populace.

'So, we come to the third video. OK, you've seen it like me,' Fred went on. 'It's a long dolly shot in some railway tunnels. Quite creepy, with yellow tones dominating. The soundtrack is classic industrial metal. It's obviously CGI, there are no real railway tunnels ten metres across, or diesel engines fifty metres high. It's well done, even very well done, it's really good CGI, but in the end it's less startling than the other videos, it could have been made at Distorted, two weeks' work, I would say.'

Bastien looked at him again. 'What's worrying about the third message isn't its content, it's the way it was disseminated. This time they didn't attack a government website, they aimed at Google and Facebook; people who essentially know how to defend themselves. And what's baffling is the violence and the suddenness of the attack. In my view their botnet must control millions of zombie machines at the very least.'

13

Fred gave a start. It sounded impossible, something orders of magnitude beyond anything they'd ever encountered.

'I know,' Bastien went on, 'but things have changed, and in a sense they've become easier for pirates. People go on buying computers out of habit, but these days they only access the web by smartphone, and leave their computers on standby. Right now, in the world, you've got hundreds of millions, maybe billions of computers in a dormant state, just waiting to be controlled by a bot.'

'I'm sorry not to be able to help you, Bastien.'

'You have helped me. I have a meeting at seven with Paul Raison, the guy from the Finance Ministry. He's at the minister's office, he's my contact on the file; now I know what I need to say to him. One: we're dealing with an attack carried out by people unknown. Two: they're capable of creating digital special effects that the best specialists in the field consider impossible. Three: the power of the calculation that they're able to mobilize is unimaginable, it's far beyond anything we've ever seen before. Four: their motives are unknown.'

A new silence fell between them.

'What's this guy Raison like?' Fred asked at last.

'He's OK. Serious, no sense of humour, even quite austere, but he's reasonable. People know him at the DGSI, in fact – or at least they remember his father, Édouard Raison. He spent his whole career in the department, he started in the old General Information section, almost forty years ago. He was well respected; he dealt with some really big cases, cases at the highest level, directly concerning state security. In short, his son grew up in the business. He might have gone to the right schools, he's been a finance inspector, usual career, but he knows the special nature of our work, and he isn't unthinkingly hostile to us.'

3

The sky is low, grey, compact. The light seems to come not from above, but from the mantle of snow covering the ground; it's fading inexorably, probably because evening is falling. Areas of frost crystallizing, the branches of the trees creak. Snowflakes swirl among people who walk past without seeing one another, their faces hardening and wrinkling, little points of wild light dancing in their eyes. Some are going home, but before they get there they understand that their loved ones are going to die, or are probably already dead. Paul becomes aware that the planet is dying of cold; at first it's only a hypothesis, but gradually it becomes a certainty. The government has ceased to exist, it has fled, or it has vanished of its own accord, hard to say. Then Paul is on a train, he's decided to go via Poland, but death is starting to fill the compartments, even though their walls are lined with thick fur. Then he understands that no one is driving the train, which is hurtling at full speed across a deserted plain. The temperature keeps falling: -40°, -50°, -60°. . .

It was the cold that dragged Paul from his dream; it was twenty-seven minutes past midnight. Every evening the heating was turned off at nine in the ministry buildings, quite late, in fact, given that most people in the government offices stop work much earlier. He had had to go to sleep on the sofa in his office just after the guy from the DGSI left. He had looked worried, personally worried, about his own fate – as if Paul was going to complain to his superiors, ask that he be taken off the inquiry or something of the kind; he had no intention of doing any such thing. In any case, since the third video the case had gone global. This time Google was the direct target: the biggest company on the planet, which worked hand in hand with the NSA. The DGSI might be kept up to date with the first results, out of politeness and because the case, inexplicably, had initially involved a French minister; but the Americans had access to far greater resources than their French counterparts, and would soon gain total control over the file. Deciding to punish that guy from the DGSI would not only be unfair, it would be stupid: the world was no longer like his father's, when dangers were local; now, almost immediately, they assumed a global dimension.

For now, Paul was hungry. He was going to go back to his place, it was the only thing to do, he said to himself, before remembering that there was nothing to eat at home, that the shelf in the fridge reserved for him was desperately empty, and the very expression 'his place' carried a whiff of deranged optimism.

Their division of the fridge was probably the most pointed symbol of the breakdown of their life as a couple. When Paul, a young official in the budget department, met Prudence, a young official in the treasury department, something else had undeniably happened in the first few minutes; perhaps not in the first few seconds, the term love at first sight or *coup de foudre* would have been an overstatement, but it had only taken a few minutes, certainly less than five, more or less the duration of a song, in fact. Prudence's father had been a fan of John Lennon in his youth, hence her first name, she would reveal a few weeks later. 'Dear Prudence' was certainly not the best Beatles song, and more generally Paul had never seen the 'White Album' as the summit of their career, and the fact remained that he had never managed to

16

call Prudence by her first name. In their tenderest moments he called her 'my darling', or sometimes 'my love'.

She had never cooked, at any point in their shared life, it didn't seem like part of her status. Like Paul she was a graduate of the *grandes écoles*, like him she was an inspector of finances and, in fact, there was something a bit off about being an inspector of finance at a stove. They were in complete agreement about value added tax, and were both so disinclined to smile engagingly, to charm, in a word, that it was probably that bond that had allowed their idyll to take shape in the course of interminable meetings organized by the fiscal legislation department, late into the night, most often in Room B87. Their sexual understanding had been good straight away, seldom ecstatic perhaps, but most couples don't ask that much, and the maintenance of any kind of sexual activity in an established couple is in itself a real success, the exception more than the rule, as most well-informed people (journalists on notable women's magazines, authors of realist novels) will bear witness, and that did not even apply only to people relatively advanced in years, like Paul and Prudence, who were gently approaching their fifties; for their youngest contemporaries the very idea of a sexual relationship between two autonomous individuals, even if it were to extend only for several minutes, seemed nothing but a dated fantasy, and a regrettable one at that.

On the other hand, the disagreement between Prudence and Paul with regard to food had manifested itself swiftly. For the first few years, however, Prudence, whether moved by love or a similar feeling, had kept her cohabitant supplied with food in line with his tastes, even though these were, in her view, annoyingly conservative. While she did not do the cooking, she did the shopping herself, and took a particular pride in seeking out the best steaks, the best cheeses, the best charcuterie for Paul. The predominantly meaty products then mingled in loving chaos with the organic

17

fruits, cereals and vegetables that constituted her personal diet, along the shelves of their shared refrigerator.

The switch to veganism, which had happened in Prudence's case in 2015, just as the word made its first in the dictionary, would provoke total nutritional warfare, the ravages of which had not been fully bandaged eleven years later, and which the couple now had little chance of surviving.

The first attack launched by Prudence was brutal, absolute and decisive. Returning from Marrakesh, where he had attended a congress of the African Union with the minister of the time, Paul had been surprised to see his refrigerator invaded not only by the usual fruits and vegetables, but by a multitude of strange foodstuffs including seaweed, soybean sprouts and numerous ready-made dishes of the Biozone brand, combining tofu, bulgur, quinoa, spelt and Japanese noodles. None of it struck him as even vaguely edible, and he made this known with a certain acrimony ('There's nothing but shit to eat,' were his exact words). A brief but intense period of negotiation followed, at the end of which Paul was conceded a shelf in the refrigerator on which to keep his 'redneck food' – to use Prudence's term – food that from now on he was to buy himself, with his own money (they had kept separate bank accounts, a detail that may prove significant).

Over the first few weeks, Paul undertook some daring skirmishes; they were vigorously repelled. Each slice of Saint-Nectaire or *pâté en croute* that he deposited in the middle of Prudence's tofu and quinoa was returned within a few hours to its original shelf, when it was not simply thrown in the bin.

Some ten years later, everything had outwardly calmed. In terms of food, Paul settled for his little shelf, which he filled quickly, having gradually given up frequenting local gastronomic artisans and settling instead for the formula, nutritionally synthetic and reliably distributed, of ready-made microwavable dishes. 'You have to eat something,' he repeated to himself sagely over his Monoprix

Gourmet poultry tagine, immersing himself in a kind of morose epicureanism. The poultry had come 'from different countries of the European Union'; it could have been worse, he said to himself, Brazilian chickens no thank you. Little creatures now appeared to him increasingly often during the night; they moved rapidly, they had dark skin and multiple arms.

Since the beginning of the breakdown they had had separate rooms. Sleeping alone is difficult when you have lost the habit, you are cold and frightened; but they had passed that awkward stage a long time ago; they had attained instead a kind of standardized despair.

Their decline as a couple had begun shortly after the joint purchase, which put them in debt for twenty years, of their apartment on Rue Lheureux, on the edge of the Parc de Bercy – a sumptuous duplex with two bedrooms and a magnificent living room, with picture windows overlooking the park. The coincidence was not accidental; an improvement in living conditions often goes hand in hand with a deterioration of reasons for living, and living together in particular. The area was 'better than brilliant', in the view of Indy, his idiot of a sister-in-law, when she visited in the spring of 2017 along with his unfortunate brother. That visit had happily remained the only one, the temptation to strangle Indy had been too powerful and he was not sure he could resist it for a second time.

The area was brilliant, yes, that much was true. Their bedroom, in the days when they shared a bedroom, overlooked the Musée des Arts Forains, the fairground museum, on Avenue des Terroirs de France. About fifty metres away, the street of Cour Saint-Émilion, running laterally across the urban rectangle known under the name of 'Bercy Village', lay winter and summer beneath a cloud of multi-coloured balloons, and featured a sequence of regional restaurants and alternative bistros. There one could reinvent the spirit of childhood as one wished. The park itself displayed the same desire for playful chaos: the plan had been to give vegetables their place, and a pavilion managed by the city council proposed gardening workshops for the residents of the area ('Gardening in Paris is allowed!', according to the slogan decorating its façade).

It was located – and the argument in its favour remained, concrete and solid – a quarter of an hour's walk from the ministry. It was now forty-two minutes past midnight – his pause for reflection, although covering the essence of his adult life, had lasted only a quarter of an hour. If he left now he could be at home at one o'clock in the morning. Or at least at the place where he lived.

4

Turning right just past his office to reach the battery of lifts on the north side of the building, Paul noticed, at the end of the faintly lit long corridor leading to the minister's apartments, a silhouette coming slowly forwards wearing the grey pyjamas of a concentration camp inmate. A few steps further, he recognized him: it was the minister himself. For two months, Bruno Juge had asked to take advantage of his staff accommodation, which had remained practically always unoccupied since the construction of the ministry. While he had not explicitly put it in these terms, he had therefore decided to abandon the marital home, thus putting an end to his twenty-five-year marriage. Paul was unaware of the exact nature of the relationship that Bruno had with his wife – although he imagined them, purely out of empathy among Western men of a similar age and background, to be more or less similar to his own. It was murmured, in the ministry corridors (how did such things end up being murmured in corridors? it was still a mystery to Paul; but murmured they were, without a doubt), that something more sordid, involving repeated marital infidelities – infidelities on the part of his wife – lay at the bottom of the affair. Some witnesses seemed to have caught unmistakable gestures made by Évangéline, the minister's wife, at receptions given at the ministry in previous years. Paul's wife, at least, kept her distance from scandals of this kind. Prudence did not, as far as he knew, have a sex life, and the more austere delights of yoga and transcendental meditation seemed to be enough to provide her with her fulfilment, or more probably they weren't enough, but nothing could have been enough, sex least of all, Prudence was not a *woman made for sex*, at least that was what Paul tried to convince himself, without real success, because he knew deep down that Prudence was made for sex in the same way, and perhaps even more, as most women, that her deepest being would always need sex, and in her case it was heterosexual sex, and even, if he had to be completely precise about it, penetration by a cock. But the sign language of social positioning within the group, however ridiculous and even contemptible it might be, had its role to play, and Prudence had been, in terms of sex as well as vegan food, a kind of pioneer; more and more people were asexual, all the surveys confirmed as much, month after month the percentage of asexual people in the population seemed to be undergoing an increase that was not constant but accelerated; journalists, with their usual liking for approximation and inappropriate scientific terminology, had had no hesitation in calling it exponential, but in fact it was not, the rate of increase was not extreme enough to merit the adjective, but it was very fast nonetheless.

Unlike Prudence and most of her contemporaries, Évangéline had assumed perfectly, and perhaps still did assume, the role of a genuine *hottie*, which could of course only have suited a man like Bruno, smitten above all with the idea of a warm, soft home, well suited to distract him from the power struggles inevitably inherent in the *game of politics*. Their marital problems were, in fact, almost irrelevant.

'Ah, Paul, still here?' Bruno did not seem to be fully awake; his tone was uncertain, slightly lost, but still happy. 'Were you working?'

'No, not really. Not at all, in fact. I went to sleep on my sofa.'

'Ah yes, sofas . . .' He had said the word with glee, as if it were a wonderful invention whose existence he had only recently rediscovered. 'I was sleeping badly,' he went on in a very different tone, 'when I remembered a file. Do you want to come and have a drink at the apartment? We must not allow the Chinese to have a monopoly on rare-earth materials,' he continued almost immediately, when Paul had already joined him. 'Right now I'm busy finalizing an agreement with Lynas, the Australian company – the Australians are tough negotiators, you have no idea; that's fine where yttrium, gadolinium and lanthanum are concerned; but there are still lots of problems, especially with samarium and praseodymium; I'm in touch with Burundi and Russia.'

'Burundi ought to do it,' Paul replied confidently. Burundi was an African country; that was more or less where his knowledge of Burundi stopped; he imagined it must be somewhere near the Congo, because of the phrase 'Congo Burundi', which floated around in a corner of his memory even though he could not connect it with any stable semantic content.

'Burundi has recently established a completely remarkable management team,' Bruno pressed, this time without waiting for an answer.

'I'm a bit hungry,' Paul said, 'in fact I forgot to eat this evening, I mean yesterday evening.'

'Really . . .? I think I still have a sandwich, or a kind of sandwich, which I planned to eat this afternoon. It's not very good, mind you, but it is what it is.'

They stepped inside the staff accommodation, and Bruno turned towards him. 'I forgot, I went out to get a file from my office. Can you wait for me for a moment?'

His ministerial office, the one where he received senior politicians, trade unionists and the directors of large companies, was in a different wing of the building, and it would take him about twenty minutes to get there and back. Bruno had put an extra desk in a little room in his lodgings: a simple board covered with fake-oak melamine, with his laptop computer on it, along with several folders and a printer. He had drawn the curtains, blocking the view of the Seine.

The kitchen was new and sparkling, and seemed never to have been used: there was no washing-up in the sink, and the huge American refrigerator was empty. The marital suite overlooking the river was also unoccupied, and the bed had not been unmade. Bruno seemed to sleep in what must have been a child's bedroom, and the room of an undemanding child at that. It was a little windowless room with grey walls and carpet, furnished only with a single bed and a bedside table.

Paul came back to the dining room–reception room which overlooked the Seine. Through the big bay windows on three sides of the room the view was splendid: the arches of the elevated metro were illuminated, and the traffic was still dense along the Quai d'Austerlitz; the waters of the Seine, given a yellow glow by the street lights, lapped against the piles of the Pont de Bercy. The magnificence of the lighting that bathed the room also suggested something chic and luxurious, like a circle of Parisian society with connections to the world of night-life, elegance, even the visual arts. None of that evoked anything for him, or at least nothing familiar – and it probably didn't for Bruno either. On the eight-seater dining table, covered with a white table-cloth, were a Daunat soft-bread chicken breast and Emmental sandwich, still in its wrapper, and a Tourtel alcohol-free beer. So that was Bruno's dinner; his disinterested service to the State did command respect, Paul said to himself. There was bound to be a brasserie open somewhere near the Gare de Lyon, there are generally brasseries open late at night, near the big railway stations, offering traditional dishes to lonely travellers, without really managing to convince them that they still merit a place in an accessible human world characterized by family cooking and traditional dishes. It was in these heroic brasseries, whose waiters, witness to so much sadness, usually die young, that Paul's last culinary hopes for the evening rested.

When Bruno came back holding a voluminous file, Paul was in the little adjacent sitting room, studying a sculpture of an animal on a windowsill. The animal, whose muscles were rendered in great detail, was looking backwards. It seemed worried, perhaps it had heard something behind it, perhaps it had sensed the presence of a predator. It was probably a goat, or perhaps a chamois or a deer, he didn't know much about animals.

'What is that?' he asked.

'A female deer, I think.'

'Yes, you're right, it must be a deer. Where does it come from?'

'I don't know, it was just there.'

Apparently it was the first time that Bruno had noticed the existence of the sculpture. As he resumed his lament about Chinese and non-Chinese rare earths, Paul wondered if he should tell him about the DGSI. That video had deeply affected him, he knew; for a moment he had even thought of withdrawing from political life. In real political life, in the heart of the reactor, Bruno was more or less an outsider. His appointment to Bercy, almost five years earlier, had not been warmly welcomed by the agencies, to say the least – one might also have talked in terms of *an outcry*, if the term had applied to finance inspectors in charcoal suits. He was not an inspector of finances, he hadn't even been to the École Nationale d'Administration, in every respect he was a pure graduate of the science-based École Polytechnique who had made his career entirely in industry. He had enjoyed genuine success, first as the head of Dassault Aviation, then of Orano, finally of Arianespace, where within a few years he had managed to eliminate competition from America and China, placing France solidly in the first global ranking of satellite launchers. Armaments, nuclear, space: all high-tech sectors, all places where a *polytechnicien* was most likely to feel fulfilled, which at the same time gave him the ideal training to respond to the campaign promises of the newly elected president. The president had in fact abandoned the fantasies of a *start-up nation* that had had him elected the first time, but had objectively led only to the creation of some precarious and underpaid jobs, on the edge of slavery, within uncontrollable multinationals. Rediscovering the charms of the economy run in the French style, he had had no hesitation in proclaiming, his arms spread wide in an almost Christ-like pose (he always knew how to do this, and even better than ever, his arms opening at an apparently impossible angle, he must have trained with a yoga coach, it wasn't possible otherwise), at the huge Parisian meeting that had closed his campaign: 'I came here this evening with a message of hope, and I am going to silence the prophets of doom: for France, today, this is the beginning of the new Thirty Glorious Years!'

Bruno Juge was, more than anyone else, born to meet this industrial challenge. Five years had passed, or nearly, and he had more than broadly fulfilled his contract. His most impressive success, the one most discussed in the media, but also the one that had left the greatest mark on people's minds, had been the spectacular recovery of the PSA group. Largely recapitalized by the state, which had almost taken control of it, the group had thrown itself into winning back the top of the range by relying on one of its brands: Citroën. These days, or at least this was Bruno's conviction, there were only two automobile markets, low-cost and top of the range, just as there were only, although Bruno refrained from saying so, and in any case it would not have fallen within his field of expertise properly speaking, only two social classes, rich and poor, since the middle class had evaporated, and the middle-ranking automobile would not be long in following suit. France had demonstrated its skill and fighting spirit in the field of low-cost vehicles – the reacquisition of Dacia by Renault had been the basis of an impressive success story, probably the most impressive in the recent history of car building. Bolstered by a reputation for elegance and a leadership trained in the luxury goods industry, France was able to face the challenge of the top-of-the-range car and set itself up as a serious challenger to German car-builders, Bruno thought. The total top of the range remained inaccessible – blocked by British car-builders, for reasons that remained fairly incomprehensible, and which would probably come to an end only with the extinction of the British monarchy; but top of the range, dominated by German car-builders, was within reach.

This challenge, the most important of his ministerial career, the one that had kept him awake for months in his office at Bercy, while his wife engaged in unlikely dalliances, was one to which he had finally risen. The previous year, Citroën had been on an equal footing with Mercedes over almost the whole of the world markets. In the highly strategic Indian market it had even risen to first place, ahead of its three German rivals – Audi itself, the unrivalled Audi, had been relegated to second place, and the economic journalist François Lenglet, not given to emotional outbursts, had wept as he announced the news on David Pujadas' much-watched programme on the LCI channel.

Reconnecting – thanks to the inventiveness of his designers, personally chosen by Bruno who, emerging for the occasion from his purely technical role, had had no hesitation in imposing his artistic vision – with the boldness of the creators of the Traction and the DS, Citroën, and France in general, had once again become the emblematic nation of the top-of-the-range car, envied and admired everywhere in the world – and the impetus, contrary to expectations, had come not from the world of fashion, but from the automobile sector itself, the final fruit of the union of technological intelligence and beauty.

Even if this success had attracted by far the most media attention, it was far from being the only one, and France had once again become the fifth economic power in the world, following on the heels of Germany to take fourth place: its deficit now represented less than 1% of GDP, and it was gradually reducing its debt; all without disputes, without strikes, in a climate of astonishing acqui-escence; Bruno's ministry was a total success.

The next presidential election would now take place in less than six months, and the president, who would easily have been re-elected, would under no circumstances be able to represent himself: since the unwise constitutional reform of 2008, no one could hold more than two consecutive presidential mandates.

Many things were already well known in this election: the National Rally candidate would be present in the second round – even if no one knew his or her name, there were five or six potential candidates – and would be beaten. One simple but crucial question remained: who would be the candidate for the presidential majority?

In many respects Bruno was the best placed. He already had the trust of the president – and that was fundamental, because the president planned to come back five years later and hold two con-secutive mandates all over again. In one way or another, the president seemed convinced that Bruno would keep his word and agree to step aside once the five years of his mandate had passed, and that he would not succumb to the intoxication of power. Bruno was a technician, an exceptional technician, but he was not a man in search of power; at least that was what the president had convinced him-self; there was, nonetheless, a Faustian-pact aspect to the whole affair, and reaching any kind of certainty was impossible.

One other, much more immediate problem, concerned surveys. For 88% of French people, Bruno was 'competent'; 89% saw him as 'hard-working' and 82% as 'upright', which was an exceptional score, never attained by any politician since the appearance of surveys – even Antoine Pinay and Pierre Mendès France had never approached such a result. But only 18% found him 'warm' and 16% 'empathetic', and only 11% thought him 'close to the people' – a number that was catastrophic at this time, the worst in the political class, across all the parties. In short, people held him in high esteem but didn't like him. He knew it, it made him suffer, and that was why that blood-soaked video had profoundly affected him: not only did people not like him, some hated him enough to stage his killing. The choice of decapitation, with its revolutionary connotations, only underlined his image as a distant technocrat, as remote from the people as the aristocrats of the Ancien Régime had been.

It was unfair, because Bruno was a decent guy, Paul knew; but how to persuade the voters? Uncomfortable with the media, stubbornly reluctant to discuss his private life, he preferred to avoid public speaking. How would he cope with an electoral campaign? There was, in fact, no obvious reason for his candidacy.

Their friendship had been relatively recent. When he was working in the tax legislation department, Paul had met Bruno several times, albeit briefly. The massive tax cuts that Bruno had opted for since the first year of the presidential term were only intended for investments directly intended for the financing of French industry – that was a non-negotiable condition on which he insisted. Such clear commitment to 'dirigisme' was not something that the department was used to, and Paul had had to fight, more or less on his own, against all the civil servants under him, tirelessly writing directives and reports in line with the minister's wishes. They had emerged triumphant in the end, after more than a year of internal warfare that had left its mark.

That shared struggle had attracted Bruno's attention to him, but relations between them had not really taken a more personal turn until the occasion of a new conference held by the African Union, this time in Addis Ababa; more precisely the evening of the first day of work at the conference, at the bar of the Hilton Hotel. The conversation had been awkward and strained at first, then everything had come to a head when the waitress came back. 'Things aren't going very well with my wife right now . . .' Bruno said just as she set a coupe of champagne down in front of him. Paul twitched with surprise and nearly knocked over his cocktail – it was a revolting tropical concoction, far too sweet, which wouldn't have been a great loss. At that precise moment, perfectly in time, two African prostitutes had sat down at a table a few metres away from them. Bruno had never previously broached a private topic; Paul didn't even know that he was married. But after all why not, yes, that happens, people do still get married sometimes, men and women, it's quite common, in fact. And a *polytechnicien*, even one who had graduated summa cum laude, even if he was a member of the Corps des Mines, the foremost technical Grand Corps of the French State, was still a man; this was a new dimension that would have to be taken into account.

Bruno sat in silence for a while; then, in a strained voice, he mumbled: 'We haven't made love for six months . . .' He had said *made love*, Paul noticed immediately, and the choice of this phrase with its sentimental connotations, rather than the term *fuck* (which he would probably have used himself) or *sex life* (which would have been the choice of many people who wished to diminish the emotional impact of their revelation by using a neutral term), was already hugely telling. Even though he was a graduate of the École Polytechnique, Bruno *made love*, or at least he had done so in the past; even though he was a graduate of the École Polytechnique, Bruno (and his entire personality, including his budgetary strictness, appeared in a new light at that moment) was a romantic. Romanticism was born in Germany, we sometimes forget, and it was even, more precisely, born in the north of Germany, in pietistic circles that also played a not inconsiderable part in the early development of industrial capitalism. That was a painful historical mystery on which Paul had sometimes brooded in this youth, back in the day when the things of the mind were still capable of holding his attention.

He had only just restrained himself from replying, with brutal cynicism: 'Six months? It's been ten years for me, my lad . . .!'

And yet it was true, for ten years he had not *fucked*, let alone *made love with* Prudence, or indeed with anyone else. But to observe as much, at this stage in their relationship, would have been out of place, as he realized just in time. Bruno was still probably imagining that an improvement, indeed a *resumption* pure and simple, was still possible; and in fact, after six months, according to most accounts, that remained a possibility.

Evening was falling on Addis Ababa, and a sound of Congolese rumba was gently filling the bar. The two girls at the next table were prostitutes, but they were high-class prostitutes, as all the evidence indicated: their designer clothes, their discreet make-up, their general elegance. They were probably well-educated too, per-haps engineers or doctoral students. Aside from that they were very beautiful, their skirts short and tight, and their low necklines promised considerable pleasures. They were probably Ethiopians, as they had the lofty attitude of the women of this country. At this stage it would all have been very simple: they would just have had to invite them to their table. That was why they had come here, and they weren't the only ones, it was the reason almost everyone had come to this stupid conference, it wasn't as if big decisions for the future development of Africa were being made here, that much was plain from the first day. Bruno might manage to place a few nuclear power plants here and there, that was pretty much his hobby, placing nuclear power plants at international conferences; in fact the contracts wouldn't be signed straight away, contracts would just be taken, and the signature would take place later, discreetly, in all likelihood in Paris.

In the more immediate future, once the two girls had been invited to their table the negotiation would be brief and polite, pretty much everyone knew the price – it would be harder with the nuclear power plants, but then that wasn't really within his area of competence. That left the question of the distribution of the girls, but where that subject was concerned Paul felt very calm: he

31

liked both girls pretty much equally, each was as beautiful as the other, they both seemed sweet and amiable, and equally willing to serve a Western cock. At this stage Paul was minded to let Bruno have first choice. And if that proved impossible, a foursome was entirely within the realms of possibility.

It was just as that thought was forming in his mind that he understood that the situation was hopeless. His relationship with Bruno might have assumed a new dimension for a few minutes, but they had not reached the point, and probably never would, when they could sleep with girls together in the same room; at any rate that could not be the basis of their friendship, they were neither one thing nor the other, and they would never be 'man-whores'; there was not even a question of him being present when Bruno decided to hire the services of a hooker – without even considering the fact that Bruno was a nationally famous politician, that journalists dressed up as congress delegates were probably, at that very moment, hanging around in the lobby keeping an eye on the lift area, and that he was already filled with a kind of protective mission towards his colleague. The absence of this masculine complicity would prevent Bruno from responding to the solicitations of the two young women in his presence, but at the same time it created a stronger complicity between them, based on reactions of modesty that established an unusual proximity between them, while at the same time removing them from the basic community of males.

Immediately drawing conclusions from this insight, Paul rose to his feet claiming vague fatigue, perhaps with a bit of jet-lag, he added (which was a bit stupid, given that there was no time difference to speak of between Paris and Addis Ababa), and wished Bruno goodnight. The girls reacted with slight movements and a brief confabulation; the shape of the situation had just altered, in fact. What was Bruno going to do? He could choose one or other of the two girls; he could also take both, which is what Paul would probably have done in his place. He could also, in a third and sadly more likely hypothesis, do nothing at all. Bruno was a man in search of long-term solutions, and that was in all likelihood as true in the management of his sex life as it was in the management of the country's industrial policy. He had never attained, and perhaps never would, that glum state of mind, which was increasingly Paul's own, and which consisted in admitting that there is only one long-term solution: that life in itself provides no long-term solution.

When this memory returned to him, four years later, the memory of the moment when he had decided, by getting up and going to his room, to leave Bruno alone to face what might have been his sexual fate that evening, Paul understood that he was not going to talk to him about his meeting with the man from the DGSI, not now, not straight away.

The day after that evening, enquiring after Bruno at reception after paying his mini-bar bill, Paul was surprised to learn that he had already checked out, early in the morning, with his luggage. That lonely dawn departure clearly did not suggest an amorous dalliance. Bruno's phone was switched to voicemail and the situation required a swift decision on his part: should he alert the diplomatic service straight away? He could under no circumstances abandon his minister, but he decided to leave him a little time, and booked a taxi for the airport.

The Mercedes minivan that took him to Addis Ababa Airport could, Paul reflected, have accommodated a large family. Since its altitude meant that it did not have the excessive temperatures of Djibouti or Sudan, Addis Ababa nurtured the ambition of becoming an indispensable African metropolis, a hub of the economy of the whole continent. After his brief stay, Paul would have tended to see this goal as a realistic one; from the point of view, for example, of extra services, last night's hookers were at a level that was more than honourable; they could have won over any Western businessman, or indeed a Chinese one.

The main hall at the airport was filled with tourists, some of whom, he learned from their conversations, had come to photograph the okapis. They had been badly advised by their travel company: the okapi lives exclusively in a small region in the northeast of the Democratic Republic of the Congo, the Ituri Forest, where a reservation is dedicated to them; besides, their discreet habits make them very difficult to photograph. At the airport cafeteria, he was hijacked by a squat and jovial Slovenian, a European Union delegate. Like all European Union delegates, the man had nothing significant to say. Nonetheless, Paul listened to him patiently, because that is the attitude to adopt with European Union delegates. He was suddenly enthralled by the violent harmony of colours emanating from a girl in white trousers and a red T-shirt, with long black hair and dull skin, who had just emerged from the crowd of tourists. Then that enthralment faded; the girl herself seemed to have disappeared, evaporating into the atmosphere, alternating between chilly and overheated, of the terminal, but it was, Paul knew, almost certainly impossible that she had vanished.

Immediately before the last call from the speakers in the departure hall, Bruno appeared clutching his suitcase. He didn't say what he had done, or what justified his late arrival, and Paul didn't dare ask him, either then or later on.

A week after their return, Bruno invited him to join him in his cabinet. It wasn't an unusual decision. Paul was more or less at the stage of his administrative odyssey where moving to the cabinet is the normal next step. What made things more surprising was that he would not, he worked out immediately, have a precise task. Managing Bruno's diary wasn't a huge burden, since it was a lot less full than Paul had imagined. Bruno preferred to work from dossiers and granted very few meetings; Bernard Arnault, for example, even though he was the richest man in France, had tried in vain to meet up with him since the beginning of his term; he just wasn't interested in the luxury sector – which in any case had no need of public support.

Paul's essential role, he gradually came to understand, would simply be to serve as Bruno's confidant as the need arose. He did not consider that peculiar or humiliating; Bruno was probably the greatest finance minister since Colbert, and the pursuit of his task in the service of the country would imply, perhaps over many years, shouldering a unique fate in which moments of self-questioning and doubt would probably be inevitable. He had no need of advisers, he had an exceptional ability to master his files, a computer brain grafted onto a normal human brain. But a confidant, someone he really trusted, had without a doubt, at this stage of his life, become indispensable.

The events of that night meant that two years later Paul no longer really listened to Bruno, and had stopped doing so some time earlier. Abandoning the topic of rare earths, Bruno had launched into a violent diatribe against Chinese solar panels, against the incredible technological transfers that China had torn from France during the previous mandate, which would now allow them to come back and flood France with their bargain-price products. He was on the point of suggesting a genuine commercial war with China, to protect the interests of the manufacturers of French solar panels. That might be a good idea, Paul said, interrupting him for the first time; he had a lot of apologising to do to ecologically minded voters, particularly for his unflagging support of the French nuclear industry.

'I think I'll be off, Bruno,' he added. 'It's two in the morning.'

'Yes . . . Yes, of course.' He glanced at the file that he was still holding in his hand. 'I think I'll keep going for a bit.'

5

Intellectually, Paul knows that he's in the ministry building, because he's just left Bruno's office; even so, he doesn't recognize the walls of the lift. Their metal is tarnished and worn, and they start vibrating slightly when he presses the button for 0. The floor is made of dirty concrete, covered with various kinds of detritus. Are lift cabins with concrete floors really a thing? He must have accidentally stepped into a service lift. The space is cold and stiff, as if supported by invisible metal bars without which it would be in danger collapsing in on itself like a saggy burst balloon.

After a long metallic groan the cabin stops at floor 0, but the doors refuse to open. Paul presses the button for 0 several times, but the doors still don't move, and it starts to get worrying. After hesitating for a moment he presses the emergency button, open twenty-four hours a day, or at least that's true of normal lifts, so surely it must be true of service lifts as well. The lift immediately resumes its descent, this time at a much faster rate, and the numbers fly past at insane speed on the control panel. Then it stops abruptly with a violent bump that nearly makes him lose his balance: he's at floor -62. He had no idea that there were sixty-two levels in the basement of the ministry, but in the end it's not impossible, he'd just never really thought about it.

This time the doors open quickly and smoothly: a corridor made of light grey, almost white concrete, faintly lit, extends into infinity in front of him. His first impulse is to step outside, but he changes his mind. Staying in the lift isn't very reassuring, since it's clearly defective. But stopping at level -62? Who would ever stop at level -62? The corridor stretching in front of him is empty and deserted and looks as if it has been that way for ever. And what if the lift sets off again without him? What if he is left a prisoner on level -62, dying there of hunger and thirst? He presses the button for level 0 again. Level -62 is not, any more than the intermediate levels in between, he realizes at that moment, listed on the control panel; there is nothing below -4.

The lift immediately leaps upwards, this time at dizzying speed, and the numbers become confused, passing by before he has time to tell them apart, he just has the sense at a particular moment of the disappearance of the minus sign. Then the lift stops with a violent impact that hurls him against the back wall; the vibrations of the cabin take about thirty seconds to subside; in spite of its brevity, the journey has seemed interminable.

He's at level 64. This time it's impossible, absolutely impossible, the buildings of the Ministry of Finance have never had more than six floors, he is absolutely certain of that. The doors open again on to a corridor with a white carpet, lined with huge windows; the light is very bright, almost dazzling; a tune on an electric organ, cheerful and melancholy by turns, can be heard in the distance.

This time Paul doesn't move, he stays completely motionless for almost a minute. Once that time has passed, the mechanism starts up again, as if making up for its docility: the doors close gently, then the cabin begins its descent at a normal speed. Even though the levels that appear on the panel (40, 30, 20 . . .) are not listed anywhere on the control board, which has nothing beyond level 6, they succeed one another with reassuring regularity.

Then the lift stops at level 0, and the doors open wide. Paul has been saved, or at least that's what he believes, but when he steps out of the cabin he realizes that he is not in the ministry building, but in a place he has never seen before. It's a huge hall, with a ceiling at least fifty metres high. It's a shopping centre, Paul intuitively believes, even though there are no shops to be seen. On the evidence he's in a South American capital, and as his hearing gradually returns he becomes aware of some music that confirms the shopping-centre hypothesis, and the hubbub of voices around him seems to consist of Spanish words, which lends consistency to the hypothesis of a South American capital. And yet the consumers, considerably numerous, in the hall, do not resemble South Americans, or even human beings. Their faces, unhealthily pale, are abnormally flat, and they barely have noses. Paul is suddenly convinced that their tongues are long, cylindrical and forked, like the tongues of snakes.

At that moment he became aware of an intermittent ringing noise, brief but unpleasant, being repeated every fifteen seconds. It wasn't a ringing noise but more of an alerting beep, and he suddenly woke up, realizing that it was his mobile telephone, warning him of the existence of a waiting message.

The message was from Madeleine, his father's companion. She had called him at nine o'clock in the morning, and now it was just after eleven. The message was sometimes incomprehensible, broken up by sobs, with a terrible noise of traffic in the background. Nonetheless Paul worked out that his father was in a coma, and that he had been taken to Saint-Luc Hospital in Lyon. He called back straight away. Madeleine picked up on the first ring. She had calmed down a little, and was able to explain that his father had had a cerebral infarction, that he had just got up, and she had chosen to spend a few more minutes in bed, then she had heard a dull thud coming from the kitchen. She went on to complain about the length of time that the ambulance had taken to arrive, almost half an hour. There was nothing surprising about that, his father lived in the depths of the countryside, in a remote village in Beaujolais, about fifty kilometres north of Lyon. No, there was nothing surprising about it, but the consequences could be very serious, he had been without oxygen for several minutes, and it was possible that the sectors of the brain might have been damaged. She broke off from time to time, succumbing to a fresh crying fit, and while he talked to her he started an internet search, the next train for Perrache was at 12.59, he could catch it easily, he would even have time to call in at the ministry to say a few words to Bruno, it was on the way, and while he was about it he booked a room at the Sofitel in Lyon, which didn't look far from the Saint-Luc Hospital, then he hung up and packed some things for the night.

He waited for a few seconds by Bruno's office door.

'I'm in a meeting with the head of Renault . . .' Bruno announced, half of his body appearing in the partly open doorway. 'Is it anything serious?'

'It's my father. He's in a coma. I'm off to Lyon.'

'My meeting's nearly over.'

As he waited, Paul consulted medical information sites on the internet. A cerebral infarction was a form of stroke – it was even the main form by some way, representing 80% of cases. The duration of the deprivation of oxygen to the brain was an essential factor in establishing the prognosis.

'They'll tell you that they don't know much, that they can't provide a prognosis . . .' Bruno told him two minutes later. 'Unfortunately it's true. He might wake up in a few days, but he might also spend much longer in this condition. My father had a stroke last year and spent six months in a coma.'

'And then?'

'Then he died.'

The Gare de Lyon was unusually deserted, and Paul had time to buy paninis and wraps, which he chewed slowly, while the train passed through a Burgundy that lay beneath an impenetrable grey sky. His father was seventy years old, it was a lot but it wasn't huge, a lot of people lived beyond that age nowadays, an argument that argued in favour of his survival; but it was more or less the only one. A regular smoker, a lover of charcuterie and robust wine, not greatly given to exercise to his knowledge, and he had everything he needed to develop a solid case of atherosclerosis.

Paul took a taxi, but Saint-Luc Hospital was only five minutes from Perrache station. The traffic on the Quai Claude Bernard, which ran along the Rhône, was taxingly heavy. He would have been better off going on foot. The rectangles of coloured glass that made up the façade of Saint-Luc were obviously intended to improve family morale, to suggest a fun hospital, a Lego hospital, a toy hospital. The effect had only been very partially achieved, the glass was tarnished and dirty in places, the cheerful impression suspect, but in any case, as soon as you stepped inside the corridors and the wards, the presence of ventilators and heart monitors brought you back to reality. You weren't there to enjoy yourself; you were there to die, most of the time.

'Yes, Monsieur Raison, your dad was hospitalized this morning,' the receptionist told me. Her voice was gentle, quite soothing, perfect, in short. 'Of course you'll be able to see him; but the senior consultant would like to have a few words with you beforehand. I'll let her know you're here.'

The senior consultant was a brisk and elegant woman in her fifties, plainly quite middle class – she gave a clear sense of being someone who liked issuing orders and regularly *dined out*, she had middle-class earrings, and Paul was sure that there must have been a discreet pearl necklace concealed under her impeccably buttoned white coat – in fact she reminded him a little of Prudence, or, rather, what Prudence could have become, what she was originally supposed to become; however one interpreted the information, it

40

was not good news. She found the file in less than a minute – at least her office was well organized.

'Your dad was brought to the hospital at 8.17 this morning.' She said 'dad' as well, it was alarming, did official instructions involve infantilizing relatives? He was nearly fifty, and it was a long time since he had called his father 'dad', maybe she called her own father 'dad', although he would have been surprised. The problem was that he couldn't bring himself to say 'Édouard' as he would have done with a brother or a friend of the same generation, in short he no longer had the first idea how to address him.

'We immediately gave him an MRI,' she went on, 'to identify the cerebral artery in question; then we carried out a thrombolysis, then a thrombectomy, to remove the blood clot that was obstructing it. The operation went well; unfortunately a secondary haemorrhage occurred to complicate the situation.'

'Do you think there are any chances of recovery?'

'It's normal for you to ask the question.' She nodded contentedly; she evidently appreciated normal patients, normal families and normal questions. 'But unfortunately I have to tell you that we don't know anything; the MRI allows us to determine the zones that might have suffered damage – in this case the frontoparietal lobe – but not the extent of the damage. There are no more medical interventions that we can try; we can only follow the situation while checking the arterial tension and the glycemia. Your dad might recover an altered level of consciousness, or a normal one in certain circumstances; but he might also move towards brain-death, anything is possible at this stage. We need to be reasonable . . .' she concluded without any real need.

'Is someone being unreasonable here?' He couldn't help himself; she was beginning to get on his nerves a little.

'Well, I must say that your father's partner . . . Her emotional manifestations, obviously understandable . . . However, since your sister arrived she has calmed down somewhat.'

So, Cécile was here. How had she managed to get here from Arras? Unlike him she got up very early, and Madeleine must have called her first, she had immediately got on well with Cécile, while she had always been a little afraid of him – perhaps because he was the older son, perhaps because she was a bit afraid of everyone.

'One last thing . . .' She had got to her feet to walk him to the door. 'Your dad had to be put on artificial ventilation, it was indispensable so that he could breathe, and I know that the sight of a tracheotomy can sometimes be a bit difficult for families. But it's not painful for him, I can assure you that he isn't suffering at all.'

In fact his 'dad', with a tube stuck in his throat and connected to a big apparatus on castors whose constant hum filled the room, a drip from his elbow, electrodes fixed to his skull and his chest, struck him as terribly old and weak – seeing him like that it was hard to give much for his chances, he looked very much as if he was dying. The two women were sitting side by side in a corner of the room, and looked as if they hadn't moved for hours. Madeleine noticed him first, and looked at him with a mixture of fear and relief, but didn't dare rise from her chair. It was Cécile who came towards him and hugged him. How long was it since he had last seen her? he wondered. Seven years, maybe eight. But Arras wasn't far, less than an hour by TGV. She had aged slightly: some white hairs, although they were hard to spot in the abundant mass of her light blonde hair. Her face had filled out a little too, but her features were still very delicate. His little sister had been one of the prettiest girls at high school, he remembered very clearly, and the huge numbers of guys who'd flocked around her. And yet she had stayed a virgin until she'd got married, he was sure of it, she wouldn't have been able to hide a romantic intrigue. Even at the time she was very pious, she went to mass every Sunday and took part in the Catholic activities of the parish. He had once happened upon her in prayer, kneeling in her bedroom, when he

42

had got the wrong door after getting up for a piss in the middle of the night. He had been embarrassed, he remembered, as embarrassed as if he'd caught her with a boy. She too had looked a bit embarrassed, she must have been sixteen at the time, and it wasn't until somewhat later that she had started saying, when he was worried about his exams – and he had been rightly worried about his exams more than once – 'I'll ask the Holy Virgin to help you', in a voice that was entirely natural, as if she was talking about a bodice that needed collecting from the dry cleaners. He didn't really know where that mystical tendency came from, it was the only case in the family. She had married a man of the same type, more ponderous in appearance – a provincial notary is ponderous in principle, that was probably what was deceptive about him, because in reality, after two or three minutes of conversation one sensed something *intense* about him, one had the feeling that he would have given his life for Christ, or for a similar cause, without a second's hesitation. He liked them both, he thought they made a fine couple – better than his own, at any rate, not to mention his brother and his bitch of a sister-in-law.

'How are you? Not too tough?' he asked at last, breaking free of her grip.

'No, it is. Very tough. But I know Dad will come out of it. I've asked God to take care of things.'

6

A few minutes later a nurse came into the room, checked the drip and the position of the respiratory tube, and jotted down some figures including the ones that appeared on the control monitors. 'We're going to give him a wash . . .' she said at last. 'You can stay if you like, but you don't have to.'

'I need a cigarette,' Paul said. Most of the time he managed to keep himself in check during the period socially required by the norms of prohibition; but this was a case of force majeure. He went out onto the embankment, and was immediately hit by a blast of bitterly cold air. About thirty people were pacing back and forth outside the hospital doorway, sucking on cigarettes; none of them spoke, or seemed to see the others, they were all locked away in their little individual hells. In fact, if there is a place that produces frightening situations, if there is a place where the need for tobacco quickly becomes intolerable, it's a hospital. You have a spouse, let's say, or a father or a son, they were living with you that morning and in a few hours or even a few minutes they could be taken from you; what could possibly be a match for the situation if not a cigarette? Jesus Christ, Cécile would probably have replied. Yes, Jesus Christ, probably.

The last time Paul had seen his father had been at the start of the summer, less than six months before. He had been on great form, busy preparing for a trip to Portugal that he was going to take with Madeleine – they left the following week, he was sorting out his hotel reservations, in *pousadas* or establishments of that kind, there were lots of places that he wanted to see again, since he had always loved the country. He was also interested in its current political situation, he had spoken at length and knowledge-ably about the revival of activity of the *black blocs*. All in all their meeting had been completely reassuring and satisfying; he was very much the active senior, taking full advantage of his retirement, and in terms of his marital situation Paul might even have envied him – he was exactly the type of senior, he reflected, who was invariably shown in advertisements for funeral insurance plans.

It was the end of office hours, and traffic had grown even heavier on the Quai Claude Bernard, in fact it was at a complete standstill. The traffic light just opposite the hotel turned red again; the first beep of a horn came, like an isolated wail, then a wave of beeps, filling the stinking atmosphere. All of these people doubtless had their own different concerns, their personal or professional worries; it wouldn't have occurred to any of them that death was there waiting for them, on the embankment. In the hospital, the *loved ones* were getting ready to leave; they too had personal and profes-sional lives, of course. If they had stayed a few minutes longer they would have seen it, they would have seen death. It was very close to the entrance, but ready to climb to the upper storeys; it was a slut, but a middle-class slut, classy and sexy. Still, it welcomed all kinds of demise, it relished the dying members of the working class just as much as the wealthy; like all whores, it didn't choose its clients. Hospitals shouldn't be put in cities, Paul reflected, the atmosphere there is too agitated, too filled with plans and yearnings, cities aren't a good place to die. He lit a third cigarette; he didn't really want to go back into that room, to see his father's intubated body; and yet he forced himself to do just that. Cécile was on her own now, she had overtly knelt down at the foot of the bed, and was praying 'shamelessly', he thought in spite of himself.

'You were praying . . . to God?' he asked without thinking, he struggled to get used to it, would the day ever come when he managed to ask anything other than stupid questions?

'No,' she said, getting up, 'that was an ordinary prayer, I was better off talking to the Holy Virgin.'

'Yes, I see.'

'No, you don't see anything at all, but it doesn't matter . . .!' She had almost exploded with laughter, her smile was luminous and slightly sarcastic, and all of a sudden he saw her in the summer when he was nineteen, just before she'd met Hervé, exactly the same smile. His little sister hadn't had much to worry about in those days, her life was impressively clear. He himself was in the middle of a complicated business, or towards the end of the middle, to tell the truth, Véronique had just aborted his baby, she had never thought of consulting him, he had learned the news the day after the operation, a bad sign in itself, and in fact she would leave him a few weeks later, it was she who had uttered the fateful phrase, something along the lines of: 'I think it's better if we stop', or maybe: 'I think it would be better if we took the time to think', he couldn't remember, at any rate it came down to the same thing, as soon as you start thinking it's always in the same direction, not only in emotional terms, in fact, reflection and life and are simply incompatible. Besides, it wasn't a particularly remarkable life oppor-tunity that had been taken from him on this occasion, Véronique was mediocre, she was responsible for all the mediocrity in the world, she could almost have symbolized it. He had no idea what had become of her, and no wish to know, but her husband if she had one would certainly not be happy, and neither would she: making another human being happy, or being happy herself, were both beyond her; she was simply incapable of love.

He was also concerned about his studies, which were also, he realized in retrospect, grimly mediocre. He wasn't sure he would be among the top fifteen graduating from the École Nationale d'Administration, or that he would be able to choose finance inspection, that was more or less what he was worried about at the time. Cécile had no problems in that department either, she simply chose not to study, she did various vague fixed-term contracts in social and paramedical work, she had already more or less decided that she would be a housewife, or that she would only work in an absolute emergency, professional life didn't attract her even slightly, and studying meant nothing to her either. 'I'm not an intellectual,' she sometimes said. To tell the truth he wasn't one either, he wasn't the kind to go to sleep reading Wittgenstein, but he was ambitious. Ambitious? Today he had trouble reconstructing the nature of his ambition. It certainly wasn't political ambition, far from it, that had never been part of his life. His ambition was to live in a duplex apartment with a magnificent living room whose windows overlooked the Parc de Bercy, to be able to walk every morning across a public garden that respected biodiversity, with ginkgo bilobas and vegetable patches, and to marry someone like Prudence.

'I told Madeleine to go back and get some sleep,' Cécile said, interrupting his reminiscences. 'It's been hard for her, since this morning.' He had forgotten all about Madeleine, and all of a sudden, thinking about her situation, he was filled with horror. Ten years before, his father had retired, and a few days later his mother was dying. Back then, Paul had been seriously worried about his father's health, and even his life. He no longer had any work, he no longer had his wife, quite simply he no longer knew what to do with himself. He just sat there for hours at a time, flicking through his old files. Washing and eating were things that no longer occurred to him; on the other hand he still drank, unfortunately, even more than before. A stay in Mâcon-Bellevue Psychiatric Hospital brought a partial solution in the form of various psychotropic drugs, which he absorbed very willingly, he was a perfectly *compliant* patient, to quote the senior consultant. Then there was the return to Saint-Joseph, to that house that he loved, which was a part of his life, but was then again only a part of his life. He'd had his job at the DGSI, the General Directorate for Internal Security, and that was gone; his marriage was gone too; his life had become simpler to a considerable degree; he still had the house, certainly, but it might not be enough.

Paul never knew if Madeleine was paid by the *département* council or by the regional council. She was a home help, able to accomplish the classic tasks (housekeeping, shopping, cooking, washing, ironing) at which his father was radically unskilled, like all men of his generation – not that men of the following generation had gained in competence, but women had lost some of theirs, and a certain equality had grudgingly taken hold, with the consequence among the wealthy and the semi-wealthy of an *externalization* of duties (a term also used by companies that assigned housekeeping and security to outside suppliers), and amongst everyone else an increase in ill humour, infestations of parasites and dirt more generally. Either way, in his father's case a home help was indispensable, and under normal circumstances things might have stayed like that. Had his father fallen in love? Can a person fall in love at sixty-five? Perhaps they can, all manner of things happen in the world. What was certain, though, was that Madeleine had fallen in love with his father, and that fact made Paul uneasy, since his father's love life was not a subject with which he wanted to be confronted. It was understandable, his father was an impressive man in his way, and Paul had always been a little frightened of him, but not very frightened because he was also a good man, that was obvious, a good man in the end, harassed and toughened by his work for the secret service, nothing to do with the circles that Madeleine was familiar with, she was just a poor thing without opinions, and her life until now had been perfectly shitty, a brief marriage to an alcoholic and that was that, you can never really imagine how trifling most people's lives are, and you can't even do it when you are one of those people yourself, and that's always the case, more or less. She was exactly fifty years old – fifteen years younger than his father – and she had never known happiness, or anything like it. She was still pretty, however, and must have been very pretty – and that had probably contributed to a great degree to her misfortune, not that she would have been happier if she had been uglier, on the contrary, but her unhappiness would have been more uniform, more annoying and briefer, and she would probably have died sooner. This happiness that had come to her late in life was now at risk of being taken from her, by a blood clot that had formed in a cerebral artery. How could she have reacted calmly? She was like a dog that has lost its master. In such cases the dog grows agitated, and howls.

'Are you staying in a hotel?' he asked Cécile at last, emerging from his solitary reflection.

'I'm at the Ibis near the station. It's fine, or at least it's convenient.'

The Ibis, yes. A feature of Christian humility, probably. That Christian humility got on his nerves a little, to tell the truth, Hervé was a notary, for fuck's sake, he wasn't homeless. Madeleine, in her proletarian simplicity, had joyfully agreed to get rid of all humility, Christian or otherwise; she had been almost childishly delighted, he remembered, by the idea of staying with his father in luxurious Portuguese *pousadas*.

'I'm at the Sofitel . . . We could have dinner tonight at the Sofitel restaurant, my treat.' He opened his hands wide, as he had seen on-line poker players do on the internet. 'It's very close to here, on the banks of the Rhône but on the other side, practically opposite.'

'Yes, show me on the map.' She took a map of Lyon out her handbag. It really was very close; just across the bridge.

'I'm going to stay until closing time, at half past seven. Can you pick up a Lyonnais sausage for me on the way? A boiling sausage,

I promised I'd bring one back for Hervé. You can go to Montaland, it's on your way, in the middle of Rue Franklin.

'Fine, OK, a boiling sausage.'

'You could even get two, one truffle and one pistachio. And get one for yourself, their boiling sausages are exceptional, one of the best charcuterie products in France.'

'Cooking isn't really my thing, you know.'

'It's not cooking . . .' She shook her head indulgently, with a hint of impatience. 'You put them in simmering water and you wait for half an hour, that's all. Well, as you wish.'

7

The Rhône was an impressive river, surprisingly wide, and he had been standing on the Pont de l'Université for at least five minutes now; a *majestic* river, it wasn't an excessive term, the Seine was a pathetic little rivulet in comparison. He had a view of the Seine from his office, one of the advantages of being a member of the cabinet, but he hardly ever looked at it during the day – and, in the presence of the Rhône, he could see why. French rivers had had their associated qualifiers, in geography textbooks for primary schools, since he was a child. The Loire was *capricious*, the Garonne *impetuous*, the Seine he couldn't remember. *Peaceful?* Yes, maybe that was it. And the Rhône? Probably *majestic* in fact.

In his room he checked his messages. He had only one, from Bruno: 'Pls keep me up to date.' He called almost immediately, and tried his best to sum up the situation – but objectively speaking he knew practically nothing. He added that he would probably be back the following morning.

The Trois Dômes restaurant was free of surprises, there was the usual display of menus with more or less humorously intended grandiloquence, along the lines of *Adagio des terroirs* or 'His majesty the lobster'. Quickly, without thinking, he chose a semi-salted Norwegian skrei fillet, while his sister went on dreamily casting her eye over the menu. Perhaps she didn't often go to Michelin-star restaurants. He caught up on the wine, opting without hesitation

51

for one of the most expensive bottles on the list, a Corton-Charlemagne. This wine was characterized by 'buttery tones and fragrances of citrus fruits, pineapple, lime-tree, baked potato, fern, cinnamon, flint, juniper and honey'. This wine was deranged.

The traffic was starting to calm down a little on the quays of the Rhône; on the horizon in the darkness two huge modern buildings could be seen, brightly lit, one the shape of a pencil, the other of an eraser. Was it the district known by the name of Lyon Part-Dieu? It was quite a disturbing sight, in any case. He had a sense that some glowing ghosts were floating between the buildings – a bit like northern lights, but their colour was unhealthy, purplish, greenish, they twisted like shrouds, like malign deities that had come in search of his father's soul, Paul said to himself, feeling more and more worried, and for a few seconds he lost contact, he saw words forming on Cécile's lips but he couldn't hear her any more, then it came back, she was talking about Lyonnais gastronomy, and how she had always loved cooking. The waiter arrived with the *mises en bouche*.

'I'm leaving tomorrow,' he said. 'I don't think there's much point in my staying.'

'No, you're right, you won't be much use.'

He gave a start of indignation. What did she mean by that? Did she imagine, by any chance, that her presence there was more useful than his? He was preparing a dazzling riposte when all at once he understood her point of view. Yes, she thought that her own presence was more useful. She was going to pray, she was going to go on praying ceaselessly for their father to come out of his coma; and in one way or another she thought that her prayers would be more effective if she delivered them by the patient's bedside; in fact magical thinking, or religious thinking if there was a difference, had its own logic. Paul suddenly remembered *Bardo Thödol*, which he had read in his youth under the influence of a Buddhist girlfriend who knew how to contract her pussy, it was the first time a girl had done that to him, in her religion a pussy was a *yoni*, and he thought that was cute; also her *yoni* had an unusually sweet taste. Her bedroom was very cheerful, decorated with brightly coloured mandalas; there was also a big painting that he'd been impressed by, he remembered. In the middle there was the Buddha Shakyamuni, sitting cross-legged under the tree of enlightenment, isolated in the middle of a clearing. In every direction all around him, on the edge of the forest, jungle animals had gathered: tigers, deer, chimpanzees, snakes, elephants, buffaloes . . . They were all staring at the Buddha, waiting anxiously for the result of his meditation, dimly aware that what was happening in the centre of that clearing was of universal cosmic importance. If the Buddha Shakyamuni reached enlightenment, they knew, not only he, not only humanity would be freed from samsara, it was the collection of all beings that would be able to follow him in leaving the realm of appearances to reach illumination.

At the same time as he successfully entered the competition for entry to ENA, Catherine was applying to get into veterinary college; she succeeded at the first attempt, but her ranking was not good enough to get into Maisons-Alfort, and she had to settle for studying in Toulouse. That separation was a real disruption for him; it was the first time that he had felt genuine sadness at the idea of a relationship with a girl coming to an end. Of course she could come up to Paris, he could go down to Toulouse from time to time, that was what they said to each other, but they hadn't really fallen for it, and of course she quickly found another guy. She was quite pretty, easy-going and cheerful by nature, and she loved fucking; how could it have been otherwise? Shortly afterwards he had slept with another Buddhist, a girl at the School of Political Science, but it was a more intellectual kind of Buddhism, more Zen, and their relationship had come to an abrupt end just after he told her he'd had a 'totally amazing' evening: while she was trying to get into a meditative state, or more precisely when she was intoning

53

the 'Sutra of the Lotus of the Wonderful Law', she was interrupted by a loud noise coming from the landing. Walking to the door and pressing her eye to the spyhole, she saw a man sitting curled up, twitching and bleeding to death. She didn't do anything, she didn't even call the police, she just sat down again cross-legged on the carpet, 'so as not to interrupt her meditation'. The mini-distribution of grave events immediately established an invisible mental boundary between them, and she didn't even seem to be aware of it, the idea that he might have been horrified by her after hearing her story didn't seem to have occurred to her. Immediately afterwards, Paul left her flat on some random pretext, and never answered her phone calls. Their carnal relationship was limited to a single instance of coition, albeit one that wasn't unforgettable, she was certainly gorgeous, but she didn't know how to contract her pussy, and her blow jobs were approximate at best, while Catherine devoted herself to them with application and enthusiasm – in every respect Tibetan Buddhism seemed superior to Zen. For Tibetan Buddhists, apart from anything else, the moment of death meant one last chance to free oneself from the cycle of rebirth and death, of samsaric existence. By now night had fallen completely on Lyon. Each of the chants of the lamas began, he recalled, with the address: 'Noble son, listen carefully and pay attention', uttered for the attention of the dying person, even the dead one; they thought that the soul of the deceased remained accessible for a few weeks after their passing.

'Dad isn't dying,' his sister cut in stubbornly. He hadn't said a word for five minutes, lost in his memories, but she seemed to have followed the course of his thoughts.

'Yes, I know, you told me, you asked God . . .' He had spoken a little too flippantly; he had no intention of hurting her, however. 'Are you going to celebrate Extreme Unction?' he asked, hoping to win her back.

'Since Vatican Two, it's been called the Anointing of the Sick,' she replied patiently. 'And the sick person must be conscious, he has to make the request himself, you can't force it on him.'

Fine, he had missed another opportunity to keep his mouth shut. He would have to do some research into this Catholic business if he wanted to resume relations with Cécile. There was a church near his flat, he remembered, Notre-Dame-de-la-Nativité de Bercy or something of the kind. They were bound to have some documentation on Catholicism, they must do.

'You don't have to worry about annoying me . . .' she said gently. 'We Catholics are starting to get used to it.' Could she really read his mind?

'I'm going to leave tomorrow too,' she went on. 'But first of all I'm going to take Madeleine back to Saint-Joseph, I think it's better if she isn't alone when she gets back to their house. And also I'll have to check some things before we settle here. I'm coming back next week with Hervé.'

'Hervé? How is that even possible? Doesn't he have a job?'

'No . . .' She lowered her head, embarrassed. 'I didn't tell you, but it's true that we don't see each other very often.' It wasn't said in a tone of reproach, but as a simple statement of fact. 'Hervé's been unemployed for a year.'

Unemployed? How could a notary be unemployed? He suddenly remembered that even though Hervé was a notary he didn't come from a comfortable background, quite the contrary. He came from Valenciennes or Denain, one of those towns in the north of France where people have been unemployed for three generations; the first time they'd met, when he had asked him what his parents did, he had replied 'unemployed', as if it was obvious.

'He was a notary on a grade 4 salary when his office went bankrupt,' Cécile went on. 'Finding a job in the region really isn't easy, the property crisis is terrible, transactions have ground to a standstill. And property is bread and butter for notaries.'

'But . . . you're OK? You'll come out of this?'

'While he's indemnified, yes; but it's not going to last for long. Afterwards I'm going to have to find something. But I didn't go to university, as you know; I've never even really worked. Apart from cooking and housekeeping I don't know how to do anything.'

It was from that point in the evening that Paul started to feel embarrassed at the thought of the eight thousand euros he made a month – not an unusual salary given his university and professional career, but he was starting to feel embarrassed. He had chosen a job and a wife that made him unhappy – but had he really chosen? The wife, yes, certainly, a little, and his job too, a little, certainly – but at least he didn't have money problems. Basically he and Cécile had gone in diametrically opposite directions, and their fates, with that painful determinism that is generally a feature of fate, were also diametrically opposite.

In professional terms, to tell the truth, things hadn't gone so badly since he had met Bruno. Bruno was a stroke of luck, the only stroke of luck in his life; he had conquered everything else by competition and struggle. Had he struggled to conquer Prudence? Perhaps he had, yes, he struggled to remember; it seemed so strange, at a few years' distance.

'And what about your daughters? You don't have any trouble paying for your daughters' studies?' For some obscure reasons, the subject of his nieces seemed easier to him, less weighted with dramatic implications – probably just because they were younger.

Deborah hadn't gone to university, his sister told him. She was a bit like her mother, she wasn't an intellectual, she was in the habit of telling him. She did little jobs, usually waitressing jobs; at the moment she was in a pizzeria. They were always short-term contracts, but in the end that was fine, she was dynamic and cheerful, and both the customers and her employers liked her, so she could easily find more work.

Anne-Lise was different, she was writing a doctorate on the

French decadent writers, particularly Élémir, Bourges and Hugues Rebell. Cécile said this with weird pride, given that she plainly didn't know anything at all about these authors, strange the pride that parents feel at the idea of their children's studies, even and especially when they don't understand a thing about it, it's a fine human feeling, Paul said to himself. What was more, Anne-Lise was at Paris IV – Sorbonne, the most prestigious of all the literature faculties, Cécile had registered that. Anne-Lise didn't ask them for anything, she refused to let them help her financially, and yet rents were expensive in Paris, but she had found a job in a publishing house and was financially independent.

His niece had been in Paris for six years and they hadn't seen each other once, Paul realized with a jolt. It was his fault, entirely his fault, obviously he should have been the one to contact her. At the same time, where could they have met? It wouldn't have been easy at his apartment; there was the awkwardness of couples coming apart, you're ashamed of displaying the pitiful, ordinary spectacle of disunity, it becomes gradually impossible to receive anyone at all, and all your social relationships end up disappearing. The *living room*, with its big picture window overlooking the park, had gradually become a *no man's land*, a neutral, deserted terrain. The only room they still shared was the kitchen; their last common piece of furniture the refrigerator; how would he explain all that to Anne-Lise?

His semi-salted Norwegian skrei steak had not yet arrived by the time the waiter brought their desserts; a slight error had been committed in service that had been perfect up until now. Paul made no attempt to play it down; he received the waiter's excuses with the half-indulgent smile of a rich man – a rich man who forgives, but who forgives *this time alone*.

As Paul had hoped, the mention of Cécile's daughters had considerably lightened the mood, since essentially young people never had real problems, serious problems, you always imagine that things will sort themselves out for young people. A fifty-year-old man who finds himself unemployed, on the other hand: no one really believes in his chances of finding another job. But you pretend to believe it nonetheless, the advisors at the job centre are good at producing remarkable imitations of optimism, it's what they're paid for, they've probably taken drama classes, maybe clowning workshops, the psychological treatment of the unemployed had got much better over the last few years. The unemployment rate, on the other hand, had not come down, that was one of Bruno's only real failures as a minister; he had managed to stabilize it, that was all. The French economy, however, had become powerful and a big exporter, but the level of work productivity had increased to insane proportions, and unqualified jobs had almost completely disappeared.

'Would you like to come with me to Saint-Joseph tomorrow?' Cécile asked him, interrupting his somewhat pointless meditations, in any case he couldn't do anything about unemployment in France, or his future in a couple, or indeed about his father's coma. '*What can I do?*' Didn't Kant ask that question somewhere, he wondered? Maybe it was more '*What ought I to do?*' He couldn't remember. It was a different question, or maybe it wasn't. Saint-Joseph-en-Beaujolais was the true home of his childhood, his father came here every weekend, and they spent all their holidays there too. 'I think it's still a bit too early for me to go there without Dad,' he replied – there you go, he was starting to say *Dad* as well; in the end it's probably pleasant to fall back into childhood, maybe it's what everyone wants to do, truth be told. Cécile nodded and said that she understood. In truth she didn't completely understand, however, the essence of the problem was that he could no longer bear the presence of Madeleine right now, she gave off a wave of scorching, intolerable pain, it would have taken a God, at the very least, to absorb such suffering. He wasn't even sure that Madeleine believed in God in the Catholic sense of the term; she doubtless believed in an organizing power that could guide or break the life of human beings – something not very reassuring, in the end, closer to Greek tragedy than to the message of the Gospels. At any rate she believed in Cécile, she doubtless saw Cécile as a kind of initiate who could use her prayers to redirect the deity. And he, this was the most surprising thing, was starting to see his sister in more or less the same way.

And resting on his hospital bed, a few hundred metres away, on the other side of the river, what was his father thinking about right now? Patients in a coma don't alternate between waking and sleeping, but do they still dream? No one really knew, and all the doctors he met would confirm it; what they were dealing with was an inaccessible mental continent.

Once again, Cécile interrupted the sequence of his reflections, which were becoming increasingly erratic. 'I'm taking the twelve past five tomorrow. That gives me three quarters of an hour to get back to the Gare du Nord. Should we leave together?'

There was a question. Two questions, in fact. Yes, between the Gare de Lyon and the Gare du Nord, three quarters of an hour should do it. Yes, he would leave with her. He would stroll about Lyon while he waited, on the quays of the Saône or somewhere.

8

Contrary to all expectations, his walk in Lyon turned out to be almost pleasant. The quays of the Saône were much calmer than the ones on the Rhône, in fact there was hardly any traffic there at all. Wooded hills stretched on the opposite bank, interrupted by groups of old buildings, probably dating from the early twentieth century, there were also some detached homes, and even some mansions. It all looked quite harmonious, and most importantly remarkably calming. Unfortunately it was impossible not to notice that a pleasant landscape, these days, was in almost every case a landscape that had been preserved from any human intervention for at least a century. He could probably have drawn political consequences from this – but given his situation at the heart of the state apparatus it was preferable to abstain from doing so.

It was probably preferable for him to abstain from thinking in general. His mother's death eight years previously had been a strange and violent moment in his life. Suzanne had fallen from scaffolding while restoring a group of angels decorating a tower in Amiens Cathedral. She had forgotten to adjust her safety harness; she was six months away from retiring. The brutality of the event, its unpredictable character, had left him numb at the time; he didn't even remember feeling real sorrow, more a profound sense of paralysis. This time, with his father, things were different; as he walked along the quays of the Saône, which were filling discreetly with mist, he felt a calm and limitless despair rising up within him, along with the idea that this time he was really entering the last part of his life, the final phase, that next time it would be his turn, or perhaps Cécile's, but more probably his.

Then he became aware that they hadn't said a word about Aurélien, that his name hadn't even been mentioned from dawn till dusk. Had someone told him, at least? Probably not, Madeleine had never had a real relationship with him. Who was going to take care of it? Cécile, obviously; when a humanly painful task was on the horizon, it automatically fell to Cécile. 'As a Catholic . . .' he said to himself vaguely, sitting down on a bench, and it was his last structured thought for a considerable time. The mist rose from the river and thickened around him, now he could only see a few metres ahead.

A comfortable luxury bus was driving at speed along a motorway crossing a desert landscape made of flat white rocks, with a few thickets of thorns and succulents, probably in a state in the American West, Arizona or Nevada, perhaps, and it was almost certainly a Greyhound bus. Sitting in the middle of the bus was a tall man, dark-haired, tough, with a satanic face. He was sitting next to another passenger, whom he might have known but probably not; either way, this other passenger wasn't in a position to intervene, because the dark-haired man symbolized Evil. The travellers knew (and Paul knew just as much as they did) that at any moment the dark-haired man could get to his feet and decide to kill another traveller; they also knew that none of them would have the opportunity, or even the idea, of putting up the slightest resistance.

The dark-haired man rose to his feet and approached an old man at the front of the bus, not far from the driver. The old man was trembling, his terror was visible, but it didn't occur to him to rebel. The dark-haired man dragged the old man violently to the door, then pressed the button and pushed the old man into the void. For a moment he leaned forward to observe the ways in which the old man had been shattered and mutilated, the shapes formed by the spray of blood on the dry ground. Then he sat back down and the journey continued. It was then that Paul understood that he was going to continue right to the end, with new interventions, spaced out and irregular, by the dark-haired man.

He immediately understood, just before he woke up on the bench, that the dark-haired man also symbolized God, and that as such his decisions were fair and final. It was a bit cold now, evening was falling, that was probably what had woken up him up; it was lucky, because it was already half past four and time for him to go to the station. Cécile didn't make a fuss about him paying for an upgrade to first class, and as regards Aurélien she herself broached the subject. Aurélien had never been close to their father, although he had been close to their mother, and even if it took a while, it was that he had chosen the career of art restorer, following her example, that he had obtained the diploma as 'restorer and conservator of cultural assets', taking the course of the Condé School; they had even chosen the same historical period – the late Middle Ages, the early Renaissance – the only difference being that his mother specialized in sculpture, and he in tapestry. In pursuing his mother's footsteps, choosing an artistic career almost identical to hers, Aurélien was tacitly, implicitly – and not always implicitly – rejecting his father's career, based on service to the state and unconditional, military adherence to the variable and sometimes troubled interests of French intelligence.

Essentially his father had never wanted a third child, this third child born several years after the others had been in a sense imposed on him, Aurélien had never been part of his project, and as a rule he was a man who preferred to stick to his projects. A couple generally forms around a project, except in the case of fusional couples, whose sole project consists in contemplating themselves for ever, lavishing a thousand tender affections on one another until the end of their days, such people do exist, Paul had heard of them, but his parents weren't among them, so they had had to develop a project, having two children was a classic project, even the archetype of the classic project, if he and Prudence had had children they wouldn't be where they were today, in fact, on the contrary, they would probably have separated already, children today aren't enough to save a couple, they tend instead to destroy it, in any case things had begun to break down between them even before they expected it. In his parents' case, in addition, there had been another project, the house in Saint-Joseph. His father knew the area well, as a child he had spent idyllic holidays there with his wine-growing uncle. As early as 1976, a few weeks after he got married, he had bought this little group of abandoned houses near Saint-Joseph-en-Beaujolais, a hamlet within the municipality of Villié-Morgon.

There were three different-sized houses which had belonged to three brothers, a stable and a huge barn. He had had the lot for a derisory sum; the walls and roofs were sound, but everything else had to be redone. He had devoted the whole of his weekends and his holidays to them over the following ten years, personally drawing up the plans even though he had not trained as an architect, doing much of the carpentry and woodwork with his own bare hands. It was he who had come up with the idea of the conservatory and the glass-walled corridor leading from the main house to the little house where the children lived. His mother had also been excited about the project, through her job she had contact with the best artistic craftspeople in every area, the house had assumed growing importance in their lives, it was the most tangible, and probably the most durable, manifestation of their existence as a couple. The result was wonderful; it was there that he and Cécile had experienced several years of the unreal and brutal hap of childhood. His bedroom window faced north-west, overlooking a rolling countryside of meadows, woods and vines that glowed red and gold in

autumn, all the way to the steep and verdant slopes of the Avenas Mountains.

That time was over for him, he would never be so happy again, it wasn't among the realms of possibility. Cécile had known, perhaps still did know, such moments of happiness, she had had children, she had become a child herself once again, she had placed her soul in the hands of the Father, as they say in her faith. He needed, he absolutely needed to imagine Cécile being happy.

He studied her, calm and tranquil, gazing at the landscape passing by the window in the last daylight. An electronic information panel showed that they were currently travelling at a speed of 313 km/h, it also showed their geographical position, and he realized with a nervous shock that they were, at the very moment when all of this was coming back to him, a little south of Mâcon, a few kilometres from the house at Saint-Joseph.

A long time, a very long time later, she turned to look at him – the train was now approaching Laroche-Migennes, and travelling at 327 kilometres an hour.

'I didn't ask how things were going with Prudence . . .' she remarked cautiously.

'You were right. You were right not to ask me.'

'I thought as much. It's a shame, Paul. You deserve to be happy.'

How did she know all that, how did she know life, when she had only known one man, and had immediately, with miraculous prescience, chosen a monster of integrity, fidelity and virtue? Perhaps life is really very simple, Paul reflected, perhaps there's almost nothing to know, you just have to go with it.

They didn't say much more until they reached Paris. The course of events was now fixed. In a week at most Cécile would come back with Hervé, and they would move into the house at Saint-Joseph. Their first task would consist in calming down Madeleine, trying to return a meaning to her days, and making sure that she didn't spend all day getting under the feet of the care workers at Saint-Luc Hospital. And after that there was nothing to do but wait; wait and pray. Might prayer be an activity for couples? Or did it need to be an individual, personal contact with God?

They hugged briefly but tightly, before Cécile set off for the metro – she had to change at Bastille, and after that it was straight to the Gare du Nord.

9

As he pushed open the door of his apartment he was surprised by whale-song coming from the living room, and realized that Prudence must have come back, that she was probably somewhere in the apartment at that very moment, since those were her usual hours. They weren't his at all, on the other hand; since he had been in the cabinet he had developed the habit of getting up late; towards midday he set off towards the ministry, strolling across the Parc de Bercy – he had almost ended up liking this park, with its idiotic vegetable patches – and then the Yitzhak Rabin Garden. Once he got to Bercy he usually had a plate of smoked fish for lunch – the cabinet had a separate kitchen from the rest of the ministry, and the chef was excellent, but at lunchtime he preferred to settle for smoked fish. This was the time of day when he would have his first meeting with Bruno.

Bruno got to his office early, at seven in the morning – and since taking up the official apartment he sometimes spent part of the night there – but he never had meetings in the morning, devoting it to background work. Probably, like his distant predecessor Colbert according to legend, he rubbed his hands with enthusiasm as he discovered the tasks of the day, the pile of files that had accumulated on his desk. Generally lunching alone with Paul – Bruno was fonder of pizzas – they went over the afternoon and evening meetings, discussing likely difficulties.

Paul usually came home late, at between one and three o'clock in the morning, by which time Prudence had already gone to bed long before. He sometimes finished his day with wildlife documentaries; he had completely stopped masturbating. In fact it was months – almost a year, he realized with horror – since he had last bumped into his wife, and even in previous years, when they bumped into each other it wasn't very often or for very long. As members of social class AB, they had no plans to stray from accepted norms, and placed great importance on the breakdown of their partnership occurring under the most civilized conditions possible. At the sound of whale song, however, he nearly fled, he nearly left the apartment to look for a hotel for the night. But fatigue took over and he opened the door to the living room.

Prudence gave a start when she saw him, which meant that she didn't feel very comfortable either. He had to act quickly and defuse the situation straight away, so he explained himself: his father had had a CVA, he was in a coma in a hospital in Lyon, which explained his own unusual time-keeping, but from tomorrow things were going to return to normal and it wouldn't happen again. She did not react very much to his promise; strangely, on the contrary, she seemed to sympathize with him, her face was wrinkled under the effect of something that looked like sadness, or at least concern. It faded, admittedly, within a few seconds; but it had happened, without any doubt. Then she said something more banal, that he had to organize things as best as he could for himself, not worry about her and so on. She wasn't far off fifty either; what was her situation with her own parents, in fact? Classic old middle-class lefties, who had spent their lives in protected sectors like higher education or the magistracy, probably fans of jogging, who liked to keep themselves fit. He had never had much time for Prudence's parents, or at least her father was all right, but her mother was frankly a pain. There was an old piece of popular wisdom that said more or less: 'If you want to marry the daughter, look at the mother'; the fact is that he had bravely refused at the time to take

69

the warning into account. Prudence, on the other hand – and this was a surprise – seemed concerned by the fate of Édouard, when she had received Suzanne's death eight years previously with indifference. 'Basically, you look like your father . . .' she had said to him one day. Was there a connection between these two pieces of information? Did this unexpected empathy for his father's fate mean that she still felt something for him, in some way? It was quite dizzying, as an idea; but since leaving Lyon the previous evening he felt he had entered a zone of great uncertainty. Only the previous day? He had a sense that it went back further, and that it was serious, that he hadn't only entered an uncertain but circumscribed area of his life, but that everything in his life had become uncertain, starting with himself, as if he was being replaced by an incomprehensible double who had been his secret companion for years, and perhaps for ever.

Be that as it may, for now he considered it preferable not to go too far with Prudence, and announced that he was going to go to his room, using the argument of a state of exhaustion easily explicable with reference to the journey and his emotions. Prudence smiled and accepted his departure with the requisite good humour, although her confusion was apparent in little circular hand gestures, as if, by creating Cartesian vortices in the ether, she could create a force of attraction between them, perhaps something resembling gravitational forces. And yet the non-existence of both ether and Cartesian vortices had been demonstrated a long time since, and there was no doubt at all on the subject in the scientific community, in spite of the last stand by Fontanelle, who in 1752 would publish *Theory of Cartesian Vortices with Reflections on Attraction*, a work which left no legacy.

She would have been better off showing him her arse, or perhaps her breasts, it's a mistake to imagine that sorrow is compromised by a directly sexual solicitation, what happens is often the opposite, a reaction occurs within the physical organism devastated by sorrow, terrified by the prospect of becoming incapable of the simplest biological functions and wishes to reconnect with any form of life, the most basic form possible. But probably it was not within Prudence's range, her upbringing had not led her in that direction, which was regrettable because few other opportunities would be presented to them as a couple.

10

As soon as he reached the office the next morning Bruno got straight to the point and asked him more or less how likely it was that his father would pull through; Paul explained the situation as best he could. Then Bruno asked him if his father was on his own. He told him about Madeleine, which made him pensive, his gaze lost its focus and seemed to disappear into some vague space; Paul was starting to become used to those moments when he was filled by general reflections, in which his usual pragmatic and precise style of reasoning disappeared behind more theoretical considerations.

'Your father was born in 1952, isn't that what you told me?' Bruno asked at last. Paul said yes. 'A typical baby boomer, then . . . You really have the feeling,' he went on, 'that people of that generation weren't only more energetic, more active, more creative and broadly speaking more talented than us in every point of view, but that they managed better in every sphere, including marriage. Even when they got divorced – they already got divorced, much less, but they did get divorced – and even when they were already old when they divorced, they managed to find someone else. I don't think that will be as easy for us. And it's even worse for the rising generation. I see my two sons, there's one who's homosexual – or at least homosexual in theory, in practice I don't think he has a boyfriend, either regular or occasional, he's more of an asexual with homosexual tendencies. I don't know about the other one, I don't think he's anything at all, or ever has been, I sometimes forget that he even exists. At least we tried to become part of a couple; we failed quite often, but we tried.'

More or less explicitly taken on with a view to bringing the thirty glorious years between 1945 and 1975 – *les Trentes Glorieuses* – back to France, it was hardly surprising that Bruno should have been fascinated by the psychology of the boomers, so unlike contemporary psychology in its optimism and its risk-taking, so different, in fact, that it seemed unbelievable that they were only separated by a single generation. His own father, as far as Paul could tell, was a moderately senior civil servant, and in this sense an atypical *boomer*. He had never met the original *boomers*, the classic *boomers*, the creators and captains of industry, the ones he hoped to see blossoming in France once more, and in any case more or less all of them were dead by now; so too were the legendary fucks of the 1970s, with their hairy pussies, who had in a sense gone with them to the grave. In terms of marriage at least, Paul had no objection to his disillusioned observation; he helped himself to some more smoked eel, and the rest of the afternoon passed more or less quietly. The chief issue at stake the following day was lunch with the trade unionists. He himself had come up with the idea of these monthly lunches, bringing the main French trade union leaders together in Bercy; they had no precise programme, they were 'informal' lunches intended to 'take the temperature of the country'. The idea of wanting to buy the goodwill of trade unionists with *lièvre à la royale, palombes confites* and the appropriate Grands Crus might have seemed simplistic, even stupid; nonetheless, the five-year term had passed in a uniquely peaceful atmosphere; the number of strike days had never been so low since the start of the Fifth Republic, while the number of public servants was falling slowly but inexorably, so much so that some rural territories, in terms of public services and medical cover, had fallen more or less to the level of an African country.

The news arrived just after 6 p.m.; Paul was informed at 6.25 by an email from the minister's press attaché. A new message had just appeared on the Web; it started, as always, with an arrangement of crudely drawn circles and pentagons; but the arrangement was different every time, with the variations in the number of circles particularly notable. Then came a text, composed in the usual letters; but this time it was considerably longer: previous messages were four or five lines long, this one was about twenty.

A click anywhere on the screen started the video. The ocean was grey and rough. The camera slowly approached a ship, a gigantic container vessel swiftly cutting through the waves without the slightest difficulty. The deck was deserted, no crew members could be seen. All of a sudden, with no apparent collision, the huge vessel rose above the surface of the ocean and fell back, cut in half down the middle. The two dislocated halves sank in less than a minute.

The special effects were perfect as usual, Paul thought to himself, and the scene was perfectly believable. After one or two minutes he called Doutremont. He was plainly on the case, and couldn't say anything for now; he promised to call him back as soon as he knew anything, even if it was late at night.

He called back at eight o'clock in the morning, and Paul got the message when he woke up. He preferred not to say anything on the phone, and suggested a meeting at the ministry in the afternoon; he wanted to be accompanied by one of his superiors at the intelligence agency.

He came at 2.00 p.m. precisely, along with Inspector Martin-Renaud; this was a man in his fifties, with short grey hair and a somewhat military appearance – in fact he reminded Paul a little of his own father.

'Are you the head of the IT unit?'

'Not exactly; I'm in charge of the intelligence service. It so happens that I had the opportunity to work with your father a few years ago. I've just found out what happened to him, and I'm terribly sorry, that's partly why I'm here; but first let's address the topic of the day.' He turned towards Doutremont.

'The message,' Doutremont said, 'differs from the previous ones in several respects. First of all in its delivery: this time it parasitized about a hundred servers all over the world – including China, which has never happened before. But most importantly the previous videos were CGI – well-made CGI but CGI nonetheless. This time we have serious doubts.'

'You mean a ship was really sunk?'

'Its registration is very legible on the image, and we've had no trouble identifying it. It's a latest-generation container vessel, built in the Shanghai shipyards. It's just over four hundred metres long and can carry up to twenty-three thousand standard units or about two hundred and twenty thousand tonnes of freight. It travelled the Shanghai–Rotterdam route, and was chartered by CGA-CGM, fourth in the world in maritime merchandise transport; they're a French operator. Of course we've asked them to tell us if one of their ships has been in an accident. What we suspect is that they'd like to avoid word getting out about the affair, and that they want a commitment from us to that effect.'

'We're far from certain that we can comply with that request,' Martin-Renaud cut in. 'They appear to be under the impression that we can control the media under all circumstances, and decide what comes out or not; that's far from being the case. There are dozens of ways in which leaks can occur, and we have no control over them, particularly since there's one strange aspect to the video: there's nobody to be seen, no crew members – exactly as if they'd warned them about the attack and they had time to leave the ship. If that's so they're bound to reappear sooner or later – and it will be impossible to keep them from speaking.'

75

'I imagine a boat of that size isn't easy to sink. It would require military capability, wouldn't it?'

'To a degree. A torpedo launcher is a difficult piece of equipment to find on the market, but it could be mounted on an ordinary boat. The method employed here is non-direct: there is no immediate contact between the torpedo and the vessel, it explodes some metres beneath. It's the rising column of water, the one sent up by the gas bubble produced by the explosion, which cuts the ship in half; it doesn't even have to be a very powerful torpedo. So no, they don't need huge funds; on the other hand, the aiming and timing of the moment of the explosion have to be very precise, and that calls for genuine ballistic ability.'

'Who could have done that?' He had asked the question spontaneously, almost involuntarily; this time Martin-Renaud smiled openly.

'That's what we'd like to know, of course . . .' They exchanged a glance with Doutremont. 'No one known to our services, at any rate. Since the first messages, in fact, we have been in a complete state of ignorance. And this time the consequences could be very serious. Of course the Chinese government can afford to protect the transport of goods produced by its businesses; but having every container ship escorted by torpedo defence will seriously increase costs. Not counting maritime insurance costs, which are bound to soar.'

'So it's going to harm global trade?' It was Doutremont who had asked the question; for Paul the answer was obvious, and the head of the DGSI put it simply: 'If you wanted to damage global trade, this is exactly what you would do.' That could obviously lead them towards certain kinds of activists, more on the far left, but far-left activists, even if they had demonstrated their capacity to ruin any kind of demonstration, had so far demonstrated no military capability, and in any case they lacked the financial means, a

76

torpedo launcher was an expensive piece of equipment, however you imagined getting hold of it.

Martin-Renaud hesitated for a few seconds before going on. 'There's another subject I wanted to see you about . . .' he said at last. 'Your father still has a number of files.' Paul was amazed: files? Even though he was retired? 'Yes, of course, but when you occupy a position like his you never retire completely,' Martin-Renaud said; and in any case those files weren't really files, in fact it was difficult to explain. 'You could read them,' he went on, 'but they wouldn't mean much to you. Yes, of course you could, they're not classified,' he added. 'In any case that's why we're not taking any precautions to keep people from stealing them; we don't think they could find any clues in there.' Essentially they weren't so much files as collections of facts or strange pieces of information, between which Paul's father had been alone in establishing a connection; there was nothing solid enough to call for an inquiry or a surveillance operation. They were more like a sort of puzzle, which had sometimes kept him busy for years at a time, in which he sensed a threat to state security, even though he couldn't specify its nature. 'There are some cardboard folders that he kept in his office in Saint-Joseph-en-Beaujolais, I went there once,' he explained. 'So, in the event of an accident, if the worst came to the worst, we would like those files to be returned to us.'

Paul's first thought was that he had avoided using the word 'death' to spare his feelings, but a glance at Martin-Renaud told him that he was really troubled and uneasy. 'I was very fond of your father,' he confirmed. 'I wouldn't exactly say that he was my mentor, he worked with a lot of other young agents of my generation; but I learned a lot from him.'

Paul had never known much about his father's professional activities; he just remembered that every now and again he would receive a call on his Teorem high-security telephone – sometimes at meal-times – and that he immediately locked himself away to reply. Afterwards he would never talk to them about the contents of the conversation, but he looked concerned, usually for the rest of the day. Concerned and taciturn. Yes, he was a man whose professional activities had been dominated by *concern*, that was all he could say.

Of course he agreed. 'Yes, I've got a question to ask you too . . .' he went on. The people responsible for these cyber-attacks – and now for this act of violence – plainly had considerable funds at their disposal; but those funds could not be limitless. He knew that in the past they had tried to close down the messages, but that they had quickly reappeared on other servers, and sometimes on the same one. Now that they had more messages to manage, they risked paying less attention to the earliest ones. The video staging the minister's decapitation had deeply wounded him, he knew; it went on undermining him; mightn't it be possible to get rid of it for good?

Martin-Renaud immediately granted his consent. 'Your reasoning seems valid to me . . . Yes, we'll look into that as soon as we get back.'

It was already late afternoon when the meeting came to an end; the early-evening early December light was sinister, Paul reflected; it really was the ideal time to die.

11

The boat's crew reappeared the next day. They had been floating off La Coruña, on the edge of Spanish territorial waters; Paul was surprised to learn that these gigantic vessels operated with a crew of about ten. They weren't able to tell the authorities much; they had been contacted by radio, and obviously the people had not identified themselves. They had fired a first torpedo which had brushed the bow of the vessel, to show that they meant business, then they had given them ten minutes to leave the ship.

Media coverage of the event had been huge at first – it was the first time that an attack of this kind had been committed – then, in the absence of any further information, it had quickly faded away. Paul gave Bruno a summary of Martin-Renaud's visit, and was surprised at the calm with which he learned what had happened. He had already been surprised by his relative indifference to the first cyber-attacks, apart from the one that directly involved him. The financial consequences had been considerable, however; a general suspicion with regard to internet security had spread around the trading floors, which had returned to the days of phones and faxes – a forty-year leap back in time; but Bruno had always held financial capitalism in a degree of contempt. It was not really possible to invent money, he thought, you would be able to tell the difference sooner or later, so the reference to a production of goods of some kind would sooner or later become indispensable, and in fact the operation of the system of production, even with a considerable slow-down in financial transactions, had remained more or less unchanged. This time, however, the real economy was affected; but to tell the truth, even though it wasn't an argument that could be publicly advanced, the brakes imposed on Chinese foreign trade were not necessarily bad news for France. Since the outset, Bruno had not really been playing the game; he was playing his own version of the game.

Paul also felt that he was becoming worried about something else, something more directly political. The situation had not really been resolved; not only had Bruno not announced his candidacy, but he was refusing to give any statement on the subject, repeating every time that the moment 'had not come'. He had no serious rival in the president's party; the possibility of his standing for the premiership was sometimes mentioned in the media, only to be immediately rejected; named since the start of the five-year term, he had never been anything other than a puppet in the hands of the head of state. From start to finish, Bruno had been the president's only confidant, the only person with sufficient weight to alter the direction of the country's politics.

One other surprising competitor had recently appeared. Benjamin Sarfati, sometimes called 'Ben', or indeed 'Big Ben', came out of the lower zones of television entertainment. He had spent the whole of his career on the TF1 channel, where he had initially presented a programme aimed at teenagers, clearly inspired by *Jackass*, except that the challenges proposed played much more on humiliation than on danger: falling trousers, vomiting and farts were the chief subject matter of a programme that would allow TF1, for the first time in its history, to rise to the top in terms of viewing figures among teenagers and young adults. His career would go on to be distinguished by total fidelity to the channel, as well as a 'Druckerization', the televisual equivalent of the gentrification of urban districts, which would conclude with his invitation to the farewell programme of veteran broadcaster Michel Drucker on the day of his eightieth birthday – one of the big moments in television in the 2020s. Soon top-ranking politicians and people with keen social consciences were jostling to get onto his talk show, weekly at first, then daily – the one who took some persuasion was heritage advisor Stéphane Bern, who was worried about the frailty of his elderly audience; but he came on too, and it was one of the greatest joys in the career of Sarfati, who had benefited at almost exactly the same time from the *leave-taking* of Cyril Hanouna. Paul couldn't quite remember if Hanouna had been accused of flashing, sexual harassment or indeed of rape, but either way he had *exploded in full flight*, he'd thought he could rely on solid support in media circles, but in the end no, he had disappeared from the airwaves and from people's awareness even more quickly than he had appeared, and no one could remember having employed him or even bumping into him. 'Bouygues has taken his revenge on Bolloré,' had been Bruno's sober commentary, referring to the notorious break-up between two telecom billionaires in the 2010s.

Without ever being too obvious about favouring the president's party – that would have been at odds with his ethics as a presenter – Benjamin Sarfati implicitly let his political positions be known, if only by his choice of the most mediocre opponents – of which he had no shortage – when it came to organizing a confrontation with an important member of the government; then he began to move closer to the most intimate circles of power. He had several hurdles to jump before he could consider standing for the presidency, but he did set about jumping them, as no one could deny. One crucial moment, without a doubt, had been his meeting with Solène Signal, head of the consultancy Confluences, which had taken charge of his communication since then.

Unlike most of her rivals, Solène was not concerned with the need to occupy ground on the internet. The internet, she liked to say, served only two purposes: downloading porn and insulting other people without risks; in fact only a minority of particularly hateful and vulgar people expressed themselves on the net. However the internet did constitute a kind of compulsory rite of passage from a fictional point of view, a necessary element of the story; but as far as she was concerned it was enough, and even preferable, to tell people that one was popular on the net, even if this was not reflected in reality. One need have no qualms about announcing figures in the hundreds of thousands, even millions of views; no one was going to be able to check.

Solène's true innovation was the second stage, the one that immediately followed on from the internet and which, under her influence, became more or less of a requirement for all consultancy firms, in establishing a modern story: that of the intermediary public figures (promising actresses, singers on the up). Their function, in the media to which they had access – usually trendy but occasionally ponderous – was tirelessly to convey the same message about the candidate: humanity, approachability, empathy – but also patriotism, gravity, attachment to the values of the Republic. This stage, which she considered the most important, was also the longest, and by far the most expensive both in terms of time and individual investment; because one had to meet these intermediary minor celebrities, talk to them and stroke their egos, both boundless and pitiful. Benjamin was particularly blessed in this regard: his position on television, his vast audience as a talk-show host, made him an indispensable point of contact for the minor celebrities. At the very worst they could imagine having only slight differences with him; but for intermediary minor celebrities, getting angry with Benjamin was not an option.

In the third part, the third stage of the rocket, Solène did not introduce any innovations, her contacts were exactly the same as those of her rivals. She knew the same senators, the same company directors, the same journalists from the *major daily newspapers*; it was particularly at the second stage that she wanted to extend her lead (and Benjamin Sarfati had clearly passed to the third some time ago); obviously she was expensive, but her consultancy was still young and she couldn't afford to price herself out of the market.

Even though he was increasingly putting himself forward as a credible candidate, Sarfati had not yet declared his intention to stand; the period immediately after the holidays would be crucial.

After their fortuitous encounter, Paul and Prudence had developed the habit of meeting up once a week – usually on Sunday afternoon. Communication between them remained difficult and mostly verbal; they never went beyond the formal kiss by way of greeting – but Paul reflected that even being able to speak to one another was quite an achievement, given that they had travelled a long way. Prudence talked almost exclusively about her work – she was still in the Treasury office. After a month Paul knew nothing more about her friendships or her leisure activities. Something new seemed to have taken root in her – something like resignation or sadness, she spoke slowly now, almost like a little old lady; physically, however, she had barely changed.

Each time she also asked him for news about his father – after all, that was what had brought them together. He told her what he could – even though he had not gone back to Lyon he often spoke on the phone to Cécile, who had moved into the house in Saint-Joseph. But for now his father was still in a coma, and the situation was stable. Cécile, however, did not seem to be discouraged in the slightest – she appeared to have a boundless trust in the power of prayer.

One Saturday in mid-December, Paul went to the church of Notre-Dame-de-la-Nativité in Bercy. It was on Place Lachambeaudie, five minutes' walk from his apartment. It was really a small church, probably built in the nineteenth century, incongruous in this modern, even post-modern district. A few metres away were the lines of the South East rail network, the TGV for Mâcon and Lyon pass by there, and his train must have passed in front of the church many times without his suspecting its existence. A brochure told him more: built in 1677 under the name of Notre-Dame de Bon Secours, the church had been demolished in 1821, because it was almost in ruins, then rebuilt from 1823. It had been destroyed again during the Paris Commune, then rebuilt exactly as before a little later. Flooded when the Seine burst its banks in 1910, then damaged in April 1944 by the bombing of the railway lines, it had been partially destroyed in a fire in 1982. All in all it was a church that had suffered, and was still not in the best of shape; that Saturday afternoon it was completely deserted, and looked as if that was the case almost all the time. If one had wished to visualize the tribulations of Christianity in western Europe, one could have done worse than the church of Notre-Dame-de-la-Nativité in Bercy.

12

The twenty-fifth of December was a Friday, which meant that Paul would be able to spend three whole days in Saint-Joseph. Prudence had left the previous Saturday, he did not know where to; probably Brittany, to her parents' holiday home, which was in fact no longer a holiday home, he thought he remembered that they had moved there some years before, after her father's retirement.

Passing through the living room – which was now the location for their Sunday-afternoon conversations, and was to a degree beginning to deserve its name again – he noticed a brightly coloured piece of paper that had been placed on the sideboard, purchased by Prudence, he remembered, who had been filled with enthusiasm for this Louis XVI sideboard, which struck her as 'ideal'; she was a woman who had been capable of enthusiasm, at certain times, on certain subjects. It was an invitation to the celebration of the Yule Sabbath which was held on 21 December in Gretz-Armainvilliers. It was illustrated by a photograph of girls wearing long white robes, their brows garlanded with flowers, frolicking in a sunlit meadow making pre-Raphaelite gestures. It looked a bit like a piece of 1970s soft porn; what was going on? What had Prudence got messed up in?

Lower down, a series of esoteric seals seemed to guarantee the seriousness of the event. A brief explanatory note, although one that seemed intended for inattentive followers, reminded the reader that the Yule Sabbath was traditionally associate with hope, with rebirth after the death of the past. That could have been said to correspond to their situation as a couple. At any rate it did not look like a very hardcore sect, more something for women, based on essential oils. Reassured, he set the sheet back down on the sideboard and set off for his train.

He had had a bad night, and fell asleep a few seconds after settling into his first-class seat – there was a headrest, which was good, and the carriage was practically empty. He was standing in the middle of a verdant meadow – the grass seemed to have been cut with scissors, dazzlingly green under the sun, beneath a perfectly blue sky set off by a few clouds, clouds without gravity, decorative clouds which could at no moment of their existence have been clouds bearing rain. He knew intuitively that he was in southern Bavaria, not far from the Austrian border – the mountains lining the horizon were the Alps. He was surrounded by a dozen old men who gave a great impression of wisdom. They were dressed in classic suits, the suits of office workers, but their office work, he grasped immediately, had only been a cover, in fact they were genuine initiates. They all agreed on one point: Paul Raison was ready for take-off, he had been sufficiently prepared. He ran down the slope, keeping his eyes fixed on the mountain ranges along the horizon to the south, but it only took a few seconds, or a few tenths of a second, at any rate less than a minute, and all of a sudden, without any premeditation, without really anticipating it, he found himself being lifted up into the atmosphere, about twenty metres from the ground. He flapped his hands slightly to keep his balance, then froze. The pseudo-office employees, who were in fact his masters, who had initiated him into the art of flight, had gathered below him to comment on his first climb, which conformed in every respect with their vision. His confidence boosted, Paul tried an initial move – he only needed to do some breast-stroke movements, altering his direction via the orientation of his arms, which worked exactly like swimming, albeit in a medium that was of course more fluid. After a few minutes' practice he was able to perform somersaults and even discreet loop-the-loops, before rising a little higher, effortlessly reaching an altitude of around a hundred metres. Moving around with supple breast-stroke motions, Paul headed for the mountain ranges; he had never been so happy.

When he woke up, the train was passing through the station at Chalon-sur-Saône, travelling at a speed of 321 km/h. His telephone was emitting a faint but insistent beep; he had nineteen missed calls. He tried to listen to his messages, but he had no signal. Signs recommended that he make his calls from the gangway between the carriages 'for reasons of courtesy'. He headed for the gangway but he still had no signal. Passing through two equally deserted carriages he reached the 'InOui' restaurant space; he had taken the precaution of bringing his ticket with him, and he had no railcard; the waiter at the restaurant space was called Jordan and served him a Paul Constant gourmet burger, a quinoa and spelt salad and a 17.5 cl bottle of traditional Côtes-du-Rhône. There was a defibrillator at his disposal should he need one, but he still didn't have a signal; the train would get into Mâcon-Loché TGV station in twenty-three minutes.

Was he responsible for this world? To a certain degree yes, he was part of the state apparatus, and yet he didn't like this world. And Bruno, he knew, would have felt equally ill at ease with these gourmet burgers, the Zen spaces where one could have one's cervical vertebrae massaged for the duration of the journey while listening to birdsong, this strange labelling of luggage 'for safety reasons', so with the general turn that things had taken, with this pseudo-playful atmosphere which was in fact normative in an almost fascistic way, which had gradually infected the tiniest crannies of everyday life. Yet Bruno was responsible for the course of the world, and to an even greater degree than he was. That phrase of Raymond

87

Aron's, about men 'not knowing the history they make', had always struck him as a weightless *bon mot*, and if that was all Aron had to say he might as well have kept his mouth shut. Beneath it there was something much darker; the increasingly obvious disjunction between the intentions of politicians and the real consequences of their acts struck him as unhealthy and even malign, and at any rate society couldn't carry on operating on this basis, Paul reflected.

Just before the train reached Mâcon the mist lifted, and the sun shone gloriously on the landscape of meadows, forests and vines, already blanched by winter. As soon as he alighted from the carriage he saw Cécile. She ran the few metres separating them and threw herself into his arms; she was in tears. There are many reasons to weep in a life, and it took her almost a moment to articulate the words: 'Dad's woken up! Dad came out of the coma this morning . . .!' before bursting into tears again.

two

1

Hervé was waiting for them by the car, smoking a cigarette. He gripped Paul's hand for a long time, and seemed pleased to see him. *People like me,* Paul said to himself with surprise; *or more precisely they appreciate me, let's not overstate the case.* Hervé loved his sister, and had done his best to appreciate, and in fact in a sense to love, the brother-in-law that fate had given him – and he had succeeded, Paul reflected; he had discovered within him aspects that were worthy of esteem and even love. That did not correspond to any objective reality, Paul said to himself; it was down to the eye of the beholder, and more precisely to Hervé's goodness, which led him to see around him a conjunction of estimable beings, and to consider that most of the time people are *good people.*

He had aged since last time: more belly, less hair, classic ageing, in the end; but he didn't look as if unemployment had done him any harm, Paul said to himself stupidly. What did he expect? That he would grow horns? At any rate he didn't look as if he spent his nights in a state of anxiety, running over in his head his fruitless attempts to seek employment; in his eyes unemployment was a widespread, natural state that had taken root for generations, accepted to some extent as fate. Difficult studies had enabled him to escape it for a while; then fate had caught up with him.

But most importantly, he was married. 'Shall we go, honey-bun?' Cécile asked, opening the front passenger door. *Honey-bun . . .? Is* it true that we don't change, even physically, for loving eyes, that loving eyes are capable of destroying the normal conditions of perception? Is it true that the first image that we leave in the eyes of the beloved is always superimposed, for ever, onto what we have become?

While the car set off along the A6 motorway, Paul remembered being present at Hervé's oath of office twenty years previously. There were about fifteen aspirant notaries, wearing a curious outfit from the eighteenth century, with black breeches, white stockings, a sort of frock coat and a bicorn hat. It was held in the old Palais de Justice in Paris and the décor was very fitting. The judge had talked about fulfilling his functions 'with precision and probity', something along those lines. In his mind's eye he saw his brother-in-law solemnly repeating 'I swear' when his name was called, which was quite impressive. Then Hervé had received a personal seal which allowed him to certify authentic documents; it was enough to make you feel a certain pride for a worker's son.

He was still going to need to find another job, Paul said to himself, sooner or later either he or Cécile was going to find another job. He had probably not gone in for insane spending – his Dacia Duster was in good condition, but it was just a Dacia Duster. The winter sun was increasingly bright, the interior of the car was flooded with light; after an easy bend, when they set off down a long shallow slope, Paul felt as if he was falling into a well of sunlight. He had sat next to Madeleine in the back seat of the car. At first they had exchanged two kisses on the cheeks, an established practice between them, they knew how to do that. Then for ten kilometres or so – until somewhere around Saint-Symphorien-d'Ancelles – he had wondered what he would be able to find to say to her, before reaching the conclusion that it was probably better if he kept his mouth shut, that Madeleine preferred silence, that right now she was very happy, and that any utterance would have reduced the fullness of her joy. Then he understood a little better, if fleetingly, what Madeleine's relationship with his father might have been like, what it must have been like to have the peaceful, almost animal presence of Madeleine by his side – and at the same moment he realized that he still couldn't help thinking of his father in the past tense.

As if she had immediately received that negative thought, Cécile began to speak, recounting her day, which had been intense. It was while crossing Paris, between the leg that had brought her from Arras and the one she was about to take to Lyon, that she'd received the phone call from the hospital – at Jacques Bonsergent metro station to be precise. Her father had come out of his coma, that was the only information she had managed to glean. She had spent the whole morning trying to get through to the hospital, but she had had no hope of getting a signal, and communication had been brief and disappointing, almost inaudible; it wasn't until she'd got to Lyon that she was able to form a precise idea of the situation. Emergence from a coma is an unpredictable and violent event that can take different forms. Sometimes the person dies, quite simply. They can also come completely back to life and recover all their abilities, and sometimes they can be released the next day. In inter- mediate cases like that of Paul's father, some functions resume, but not many. He had opened his eyes, which was the major criterion for coming out of a coma; he could also breathe normally; but he was completely paralysed, unable to speak or to master his natural functions. He was in a state that was formerly called 'vegetative' by medical practitioners, but most of them now rejected the term, fearing that it recalled the usual metaphor of likening their patients to vegetables, that it might be a semantic trick intended to justify their euthanasia in advance; they preferred to use the term 'non- responsive awakening', which was more precise, apart from anything: the patient had recovered his capacity to perceive the world, but not to interact with it.

The car was coming into the suburbs of Lyon; the traffic jams promised to be interminable. Hervé drove calmly, nothing seemed capable of annoying him this morning. There wasn't a cloud in the sky now, and even the mist had lifted.

Once they had parked in the hospital car park, Madeleine turned to him. 'I should let you see him alone,' she said. It was important for her, he being the eldest son, she wasn't joking about this, she would probably never be able to shake an attitude of fearful respect with regard to him.

'Come with me, Cécile . . .!' Paul called to his sister in a desperate, almost pleading voice, unpremeditatedly. It was only at that moment that he realized he was afraid.

2

His father had changed rooms, and even floors; that was the first discovery that Paul made after visiting reception at the medical centre. 'It's normal, he's no longer in resuscitation . . .' Cécile said to him. 'I saw the senior consultant this morning. She isn't there now, she had to leave early today, but she'll be able to see us on Monday, and she doesn't take any holidays between Christmas and New Year. Could you be there on Monday?' He didn't know, they would see later, he replied, it wasn't the most important thing at the moment. Probably yes, he reflected almost immediately: between Monday 28th and Thursday 31st there was a new four-day week, what is known in French as the 'Confectioners' Truce'. Bruno would doubtless be at his desk, he couldn't remember ever knowing Bruno to take a holiday, but he wouldn't have any meetings, he wouldn't need Paul, he would alone with his files, he would be happy. Work is diverting, Paul said to himself. The nurse who walked ahead of them down the corridor was striding quickly, and in less than a minute he would be in the presence of his father once more, his heart was beating faster and faster, a wave of terror rose up in him, and he almost stumbled as he reached the door of the room.

The change was radical: propped up on two pillows, Édouard was almost sitting in his bed. He no longer had a tube in his throat, and the noisy machine had disappeared. He no longer had a drip either, or any electrodes fixed to his head. He was his father again, with his serious, even austere expression, and most importantly his eyes were wide open, staring straight ahead without moving, without blinking.

'His natural breathing has resumed, he doesn't need the respirator any more. The respirator is what families are usually most impressed by,' the nurse observed. Frozen to the spot, Paul couldn't look away from his father's eyes.

'Can he see?' he asked at last. 'Can he see and hear?'

'Yes, he can't move or speak, he's completely paralysed, but his senses of sight and hearing have returned. On the other hand we can't tell if he is able to interpret his perceptions, to connect them with things that he knows, with ideas or memories.'

'Of course he remembers us!' Cécile cut in confidently.

'Generally speaking, patients in a vegetative state react more to familiar voices than to faces,' the nurse continued, untroubled. 'So you've got to talk to him, don't hesitate to talk to him.'

'Hello, Dad,' Paul said while Cécile, very much at ease, began to stroke his hand. Paul thought for a minute before asking, 'Is he going to stay like this for a long time?'

'That we can't tell,' the nurse said with satisfaction; she had been waiting to hear that question, families generally ask it straight away, and the fact that Cécile had not broached the subject at all had bothered her since the start of the morning. 'We've carried out all possible tests: MRI, PET scan and of course the ECG; we're going to continue, but at the moment there is no test that would allow us to predict with any certainty the progress of a patient in a vegetative state. He could come back to normal consciousness within a few days, but he could equally stay like that for the rest of his life.'

'Of course he's going to come back, but it might take more than a few days . . .' Cécile broke in. Her self-assurance was incredible, she expressed herself as if she received her information directly from a supernatural power; his sister's mystical manifestations had definitely assumed new proportions, Paul said to himself. He gave the nurse a sidelong glance, but she didn't even look angry, she was simply surprised.

His father, in any case, appeared to be beyond all of these concerns. Those eyes staring at an indeterminate point in space, those eyes that saw but could no longer express anything, were endlessly troubling, as if his father had entered a state of pure perception, as if he had become disconnected from the emotional labyrinth, but Paul said to himself that this was bound to be wrong, his father must have retained his full ability to feel emotions, even if he was no longer in a state to express them, but it was strange to imagine pain or joy that could not be translated into facial expressions, groans, smiles or laments. The nurse seemed to be full of goodwill, and willing to communicate whatever medical information she had at her disposal. Out of caution she reminded them several times that she would have to check with the senior consultant, but she seemed to be in complete control of her subject. His father's mind was functioning, yes, no doubt about it, she said to Paul. The electroencephalogram had allowed them to detect delta waves, typical of dreamless sleep or deep meditation, but also theta waves, more associated with drowsiness, and even on two occasions alpha waves, which was very encouraging. He alternated between waking and sleeping, even if he did so much more quickly than a man in good health, and did not follow the usual nychthemeral rhythm at all; it was impossible to tell if he had dreams.

At that precise moment, his father closed his eyes. 'There . . .' the nurse said with satisfaction, as if his father had played his role as patient to perfection. 'He has just gone to sleep. That will last a few minutes, an hour at the most. It may be that your visit, the fact of seeing you again, has tired him.'

'Do you think he recognized me then?'

'Of course he recognized you, that's what they're telling you!' Cécile cut in impatiently. 'Anyway, they're going to let him rest for this evening. Besides, I have to go back and cook dinner.'

'Already?'

'It's Christmas Eve tonight. Had you forgotten?'

3

Yes, he had completely forgotten that it was Christmas Eve. The technical terms that the nurse had used, his father's gaze, which had immediately evoked for him what he imagined a ghost's gaze might look like, that gaze clinging both to life and to death, very remote from and very close to humanity, the actual inability to know anything at all about his mental state, it had all plunged him into a general state of confusion and gave him the sense of coming out of a television series about the paranormal. Night had fallen long before they reached Villié-Morgon, with its Christmas lights, before taking the D18 towards the hill of Fût-d'Avenas.

Hervé parked in front of the main house. Beneath the stars it seemed even bigger, more imposing than he remembered.

'I forgot to tell you . . .' Cécile said, getting out of the Dacia. 'Well, just in case you could stay next week. We're having a visit from Aurélien, he should arrive on the thirty-first.'

'Is his wife going to be there?'

'Yes, Indy will be there. And their son, too.' He had hesitated as she uttered the last word, she really couldn't get used to it.

'We'll probably put him in Aurélien's old room,' she went on. 'Which means that you'll be in the guest room, the blue one – I'm in the green one. Unless you'd rather sleep in the little house.'

'Yes, I'd rather.'

'I suspected as much. In fact I've already made up the room for you, I've turned on the heating.'

It was odd that she'd suspected that, because he himself hadn't anticipated it at all. He had visited his father several times over the last few years, but every time he had preferred to sleep in a guest room, he had never set foot in the bedroom that had been his as a child, then as a teenager, and he hadn't seen it again for twenty-five years. It was probably a bad sign that he wanted to plunge back into the years of his youth, that's probably what people do when they realize that they've failed in life.

'Do you want to sort yourself out now?' Cécile asked. 'I'm about to make dinner, then we'll go to mass and eat when we get back. You can rest for a couple of hours, if you like.'

'No, I'd rather stay in the sitting room.'

What he really needed, in fact, was a glass of something, or several. The bar was where it had always been, and there was Glenmorangie, Talisker and Lagavulin; so the quality hadn't deteriorated. After his third Talisker, it occurred to Paul that he would be slightly drunk at midnight mass, which wasn't necessarily a bad thing. Cécile hadn't left the kitchen for an hour, and various aromas were starting to fill the sitting room; he recognized the smell of bay leaf and shallots.

Perhaps he should light a fire, he thought, it seemed like an appropriate idea for Christmas Eve, there were logs and kindling beside the fireplace. Just as he was imagining the arrangement with some uncertainty, trying to remember fires that he had lit in the past, Hervé came into the room; Paul was glad to see him. He accepted a glass of Glenmorangie, and as Paul expected, he launched into the matter of the fire swiftly and competently, and a few minutes later high, bright flames were already rising into the chimney.

'Oh, you've made a fire, that's nice,' Cécile said, coming into the sitting room. 'We've got to go.'

'Already?'

'Yes, I got the timing wrong, they've brought it forward by half an hour this year, it's at 10 p.m.'

As he put his coat back on, Paul wondered for a moment where Prudence could be at that moment; had the celebration of the Yule Sabbath finished? Cécile hadn't asked him anything about his marriage and Hervé wouldn't either; in all likelihood Bruno would be the only one to broach the subject with him. Couples who are getting along don't generally like to enquire into the fate of couples who aren't, it's as if they feel a kind of fear, as if conjugal disharmony were a contagious condition, as if they were frozen with fear at the idea that these days any married couple is almost inevitably a couple on the brink of divorce. Aligned with this instinctive, animal unease, a touching attempt to evoke the common fate of separation and a lonely death, there is the crushing sense of their incompetence; a little like people who don't have cancer, who always have difficulty talking to people who do, striking the right tone.

His father was well integrated into village life, he realized as soon as they entered the church; he felt surrounded by a confused but benevolent atmosphere, with a least twenty or so of the faithful gesturing discreetly in their direction. He suddenly remembered that his home was supposed to have been 'neutralized' by the DGSI; they paid all the bills and local taxes to prevent his father from being located. That protection continued after this retirement, and would in fact do so until his death. His father had explained that to him a few months before he sat his baccalaureate, during his only attempt to talk to his son about his professional future, in the vain hope that he might choose the same path as himself. That protection seemed to him, in the church of Villié-Morgon, where the priest was already on stage for this vaguely absurd ceremony — the phrase came to him in spite of himself, and he regretted it, but there was nothing he could do about it: in any case, all the villagers knew him, and must know that he worked 'in the secret services', it added to the romance of their lives, of course they knew nothing more about it, but essentially he himself had never known that much more; either way, though, a simple act of local reconnaissance would have been enough to locate him. At the same time, perhaps it wasn't that absurd: acts of local reconnaissance are expensive, you need to send agents on site, and it's certainly more difficult than employing a mid-level hacker to go through badly protected files like electricity bills or local taxes.

The crib scene was very skilfully done, the village children had put their hearts and souls into it, and the ceremony itself went well, as far as one could tell. A saviour was born into the world, he knew the principle, and the effect of the Talisker even allowed him, for a few moments, particularly during the carols, to consider that it might have been good news. He knew the importance that Cécile placed on the fact that their father had come out of his coma just in time for Christmas; he was ironic about it in spite of himself, but essentially he didn't want to be. Did the Yule Sabbath celebrated by Prudence make more sense? Probably less. It was probably a more or less pagan thing, perhaps pantheistic or polytheistic, he got the two mixed up, a vaguely disgusting, Spinoza-like thing. Even God struck him as difficult to reconcile with his personal experience; but several became a joke, and the idea of deifying nature frankly made him want to throw up. As to Madeleine, she had sided completely with Cécile; she wanted to get her husband back and resume their life, her ambition went no further than that; Cécile's god seemed powerful, he had obtained an initial result, she put herself unhesitatingly on the side of God and Cécile, and fervently took Holy Communion.

He himself abstained from taking Communion, which struck him as the orgasmic moment of a well-conceived mass, in so far as he understood anything at all about their cult, and in so far as he even remembered what an orgasm was. His abstinence was due

102

to the respect that he felt for Cécile's faith, or at least that was what he tried to convince himself.

Shortly afterwards, to use the time-honoured expression, the mass was said – everyone was to return to their own hearth and enjoy themselves amidst their family, to the best of their means.

As he left the church, he had an even better understanding of the extent to which his father had been (he couldn't help himself from saying 'had been' in his head, when he should have been thinking 'was'; he really wasn't good at being hopeful) . . . the extent to which his father was popular in the village. Almost all the members of the congregation who had been at the mass came towards them, addressing Madeleine most of all, but also Cécile, whom they seemed to know; she must have visited their father more often than he did. They had all learned of his cerebral vascular incident, and the fact that he had fallen into a coma; Cécile gave them the news that he had awoken from it that very morning. It was good news, and Christmas Eve felt better for many of them, Paul understood immediately. It's never pleasant for men to die, he said to himself stupidly, he was plainly struggling to leave the mindless state that he had fallen into since visiting the hospital.

'The people here are nice . . .' Hervé said simply as he got back into the car.

'Yes, it's true, it's a nice part of the country,' Cécile said thoughtfully. 'Where we live, in the North, people are quite hospitable too, in principle, but it's also true that people are so poor that it ends up creating tensions.'

The conversation was about to split, ineluctably, towards politics over the course of dinner, Paul readied himself for it resignedly, he didn't even imagine trying to avoid it, political discussions have been an inevitable part of family dinners since politics and the family have existed – a long time, in other words. He himself, to tell the truth, had never really been able to take part during his own childhood, his father's work at the DGSI seemed to numb political conversations as if they forced him into a flawless allegiance with whoever happened to be in power. It wasn't the case, however, he could vote 'like any other citizen', he sometimes reminded him good-humouredly, and Paul remembered hearing him express especially acerbic criticisms of Giscard, Mitterrand, then Chirac – which amounted to more than thirty years of political life. His criticisms, thinking about it, were even so violent that it was hard to imagine him voting for them. Who could his father have voted for? Another thing about him that remained mysterious.

Cécile and her husband both voted for Marine, obviously, and had done for quite a long time, ever since she had replaced her father at the head of the movement. Given his occupation, Cécile will have assumed that Paul voted for the president – and this assumption was correct, he had voted for the president's party, or for the president himself, in every election; it seemed to him to be 'the only reasonable option', in the time-honoured phrase. Cécile would therefore take care to keep the political discussion from going too far, to avoid clashing with him, and she had probably given a warning to Hervé – who, as Paul knew, had in his youth been part of tougher movements, like the Identitarian Bloc. In fact he didn't hold it against them at all – if he had lived in Arras, he too would probably have voted for Marine. Apart from Paris he only really knew Beaujolais, a prosperous region; wine growers were probably the only French farmers, apart from some cereal growers, who were not constantly on the brink of bankruptcy, and in fact benefited from the present situation. Along the Saône Valley there were also many precision-engineering companies, and sub-contractors in automobile production, who were doing well and standing up victoriously to their German competitors – even more so since the arrival of Bruno at the Finance Ministry. Bruno had never been reluctant to ignore the regulations of European free competition, whether it was a matter of awarding public contracts or the introduction of customs duties when convenient for certain products; in this respect, as in every other, since the very beginning, he had behaved entirely pragmatically, leaving the president with the task of defusing the situation, reasserting his attachment to Europe at every available opportunity, and pressing his lips to the cheeks of every German chancellor that fate gave him to kiss. The relationship between France and Germany was sexual, though, it was weirdly sexual, and had been for some time.

Cécile had made lobster medallions, a wild boar daube and a *tarte aux pommes*. It was all delicious, she really was incredibly gifted, the tarte in particular was to die for – the delicacy of the pastry, crunch and then soft, the precise balance between the flavours of melted butter and apple, how had she learned to do that? It was heart-breaking to imagine that she would soon probably have to turn her hand to a different set of skills, it was a bad use of her abilities, a tragedy on every level – cultural, economic, personal. Hervé seemed to share his diagnosis, and started grimly shaking his head immediately after the tartes aux pommes – obviously he would be the first victim. However, he too accepted a Grand Marnier, which Madeleine was delighted to serve him – where had Cécile gone? She had disappeared in the middle of the tarte aux pommes. Grand Marnier is an exceptional spirit, and too often overlooked; however, Paul was surprised by the choice, since he remembered Hervé as being more inclined towards harsher sensations, those provided by Armagnac, calvados and other powerful and obscure regional liqueurs. Perhaps Hervé was becoming a little more feminine as he grew older, and that seemed to him like quite good news.

Cécile reappeared a moment later, bringing a little parcel with a ribbon around it, which she set down in front of him with a shy smile, saying, 'Your Christmas present . . .'

A Christmas present, obviously, they were giving each other Christmas presents, how had he managed to forget? He really was useless at family relationships in general – and he didn't get on very well with animals either. He untied the ribbon and found a beautiful metal case, with discreet silvery reflections, containing a Montblanc fountain pen – a Meisterstück 149 – which seemed to be specially decorated, probably with what is called red gold.

'You shouldn't have . . . It's really too much.'

'I bought it with Madeleine, we pooled our funds – you need to thank her as well.'

He kissed them both, filled with a strange emotion; it was a beautiful present, incomprehensible.

'I remembered,' Cécile said, 'that in the old days you used to copy out phrases into a notebook, phrases from writers, the ones you thought were the best, and every now and again you would read them out to me.'

It came back to him all at once: yes, he had done that. It had started at the age of thirteen and continued until the year of his baccalaureate; he wrote the phrases out with great care, he spent hours doing it, practising several times, on loose pages, before copying them into his notebook. In his mind he saw the notebook itself, with its stiff cover reproducing an Arabic mosaic. What could have become of it? It was probably still there, in his teenage room; on the other hand he had no memory whatsoever of what he might have copied out in those days. All of a sudden something came back to him, but it was not a phrase, more a verse from a poem; it had re-emerged, all by itself, from the depths of his memory:

What remains to him today,
That kindly dauphin,
Of all his fine kingdom?
Orléans, Beaugency,
Notre-Dame de Cléry,
Vendôme,
Vendôme.

Immediately afterwards he remembered the song by David Crosby that used the same lyrics – it wasn't really a song, more one of those strange combinations of vocal harmonies, without a real melody and sometimes without words, that Crosby had composed towards the end of his career.

They parted company after the end of dinner; Paul remembered that he had forgotten to call Bruno. He would do it the next day; he didn't know what Bruno might be doing for Christmas. Probably nothing: Christmas Day would probably annoy him more than anything else. Or maybe he would be doing something, maybe he would be seeing his children, maybe he would be making one last attempt at reconciliation with his wife, and it would be better to wait for the 26th. But in any case he was going to tell him that he planned to stay in Saint-Joseph all week.

Pleasantly drunk, without even thinking about it he walked along the glass corridor leading to his bedroom. The first thing that struck him as he stepped inside was the poster of Keanu Reeves. The image was taken from *The Matrix Revolutions*, and showed Neo blind, his face covered by a bloody bandage, wandering in an apocalyptic landscape. It was probably symptomatic of something that he should have chosen this picture rather than one of the many that showed him demonstrating his prowess in the martial arts. He slumped on the little bed; terribly narrow, but he must have slept with girls in that bed; well, with two.

The Matrix had come out a few days before Paul's eighteenth birthday; he had been excited about it straight away. The same thing would happen to Cécile two years later, with the first episode in the *Lord of the Rings* series. Many people had gone on to think that the first episode in the *Matrix* trilogy was the only really interesting one, with its innovations in terms of visual effects, and that the ones that followed were a bit stale. Paul didn't share this point of view, which in his mind did not take sufficient account of the construction of the screenplay. In most trilogies, whether *The Matrix* or *The Lord of the Rings*, there's a waning of interest in the second part, but a resumption of dramatic intensity in the third, even an apotheosis in the case of *The Return of the King*; and in the case of *The Matrix Revolutions*, the love story between Trinity and Neo, at first a little incongruous in a film for nerds, ended up by becoming genuinely overwhelming, to a large degree thanks to the performances of the actors, or at least that was what he had thought at the time, and what he still thought the next day when he woke up, this 25th December morning, almost twenty-five years later. The sun had almost risen on the frost-covered meadows, and he went to the common area to make some coffee. He felt a little foggy, but he didn't have even a slight headache, which was surprising given the quantity of alcohol consumed the previous evening. Cécile planned to go back and see their father in the early afternoon; that was the only thing planned for the day. As he took his first sip of coffee, remembering *The Matrix* again, he was struck by something blindingly obvious, which froze him to the spot and took his breath away: Prudence looked very like Carrie-Anne Moss, the actress who played the part of Trinity. He dashed to his bedroom and easily found the file in which he had kept the photographs of the film: it was obvious, flagrantly so, how had he managed not to make the connection before? He was stunned, he would never have imagined that he was that kind of person, he saw himself as someone rather cold and rational. The light was rising more and more into the room, and now he could make out all the elements of his bedroom as a boy, starting with the huge Nirvana poster, which was even older than *The Matrix*, it probably went back to the beginning of his adolescence. He would probably have enjoyed seeing *The Matrix* again; Nirvana was more doubtful, he hardly ever listened to music these days, sometimes a bit of Gregorian chant when he had had a difficult day, something along the lines of *Christus Factus Est* or *Alma Redemptoris Mater*, a long way from Kurt Cobain, on some points we change and others not at all, that was the feeble conclusion he felt he was able to reach on that Christmas morning.

Carrie-Anne Moss, on the other hand, he found just as attractive, even more attractive than ever; seeing the photographs from the film he found all his emotions as a young man still intact, and couldn't work out whether this was good news or not. He took a second coffee, and it occurred to him to try and find the notebook that Cécile had talked about the previous day, the one in which he'd recorded his favourite phrases. After a quarter of an hour of fruitless effort he remembered that he had thrown it away just after deciding to prepare for the ENA entrance exam, after a troubled night the course of which he was not able to reconstruct in its entirety, but he could see the dustbin on Rue Saint-Guillaume where he had got rid of the object. It was a shame, he said to himself, he might have learned more about himself, there had certainly been some telling early signs, alerts to his destiny, perhaps, which he might have been able to decipher beneath the surface in his choice of certain phrases; the only ones that he had managed to remember so far were not very encouraging, there was something about an unhappy king, a king beaten and humiliated by the English, who had lost almost everything of his kingdom. And Neo's fate wasn't very enviable either; not to mention that of Kurt Cobain.

It was broad daylight now, once again it was going to be a fine winter day, clear and radiant. The waves of the past that were rising within him as he rediscovered the objects in the room finally made him feel a bit sick, and he went outside. The house was magnificent in this light, its gilded limestone walls lit by the big winter sun, but it was still very cold. He didn't feel like going back to his room, not straight away, so he headed off instead towards Cécile's room, which would at least be less gloomy. He knew she wouldn't mind, she had never had much to hide, it wasn't in her nature.

Not Nirvana now, but Radiohead; and not *The Matrix*, but *The Lord of the Rings*. There were only two years between them, but that might have been enough to explain the difference, things still

109

moved quite quickly in those days, much less quickly than in the 1960s, of course, or even in the 1970s, the deceleration and immobilization of the West, heralding its annihilation, had been progressive. While he no longer ever listened to Nirvana, he suspected that Cécile still listened to old songs by Radiohead from time to time, and he suddenly remembered Hervé at the age of twenty, when he had met Cécile. He too was a fan of *The Lord of the Rings*, he was even a *total fan*, he knew certain passages by heart, particularly the part where the Black Gate opens just before the final confrontation. At that moment he saw Hervé standing in front of them, reciting by heart the speech by Aragorn, son of Arathorn. First there was the moment when, in front of the gate, accompanied by Gandalf, Legolas and Gimli, his first companions, Aragorn delivered this last generous and chivalrous request:

> *Let the Lord of the Black Land come forth.*
> *Let justice be done upon him.*

The gates actually opened, and the armies of the evil powers spread out over the plain – vast, infinitely greater in number, the armies of Gondor were filled with terror. Aragorn consulted with his companions before delivering his address to his troops, and this exhortation by Aragorn was certainly one of the finest moments in the film:

> *Sons of Gondor and of Rohan, my brothers.*
> *I see in your eyes the same fear that would take the*
>   *heart of me.*
> *A day may come when the courage of men fails,*
>   *when we forsake our friends and break all fellowship,*
>   *but it is not this day.*

Here, after speaking in French, Hervé switched to English, the only way to convey the intonation of Viggo Mortensen, that awareness that the battle was almost impossible but nonetheless indispensable, that desperate obstinacy, that courage: *BUT IT IS NOT THIS DAY!*

Why did he have such a clear recollection of that episode, which didn't even concern him directly? Probably because it was the exact moment when he worked out that his little sister was falling in love with Hervé. He himself had never been in love; he had slept with half a dozen girls, and he had found them likeable enough, nothing more, but in the looks that his sister was giving to Hervé he discovered an obvious and powerful strength with which he himself was unfamiliar.

> *An hour of wolves and shattered shields,*
>   *when the age of men comes crashing down!*
> *BUT IT IS NOT THIS DAY!*
> *This day we fight!*
> *By all that you hold dear on this good earth.*

Once again Hervé added the original version, the French wasn't bad but the English text was really something else. Then came the final phrase, the call to arms:

I bid you stand, Men of the West!

Hervé must definitely have been a member of the Identitarian Bloc at the time, and have thought that the powers of Mordor offered an appropriate representation of Muslims, the *Reconquista* had not yet begun in Europe, but it already had its film, that was doubtless how he saw things. Had he taken part in actions that were actually illegal or violent? Paul didn't think so, but he wasn't really sure, Cécile probably knew, but he wouldn't ask her about it. Either way, his studies to become a notary must have calmed him down. Perhaps not entirely, though; there was still something weirdly rebellious about him, something not entirely domesticated, hard to define. His father had always liked him, he wasn't *disappointed by his son-in-law*, and the wedding had been a sumptuous one, with horse-drawn carriages crossing the mountains of Beaujolais, that kind of thing, completely out of proportion to his own treatment. His father had always preferred Cécile, that was the truth of the matter, Cécile had been his pet from the beginning, and in the end he couldn't argue with that because Cécile *was* preferable, she was just a better-quality human being.*

Things had been turned violently upside down; his father was now in the role of the child, even the baby, but Cécile would be a match for the situation, she was in her prime and she would not be defeated, Paul was sure; his father would never find himself in the same situation as those little old women who are left to soak in their own shit and urine for hours, waiting for a nurse or more probably a care worker better disposed than the others to come and change their nappy. Thinking of what might have awaited his father, what his father's fate might have been if Cécile and Madeleine had not been there, Paul felt slightly oppressed, and decided to take a walk among the vines. The vines didn't look like much at this time of year: twisted, black and mediocre, rather ugly,

* When you come to look at questions of this kind (and sooner or later we always end up examining questions of this kind), we must take into account the fact that one always places oneself at the exact centre of the moral world, that one always considers oneself as a being that is neither good nor bad, morally neutral (I mean in the true heart, the secret nook of one's being, because officially one always describes oneself as 'quite a good guy', but deep down one is not deceived, deep down one always has that secret scale that places one at the exact centre of the moral world). Thus a methodological bias is created in the observation, and a translation process proves necessary almost every time.

trying to preserve their essence throughout the winter, it was impossible to imagine that such wretched little things might later give birth to wine, the world was strangely organized, Paul said as he strolled among the penny-bun mushrooms. If God really existed, as Cécile thought, he could have provided more clues about his opinions, God was a very poor communicator, such amateurism would not be allowed in a professional context.

4

The hospital was full of people that Christmas Day, not surprising in itself, for most visitors it was their moment of annual generosity, which would finish by the next day at the latest, or more probably that same evening. The nurse was the one from the previous day (was she permanently employed throughout the whole holiday period?), she looked tired, but still just as helpful and competent. The door to the room was closed. 'The carers are washing him,' she said, 'it will be a quarter of an hour.'

Madeleine had brought a present, a box of cigars, Gold Medal No. 1. Paul remembered those cigars, long and quite slender, panatelas, which his father had had difficulty finding, they were made by La Gloria Cubana, a relatively unknown little factory, and which he thought were the best cigars in the world, far superior to Cohiba or Partagas. 'I just want to show them to him and let him smell them, of course,' Madeleine explained, 'I'm not going to leave them at the hospital'; she plainly didn't place much trust in the hospital staff.

This surprising present was not unjustified; in principle, his father's sensory capacities had completely returned, including his sense of smell. In any case, he could see, the nurse had been categorical on that point, and he recognized what he saw. He could also understand spoken words, Cécile at least was sure of it, and she started to tell him about their Christmas evening, the whole village had asked after him, she talked to him about their dinner menu, and the present that they had given Paul; she also talked about Hervé, without mentioning the fact that he was unemployed. Paul listened to his sister more and more distractedly, and made his mind up all of a sudden. 'Can you leave us?' he asked Cécile. 'Can you leave us for a moment?'

She said yes, of course, and left at once with Madeleine. He took a long breath and stared his father right in the eyes before he started talking. He had planned nothing, nothing in particular, and he felt as if he was sliding down a slope, his eyes still fixed on his father's eyes. He talked about Bruno first, that was important for him. He talked about him for a long time, spoke about the next presidential election, and also broached the topic of the strange messages that were troubling websites all over the world, he imagined that that might interest him, as a former member of the DGSI. He also talked about Prudence, that was the most difficult part, given that his father had never liked Prudence very much, Paul was aware, even if he had almost always been careful not to say so. Once, just once, very late at night (what were they doing still up together at three in the morning? impossible to remember), he had let slip: 'I'm not sure she's the woman for you.' But immediately afterwards he had added: 'Neither am I sure that ENA is the right school for you. Right now I don't really understand the direction that you are trying to give to your life. But it's your life, of course.'

Finally, Paul added that he regretted not having children, and it was a real shock when he heard those words coming out of his mouth, because it was something he had never said to himself, and what was more it was completely unexpected, he had always been sure of the opposite. He had never spoken so intimately to his father when he was in full possession of his faculties, and he had been sorry about it at many times in his life. He had tried, but he simply hadn't succeeded. With his face frozen in a priestly expression, his eyes staring at an indeterminate point in space, his father no longer belonged entirely to humanity, there was definitely something spectral about him, but also something oracular.

He went on talking for a long time, and came out in a state of great mental confusion. Cécile and Madeleine were no longer in the corridor, and the first person he happened upon was the nurse. She looked anxious when she saw him.

'It doesn't look as if it's working . . .' she said. 'You've been . . . Was it difficult?' Obviously, Paul said to himself, she must be used to families going into tailspins after visiting their parents, their brothers or their children in a coma, that kind of thing was her daily bread. 'Do you want to rest in our free room for a moment?'

He said no, that he would be all right in a moment. In fact he wasn't entirely sure.

'Your dad won't be with us for long, you know . . .' she said, more solicitous than ever. 'You're seeing the senior consultant on Monday, is that right?' Paul said he was.

'He's in a Stage 2 coma, almost Stage 1; they'll definitely try and find him a place in a PVS/MCS unit.'

'What's a PVS/MCS unit?'

'PVS is persistent vegetative state, your father's condition at the moment: no reactions, no interactions with the world. MCS is the minimally conscious state, when the patient begins to react a little, to have voluntary movements, generally beginning with the eyes. I worked in a PVS/MCS unit for several years; I liked it, they're generally run by good people who take the time to be interested in each patient. Here we can't, we're in A&E, then resuscitation; the patients don't stay for long, it's not possible to get to know them. I'm sure your dad is an interesting person.'

She had said 'is' and not 'was', that was worth noting; but anyway, what could she know?

'He has an interesting face, I think, a handsome face. You look very like him, by the way.'

What did she mean by that? Was she flirting with him? She was a pretty girl, she must have been about twenty-five or thirty, she had tousled, curly reddish-blond hair and a good figure, you could see that quite clearly under her doctor's coat – but she didn't look well, her nervous gestures betrayed her desire for a cigarette, she must have been worried at the moment, tobacco didn't lie, he himself had been smoking a lot since his father's CVA, particularly when he had to go to the hospital. Was she having problems with an untrustworthy boyfriend? Was she looking for a reassuring man in his forties who was settled in life, a man rather like himself, in fact? None of it made any sense, and he went to find Cécile.

'Your sister went down to the cafeteria, I think, with your dad's companion . . .' the girl said, as if she had been following the course of his thoughts. He took his leave, reflecting that his father was twenty or twenty-five years older than Madeleine, and that he certainly wouldn't have hesitated; he went down the stairs leading to the cafeteria level, with a growing sense of having been an idiot.

Madeleine and Cécile were sitting with slices of apple clafoutis and fizzy drinks. Hervé had joined them, with a hot dog and a beer. Cécile seemed to be waiting for him, she noticed him as soon as he came into the room and watched him as he approached their table.

'You had a lot to say to Dad . . .' she said as he sat down.

'I did?'

'You stayed with him for more than two hours . . .' It wasn't a reproach, she was just intrigued. 'Well, I'm sure it's a good thing that you did, I'm sure you needed to, and he probably needed it even more. We're going up to say goodbye, and then we'll head back. We have a meeting with the senior consultant at nine o'clock on Monday morning.'

5

The weather was worse on Saturday morning, but Paul still loved the landscape just as much when it was covered with mist, and took a long walk around the hills and the vineyards. When he got back, he called Bruno and explained the situation; as he expected there was no problem with him taking the whole week. Nothing important was due to happen in the immediate future, but things would probably start up again in early January, so he couldn't wait longer than that; the president might also allude to the issue of his successor during his New Year's speech, it wasn't impossible. Besides, the video staging Bruno's decapitation had disappeared completely, and couldn't be found anywhere on the internet; Martin-Renaud had kept his promise.

To make his call he had gone to sit in the conservatory, a little octagonal room filled with rubber boots, begonias, hibiscus and other more or less tropical plants whose names he didn't know. He was able to take his coffee there thanks to a little marquetry table. The room, glazed on all sides, offered a magnificent view of the surrounding countryside. Bruno 'hadn't done much' over Christmas. So he was wrong: Bruno hadn't seen his children or tried to make things up with his wife. He probably wouldn't, and would never talk about it again; people rarely announce their impending divorce. He would have been better off divorcing quickly, before the electoral campaign really started up, but it was probably too late to deal with it; Paul avoided the subject. As he hung up, he suddenly felt very alone. He even thought of calling Prudence, who would by now have returned from her Sabbatical weekend, is that what you would call it? Something held him back at the last moment.

Madeleine and Cécile came back at around midday. The sun appeared after lunch, gradually dispersing the mist. Madeleine announced that she was going for a cycle, she often went cycling, summer and winter, there were several passes around here, not very difficult passes, but still. 'Your dad often came with me,' she said to Paul, 'he was a good ride for a man of his age.' He looked at her blankly before realizing that she was talking about cycling; amateur cyclists were a little tribe, united by shared values and strong rituals. He had no idea that his father engaged in that kind of leisure activity, and he felt a burst of admiration for his willingness to integrate socially. In certain cases perhaps the end of life wasn't entirely unhappy, he reflected; that was surprising. Madeleine was starting to talk to him, to be less intimidated by him. Seeing her coming back in her jersey and tight-fitting cycling shorts, Paul was suddenly certain that his father still had a sex life, at least before his CVA.

Why hadn't he fucked any women other than Prudence over the last six years? Because his professional life didn't encourage such things, he thought to himself at first. A few seconds later he became aware that this was only an excuse, some of his colleagues, a small minority, but some nonetheless, still had an active sex life. He remembered the act itself, you don't forget something like that, it's like cycling, he thought with a certain lack of relevance as Madeleine left the room; it was the procedures leading up to it that seemed extremely remote and phantasmagorical, they could have belonged to a mythological tale or a previous life.

Late that afternoon he bumped into Hervé, who suggested having a glass before dinner. He accepted straight away, he was always up for a glass, perhaps a bit too much, it was starting to become excessive, tobacco and alcohol might kill him quickly, and the end-of-life problem simply wouldn't arise. Hervé had also been for a walk that morning, he had talked to several people he recognized; in the end he was very keen on the region and wondered if he and Cécile mightn't move there. He was born in Denain, his parents were born in Denain, he had never left Nord-Pas-de-Calais, but you had to give in to the fact that Nord-Pas-de-Calais was fucked, he had no chance of finding anything in Nord-Pas-de-Calais, whereas here he might. And there was also the fact that their daughters were grown up now, they had their own lives, he said with some sadness. Paul wondered where they could be, those nieces that he hadn't seen since they were six or seven, if they had a 'boyfriend', as people maybe still said, and then it occurred to him that their father probably knew nothing about it. Cécile, at any rate, had a career plan, Hervé went on, a job doing home catering, she had looked on the internet, there were lots of offers in Lyon and she'd been taken on, she'd always been good at cooking, no doubt on that score. Paul didn't even know that that kind of job existed; it had been new to Hervé too. Middle-class people, meaning rich people who wanted to invite friends to dinner at their house but who didn't know how to cook, could hire the services of a cook for the evening. And there was no shortage of rich people in Lyon – not like in Valenciennes or Denain.

It was all a bit depressing, and Paul went to bed. He was on the ground floor of a huge, old-fashioned building, in the company of a middle-aged woman, with a round face and sturdy limbs, who belonged to the popular classes. He too, in any case, belonged to the most wretched stratum of the proletariat in the dream, and he was talking to the woman about the impossibility of attaining access to the upper floors, reserved for the most elevated classes of society. Then an audacious young man with very black hair appeared, who was perhaps a corsair or had more likely been one in a previous life. The upper floors were not guarded very much in fact, he explained to them, and even an encounter with the guards did not pose any real danger. He spoke confidently, as if he made this journey every day. Then they set off towards the upper floors, but at each landing they had to jump over piles of suitcases accumulated at random, separated by gaping holes; the danger was very present and the young man had disappeared. Now Paul found himself obliged to assume the role of guide.

At last they reached the final landing, the most dangerous, this time with a wide empty space to cross. Paul managed the leap successfully, then turned to help his companion, but it was no longer the working-class woman, she had been replaced by a dynamic and modern young woman who looked after her skin and worked in business management. The woman was accompanied by two young children. At the risk of his own safety, Paul held out his hand over the gap, but he felt confused by the substitution. She managed the leap successfully, and then it was the turn of the older of the two children, but the gap had shrunk, and so had the danger of the jump. Then came the turn of the younger one, but Paul was disgusted to notice that the empty space had completely disappeared, replaced by a patch of parquet on a slight slope that the child was easily able to cross on all fours. Then, on the instruction of its mother, he had to congratulate the child, which now appeared to him with the features of a dog, a very pretty, clean, white dog.

The last landing in fact consisted of a holiday resort, a vast beach as far as the eye could see, unfortunately occupied by a crowd of athletic holidaymakers, very noisy and vulgar. They seemed to be enjoying themselves hugely, constantly uttering animal cries, while the sky was darkened with big dark clouds, the sea was rough and the weather quite cold. Walking several kilometres, he was finally able to escape the crowd of holidaymakers and reached the edge of a valley where an almost-dry stream fed into the ocean. The walls of the valley consisted of large surfaces of rough concrete, at quite a steep angle. Throwing himself into the void, he froze a few centimetres from the surface, then began turning anti-clockwise, floating just above the valley wall; the exercise brought him huge relief. Standing on a bridge across the dry stream a tense-looking young man, clearly in search of a revelation, was studying him with an expression of respectful admiration. Paul then rose into the air and did his best to explain the mechanics of weightless rotation, but soon had to leave him to get back to a glass house, which contained holiday aimlessness in a concentrated form. It was a mansion located in the middle of a well-maintained French-style garden with one curious quality: inside the mansion there were only athletic holidaymakers, noisy and vulgar; but as soon as they came out they turned into happy little white dogs. Just as Paul became aware of the identity of the two forms, he also understood that the glass mansion was only another form of the huge old-fashioned building from which he had previously escaped. He was filled once again with a keen sense of disgust, but he very soon found himself once more in a large alpine chalet, this time accompanied by an Austrian instructor who he knew would become his mistress over the next few hours, at least before nightfall. They had entered the chalet illegally, and were eating to regain their strength. The weather hadn't changed, the sky was covered with dark clouds, once again there was a sense that it was going to get still darker, and the atmosphere was heavy with snow; they weren't happy about that, and their initial plan was to go towards the sun. Paul's father was there too, but unlike them there was a sense that he had always been there, and that he was resigned to it, that he even liked it. This huge house, this dark wooden furniture, this sad mountain, these short, icy days: one had a sense that he was going to stay there for his whole life, that he would never imagine living anywhere else. The illegality of their presence in the chalet was also an unimportant detail, because the owners had gone travelling and would never come back. The Austrian instructor had disappeared now, and Paul realized that she would never be his lover, and that he, too, would be staying in this house, with his father, until the end of his days.

*

122

That morning a very thick fog covered the countryside. When he stepped into the kitchen, where breakfast was being served, Cécile asked him if he wanted to go with them to mass. No, maybe not, two masses in a week was a lot for a non-believer, or an agnostic at any rate, he argued. He added, however, that he had 'liked' Midnight Mass, which didn't mean much, he was aware. Instead he decided to take a walk. As soon as he was outside he started walking in the middle of a white mass, milky and palpable, he could only see a few metres, two or three at most, it was an unreal but quite pleasant sensation; he walked on for a quarter of an hour before becoming aware that he ran a serious risk of getting lost if he continued walking. Then he turned back towards the house, which he felt he found somewhat by chance. He took a key from the rack and made his way towards his father's office, which he hadn't seen for about twenty years, maybe more, he had only gone inside once in his life, in fact, on that occasion when his father had given his enlightening advice about his career. That was exactly thirty years earlier, almost to the day – his father had chosen 1 January for his explanation. But he remembered the moment perfectly, and noted that hardly anything had changed in the furniture of the room – a computer and a printer had been added, that was all. Some reference works were lined up on the library shelves – professional directories, thematic atlases of the planet's mining or hydrographic resources. There were also, isolated on the top shelf, some files – certainly the ones that Martin-Renaud had mentioned. Five anodyne-looking cardboard folders. So that was the hiding place of the mysterious clues that had kept his father's speculations busy until the end. He wasn't tempted to open them; he knew that he wouldn't understand a thing. But he carefully closed the door, returned to the main house, put the key back on the rack and took another one.

The former barn, which had been his mother's studio, had been something else, he had stepped inside it several times, without any

123

real pleasure, when he had to go and get her to join them at meal-times – by the end she had completely given up addressing household tasks, and Cécile had taken care of everything. After spending almost her whole life restoring gargoyles and chimeras in many of the churches, abbeys, basilicas and cathedrals of France, at the age of almost forty-five she had decided to throw herself into creative work, and had lost interest in her home. The wall to the left of the door of the barn had been sculpted by another artist, a relative of his mother's; Paul remembered her stay, she was a tall, thin woman, very ugly, who barely spoke, but who was gripped by a passion for the stones of the region, the golden limestone so typical of Beaujolais. She had used the stones that made up the walls of the barn – large stones, about twenty centimetres across. She had carved in each a different human face – with expressions that were sometimes terrified, sometimes hateful, sometimes in the grip of death throes, more rarely sniggering or sarcastic. It was an impressive and highly expressive body of work, the suffering given off by the wall took you by the throat. Paul did not, on the other hand, like his mother's sculptures, many of which were still stored in the barn, and never had. The gothic figures that she had spent most of her career restoring had doubtless influenced her; they were essentially chimerical creatures, monstrous combinations of animals and humans, with a large freight of obscenity, enormous vulvas and penises, like the ones that some gargoyles actually had, but there was something arbitrary, something artificial in their treatment that made one think less of medieval sculptures than of manga, in the end it was probably down to the fact that he knew nothing about art, he had never taken an interest in Japanese comics that some people held in such esteem, and in any case his mother's works had enjoyed a certain success, without reaching a huge market value, but some of them had been bought by the French Regional Fund for Contemporary Art, or by regional councils, sometimes to decorate roundabouts, and she had had a few articles in specialist magazines, in fact it was through one of those articles – and this was essentially the greatest reproach that could be levelled at his mother's sculptures – that his brother Aurélien had met his future wife. At the time Indy was a relatively young journalist – in so far as a journalist can be young – her article had been laudatory, even dithyrambic, his mother's work had been presented as the most emblematic example of a new feminist sculpture – but this was a differentialist, wild, sexual feminism, worthy of comparison with the *witch* movement. This artistic trend did not exist, she had invented it for the requirements of the article, which was itself displeasing to read, the slut had a certain way with words, as they say, and would soon jettison that second-rate art magazine to work instead for the society section of a major centre-left news magazine. Having said that, she felt a real admiration for his mother, and that was probably the only sincere element of her manoeuvres; Paul had never believed in that woman's love for Aurélien, not for a second, no way was she a woman who could have loved Aurélien, she was a woman who hated weak people, Aurélien was weak and had always been, filled with admiration for their mother, incapable of doing anything at all to assert his existence or even to exist, Indy would have no trouble dominating him, that much was certain, but that still wasn't reason enough to marry a man, one might wonder. Perhaps she had thought that Aurélien's mother's market value might take off, might reach stratospheric levels, and that in the future she herself would end up benefiting from a considerable legacy, yes, that must be it, she was enough of an idiot to have come up with that hypothesis. The hypothesis had not come to anything, his mother's market value had remained at reasonable, respectable levels, but in the end there was nothing to get wildly excited about. So Indy began to show a degree of disappointment, conveyed by an increasingly contemptuous attitude towards her husband.

Paul had never really liked Aurélien, he had never hated him either; basically he didn't know him very well, and had never felt very much for him except perhaps a mild contempt. Aurélien was born a long time after him and Cécile, he had grown up with the internet and social networks, he was a different generation. When exactly was he born? Paul was embarrassed to note that he had forgotten his brother's birthday; at any rate, there was a large gap. Cécile had sometimes tried to fill that gap; he had not. When he left home Aurélien was still a child, something that he failed to distinguish to any great degree from a domestic animal; he had never really had a sense of having a brother.

They would probably turn up on the afternoon of the 31st with their tiresome little brat of a son; it was just a bad moment to endure – quite a long moment, admittedly, as the idea of going to bed before midnight on the 31st is unthinkable, but it was still manageable, he might be drunk from mid-afternoon, and alcohol enables you to bear pretty much anything, that's one of the problems with alcohol.

He came back out of the barn a little later without looking, he realized as he closed the padlock, at any of his mother's works. It was three o'clock in the afternoon and he had forgotten to have lunch, as Cécile reminded him when he entered the sitting room. It was true, he had forgotten, and he accepted two slices of *pâté en croute*, accompanied by cornichons and a half-bottle of Saint-Amour. Cécile and Hervé had settled in front of Michel Drucker's Sunday programme; he was witnessing a rite of coupledom, one that they shared with millions of couples of similar age or older, across the whole of France. That afternoon, apparently, it was Michel Drucker or nothing; as far as he was concerned it amounted to the same thing, more or less. He left them, hand in hand, in front of the popular presenter.

6

'I have some good news for you,' the senior consultant said; then she paused, as if she had forgotten the rest of her sentence. She herself didn't seem to be doing very well, not well at all, in fact, perhaps she'd had a dreadful Christmas Eve, perhaps unfathomable family conflicts had come to light during the evening of 24 December, perhaps they had continued to rankle during the days off that followed. Having said that, her bourgeois smugness was still present, and it was going to take the upper hand, or at least that was what Paul hoped, on that Monday 28 December, when Saint-Luc Hospital was very calm, and the patients themselves, if they were still dying, seemed to be doing it in slow motion.

'Your father's continued presence in our unit can no longer really be justified,' she said, slowly regaining control of herself as she refocused on her area of competence, 'and that's the first piece of good news, the question of resuscitation does not arise, the patient's condition is no longer life-threatening.'

She had said 'father' and not 'dad', Paul reflected, perhaps she really had had family problems over Christmas, he was starting to find her almost sympathetic, bourgeois idiot that she was.

'Your father now has a place in a dedicated unit.'

'Yes, a PVS/MCS . . .' Paul added involuntarily. The face of the senior consultant darkened.

'What do you know about that?' she said frostily 'What do you know about PVS and MCS?'

'Oh nothing, I must have read something on the internet . . .' he replied quickly, suggesting stupidity and incompetence. The senior consultant's face calmed and darkened further at the same time, it was quite pretty. 'Yes, the internet, that Doctissimo website, I know, it all does us a lot of harm . . .' Paul nodded with a mixture of contrition and enthusiasm, he was delighted to play the role of the modern fool high on Doctissimo, on conspiracy theories and fake news, he felt ready to do all kinds of things, right now, to appease the senior consultant. She circled the issue for some time, however, before finding the thing that she wanted to tell them.

'The big news,' she said at last, 'is that we've found a place in a PVS/MCS for your dad.' 'Dad' again, that might be a good sign, Paul thought, or at least it was a sign. 'A place has come available at the hospital in Belleville-en-Beaujolais,' she went on. 'I think that should suit you, Belleville-en-Beaujolais isn't too far from you, is it?' She clearly hadn't had time to check the file, Belleville was ten kilometres from Saint-Joseph, they could never have hoped for that, and the conversation was interrupted by a long wail from Madeleine, but it was a wail of joy, the senior consultant finally grasped that and stopped talking, just waiting for the end of the wail. They had wondered about whether or not to bring Madeleine along, but Cécile had given in. 'After all she's the most important person involved,' she had pointed out, and of course she was right, although that didn't mean that there wasn't a *gap*, a cultural gulf between the senior consultant and Madeleine, and Paul was grateful to Cécile when she picked up the thread, summing up the emotions in play: 'Yes, we're very happy, we couldn't have hoped for more. When could the transfer take place?'

The senior consultant looked pleased, but at the same time she hadn't finished her talk, and she liked to finish her talks. 'It's a small unit of about forty beds, set up after the Kouchner circular of 3 May 2002 . . .' she began softly, and no one could have realized, but that circular was the last signed personally by Health Minister Bernard Kouchner just before he had to leave his office for the presidential election, the second round of which was held two days later, on 5 May, and this had been overwhelming for her because she had been in love with Bernard Kouchner throughout the whole of her teenage years, *seriously* in love, and that had played a big part in her decision to study medicine, she even had a slightly shameful half-memory of having, on the evening of her enrolment at the medical faculty, masturbated over a poster decorating her bedroom of Bernard Kouchner, in a meeting, and not carrying a bag of rice as he famously did in a photograph taken on a visit to Somalia. 'Like many PVS/MCS units it's attached to a PEoLC centre, meaning Palliative and End of Life Care,' she went on as she struggled to regain control of herself, feeling something worryingly moist filling the space between her legs, it was really in her interest not to mention Bernard Kouchner. After thirty seconds of coordinated breathing, she continued. 'Yes, I know,' she said, turning towards Cécile, 'PEoLCs have a bad reputation, and it's not wholly unjustified, it's true that overall they are wretched places where people go to die, I should say that, but in my view PEoLCs are one of the great scandals of the French medical system. Having said that, as it happens, the PVS/MCS unit is managed independently, at least at a therapeutic level. As it happens, I know the doctor who runs it, Dr Leroux, and he's really very good. Your dad will be looked after perfectly, I'm sure of it. He doesn't need a tracheotomy to breathe, and that in itself is very important. The downside, on the other hand, is that there is no ocular movement – it's the ocular movements that allow us to re-establish communication, and that is often the first thing that they get back.'

She didn't add that in many cases it was also the last, to tell the truth she still had quite a worrying memory of visiting the hospital in Belleville-en-Beaujolais, when she had found herself in the common room in the middle of twenty men motionless in their wheelchairs, motionless apart from their eyes that clung to her and followed her as she crossed the room. 'They have several weekly sessions of kinesitherapy and speech therapy,' she went on, dispelling that memory, 'and Leroux works with good professionals, the same ones as he has worked with for years, I was impressed when I went there. They are bathed regularly, and they often go out in their wheelchairs. There is a park, well, a kind of little park, inside the establishment, but often they go further, to the banks of the Saône. As regards the transfer date,' she went on, this conversation with the *family* was going as she wished now, she was completely in control, 'well, it's Monday today. Leroux called me this morning to tell me; the room has already been vacated, it just needs to be cleaned, it seems entirely possible to me that they could take your father in on Wednesday. Would you be available on Wednesday to meet the team?' Madeleine and Cécile enthusiastically agreed, everything was decided, overall, and the meeting could come to an end. Paul smiled suavely as he said goodbye to the senior consultant, but couldn't keep some unpleasant thoughts from running through his mind. So on Wednesday 30 December of this year, Édouard Raison would enter a new phase of his existence – and everything suggested that it would be the last. If a place came free in that unit in Belleville-en-Beaujolais, if a room had been vacated, and was going to be cleaned, it was obvious that another resident had *left* – or, to put it more clearly, that he had died.

He kept from talking about it, sitting next to Hervé in the car that brought them to Saint-Joseph – Hervé had been given an account of the discussion and of its happy conclusion, and he drove calmly, as he always did. Cécile and Madeleine, in the back seat, were bathed in an almost ecstatic feeling of relief – at one point Cécile even began to hum something, perhaps by Radiohead, he seemed to recognize the tune.

7

It was almost thirty years since Paul had set foot in Belleville-en-Beaujolais, which had at the time been called Belleville-sur-Saône – the council, he knew from his father, had lobbied the Departmental Council to be rechristened Belleville-en-Beaujolais, a name that struck it as carrying more weight among Indian and Chinese tourists. At any rate, even during his adolescence, even at a time when he was happy to travel to some place or another, in search of opportunities to live and, more importantly, to fuck, he had never been particularly interested in Belleville-sur-Saône. He had a vague memory of a late-opening bar called Cuba Night, that was plausible, but there were probably late-night bars called Cuba Night everywhere, it could just as easily have been in Addis Ababa. He was sure in any case that he had not had a significant encounter there, meaning a sexual one, he remembered all of his sexual encounters, even the briefest, he even remembered a blow job in a night-club toilet, it had happened once in his life, in the Macumba, and the girl was called Sandrine – her face, her mouth, the way she had of kneeling down, he could see it all perfectly, when he closed his eyes he could even remember the movements of her tongue. Conversely, though, he couldn't remember anyone he could have called a friend in his youth, not to mention any of his teachers, he remembered absolutely none of them, not the slightest image, nothing at all. Sexuality hadn't played an important part in his life, however, or perhaps it had, maybe at an unconscious level, at least one could imagine that it did, but either way he had never fucked that much, he had never been what one might call a *swordsman*, although he had probably shown interest in philosophical and political questions without ever being a militant, he had still been through Sciences Po, he had probably had general discussions with his fellow students, but he couldn't remember those either, his intellectual life didn't seem to have been very intense over all. Could one conclude from this that he had only been a hypocrite, hiding his exclusive interest in sex behind other more acceptable concerns? He didn't think so. Rather the truth was that, unlike a Casanova or a Don Juan (yes, to put it more clearly, a *swordsman*), for whom sexuality is part of daily life and to some degree the air that he breathes, every sexual moment in his life had been incongruous, a rupture with the normal order of things, and consequently provoked the memory, starting with that blow job in the toilets of the Macumba in Montpellier, what he was doing in Montpellier he had not the slightest idea, he had been talking to Sandrine for a few minutes and she had dragged him into the toilets, he still wondered why she had done that, she had probably read something like it in a novel and set herself the challenge of doing the same thing, and besides she was probably drunk, or else she was going through a Sartre moment, but involving cocks, 'a whole cock made of all cocks, worth all of them and any one of them', so one had only to be a man and in the right place to enjoy the windfall.

That evening, however, even if like any man 'made of all the others and worth all of them', it would never have occurred to him to refuse a blow job, one might even have said that he was in pursuit of love more than sex, his mother had never really been affectionate, yes, that was it, he must have felt an unsatisfied need for love. Be that as it may, he hadn't satisfied it in Belleville-sur-Saône, and he was surprised to have the sensation that the little town had changed when in fact he could barely remember it. It took him some time to work out the reason: there were Arabs, a lot of Arabs in the streets, and that was certainly a novelty in terms of the general atmosphere of Beaujolais, and of France as a whole. The address of the hospital was Rue Paulin-Bussières, but the entrance was really on Rue Martinière, it took them quite a long time to find it, and not before they had noticed several signs showing them the direction of the Ennour Mosque, so there was a mosque in Belleville-en-Beaujolais, it was amazing. It wasn't a Salafist mosque, at least no information to that effect had filtered through to the press, as it would certainly have done, in spite of their recent military setbacks the Salafists remained a popular subject, but in the end it was a mosque. The hospital in Belleville – chiefly PEoLC, if he had understood the senior consultant's words correctly – was at any rate a closed space, a set of light-coloured modern buildings, right in the middle of the little town, clearly isolated from the urban fabric and no perceptible relationship with it. Approximately three hundred people ended their lives there, mostly of old French stock, as they say, but maybe also some Maghrebis, probably very few, solidarity between the generations remained strong in those populations, old people generally died at home, for most Maghrebis putting their parents in an institution would have meant dishonour, or at least that was what he had been able to conclude from his reading of various magazines on social issues.

They arrived at a quarter past midday; Dr Leroux was waiting for them in his office, drinking a coffee with milk and eating a sausage sandwich. 'Haven't had time to catch breakfast, I'm having lunch at the same time . . .' he explained. 'Would you like a coffee?' He was a man in his fifties, with astonishingly lush, curly hair and a childish expression on his face, a bit boyish, but at the same time one sensed that he must have been a meditative child, rather sad and lonely. His white doctor's coat had been hastily slipped over a royal-blue jogging suit, and he was wearing trainers. 'You're almost on time, but your father is very late,' he went on, 'or rather I mean that the ambulance from Lyon is late, they're always late, I don't know why.' Then he fell silent and looked carefully at the four of them without saying a word for almost a minute. 'So, you're the children. The family . . . And you . . .' he turned abruptly to Madeleine, 'you're his wife, aren't you?' He had said 'wife' and not 'companion', Paul noted. Madeleine nodded silently and Paul understood that the situation had just tipped, he was now a negligible quantity in the eyes of Dr Leroux, and Cécile herself seemed a bit irrelevant, it was Madeleine, and Madeleine almost alone, that he was going to deal with, he had worked it out, how had he worked it out, though, how had he worked out that Madeleine was his wife and they were the children, he hadn't had time to acquaint himself with the file and in any case it wasn't written in the file, he had worked it out, that was all, and it was Madeleine that he addressed first when he invited them to follow him, the room was ready, he said, it had been ready since this morning, it was Madeleine that he took by the shoulder to guide her along the corridors. He, Cécile and Hervé followed on two paces behind, the corridors were bright and clean but not empty, on the contrary there were quite a few people moving about, people of all ages and all backgrounds, probably families, Paul said to himself. It was in these buildings that his father was going to live out his last days, he also said to himself, they would make up his last horizon, his last landscape.

The room itself was quite large, around six metres by four, and the walls were painted a shade of baby-chick yellow, a light, warm note, Paul couldn't remember the last time he had seen a baby chick, he probably never had, you seldom have the opportunity to see such things in real life, but in any case it was a pleasant colour, and a pleasant room, with shelves fixed to the wall waiting to be filled. 'You can bring whatever you like, put up photographs or drawings, arrange the space to your own taste, this isn't a hospital, it's a place of life, a place of life for disabled people. People with a disability, and you're at home here, families are always welcome among us, that's what I wanted to tell you.' He was sincere, Paul was immediately sure of it, the senior consultant was right, he was a good person. 'Will I be able to sleep in his room?' Madeleine asked suddenly. Well, yes, he replied, it was unusual but he had no objection in principle, they could even set up a camp bed for her. She just needed to be aware that the rooms had no wash basins or toilets, they would have been no use to the patients in their condition, but she could use the staff units at the end of the corridor. She would also have to take care of her own meals, the staff of the unit ate with the staff of the old people's home, and she wouldn't have access to the self-service cafeteria. Madeleine nodded vigorously. 'Are you sure you want to do that, Madeleine?' Cécile broke in. 'It isn't really very comfortable. We can bring you here every morning if you like, it's really not very far.' Madeleine was sure, she had made her mind up, she would go back to Saint-Joseph once a week to have a shower and get a change of underwear, it was fine like that.

'Well, all that remains is to await the entry of the star . . .' Leroux concluded. 'Will you excuse me for a moment? I have some meetings this afternoon, and in any case they will beep me as soon as he gets here.' At that moment Cécile's phone rang; she went out into the corridor to answer it, the conversation lasted a minute or two and she returned with a worried expression. 'It's Aurélien,' she said, 'they're arriving earlier than planned, it'll be today, in two hours they'll be at Loché station. I'd prefer not to go, I'd rather be here when Dad gets here . . .' There was a moment's silence, then Hervé said heavily, 'I can go if you like.' His wife looked at him doubtfully; she had managed to maintain more or less acceptable relations with Indy most of the time, but it had been ages, their last meeting was five years ago and she had no trust in Hervé's abilities to demonstrate the same diplomacy.

'I can go,' Paul broke in, 'if you lend me your car.'

'Yes, you go, it'll be better,' she replied with relief.

Paul had left the car park only ten minutes earlier, and Hervé was finishing his cigarette, when the ambulance arrived. Leroux immediately came out of the building to go and meet him; he plainly preferred to greet patients personally. The two orderlies attached a little sloping ramp to the back of the ambulance and rolled the hospital trolley into the car park. Édouard was wide awake with his eyes wide open – but still staring. The doctor bent down to his level. 'Hello, Monsieur Raison,' he said gently, looking him straight in the eyes. 'I'm Dr Leroux, I'm in charge of the medical unit where you're going to be living. I'm happy to welcome you.'

The next two hours, once Édouard was settled in his room, were devoted to an account of the treatment that would lend a rhythm to his week – to be on the safe side, Leroux preferred to act as if the patients understood everything that was said to them, and explain the purpose of each of the treatments that they would be receiving. First of all there was kinesitherapy – two sessions a week – aimed at avoiding muscular contractions, the retraction of the extremities. Then, and this was also very important, two weekly sessions of speech therapy to get the tongue and the lips working.

'Does that help them learn to speak again?' Cécile asked.

'Yes . . . Or rather that's the very optimistic version. Language is a sophisticated function, it involves different zones of the brain, contrary to what was believed for a long time. But the Broca area remains important, even if it isn't the only one, and on your father's MRI scans I can see that it was affected, but honestly I don't really believe it. Apart from language, however, speech therapy also helps to retrain the patient in swallowing, which means that gastrostomy can be avoided, to return to normal feeding.'

'Normal in what way?' Cécile looked surprised.

'Completely normal. All foodstuffs are permitted; as long as they are blended and reduced to a purée, he will be able to rediscover all the flavours he used to know.'

Seeing that Cécile looked delighted, and that his words seemed to have opened up some horizons for her, he thought it best to add a caveat: 'But be warned, I didn't say we would succeed; but I promise you we'll try. Then,' he went on, 'there is sensory stimulation in general. Every week we hold a session in music therapy for those who want it. And last of all, this is more recent, it's done by an association, there are the domestic animal workshops. They come once every two weeks, with cats and little dogs that are placed on our patients' laps. They can't even stroke them, we don't have a single resident who can really move their fingers, but it's incredible how much good some of them get from just putting their hands on an animal's fur. And of course,' he continued, 'we don't leave them lying down all day, that's the most important thing in my view. That alone avoids bedsores, in five years I've never had a single bedsore in my unit. They are taken out of bed every morning, and put in a wheelchair – the wheelchair is very important, we'll have to make one in your father's size as soon as possible – and they stay in the chair until the evening – we can move them, depending of course on the availability of carers. We have a park, well, park is a big word, we have a few trees, it's not really the season at the moment of course but in the summer most patients prefer to stay there, in the open air, rather than inside. And then we try and take them for longer walks, we take them out every day, sometimes into town, sometimes to the banks of the Saône. It's import for them to be able to see other things, listen to different sounds, smell different smells; but obviously that's more expensive in terms of staff, you need a carer to push each chair, it's a rolling process, we try to make sure that everyone has their outing at least once a week.

'Oh look, our patient has gone to sleep . . .' he said, breaking off. Indeed, Édouard's eyes were closed, and his breathing had become slow and regular. 'That's normal, it often happens after they've been transferred, it's a change of surroundings and it's tiring for them; he'll wake up soon, in an hour or two, I would say. I'll be off, but you can stay and wait for him to wake up, or rather you can stay as long as you like, make yourselves at home, really,' he said again before letting them into the room.

8

Meanwhile Paul had become embroiled in an inglorious struggle with the sweet dispenser at Mâcon-Loché TGV station, deserted apart from him. A few minutes later he gave up, abandoning his two euros to the recalcitrant machine; the Paris train had just been announced. Reaching the platform, he was filled with sudden doubt; would he recognize his brother and sister-in-law? They had last met some years ago, he had a memory of it that was as materially vague as it was emotionally unpleasant, but it would still be embarrassing if he failed to recognize his own brother. The previous day he had had a disturbing dream. He had a meeting with his Russian lover in Bourges station, he had never had a Russian lover but in his dream he had one; he had never been to Bourges either, for that matter. They called each other on their mobiles to try and meet up at a particular spot in the station, opposite the Relay newsagent in the entrance hall, they got there at the same time, confirmed on the phone that they were there, and yet they couldn't see each other. Then they tried another meeting place, spot G on Platform 3, but even there, even though the place was clearly identified, telephone communication was excellent and they confirmed their presence several times, they didn't manage to meet up, which was all the more striking since Platform 3 was deserted, they told each other on the phone that they were surprised. At that point in the night, Paul took the scriptwriter of the dream to task: the story of parallel planes of

139

reality might have been interesting in theory, but in reality, he told him, in the reality of the dream, that is, he had still felt painful regret over the loss of his Russian lover; the scriptwriter of the dream seemed sorry, but without really apologizing.

Nothing of the kind happened at Mâcon-Loché TGV station; his brother, his sister-in-law and their son were the only passengers to get off the train from Paris. But even so Paul would have had no difficulty recognizing Aurélien, he hadn't changed at all; his face, with its delicate, rather harmonious features, had a hesitant, indecisive quality that gave him a fragile appearance; he went on trying, without great success, to make himself look more manly by growing a beard which remained sparse. Indy was ten years older than him, and that was starting to become obvious, he couldn't help noticing: she had aged terribly; that couldn't have made her more lovable. Their son was very tall for his age – nine? he couldn't remember exactly. Their son was the worst, he couldn't get used to him, any more than Cécile could. It wasn't a matter of racism, he had never had particularly strong feelings either way about the colour of anybody's skin, but in this case there was something not quite right. He could of course have understood Indy wishing to resort to medically assisted reproduction on the grounds of her husband's sterility; the fact that she also chose to resort to surrogacy was more questionable, in his eyes at least, but perhaps he had fallen victim to outdated moral conceptions, and the commercialization of pregnancy was entirely legitimate, he didn't think so, to tell the truth, but as a rule he avoided thinking about these matters too much. That she should go to California to undertake all these operations, perfect, that was the most reliable option from a technical point of view, and it was also the most expensive – but she seemed to have the funds, he did wonder where the money might come from, it certainly wasn't her wages as a journalist writing on social issues that allowed her to indulge these fantasies, and even if she had 'had a wicked turn of phrase', as they say, it would have been beyond her range. It was probably her parents who had paid, she herself was more tight-fisted, the kind who would have gone to Belgium or Ukraine. All of that's fine, let's admit it, but what could have led her, among the huge catalogue of donors placed at her disposal by the Californian biotech company whose services she had used, to choose a black donor? Probably the desire to assert her independent spirit, her non-conformity and her anti-racism all at the same time. She had used her child as a kind of advertising billboard, a way of displaying the image that she wanted to give of herself – warm, open, a citizen of the world – while he knew her to be rather selfish, greedy and above all conformist to the highest degree.

Or else – and this possibility was even worse – she had made this choice specifically to humiliate Aurélien, to let the world know from the first second that he was not, could under no circumstances be the real father of her child. If that had been her intention, she had completely succeeded. Biological paternity is of no importance, the important thing is love, or at least that is what is generally asserted; but there has to be love, and Paul had never had a sense that there was any kind of love between Aurélien and his son, he had never spotted any warm gestures, or even simple protective attitudes that he might have had towards him, and all in all he couldn't remember ever seeing Aurélien and Godefroy so much as speak to one another – she had also insisted on giving him that ridiculous medieval first name, which was incongruous in terms of the boy's physique. Paul had the repellent impression that the name was intended humorously, an example of *second-order signification*. Nonetheless, he managed to give him the requisite couple of kisses required, even brushing his lips against the child's cheek. Not only had he grown a lot taller and broader, physically the opposite of his *papa*, but his skin seemed to have become darker than last time.

With a sigh of relief, Aurélien took his seat next to Paul in the front of the car. As soon as they had left the station car park,

Godefroy turned on his iPhone to hurl himself into what seemed to be a video game.

'What game are you playing?' Paul asked in an attempt, which he sensed would be the last of the weekend, to take an interest in him.

'Ragnarok Online.'

'Is that a Scandinavian game?'

'No, Korean.'

'And what does it consist of?'

'Oh, it's very classical, I have to kill monsters to collect experience points, that lets me rise through job levels and change class. But it's a good game, it's well designed, very fluid.'

'And what class are you now?'

'Paladin,' the boy said modestly. 'But I'm not far off becoming a Rune Knight, at least that's what I hope.'

In fact nobody could have said that the Korean designer had revolutionized the genre, and that was the end of the conversation, but Paul had a feeling that he and his nephew had *had a good conversation* this time. Once they were on the motorway Aurélien wanted to know what sort of state his father was in from a medical point of view; Paul told him as best he could, without concealing the fact that his chances of improvement were slim.

'Yeah, he's going to stay a vegetable . . .' Indy said wearily in the back seat. The word 'vegetable' quite stupidly made her son laugh. Paul glanced at them furiously in the rear-view mirror but avoided replying. Stay as calm as possible, avoid poisoning things as much as possible, breathe slowly, regularly, he told himself over and over again, although he had involuntarily put his foot down on the accelerator, and he braked abruptly just before he tail-ended a lorry. He had almost retorted to this tart that she had liked the vegetable patches laid out by Paris city hall the last time she had visited the Parc de Bercy on her first visit to their apartment – which he hoped more than ever would be the last. Where was Prudence?

He wondered by association, where might Prudence be now? Definitely, he would try to bring her along next time.

Paul was still quite nervous when they reached the hospital, and after parking Hervé's car in the car park leading on to Rue Paulin-Bussières he had a swift moment of hyperventilation, before walking ahead of them down the corridors. Not wishing to involve himself in the reunion he took a few steps back once they arrived at their destination, letting Aurélien and Indy step ahead of him into the room where Édouard had just woken up, and had opened his eyes. Madeleine and Cécile, by his bedside, were engaged in a heated discussion about how they were going to decorate the room, while Hervé appeared to be dozing. Godefroy had stayed in the car, refusing to abandon his video game. Obviously he didn't care a damn about his grandfather, which was normal in a way, not least because his grandfather didn't care much about him either. Édouard wasn't racist either – on the contrary, Paul remembered that he had particularly warm relations with one of his Caribbean colleagues, whom he had once invited home for dinner; but he thought, and he had never hidden the fact, that his daughter-in-law had as usual had an absurd idea that could 'only cause no end of trouble and woe', an expression dear to his heart, which he used often about the leftist groupuscules that he had spent most of his professional life keeping under surveillance and sometimes dismantling, 'makers of trouble and woe'. In any case Godefroy, as Paul had sensed the moment the boy declined his suggestion that he come with them, had probably guessed the existence of a thorny family problem that he didn't want to get involved with. This boy, he sensed, despite his obviously muscular physique, was by no means stupid, and his intelligence plainly didn't come from his mother – Paul imagined Indy flicking through the catalogue of donors put at her disposal, she might have chosen a Black man, but doubtless a Black graduate of Harvard or MIT, he could clearly see her line of thought.

With some hesitation, Cécile got to her feet and walked towards them, even managing to produce the kisses required by family decorum, but found absolutely nothing to say to them; after two minutes she had only managed to come out with a frankly minimal 'Did you have a good journey?' Hervé and Madeleine, peacefully settled in their hospital chairs, showed no intention to come to her aid.

It was Aurélien who approached his father first, and gazed into his eyes, which maintained a stubborn stare. He took his hand and gripped it hard – he wanted to kiss him on the cheek, but he didn't dare. Then he broke off his contact and took two steps back, his eyes still fixed on his father's; his lips trembled slightly, but he didn't utter a word. Indy approached the medical bed in turn, with an expression of resignation. As soon as she entered his field of vision, slowly but indisputably, Édouard turned his eyes towards the left – towards Madeleine, who was sitting next to him. Cécile uttered a kind of cry, like an unarticulated 'Ah!' Madeleine said nothing, but her face was frozen with amazement.

'Well, you see . . .' Paul said, stepping away from the wall to approach Indy, 'it was good that you came, you've already accomplished a miracle . . . He turned his head to avoid seeing you, it's the first time he's moved his eyes since he came out of his coma.' He didn't know what had come over him, that flash of mischief wasn't typical of him, but Indy had turned purple and clenched her fists, and Paul thought she was going to slap him, may even deliver a right hook, and he braced himself to anticipate the blow while at the same time cupping his right hand to catch it level with his ear. For almost a minute she remained frozen in front of him, trembling with fury, then turned on her heels and violently slammed the door behind her. Aurélien had followed the scene with horror but didn't move.

It was Cécile who broke the silence that had fallen. 'You shouldn't have said that, Paul,' she said sadly. He chose not to reply, but essentially he didn't agree. Not only was what he had said factually true, that increase in the level of violence had done him good, he breathed more easily. When she stared at him with her fists clenched in fury, he had almost come out with something sarcastic like 'the vegetable fights back', but he hadn't had time. At that moment Aurélien had made a muffled noise in his throat, which had had more or less the same meaning as Cécile's reproach, and then Paul had been filled with remorse. He really couldn't stand Indy but he felt sorry for Aurélien, he was the one who would pay the price, this evening, probably, in their shared bedroom, he would have a bad night. Basically, yes, perhaps he would have been better off holding his tongue.

At that moment, Édouard closed his eyes again. 'He's tired,' Cécile immediately interpreted the fact. 'It's all been tiring for him, we should leave him alone.' Everyone mumbled agreement, and in fact in terms of a *family reunion* that was quite enough for today. They withdrew from the room, leaving him alone with Madeleine, who had taken his hand and was studying his breathing, increasingly slow and peaceful.

'We'll have to sort out some transport,' Hervé said as they got to the car park. Basically they wouldn't all fit in the car, he'd have to make two trips.

9

They found a café open on Rue du Moulin where Aurélien and his family could wait for him to come back; Paul would sort out their transport. It didn't bother him, he was sure that his firmness would pay dividends with Indy, he thought he was capable of managing her. He knew she was slightly scared of him, particularly since he had been part of a ministerial cabinet, after all it was a place of power, and she respected power almost as much as money.

He got back to Belleville-en-Beaujolais twenty minutes later, in fact it was a very short journey, and as he expected Indy was all smiles, she seemed to have forgotten the incident, or at least she pretended she had. She sat down beside him in the front seat and started a conversation about the presidential election. Ah, so that's it, he said to himself with amusement, he should have expected that, it was probably even the reason that had led her to accompany Aurélien on his visit to his father: she was going to try to press him for information about his intentions. In fact nothing had trickled into the press, for one or two months he'd even refused all interviews, which was bound to annoy plenty of people in the circles in which the silly bitch moved. He suddenly remembered that she had changed employer for the second time within two months, and they weren't anodyne changes, she had moved from the *Nouvel Obs* to *Le Figaro*, then from *Le Figaro* to *Marianne*, who had told him that? Probably Bruno's press attaché, given that

146

she knew they were connected. At the same time it was the point of view of a press attaché, used to establishing byzantine distinctions between indiscernibly different newspapers and magazines.

'I was surprised that you moved to *Figaro*, particularly when you went to *Marianne* immediately afterwards . . .' he said none-theless, without any real conviction.

'Oh really, why?' She had reacted very quickly, tit for tat, but she was knocked off balance, he sensed, she was trying to justify herself, and all he had to do was be silent and wait.

'I really had trouble with Zemmour's editorials,' she went on as if by saying that she was accomplishing a meritorious act of civic courage. 'Zemmour is a bastard,' Godefroy cut in briefly before diving back into Ragnarok Online. Even though the remark was quite banal in itself, it allowed his mother to regroup and to add, this time in a tone distinctly more convinced and almost emotional in the broadest sense: 'But I think it's important for him to be able to express himself, to defend his point of view. Freedom of expression is still the most fundamental thing we have.'

'He's a fucking bastard,' Godefroy added, completing his thought. Paul nodded seriously to show that he was taking an interest in this exchange of views, they had just passed Villié-Morgon, they would be at their destination in less than two minutes, and his attempt at diversion had worked wonderfully well, it's true that Zemmour always works, you just have to say his name and the conversation starts purring along brightly signposted and pleasantly predictable tracks, a bit like Georges Marchais in his day, everyone finds his social markers, his natural place, and draws calm satisfaction from it. What surprised him now was that he might have imagined for a moment that Indy practised her profession as a journalist out of conviction, or that any kind of conviction had ever at any point passed through her mind; nothing he knew about her confirmed this hypothesis. At *L'Obs* she had dealt mostly with trans people, with protestors, indeed with trans protestors, that was her role as a journalist writing about social issues, but she could equally have devoted articles to neo-Catholic Identitarians or vegan Pétainists, it wouldn't have made any difference in her eyes. For now she was quiet, so that was something. He took his eyes off the misty road and saw Aurélien's face in the rear-view mirror. He seemed to be lost in contemplation of the landscape of vines blackened by winter, but he turned sharply towards him and for a few seconds their eyes met; Aurélien's expression struck him as hard to decipher at first, but then all of a sudden he understood: it was, purely and simply, an expression of *boredom*. Aurélien was bored, he was bored with his wife, he was bored with his son, and he had probably been constantly bored for years with what he had instead of a family. He must, Paul thought, already have had quite a sad childhood, since their father had never been a particularly affectionate or tactile person, his family mattered to him, certainly, but his work and his service to the state came before everything else, that much had been obvious from the beginning, it wasn't negotiable. As to his mother, she had purely and simply dropped them as soon as she had discovered her vocation as a sculptor. Cécile might perhaps have looked after him a bit, but he was still very young, not yet ten, when she had gone off to join Hervé in the North. Yes, he must have been very lonely. And now he was just as lonely, between a wife that he didn't love and a son that he tolerated, who probably despised him a bit and who wasn't his in any case. Embarrassed, Paul broke eye contact with Aurélien, who went on staring at him in the rear-view mirror. They reached their destination a few moments later.

It struck him as soon as he entered the dining room, warmed by a splendidly blazing fire: Madeleine, Cécile and Hervé were all feeling good together, they had developed shared habits, and as he came in he had a sense that he and Aurélien were intruders. In fact, in two days they would set off again to their respective Parisian activities, while the others would stay put, they would be in touch with the medical team and would really be managing the case. For now, to tell the truth, everything was going well, Dr Leroux had made a good impression on everyone and Cécile, constantly ferrying between the kitchen and the dining room, was in an exuberantly good mood that was barely troubled by Indy's arrival; Paul even wondered if she had seen her. Godefroy disappeared very quickly to his bedroom, still clutching his iPhone, after swiping two tins of Coke and a slice of pizza from the fridge. 'Do you want me to heat it up for you?' asked Cécile, who must have noticed their arrival after all. She received no reply; the boy's manners definitely left much to be desired.

During the meal, Indy tried to come back to the question of the presidential election; Paul wasn't bothered, he was used to keeping his silence, after all he had been in the profession for some years. In the end she got a bit annoyed and said, 'Fine, I know you're not allowed to say anything anyway . . .' That was absolutely right, in fact it was the first thing she had said since the start of the evening that was: if he had known anything, he would have been obliged to keep his mouth shut. But he knew nothing about Bruno's intentions, and in fact he suspected that Bruno didn't yet know anything himself. He tried to imagine him in full electoral campaign, replying to questions from journalists, people like Indy: yes, it was anyone's guess, his decision was going to be a difficult one.

Predictably enough she launched off into the recurrent but increasingly imminent danger of the National Rally. Hervé maintained a prudent silence, peacefully chewing on his roast lamb, and topped up his glass a little more often than usual, the only clue that he might be slightly irritated; a lesson that Cécile must have taught him with some firmness; and as to Aurélien, he had never had anything to say on these subjects; perhaps he was thinking about his medieval tapestries, which he would soon be seeing again, the beautiful aristocratic ladies waiting for their lord to come back from the crusades – childish and inconsequential matters, then. Indy was, in short, the only person talking, but that didn't seem to bother her at all, in fact she probably hadn't noticed. They went their separate ways with relief, however, once the meal was over.

10

Paul is an internationally famous star, but he doesn't know in what field. He is walking, with his wife and his agent, down a muddy street in the fifth arrondissement of Paris (his wife isn't Prudence, she's a young Black woman who looks like the two Ethiopians from Addis Ababa; but unlike them, his supposed wife has no modesty, on the contrary, she is determined to flash her genitals under all circumstances, an action that seems to fill her with strange pride); the rain is torrential, all the traffic lights are flashing amber; the layer of slippery mud, thicker on the pavements, makes walking difficult and even dangerous.

Paul is surprised that his agent doesn't turn right, towards his home; in fact he wants to grab a drink in a nearby bar called Le Café Parisien. Paul works out then that they are near Rue Monge, but it doesn't matter. They enter the establishment. Paul's supposed wife has disappeared. After some time, since no one seems to want to come and serve them, Paul's agent heads for the counter at the back. It's then that a pseudo-waiter sits down at Paul's table. He behaves with shocking familiarity, and his dangling legs force Paul to move his own to the side.

Paul's agent is late, and it's taking him for ever to make his order. To his great surprise, the pseudo-waiter asks him to take him in his arms and, acting out his words, presses himself against him, waiting for more intimate contact. Paul refuses, but the pseudo-waiter's arms seem to have some kind of adhesive power, and he finds it harder and harder to reject his embraces. Turning his head to one side he suddenly becomes aware of the presence of a film crew from the TF1 television channel. There are two cameramen, a sound-recordist and a director – Paul identifies him as the director because he is holding a rolled-up typescript that must be the screenplay for the sequence, and which bears the title 'Tenderness'.

Paul's agent glances in his direction; the orders seem to be coming along. At the same moment he notices the existence of a second typescript, entitled 'Aggression'. Luckily his agent comes back to the table holding two glasses. 'François-Marie . . .' Paul says anxiously (François-Marie is his agent's name), 'François-Marie, I think it's time for a serious intervention.'

Paul's agent has assessed the situation in a glance, and throws his arms out and upwards. The shoot is halted immediately. Then he makes for the back of the bar, followed by the whole film crew, who are sheepish and humble, aware that the situation has just changed dramatically.

The counter has disappeared. Paul's agent goes and sits in a relaxing armchair, more of a chaise longue really, which has taken the place of the counter – some green plants have also appeared, and the modified lighting suggests the swimming pool of a tropical resort. Very calmly, in a long and detailed speech, Paul's agent retraces the history of image rights. Gradually, regretful exclamations burst from the film crew. 'We're in big trouble . . . We had no idea! We're fucked . . .' Such are the words on everyone's lips. Paul's agent confirms that their situation is actually unfortunate; he doesn't try to conceal the huge extent of the damages that he is going to demand – and that he will obtain, for jurisprudence is unbending on the subject – from the offending channel. Neither does he conceal the deadly blow that will be dealt to the careers of the incriminated technicians.

*

Paul started awake at four o'clock in the morning; the light of the full moon had filled the room, and one could see almost as if it were broad daylight. He staggered to the window to close the shutters before going back to bed and went to sleep almost immediately. He woke again, more gently this time, a little before seven in the morning; he had dreamed again. He only had a dim memory of it, but the dream had something to do with Prudence, and with the Sabbath celebrated in Gretz-Armainvilliers. At the end the name of the religious grouping that organized the event had come to his mind; it was something like 'yucca'. He turned on his laptop and undertook some brief research: no, it wasn't that, a yucca was an ornamental plant. He made two further attempts before getting it right: it was Wicca, a new religion that was developing swiftly at the moment, particularly in the Anglo-Saxon countries. The rest was neither very interesting nor very clear: apparently, members of Wicca worshipped a god and a goddess, hence a male principle and a female principle, which they held to be necessary for the balance of the world; the idea wasn't overwhelmingly original. Did Prudence by any chance take part in ritual orgies? He would have been amazed, to be honest. He went back to sleep a little later. He would have liked to have erotic dreams every now and again, young goddesses in transparent robes rolling in the grass of sunlit clearings, celebrating their god, why not, but he had no control over his dream-life, it didn't work like that.

He woke again at about eleven o'clock. Under a dome of the purest blue, a generous sun lit the woods, the meadows and the vines, 31 December was going to be another beautiful day. Waking late like this was rather a good thing, as he had no great desire to meet the others; he had however decided to talk to Aurélien, he thought he and Aurélien needed to talk, but he didn't know what about, or even if he really wanted to, and in the end it was something of a relief, when he turned up in front of the house, to come across not Aurélien but Madeleine, who was filling the

153

boot of Hervé's car. 'We're going to the hospital to decorate the room,' she told him. In among the potted plants and the many photographs that filled the boot, he saw the five files that had been lined up in his father's office, the ones he had kept until the end. 'Are you bringing him his work files?' he asked, surprised. 'Yes, it was my idea,' Madeleine replied. 'His work was his whole life, you know.'

There she was being too modest, Paul said to himself, she too had a place in his life, probably even a more important place than his mother had had. At that moment it occurred to him that their trip to Portugal the previous summer would have been their last trip; they planned to go to Scotland the following summer, another country that his father wanted to see again and that he had loved. That trip would not take place, and seeing Madeleine arranging the objects in the boot, thinking of Madeleine's broken life, he was filled by a wave of compassion so violent that he had to turn away to keep from crying. Luckily Cécile arrived at that moment; she too seemed cheerful and in a good mood, women are so brave, he said to himself, women have an almost incredible courage. He would join them later at the hospital, he announced, he would take the Lada.

He had never really understood what had led his father to buy that expensive Russian 4 x 4, which had become a paradoxical fashion icon in the late 1970s. Such dandyism, further emphasized by the fact that it was a special 'St Tropez' series, was not his style; generally speaking he didn't like to stand out, and systematically went for more usual models. He had another coffee then went to the garage, which had once been a stable. The car started imme- diately after a quarter-turn of the key. At that moment he remembered that his father had bought it in 1977, the year of his birth, as he frequently reminded him, as if to establish an implicit parallel, and the car's longevity suddenly became slightly worrying. Essentially, there had probably been no dandyism in his purchase, he had simply chosen a Lada Niva because it seemed like a good car, sturdy and reliable.

He wanted to see certain landscapes again, and passed through Chiroubles, then Fleurie, before taking the Col de Durbize, and the pass at Fût-d'Avenas, and then driving back down towards Beaujeu. He stopped halfway, at a panoramic rest area that he remembered. It was only a few kilometres from Villié-Morgon, but the vines had disappeared. The absolutely deserted landscape of forest and meadows seemed to him to be immersed in a religious silence. Certainly, if God was present in his creation, if he had a message to communicate to human beings, it was here rather than in the vegetable patches in the Parc de Bercy that he would choose to do it. He got out of the car. What's the message? he wondered, and he felt on the verge of shouting the question out loud, he only just restrained himself from doing so, in any case God would remain silent, it was his usual way of communicating, but without a doubt it was quite something, this splendid, empty, silent landscape bathed in total silence; that was very different from life in Paris, with the *political game* in which he was going to find himself once more in a few days' time. The message lay in a clear meaning, but it was difficult to connect it with the life on earth of Jesus Christ, which was marked by many human relationships, and many dramas too, blind people seeing, paralytics walking again, he was even some-times interested in the poor, in places it was almost political. Neither did this peaceful landscape of the Haut-Beaujolais evoke the male and female divinities apparently worshipped by Prudence, there was nothing male or female in sight, but something more general, more cosmic. It looked even less like the God of the Old Testament, disputatious and vindictive, always whispering to His chosen people. It was more like a single, vegetable deity, the true deity of the earth before animals appeared and started running about in all directions. The deity was now at peace, in the calm of this beautiful winter day, there wasn't a breath of wind; but within a few weeks the grass and leaves would come back to life, would feed on water and sunlight, would be stirred by the breeze. There was still, or so he thought he remembered, a kind of plant reproduction, with male and female flowers, and the wind and insects had something to do with it, on the other hand plants sometimes reproduced by simple division, or by throwing new roots into the ground, to tell the truth his knowledge of plant biology was from a long time ago, but even so it mobilized a set of dramas less intense than rutting stag battles or wet T-shirt competitions.

He returned to the steering wheel in a state of total intellectual uncertainty, before continuing, still without meeting anyone, his descent towards Beaujeu, 'the historical capital of Beaujolais', Beaujeu, where he also kissed a girl for the first time in his life, the summer when he was fifteen, it was so long ago, so desperately long ago, the warm moistness of that kiss now seemed almost unreal to him, the girl was called Magalie, yes, that was it, Magalie, he had had an erection immediately and they had pressed so close to one another that she was bound to have felt it, but she didn't do anything to go any further, and nor did he, he didn't know how to go about it, there was no internet porn at the time, he only made love for the first time two years later, that time it was in Paris and the girl was called Sirielle, the fashion for strange first names had already begun to spread, in urban circles at least, but there was still no internet and human relationships were simpler. *Love was such an easy game to play*, as the other Paul said, and all of a sudden he wondered if he didn't, like Prudence, owe his first name to The Beatles. That seemed very unlikely, however, his father had never shown any particular interest in their music, or in any music, for that matter, but at the same time he was a very secret person, as if his professional obligation to secrecy had extended to every aspect of his life. So he was surprised to discover, on his last visit, that one of his father's bedside authors was Joseph de Maistre – when he had never demonstrated the slightest royalist conviction in his presence, and had on the contrary always presented himself as a faithful servant of the Republic, however reprehensible his behaviour in other respects.

He drove slowly, very slowly, along local roads that were still just as deserted; he even stopped a few times, feeling indecision rising within him, like a sly illness, so that it took him almost half an hour to reach Belleville.

The little town was just as deserted as the surrounding countryside, as if it were regrouping itself, gathering its strength before leaping into 2027, which it celebrated on a curious banner on Rue du Maréchal Foch: 'Belleville-en-Beaujolais welcomes you in 2027'.

Night had almost fallen when he parked in front of the hospital, and the first corridor he stepped into was badly lit, the ceiling lights couldn't have been working properly. As he took the first turning to the right he found himself face to face with an old woman who was walking in his direction pushing a Zimmer frame. She was at least eighty, her long, dishevelled grey hair floated over her shoulders, and she was completely naked apart from a soiled nappy, with shit dripping down her right leg. As he stopped, unsure about the right way to respond, he was overtaken by a nurse walking quickly and pushing a trolley of medicine. He didn't have time to gesture to her, and in any case she must have seen the woman, but she passed her without slowing down. The old woman kept advancing inexorably towards him; he had trouble taking his eyes off her flabby breasts, and she was three metres away when he managed to emerge from his frozen state and set off again, almost running, back down the corridor from which he had just come. The entrance was now blocked by a hospital trolley. At that moment he understood: he should have turned left at the start to get back to the PVS/MCS, and by turning right he was heading towards the care home. He approached the hospital trolley: a very old man with an

157

emaciated face, hands crossed over his chest, was breathing feebly, he looked almost dead, but Paul thought he could hear a faint croak. Near the main door, a nurse or an orderly, he couldn't tell the difference, was wedged into an armchair with his eyes fixed on the screen of his mobile phone. 'Did you see, there's someone . . .' he said, feeling completely stupid. The other man didn't reply, his fingers went on tapping on the touch screen, which made a faint 'plop' sound from time to time, it must have been a video game. 'Shouldn't something be done?' Paul pressed. 'I'm waiting for my colleague,' the other man said irritably, bringing the conversation to a close.

At the end of a glass-walled passageway, Paul emerged into the common room of the PVS/MCS unit; he now recognized his father's room and reached it without difficulty. Cécile and Madeleine had done good work: pot plants decorated the windowsill and the top of a low bookshelf. His father's affection for his plants was a curious feature, given that he had never owned a pet: he looked after them himself, he watered them and regularly changed their position so that they had the requisite amount of light. The book-shelf contained the files, which he recognized, and some books that he didn't remember, a mixture of contemporary detective novels and classics, particularly Balzac. Those books must have come from his bedroom; he mostly read in the evening before going to sleep, and Paul had never gone into his parents' room. The wall facing the bed had become a real mosaic of photographs. He was struck first of all by a photograph of his parents with their arms around one another on a sea-front terrace that might have been in Biarritz; it showed his father and mother as he had never known them, very young, certainly not much more than twenty, he didn't exist at the time, not even as a plan. Then lots of photographs put the spot-light on Cécile, the naive pride with which her father held her in his arms when she was still a baby, six months at the most, left no doubt about his preference and his love. Still, Paul himself appeared in a photograph beside his father; it had been taken on the terrace in front of the house in Saint-Joseph; they had both dismounted from their bikes and were smiling towards the camera. He must have been about thirteen. He remembered his bicycle, a 'semi-racer' with racing handlebars but also mudguards and a luggage carrier – that kind of hybrid bicycle seemed to have disappeared, you couldn't find semi-racers in the shops any more. Other pictures showed his father being involved in the construction of the house, beside a half-built stone wall, or engaging in carpentry work with tools in his hand, he looked happy, the house had plainly meant a lot to him. Most of the pictures, however, showed him at work, with colleagues, sometimes in an office setting, sometimes in places that were harder to identify, often places for passing through – airports or railway stations. One surprising photograph showed him in the middle of a group of men wearing padded black overalls, all holding assault rifles, they were standing at ease, the barrels of their rifles pointing at the ground, and smiling into the lens. He was the only one looking serious, which led Paul to a question that he had asked himself for a long time: had his father directed or, which was more likely, given the order for *ground offensives*? Had he taken the initiative for *physical eliminations*?

'Do you like it?' Cécile had asked the question very gently; he gradually returned to the reality of the moment, and realized that he had spent a long time, half an hour, perhaps even an hour, standing in front of the wall of photographs. He looked once again at his father, indecipherable, propped up in an almost seated position in his medical bed. 'Yes,' he replied, 'I think he's going to like that a lot, he's going to spend his days looking at them.' Madeleine, he noticed as he said the words, was missing from the photographs; her work had been completely selfless. That was probably normal, he said to himself, his father must have reached an age when one no longer really wants to take photographs, or at least photographs of oneself, to capture evidence of the passing of time; but when one still wants to live, perhaps more than ever. Madeleine was there at any rate, she would always be there, until the very last second, his father had no need of photographs of Madeleine.

Someone knocked at the door and Cécile told them to come in. A young Black girl came into the room, a nurse or a carer, it seemed to Paul that they had the same uniform – in the hospital in Lyon it was different, but here you couldn't tell them apart. She must have been about twenty-five and she was absolutely ravishing, with long, smooth, shiny, perfectly straightened hair that set off the purity of her features, he had never understood how they managed to do that but the result was impressive. 'My name is Maryse,' she said, 'I'll be looking after your dad, most of the time, well, with my colleague Aglaé, we alternate. And with Madeleine of course, because she'll be staying with us. So now we're going to put your dad in a wheelchair to bring him back to the common room, it's our New Year's Eve party with the residents and the staff. You can come too, if you like. Then there will be a concert of classical music for those who want one.'

It was not until that moment that Paul had noticed the presence of the wheelchair in a corner of the room. It was huge, though, with lots of padding; it had been clearly made to measure, and looked like a business-class aeroplane seat. 'The wheelchair has an adjustable back,' Maryse said, 'it goes from a seated position to an almost reclining one. And it has a powerful motor with four hours of battery life, so that you can go on nice long outings.' She rolled it to the bed and pressed a button to lift the bed about twenty centimetres. 'Grip him under the knees,' she said to Madeleine. She wrapped her arms round his shoulders, seeing them working like that it looked very simple, and in less than thirty seconds they settled him in the wheelchair. In spite of its large size, the appliance looked manageable, and it was easily manoeuvred along the corridors. About twenty patients had already assembled in the common room, and their wheelchairs were arranged more or less in a circle. His father was assigned his place in the circle; his two neighbours were young, Paul was surprised to note, and the one on the left was a teenager. Dr Leroux went from one wheelchair to the other, saying a few words to each, he looked as if he believed it, Paul said to himself, he seemed to think that everything he said was understood, even if the patients were in no condition to reply, and after all he must have been right, he was the doctor, but even so it can't be easy to speak without ever getting a reply. Paul made his way to a trestle table set up at the back of the room, with bottles of sparkling wine and plates of sweet and savoury biscuits; there were mostly carers there, but also some ordinary people, probably family members, or at any rate people in the same situation as them, but he couldn't see how to make contact and drank down three glasses of sparkling wine in a row in the hope of finding a topic of conversation. Luckily Cécile joined him at that moment, followed closely by Hervé. She would save the situation, she knew her way around human relationships.

Having said a word to each of the patients, Leroux was now talking to the carers; last of all he turned to the families, and spoke first to Cécile, who was just beside him. 'You are our latest arrivals,' he said. 'I hope you like the place, and that it comes up to your expectations.'

'Thank you, Doctor. I really want to thank you for everything you're doing.'

'It's less hard for me than it is for you. For me it's my job, I just try to do the best I can.'

Loving isn't exactly a job, in fact, Paul said to himself, but the job is also necessary. It occurred to him that it was probably normal for him to drift off into slightly confused general reflections on New Year's Eve. At that moment the musicians came in through the door at the back, and he realized that there was a grand piano on a raised platform at the back of the hall, and a cello right beside it, on its stand. They were immediately followed by two violinists, carrying their instruments, and then a fifth musician, a woman, also with a kind of violin but a bigger one. Was it what people called a viola? Was the formation a *string quartet*? He knew no more about string quartets than he did about farm animals, he just knew that the string quartet provided access to an enormous repertoire in Western music. Then he noticed Hervé two metres away from him, immersed in his study of a photocopied sheet that was obviously the programme for the musical evening, and went over to study it with him. The musicians tuned their instruments, it took quite a long time, but no one seemed to be in a hurry, Leroux was still going from one family to another, exchanging a few words with everyone. 'Right!' he said at last in a loud voice to cover the surrounding hubbub, 'I'm off now, I'm needed at home. Good luck to everyone who's on watch tonight. Good evening, and Happy New Year to you all.'

'What time is it? Do you know the time?' Cécile had turned back to face Hervé.

'A quarter past nine.'

'Hervé, we've forgotten! We've completely forgotten the others! And I didn't buy anything to eat, we absolutely have to go back.'

'I'd heard a lot of good things about Bartok . . .' Hervé said thoughtfully, turning the programme around in his hands.

'No, listen, darling, we've really got to go, this mustn't happen on New Year's Eve.' She looked traumatized, and he went along without protest, apart from murmuring vaguely: 'The others could come with us . . .'

They joined Dr Leroux in the hall and left the hospital buildings at the same time as he did. They stopped, startled by the cold. The night was bright, with lots of stars and an abstract beauty.

'I meant to ask you . . .' Paul said to Leroux. 'I couldn't help noticing that many of your patients are very young.'

'That's true. In fact I even think that your father will be the elder of the unit. Often PVS/MCS results from cranial trauma, so we have lots of patients who have had motorbike or moped accidents. It's . . . What can we do?' He made a complicated movement with his right hand, a mixture of flights and retractions, which seemed to indicate all at once the need to pay attention, the importance of wearing a helmet, the wisdom of road safety measures and the intoxicating effect of riding bare-headed at the controls of a two-wheeler hurtling at full tilt down a winding road. 'I didn't come to judge, but to cure,' it wasn't really his style to say that, but Paul had a sense that the phrase was there, hanging in the atmosphere, so clearly that one could have imagined one had heard it. They wished each other a Happy New Year again, then Leroux headed for the car park.

Madeleine had decided to spend the night at the hospital; her camp bed hadn't arrived, but she made do with a pillow and some blankets; she was no longer fully with them, she had already settled into her new life. A chord on the strings reached them, very much muted by distance, in the middle of a particularly fast allegro. They stood there for another few moments, in the courtyard of the hospital, beneath the starlight, then Cécile rested her hand on Hervé's shoulder. He nodded in silence and got out his car keys.

11

He should perhaps have tried to talk to Aurélien, as he had planned to do, Paul said to himself as he got to Saint-Joseph. They called but the house was empty, they must have taken a taxi to go and eat somewhere; it was easy to find taxis, he had been surprised to realize; Beaujolais presented the now unusual situation of being a living countryside, there were small shops, doctors, taxis, home nurses, it was probably what *the world from before* had looked like. For some decades France had been transformed into a random juxtaposition of conurbations and rural deserts, it was more or less the same thing everywhere in the world, except that in poor countries the conurbations were megalopolises and the suburbs shanty towns; be that as it may, Aurélien and his wife had left. He exchanged a regretful glance with Cécile; she gave a resigned shrug and set about preparing the meal; she found some preserves in the larder and enough to make a salad in the fridge.

As far as wine was concerned, they were very well supplied. On one side of the kitchen, some steps led to a cellar dug into the basement. Paul had never gone down there, it was always his father who took care of it. Turning on the fluorescent lights that illuminated the shelves, he was dazzled: there were hundreds of bottles lined up at an angle; the room was cool and dry, probably ideal storage conditions, he had no doubts on that score. Trying to get his bearings, he quickly concluded that they were classified by region. There were Burgundies that looked ancient, clarets that were certainly no less so. Another of his father's hobbies – and even a passion, it was no exaggeration – that he knew nothing about. After dithering for a few minutes between the Puligny-Montrachets and the Château Smith Haut-Lafittes he felt a wave of discouragement and decided to appeal to Hervé; he'd had enough of playing the man of the house; since his arrival he'd had the strange sense that Cécile was now the elder sibling and he the little brother. She had lived, she'd had children, the things that matter in life, while he had only written obscure reports designed as corrections to financial laws, so obviously it was up to Hervé to choose the wine. He too was open-mouthed as he entered the cellar. 'This really is serious stuff . . .' he observed. 'But to tell you the truth I don't know any more about it that you do. How can we choose?'

Paul shrugged. 'I don't know . . . The only option is to take several.' The cellar was an extra mystery with regard to his father's personality, he said to himself as he climbed the steps again; it seemed oddly out of kilter with the lifestyle of someone who had retired from the DGSI, which he imagined as being more or less equivalent to that of a policeman. Or maybe not, maybe he was the custodian of secrets of state which justified a supplement; there were sums called things like special funds whose circulation within the state apparatus remained an enigma; Bruno himself had given up finding out anything out anything more, it wasn't worth getting angry with his colleagues in the Interior and Defence ministries, he decided, it was just 'pin money'; in general, as far as he was concerned, anything less than a billion euros was pin money.

In the middle of the meal he developed a headache and a bad taste spread in his mouth, something fetid, and he couldn't wait for New Year's Eve to finish, but there was still cheese to come; trying to bite into a piece of parmesan he felt an acute pain in his molars, on the left. He cautiously touched his jaw, the pain persisted, he must have another abscess, the old dentist that he consulted at the time, on Rue de la Montagne-Sainte-Geneviève, was retired or maybe dead, he would have to find another one, in all probability a young man who would try and sell him implants, implants were an obsession among dentists, that was obviously how they made their living, but still they overdid it with their implants, he didn't want implants under any circumstances, if he could have avoided it he would even have preferred not to have any teeth any more, teeth struck him as being a source of problems more than anything else, while as regards implants, no thank you, but he knew that the suggestion would be made and he was exhausted in advance by the prospect of having to refuse.

They were finishing dessert, and Hervé had just taken out a bottle of Benedictine, when the sound of a click came from the front door, followed by footsteps on the stairs. Cécile immediately froze, and her face turned very red; Hervé rested a hand on her shoulder, stroking it gently, without managing to calm her down.

It was them, in fact. Godefroy disappeared almost immediately in the direction of his room, bright and nimble as a trout; family conflicts plainly weren't his thing. Indy, on the other hand, sat down heavily opposite Paul, spreading her knees like an old woman, the image of goodwill ridiculed – but her eyes were alert and almost intelligent, she was at a hundred per cent capacity for mischief, he understood immediately. Aurélien sat down beside her, opposite Cécile; he cast a quick glance at his big sister, and seemed to be on the brink of tears. Hervé sat back in his seat and very slowly poured himself a glass of Benedictine without offering any to anyone else.

'We got a bit held up, at the hospital . . .' Cécile said awkwardly.

'We noticed. It doesn't matter, we found a place to eat.' Indy let a few menacing minutes pass before continuing. 'We're still going to have to address a few topics.' She nodded towards Aurélien;

he must have rehearsed his speech in the car and began quite easily: 'Dad plainly wasn't in a state to manage his financial affairs. In these conditions we think it would be appropriate to appoint a guardian.' Then he fell silent.

Indy gave him an encouraging glance, but he remained silent; he had obviously forgotten what came next. Three sentences of a speech and he couldn't memorize them; she shook her head with disgust.

Paul picked up the bottle of Benedictine, poured himself a glass and turned the liqueur slowly around before his eyes. He liked the atmosphere, the vibrations of hatred that he felt developing, and the spirits slightly anaesthetized his toothache, but the problem now was that he was starting to sweat. He collected himself and let a few moments pass before asking, separating his words clearly: 'What, in your eyes, makes this guardianship necessary? Do you think there might be a danger of malpractice?'

Indy didn't say anything at first, and only darted an imperious glance at Aurélien, unsuccessfully; not only had he forgotten his lines completely but he seemed to have left the stage, his eyes focused on some indeterminate point in space that could have been the omega point, or the reincarnation of Vishnu.

'Do you think, for example, that Madeleine might take advantage of the situation to deprive us of our due?'

'Absolutely not! Obviously we're not accusing anybody!' She had reacted vigorously, as if roused into action by a whipcrack, and found one of the sequences that she had learned by heart, one of those successions of sentences that she had anticipated drawing up. 'It is true that your father has a joint account with Madeleine, which is a bit unusual.'

'That's up to Dad . . .' He had lowered his voice emotionally on *Dad*, saying the last word on a breath. Indy fell silent immediately, she was increasingly losing her footing and he was really beginning to enjoy himself, but at the same time he hadn't even been simulating, he was sincerely moved by the thought of that joint account, he himself had never reached that stage with Prudence, his father had plainly had access to levels of human experience that remained unknown to him. He got to his feet and walked to the window; the full moon lit the meadows surrounding the house, but moonlight is never calming in reality, it is more likely to exacerbate neuroses and madness. He came and sat down again, still a little worried about how the rest of the evening was going to go.

'A guardian is often appointed in cases like this.' Aurélien had started speaking again, to general surprise. He had uttered these words mechanically without addressing anyone in particular, in fact he had just happened to remember the next sentence from his lines, before lapsing immediately back into silence again.

'That's true. In situations of this kind, guardianship is very often requested by the children. I've seen this on many occasions in my professional life.' Hervé had spoken in a strong, steady voice; Indy, surprised, turned to face this new adversary. 'The designation of the guardian is the responsibility of the district court within whose jurisdiction the address falls – in this instance the high court of Mâcon. The guardian's responsibility is extensive; it is also up to him to decide, if necessary, if life is to be medically prolonged. The law is clear on the matter, in fact: the judge will always designate the child who is closest in personal and geographic terms.'

'Obviously!' Indy replied with some violence. 'We have work to do in Paris, we can't . . .!' She came to an abrupt halt. She hadn't said, 'We can't spend our time kicking our heels in the sticks . . .' but it wasn't far off. Hervé let the implied words form slowly in the atmosphere before replying in a pleasant voice: 'That's what I meant. You are unable to ensure sufficient geographical and emotional closeness.' Then he poured himself another Benedictine.

She flapped her hands around feebly in search of a second wind and turned her head towards Aurélien – to no avail, he was still motionless with his eyes lost in the distance – but she did manage to recover and launch a fresh assault – her pugnacity could not be denied. 'It still seems to me, though, that this doesn't resolve everything. In the case, for example, of Suzanne's sculptures, they are mouldering away there in a barn, the public have no access to them, and I don't think that's what she would have wanted. Aurélien is the only one who understood his mother's artistic projects, they had a genuine complicity on the matter, and I think that does give him, in fact, a certain moral right.'

At the words 'moral right', Hervé sat back in his chair with a broad smile. He waited another thirty seconds, as if allowing the notarial spirit to flow into him, before continuing fluently, his glass of Benedictine in his hand: 'Moral right may be broken down into the right of withdrawal, the right of publication, the right to the respect of the work's integrity. The right of withdrawal is a particular one, because it dies with its author, unless otherwise indicated in the terms of the will; but the possibility of exhibiting these sculptures has primarily to do with the right of publication. In the case of *succession ab intestato*, the right of publication in fact benefits from anomalous rules that overrule common inheritance law. The children are, jointly, the prime beneficiaries, followed by the ascendants, should there be any remaining, the spouse coming only in third position. As to the other two aspects, it is ordinary inheritance law that applies.'

He left a pause before continuing: 'With regard to property law – which I assume is the one you really care about – once again it is the rules of common inheritance law that should be taken into account.'

A prolonged silence followed. Paul had lowered his head, he didn't even want to look at Indy; a hoarse sound of breathing came from her direction. This time she really seemed to have been crushed. He almost felt sorry for her: not only was she a predator, but she belonged to a species of predator with low intelligence; everyone knew more or less, albeit not in such detail as

Hervé, that inheritance is shared just about equally among the children; what was this silly bitch hoping for? All of a sudden Aurélien got mechanically to his feet, turned on his heels and set off for their bedroom. Indy turned towards him, open-mouthed and stunned by his defection, but unable to react. Cécile twisted a napkin in her hands, and it was clear that she was an inch away from bursting into tears. Still, it was crazy that she was so bad at coping with conflict, Paul thought; she had had two daughters, after all, two girls of almost the same age, and there must have been rows about clothes or websites, so how come she was still so fragile?

Indy seemed completely stunned, it took her a good minute after Aurélien's departure to recover and try to go on the attack once more, like a sick old water buffalo. It was baffling, she tried to argue, that Suzanne's husband should still have a right of access to her works, when he was visibly . . . Here she looked in vain for an alternative to the word 'vegetable', and ended up explaining that he was now incapable of any kind of expression, any kind of human communication, in fact he was no longer really a person, 'except a moral person, of course'. What did she mean by that? Probably nothing, she was getting her terms mixed up.

Paul raised his hand calmly before answering that she hadn't fully understood Hervé's explanation: the right of publication was distinguished by the priority that it granted to the children, and even any possible ascendants, over the spouse. Furthermore, this idea of communication was very relative, he stressed affably. Her son Godefroy, for example, was not in a vegetative state; could one still say that one communicated with him?

She bent double with a groan as if she had just taken a punch to the solar plexus, and it was in that bent position that she rose a few seconds later before leaving the dining room. The blow had clearly landed, she even had trouble walking. There, the family New Year's Eve party was over. Paul glanced at his watch: it was five to midnight, he really needed to go to bed, he was sweating more and more, his tooth was beginning to ache again, and his eyes were blurring a little. He could probably hold out for a few more minutes.

Cécile sighed wearily, and he immediately reacted, without giving her time to speak: 'Wait, let me stop you right there. Hervé did the right thing. What you need to do with her is be firm, it's the only solution. She'll be completely lovely tomorrow morning. In any case, she needs our agreement if she wants to sell those sculptures.' He had nearly said 'that crap' but restrained himself just in time, and congratulated himself on his own moderation.

She shook her head and gazed at each of them in turn. 'You don't understand . . .' she said at last. 'Her claims were ridiculous, of course they were, and she had to be told; but did she really need to be humiliated?'

Perhaps she was right there, Paul thought to himself. 2027 hadn't begun, there might be problems, decisions to make; perhaps it wasn't very smart to antagonize Indy right at the start, she had a real power to do mischief. Still, he was sure that her motivations were purely financial, and that they would be able to agree on the basis of their common interest, the sale of the sculptures.

'Are you really cross with me, honey-bun?' Hervé put his arm around her shoulders, and now he looked very apologetic, even sheepish.

'No, I'm not really cross, she really is unbearable, that cow . . .' she said with resignation, 'and your notary act was quite funny.' Hervé managed not to reply that in his mind it wasn't a notary act, but a reminder of the law. 'But it's always the same thing, there's Aurélien, and his situation can't be easy . . .'

True enough, Paul thought, I'm sure it isn't, and she hadn't left to become a nicer person. It was two minutes past midnight, the year had really changed. He hugged Hervé tightly and kissed him on both cheeks. They had got quite a lot closer over those few days, they'd worked out some sort of deal between them, like an alliance – and without really making things explicit he felt that he was going to need an alliance, that there was something dangerous and dark about this new year. He immediately went off to bed, but he couldn't get to sleep, his toothache took over again in spite of all the alcohol he had absorbed, and he started thinking about 2027 again. He really didn't like this year, there was something repellent about the combination of those figures. 20 and 27 were both obviously multiples, two elementary products of the multiplication table that they had still learned at primary school in his day: four times five is twenty, three times nine is twenty-seven. Was it possible that 2027 was a prime number? He turned on his computer and checked quickly: true enough, 2027 was a prime. That struck him as monstrous and unnatural, but in a way that abnormality was typical of prime numbers. The distribution of prime numbers had driven quite a few people mad throughout Western history.

three

1

The following morning Indy was in an affable mood; she apologized for losing her temper, and even thanked Hervé for his remarkable explanation of inheritance law – there, she was going a bit far, Paul said to himself. 'In any case, I have a sense that we all agree on the sale of those sculptures . . .' she said cheerfully.

'We don't really know what Dad would think . . .' Cécile suggested. 'Or Madeleine . . .'

'Yes, in fact, we know,' Paul replied calmly. It was true, Cécile immediately agreed; in fact they did know. After putting a padlock on the door of the barn, Édouard had completely lost all interest in the matter. As to Madeleine, it was quite possible that she had never even set foot in the barn, in fact he wasn't even sure she knew the sculptures were stored there. Édouard's attitude towards his wife's late-blossoming artistic ambitions had always been curious: he hadn't shown any disapproval, or any real interest, he had simply never talked about it, and everything suggested that he didn't think about them very much either. His reserved attitude, thinking about it, extended to a large part of humanity's artistic productions in general, particularly in the field of the visual arts. Paul remembered the few cultural outings that they had made as a family, particularly to Vézelay Abbey, when he must have been ten years old. As soon as they entered one of those religious buildings to which she had devoted her professional life, his mother turned into

a voluble and enthusiastic guide, commenting on each of the orna-
mentations and sculptures – they could spend hours just in a
baptistry. His father would stay silent throughout the whole visit,
maintaining an awkward attitude of respect; he behaved exactly as
if he was in the presence of an important file, but one that had
some elements missing. Western Christian art was an important
and respectable thing that had its place in children's education, he
had no doubt about that; but it was a thing that remained alien
to him. Several times, on the other hand, Paul had wondered
whether those visits to religious buildings, quite unusual among
children their age, might not have played a part in unleashing
Cécile's mystical crises; but basically he didn't believe it. His little
sister had never been an aesthete, the pious images of the Virgin
handed out at catechism had delighted her every bit as much as
the reproductions of Italian Renaissance masterpieces. That wasn't
what had made the difference in her case, it had been a burst of
humanitarianism, a compassion and love directed at humanity in
general. He remembered that she had, with other impassioned
young Catholics, been a member of an association, the 'Awakers
of Joy', or something of the kind, and that they had spent their
weekends visiting old people in retirement homes, before they were
called PEoLCs. Then they had thrown themselves into a project of
washing the feet of the homeless, they'd trudged the streets of Paris
with basins and jerry-cans of hot water, antiseptic products and
new socks and shoes; the feet in question were, in fact, usually in
a terrible state. Her father observed these activities with a slightly
baffled respect, and essentially he couldn't have been entirely reassured by this strange genetic detour that seemed destined to make
him the father of a saint, and he was genuinely relieved when Cécile
showed, for the first time, signs of interest in one man in particular –
Hervé, as it happened.

Still, twenty-five years later, it was Cécile more than anyone else
who had an interest in the sale of these sculptures, she was the one

who needed the money even more than they did, and she would finally realize as much, or at least Hervé would. Paul had always thought that his sister-in-law overstated the profit likely to be made from them, but in the end that was mostly because he did not hold his mother's artistic productions in particularly high esteem; at first sight things seem to suggest that Indy was right. The last time one of the works had been sold, he remembered a relatively high figure, something like twenty or thirty thousand euros. Allowing that the market value hadn't changed, that would mean not far off ten thousand euros for Cécile; there were about thirty, maybe forty sculptures in the barn. To them that was a considerable sum, certainly more than their house in Arras, and perhaps more than their assets as a whole. They would have to draw up a precise list, write up a detailed record for each of the works and contact dealers. Aurélien would take care of it, he promised, he would come down at the weekend and was happy to do so. He was happiest of all, Paul said to himself, to have an excuse to get away from his wife.

The Saône Valley was drowning in thick fog, and they were nearly late in arriving at Mâcon-Loché TGV station. For a while Paul had thought about changing his ticket on the internet to avoid travelling on the same train as Aurélien and Indy, but in the end he had given up. They were in first class too, but not in the same carriage; it was only Friday 1 January, the weekend was far from over and the train was almost empty. He nodded politely in their direction and then went to his seat. Two minutes later they had set off. Travelling at 300 km/h through an ocean of thick fog as far as the eye could see, which revealed nothing of the surrounding countryside, wasn't really a journey; he had more of a sense of numbness, of falling motionless into an abstract space.

They had set off about an hour before, and he hadn't moved, not even to put his suitcase on the rack, when he spotted Aurélien hesitating in the doorway to the compartment, holding a packet of sweets and a tin of Coke. He came over and asked, 'Would you like some M&Ms?' Paul refused with an incredulous shake of the head; had he really come here to offer him some M&Ms?

'Can I sit down?' he asked.

'Yes, of course.'

'You know . . .' he continued after a few moments, 'I don't always agree with Indy.'

At first, Aurélien went on, he hadn't wanted to put the sculptures on sale, he would rather have brought them together in a museum. But establishing a museum was complicated, they would have needed to set up a ticket office and a security system. Also, Paul thought, probably not many people would have been interested in it; but he refrained from saying so. If he came down to deal with it at weekends, Aurélien went on, it might give them the chance to see each other. 'Recently,' he said, 'I'd got a bit closer to Dad.' He went into greater detail, and in fact Paul was surprised to realize that over the last two years Aurélien had come to Saint-Joseph more often than he had. 'Things with Dad weren't always easy, you know . . .' he added. It was a euphemism, hardly anything had happened between them during the first twenty-five years of his life, apart from mute hostility. 'And then there's Cécile, I talked a lot to Cécile . . .' Yes, of course, there was Cécile. Paul was horrified to realize that he expected him to talk to him like a big brother, which he actually was. But what could he say to him? There was nothing, absolutely nothing, that he could say openly without upsetting him. Obviously he needed to get divorced, it was the only thing to do, but it wasn't possible in the immediate future, she would cling to him fiercely until the money from the sculptures had been transferred, and then she would let him go, he could draw a line under it, after all he was still young and not bad looking, he had a decent position in a cultural administration, and fortune was on his side, he would only have lost about ten years. Thinking about it, there were some things that he could have said to him, but for now their intimacy had not yet reached that level, and Aurélien took his leave, expressing the hope that they would soon have the opportunity to talk again. Paul slumped into his seat. The conversation had made him somewhat tense, and his neck muscles hurt. The fog outside was still just as impenetrable; where could they be now? Montbard, Sens, Laroche-Migennes? It would probably clear as soon as they reached the first suburbs.

2

The fog did in fact partially clear around Corbeil-Essonnes, and the wearying algebra of high-rises, detached houses and towers was enough to stamp out any spark of hope. More than ever, the imposing buildings of Bercy rose like a totalitarian citadel grafted onto the heart of the city. Bruno was probably there, at that very moment he might be wandering along the deserted corridors between his work apartment and his office; apart from him there must have been about thirty agents in the whole ministry, to ensure the surveillance and maintenance required. Paul felt a bit better when he stepped into Yitzhak Rabin Garden: patches of fog floated among the trees, lending a vague quality to the garden, almost empty but for a few isolated Chinese tourists, perhaps looking for the nearby cinematheque, or else they were lost, they had been imprudent enough to leave their group in a moment of excitement after the New Year's Eve celebrations. They would soon regret it: Paris was a city with a weak level of social control and a high rate of delinquency, they had been told that a hundred times before they left Shanghai. Walking around a clump of trees he found himself facing two Chinese women who emitted terrified shrieks; he raised his hand in a pacifying gesture before continuing on his way across the Parc de Bercy.

As he stepped into the living room of the apartment, a ray of sunlight filtered through the clouds, illuminating the sparse fog that lay on the park. The room suddenly appeared unusually welcoming; Prudence wasn't there, but even though he didn't know why he had the sense that she wasn't far away, that she would come back at any moment; then he noticed the tree.

It was a little Christmas tree, about fifty centimetres tall, in a corner of the room, decorated with garlands, silver balls and luminous blue, red and green candles that blinked on and off in alternation. What could have possessed her to buy this tree? She had probably had a visit from her sister, and her sister had a little daughter, he had met her a long time ago. He had an uneasy memory of the greed with which Prudence had taken the baby, rocked her and walked her around the apartment, holding her against her chest. There was probably a lack, something biological that was unleashed in women, and which he had neglected to take into account. He didn't know much about female hormones, any more than he did about chamber music or farm animals; there were so many things in life that he didn't know, he said to himself as he slumped on the sofa, suddenly discouraged. He went to the sideboard where he seemed to remember there were some drinks. Yes, there was some left, there was even an unopened bottle of Jack Daniel's. He poured himself a big glass, right to the brim, and looked once again at the living room; the tree was pretty, in fact, particularly with a glass of Jack Daniel's. On the low table alongside the corner sofa he saw a pile of issues of *Sorcery Magazine*, a journal that he had never seen before. It probably had something to do with Prudence's new activities in yucca, or rather Wicca; the copy on top of the pile was a New Year issue, probably the most recent. The cover had an enticing headline: '2027, the year of all the changes'.

Flicking quickly through the magazine, he happened on an article devoted to the forthcoming presidential elections. Since 1962, the author stressed, that is since the crucial institutional development that had been the election of the president of the Republic by universal suffrage, 2017 was the first election year that had been a prime number; it was not a matter of chance, the author suggested, that it had coincided with an upheaval, a complete rearrangement of the political field, sweeping away all the traditional parties. After 2022, an even-numbered year, the 2027 election once again aligned with a prime number; could we expect to see an upheaval of the same kind? The next instance, in any case, would not happen until 2087. The article was signed by one Didier Le Pêcheur, who introduced himself as a former student at the École Polytechnique. Paul could easily imagine the type: a second-rate *polytechnicien*, who had spent his whole career in a public organization of minor significance, like INSEE, who had then taken an interest in numerological speculations. It is a mistake to imagine that scientists are by their very nature rational people, they are no more so than anyone else; scientists are above all people who are fascinated by the regularities of the world – and by its irregularities and quirks, when they appear; he himself, on the night of 31 December, had succumbed to this kind of arithmetical reverie. He promised himself he'd ask Prudence if he could cut out the article, which might amuse Bruno.

The previous issue of *Sorcery Magazine*, published just before Christmas – it seemed to come out bi-monthly – was essentially a 'Wicca special', and he paid it more attention. According to the editorial, which quoted at length a certain Scott Cunningham, 'Wicca is a joyous religion springing from our kinship with nature. It is a merging with the Goddesses and Gods, the universal energies which created all in existence. It is a personal, positive celebration of life.' Plainly we were dealing with an American; nonetheless, he continued reading; even though it was increasingly clear that they had lost the game in which they had unwisely engaged against the Chinese, the Americans still perhaps had something to say to us, after all they had dominated the world for almost a century, they must have accrued a certain wisdom, or else the situation was hopeless.

A narrowly feminist vision of Wicca had unfortunately developed, one that placed exclusive stress on the celebration of the goddess rituals, the author bemoaned. It was, he immediately agreed, a normal reaction to centuries of oppression by patriarchal religions; however, a religion that completely adopted the female principle would be just as unbalanced as one based solely on the male principle; a balance between the two principles was required, he concluded. This was what was quite reassuring, particularly from the point of view of an American, doubtless politically correct to the bone; the celebration of masculinity was as welcome as it was unexpected.

The problems became apparent with the first feature article. Paul definitely couldn't identify with the triumphant erections of the young god Ares; it was similarly difficult to establish a relationship between Prudence and the ample breasts of the young Aphrodite. But something had happened in their lives that might bear some resemblance to that, he immediately remembered their first summer in Corsica, on that beach just south of Bastia, was it Moriani? He was embarrassed to realize that the memory brought tears to his eyes. Prudence had grown thinner since then, and life had flattened out in some way. He turned a few pages and happened on an article that consisted of a summary of the Wicca year. The Yule Sabbath, in which Prudence had taken part just before Christmas, was followed by Imbolc on 2 February, then Beltane on 30 April and Lughnasadh on 1 August. A cycle seemed to conclude with the Samhain Sabbath on 31 October, which corresponded, the article stressed, to Halloween – and All Saints' as well, Paul said to himself, they were firmly Anglo-Saxon in their references. Samhain was a time of reflection, a moment to consider the year that had just finished, and accept the prospect of death.

Scott Cunningham was not only a theorist, and another article picked up on some of his practical tips, adapted to different circumstances of life. 'When you're afraid,' he recommended, 'play a six-string or listen to pre-recorded guitar music while visualizing yourself as confident and courageous. Invoke the God in his Horned, aggressive, protective aspect.' Financial difficulties? 'Sit quietly dressed in green and slowly thump a drum, visualizing yourself bursting with cash while invoking the Goddess in her aspect of provider-of-abundance.'

Immersed in his reading, he hadn't heard the door open, and was surprised to see Prudence in the doorway to the room. She stopped, also surprised, her face frozen in a hesitant smile, but she looked pleased to see him; and he, he realized, was pleased as well. 'Ah, you've found that . . .' she said, pointing to the magazine. 'You'll laugh at me . . .'

'No . . .' he said softly. He was surprised, certainly, he didn't really know what to say about it, but he really had no desire to laugh. 'Any news of your father?' she asked; he was grateful to change the subject because in fact he did have some news, and even good news. He picked up his bourbon, she poured herself a tomato juice to keep him company, and he told her at length about the emergence from the coma, the transfer to Belleville-en-Beaujolais, and Dr Leroux; he refrained, however, from talking about Aurélien and Indy. She listened to him carefully, shaking her head. 'You've actually been very lucky . . .' she said, and he wondered once again how things were with regard to her own parents, who she hadn't mentioned to him for years. 'Have you seen your sister over the last few days?' he asked. No, she replied, surprised by the question, her sister had moved to Canada, had he forgotten? They hadn't seen each other for almost five years.

'It's because of the Christmas tree . . .' he explained. 'I thought . . .'

'Oh, the Christmas tree . . .' She looked at it with amusement. 'I thought it would be more cheerful for when you came back.'

He said nothing for a very long time, slightly flummoxed by the turn that events were taking. Prudence rose nimbly from the sofa. 'I'm going to read a bit before I go to bed . . .' she said. Looking around him, he was surprised to notice that night had fallen, and for some time, in fact, they must have been together for several hours, she had clearly turned on the lights in the room at some point without him noticing. He got up in turn and gently planted a kiss on her cheek. She smiled at him once again before leaving the room. He stood for a long time, maybe ten minutes, in the middle of the room, then picked up the bottle of Jack Daniel's before taking the stairs to his room.

3

The next day Paul went out early; the shops on the Cour Saint-Émilion were closed, and even the hipster cafés, trying to imitate a New York vibe, were operating in slow motion. He liked those moments when the year paused, when life seemed to stop as if at the top of a big wheel, before plunging back down into a new cycle. This almost always happened on the 15 August holiday, and often in the period between Christmas and New Year's Day, when the calendar allowed.

It was Saturday 2 January, and the next day the atmosphere would be more or less the same, but would degenerate towards the evening, contaminated already with the anxiety of things resuming. This morning everything was perfectly calm. It wasn't yet quite the moment, he felt, to take things further with Prudence. He would have to wait a little longer, and allow a stream of hope to flow through them – the way blood starts circulating again in a bruised organ. Then perhaps something caring might happen, something that would go with them towards the end of their lives, and they would know some pleasant years again, perhaps many years.

The prospect almost took his breath away; he stopped, trembling, in the middle of an avenue, near a bank of hydrangeas, and let his breathing gradually calm down. Then he headed eastwards, towards Notre-Dame-de-la-Nativité de Bercy. The church was still just as empty. He put two euros in the collecting box, and lit two candles, which he placed in the holders. He didn't know exactly who or what they were meant for, but two candles seemed necessary. He crossed himself hastily, not entirely sure what gestures you were supposed to make – you started at the top, then the bottom, but after that was it left or right? – before noticing that the statue of the Virgin was on the other side of the church. He picked up his candles, began the whole operation all over again and sat down in a pew, closed his eyes and fell asleep almost immediately.

The young man gave his name as Erwin Callaghan, he had the dynamic and enthusiastic expression associated with insurance salesmen in the American films of the 1950s, but in fact he was probably Louis de Raguenel, a French journalist whom Paul had seen in various televised debates – he had interviewed Bruno several times.

The bearer of a business card in his name, the pseudo-Erwin Callaghan visited various New York families of modest circumstances to tell them that they were completely ruined, and that the insurance company that he represented planned to cynically enrich itself on the back of their bankruptcy. Naturally the news was not received well, with wailing and tears; but he made renewed attempts several years apart, driven by a higher necessity.

Louis de Raguenel, alias Erwin Callaghan, was now a very old man, wearing a suit and a black hat, his face was a whitish grey and furrowed with fine wrinkles. He looked a bit like Professor Phostle, the old astronomer in the Tintin story *The Shooting Star*, but also a bit like William Burroughs. He moved with the greatest difficulty, his limbs were stiff with arthritis, but in spite of everything he decided to assume the name Erwin Callaghan one last time, to announce the bad news.

Having reached the antechamber of the house, he realized that this time he wasn't dealing with a poor family, and that they probably weren't from New York. He was welcomed by a pious and devout young woman who began by carefully cleaning a table as if to wipe away fingerprints, and who then swept the floor with

187

two brooms simultaneously. Finally she informed him that the inhabitants of the house were genuine demons, but that they had nothing to fear, for God was on their side. It was apparent then that Erwin Callaghan, with his obstinacy, represented a form of rightness and justice.

After that he found himself in a sparsely furnished sitting room in the company of a man in his fifties, very tanned with a harmoniously muscular physique, and a woman in her thirties with a voluptuous figure, naked under a light-coloured dress. Lying stretched out on the floor was a very long, very thin dog, a lurcher type, but with the cruel features normally associated with the weasel. The man spoke at length, saying nothing, then gave the woman a sequence of orders in a level voice. Even though each one began with the words 'Would you like to . . .?', it was plain that these orders were not to be questioned; they sounded incoherent, leading nowhere, but the woman responded by progressively letting her dress slide off, at the same time speaking to the dog in a hoarse voice, in a semi-human language. The dog gradually woke up and seemed to be in a bad mood. At last the woman was completely naked and rose from her sofa. The dog, now completely awake, stood up on its hind legs. Then the woman pressed a little fleshy swelling just below the dog's throat, and it was plain that the animal was about to fly into a mortal rage.

Callaghan, the man and the woman were now near the door; the woman held her dress under her arm. The man, himself naked to the waist, was speaking in an affected voice, pretending to regret the fate that had befallen the pseudo-Erwin Callaghan, really Louis de Raguenel, who was going to be torn to pieces and then devoured by the furious dog. Callaghan, apparently resigned to his fate, shook his head sadly. Then the man opened the door and went out, accompanied by the woman. At that moment it was clear that the scene was being played out on a yacht, crossing a pleasant sea.

When Paul came out of the church it was two o'clock in the

afternoon, and the Parc de Bercy was bathed in dazzling sunlight. He wasn't hungry, and went on walking with no precise destination, along the Quai de la Rapée, then crossing the Pont d'Austerlitz towards the Jardin des Plantes; there were rather more people around now. Towards the end of the afternoon he decided to phone Bruno. He answered after a few rings, and immediately enquired about Paul's father. Paul summed up the situation, more briefly than he had with Prudence. Bruno had some news of his own, it was complicated on the telephone, so they arranged to meet the next day.

He reached Bercy at about one o'clock and held his card out to the doorman. The lift was empty, and so were the corridors; still, there was something weird about never leaving the ministry, even on Sundays, he said to himself. Bruno was sitting in the dining room, he had opened a bottle of Pomerol, put out a plate of foie gras on toasts, almost a *fiesta* by his standards. He seemed to be in a very good mood. 'I'm happy about your father, really,' he said as he welcomed Paul in, 'there are even still some things that work well in France . . .' Paul had never seen him so perky before. 'Right . . .' he went on, 'I'll get down to it right away: tomorrow I'm having lunch at the Élysée. With the president and Benjamin Sarfati. He called me on the night of the thirty-first, just after his New Year's Eve address.'

'Do you think he's made a decision?'

'Yes. I don't know what, but he has made one. To be honest I'd almost had enough of the uncertainty.'

Then Paul understood, or at least he thought he did: Bruno wasn't telling him the whole story. The president had opted in favour of Sarfati's candidacy, or at least that was what Bruno imagined after their exchange, and he was relieved. He had never really wanted to throw himself into a presidential campaign, or to become president of the Republic; the position of Finance Minister was in line with his wishes, his deepest aspirations.

'Will you keep me up to date?'

'Yes, of course. I suggest that we meet up here at three o'clock tomorrow, I should be back by then. We need to get organized, and sort out my diary for the next few weeks. I'm not worried at all, I'm in a perfect position to have my voice heard: the growth predictions are excellent for 2027, the deficit is as low as it's ever been, if we sort ourselves out we could even end the year on a slight surplus.'

'Has something major happened? You were optimistic before Christmas, but not as optimistic as this.'

'No, not really. Or rather yes, something major has happened, but that's certainly not what's making me optimistic: there's been another attack on a container ship.'

'Nobody's mentioned it.'

'No, this time a Chinese shipowner was targeted directly, the China Ocean Shipping Company, the third-biggest in the world, and the authorities managed to maintain a total block. It was Martin-Renaud who called to tell me, and the French secret services themselves didn't know about it, they were told by the NSA.'

'The Americans? Is that normal?'

'No, it's not normal at all. In fact it's surprising that they managed to penetrate the internal communications of the Chinese government; but it's also strange that they're behaving as if we're all allies.'

'Aren't we their allies?'

'I for one don't see myself as their ally. The economic war between the United States and China has never been so heated, it's been going on for almost twenty years now, and it seems like it's set to go on and on, that it will never end except with a real disaster, a military confrontation. Commercially the Chinese are our enemies, that much is certain, but equally it doesn't make the Americans our allies; it's a war in which we don't have any allies.'

'Is there nothing on the internet either?'

'No, and that's the most worrying thing in my view. The

terrorists haven't posted anything, either a message or a video, as if it's become a normal operation. And they didn't attack at random. After the first one, the Chinese have had all the maritime transports leaving their territory accompanied by an anti-torpedo boat; that was expensive, obviously, and after a month they decided to stop. The first transport that they organized without an escort was attacked; the Shanghai–Rotterdam line, like the first time, but this time the ship was sunk off the Mascarene Islands; again, the crew were told a quarter of an hour beforehand so they could abandon ship: non-contact torpedo launch, perfect aim. They really are very skilful. And very dangerous.'

'So we still don't know who they are?'

'We haven't the faintest idea. Global maritime transport systems are on the alert, the situation is unprecedented. That's where we are as we speak: more or less nowhere.'

A complete silence followed; Bruno poured himself a glass of Pomerol. So the configuration of the world is changing right now, Paul said to himself. Generally speaking, the configuration of the world remains stable, things continue on their course; but sometimes, rarely, an event takes place. It's much the same, he thought more generally and more vaguely, with the configuration of human lives. Human life consists of a sequence of administrative and technical difficulties, interspersed with medical problems; as age advances, medical aspects take the upper hand. Then the nature of life changes, and starts looking like a steeplechase: increasingly frequent and varied medical examinations study the state of your organs. They conclude that the situation is normal, or acceptable at least, until one of them delivers a different verdict. Then the nature of life changes again, to become a more or less long and painful journey to death.

'Martin-Renaud asked me for news of your father,' Bruno went on. 'It seemed to mean a lot to him, and I think it would be better if you called him yourself. Your father seems to have been really important in their organization, I don't know exactly how they work, those secret service types are quite weird.'

'I don't really know either; my father never really talked to me about it.'

'I understand that. You know, it's true what they say, power is isolating; the more responsibilities you have, the more alone you are. What I've just told you, I would never have spoken about to my family – well, if I still had one.'

'From that point of view, nothing's changed?'

Bruno shook his head for a long time without saying a word. Paul waited in vain for him to speak, gradually becoming more and more aware that in fact he would probably be left alone, he would take his work to its conclusion, the work that he had set himself, but he would remain alone now, perhaps it was a shame but that's how it was, it is not good for man to be alone, God said, but man is alone and there's not much that God can do about it, or at least he doesn't give the impression of being all that concerned about it, Paul felt it was time to take his leave; he took another piece of foie gras on toast, gradually filled by the crushing awareness of his uselessness. Men struggle to maintain social relations, and even friendly relations, which are of almost no use to them, it's a rather touching feature of men. The president wasn't like that, he seemed to be exempt from weakness, and other men seemed to have little importance in his eyes. Paul had only met him once, briefly, coming out of a special committee meeting; the president had talked to him for a minute or two about his 'fine years' in Inspection of Finances; he had spoken about it without any real need to, as if talking about an imaginary Arcadia in which they were both bathed in the most exquisite delights. He had probably got him mixed up with somebody else.

4

Waking up the next day, Paul realized that he had slept for twelve hours, deeply and dreamlessly – or rather apparently we dream all the time, but most of the time we don't remember. Stepping into the bathroom, he made the disagreeable discovery that the water heater had stopped working; he tried to manoeuvre a flap and obtained a long groan from the pipes but no hot water. Going to the ministry without having a shower wasn't a good idea, and he had a feeling that it was going to be a long day. He would use Prudence's bathroom, that was the only solution.

It was at least five years since he had gone into her bedroom. He had a shock at the sight of her pyjamas neatly folded on a chair at the foot of her bed; thick and very modest, they looked like a child's pyjamas. She was reading Anita Brookner, he noticed; that was hardly likely to boost her morale.

The bathroom was worse: two thin and not particularly soft towels, no bathrobe. An ordinary Marseille soap on the wash basin. Monoprix shower gel and shampoo on the side of the shower. No beauty products, apparently, not even moisturizer, she seemed to have forgotten that she had a body. That wasn't a good thing, he said to himself, not a good thing at all.

After a quick shower he sat down to write her a note, first to apologize for using her bathroom, then to ask her if she could sort out the water heater – he seemed to remember that she knew a decent plumber. He hesitated for some time about how to address her. 'Prudence' was cold. 'Dear Prudence' was better, but it wasn't exactly right. He nearly wrote 'My darling' but then thought better of it with a shudder and settled for 'My dear Prudence', that was good, that would do. 'Kisses' as a salutation wasn't overstating things, after all they had kissed each other's cheeks, as recently as the previous evening. He came outside feeling almost pleased with himself; the cafés of the Cour Saint-Émilion were open, and even seemed to be working at full power; he imagined eating something at Coney Island, the name was ridiculous but the bagels were acceptable. He immediately recognized the waiter, a big cretin who shouted 'full steam!' about everything and made a point of addressing the customers in English. He was horrified to hear him reply 'OK, man' to a Chinese tourist who was trying to order a *café au lait*. He couldn't stay there, and in any case it was packed, it would take him hours to be served; he got back up and settled for a coffee at the bar. There was bound to be something to eat at the ministry, and if the worst came to the worst Bruno had a butler and a cook at his service, there was no reason not to take advantage of the fact, he said to himself, absolutely none.

He got there on the dot; the butler was waiting outside the door to the apartment. 'The minister will be a little late,' he said, 'he asked me to show you in.' He should have suspected as much: three o'clock – Bruno had been too optimistic, it was about a presidential election, after all, and it wasn't going to be sorted out in three sentences.

The foie gras toasts and the bottle of Pomerol were still on the dining table, nothing had changed since yesterday. The toasts were stale now, too dry. He took a walk around the kitchen; there were gluten-free Heudebert biscuits, an open Caprice des Dieux cheese in the fridge; that might do in the end, he didn't feel much like calling the butler.

The little sculpture of the doe was still there, standing on its window sill; yes, it was definitely a doe. Could you say it was a 'doe at bay'? What did that really mean, being at bay if you were a doe? It struck him as vaguely sexual, although this one wasn't, it just looked worried; but perhaps that was the same thing, does couldn't have many expressions at their disposal, their lives weren't very varied.

Human lives weren't that varied either, to tell the truth, he said to himself, looking through the picture window, the traffic was already busy on the Pont de Bercy. It was five o'clock in the evening, he realized with surprise, he must have been miles away for a long time, that was happening to him more and more often, being miles away, and Bruno was definitely late.

He arrived less than ten minutes later. 'Yes, I'm sorry . . .' he said, sitting down on the sofa opposite. 'It took longer than expected.'

'But . . . it went well?'

'Yes. Or rather I think it did. Sarfati will actually be the candidate, he's going to announce it this evening, he's a guest on the eight o'clock news programme on TF1. He's right at home on TF1, it's his channel, so they're probably going to be quite kind.'

'What did you think of the guy?'

'Well, he's certainly not stupid.' Bruno paused and frowned as he tried to think of the appropriate phrase. 'Having said that, he seemed pretty good. He set out a whole theory for us, it took almost half an hour, according to which the media sphere and the political sphere really started coming closer together in the early 2010s, at a time when they were losing all real power. The media sphere because of competition from the internet, because no one thought of buying a newspaper any more, or even watching television; the political sphere because of the European government and the influence of social lobbies. Well, I wasn't completely convinced, but he expressed himself confidently and it flowed well.'

'And what do you think the president thinks of him?'

'I'm sure he's not too happy to be told that the political sphere has lost all its power, after all, you know him – no, you don't really know him, but imagine you do. And also it's not entirely true; or rather it is, social lobbies are incredibly important for some ministries; but in the case of Europe it isn't true, I'm well placed to talk to you about it, for five years I've paid hardly any attention to European directives, France is too important a country to be sanctioned, that was all you needed to know, the theory of 'too big to fail' is basically quite accurate. So the president is convinced that Sarfati would be easy to manoeuvre because he has no political ideas, he just wants to be president for the status, for the fun: the apartment at the Élysée, the presidential plane, the official visits to Kyrgyzstan, with dancing girls and swords and all that nonsense. And then in five years he'll obediently disappear off again, former president of the Republic must count for something, he'll still have a chauffeur, an office, secretaries and bodyguards, and he'll still be able to show off in front of his old pals from TV.'

'Do you think that's true? Do you think that's all there is to Sarfati?'

This time Bruno thought for ages, almost a minute, before replying.

'That's what he wants you to think, at any rate. Is it true or not? It's hard to say. On the one hand the guy is clearly impressed by the splendour of the Republic, the glamour of the thing. The president received us in the golden office just before we went for lunch, he was impressed, I'm sure he wasn't pretending, he was practically dribbling. On the other hand, I can tell you, he gave me the impression of being an exceptional liar; not in the same way as Mitterrand, but on the same level as a liar. So it's a bit of a wager. By the way, did you see the president give his New Year's address?'

'No, I forgot to watch. How was it?' Paul remembered 31 December, Indy and Aurélien in the dining room at Saint-Joseph, the difficulty he had stopping himself from insulting his sister-in-law. His toothache hadn't helped either, he'd definitely need to see somebody.

'He was very good,' Bruno replied. 'Excellent, in fact. That thing of his: "I have had the honour to be the captain of the French ship, but the captain is only the first sailor", it was clever, really, and then physically you can imagine him in a little sailor suit. And then at the end, "I'll miss you", right in the eyes looking into the camera, people were moved, I think.'

'And what about you? What happens to you in this arrangement?'

'Me? The same, I stay Finance Minister. Or maybe a bit more, maybe I'll be appointed Prime Minister at first, but not for long. The president's idea, it's not absolutely certain but I think he's very tempted, would be to change the constitution, and to do it very quickly, within the three months after the election at the very most. He wants it to be announced as soon as the campaign begins, he wants it to be made one of the axes of the project. The idea would be to move to a real presidential regime: get rid of the post of Prime Minister, reduce the number of MPs and hold mid-term elections like they do in the United States.'

'And get rid of the Senate as well?'

'No, he thinks attacking the Senate would be bad luck; the historical examples suggest that he might be right. So you keep the two chambers, but the power of parliament will be further reduced. It's a bit post-democracy, if you like, but everybody's doing that now, it's the only way that works, democracy is dead as a system, it's too slow, too ponderous. In short . . .' Bruno resumed after a moment, and for the first time his face looked slightly tired, 'I would stay in Bercy, but my power would have grown, of course, because I would no longer have to refer what I did to the prime minister, only to the president; and on the economy, Sarfati is in the slow lane. For now, the problem is that they want me to intervene in the campaign. They want to sell a kind of president vice-president ticket, which is quite American as well. To tell the truth Sarfati spent almost all of lunch flattering me, as if he was apologizing for being the candidate in my place; he doesn't yet feel entirely legitimate, that much is obvious, and it's also obvious that the president is counting on that to control him. But most importantly they want to stress the economic balance, that's one of their main planks; they aren't thinking that much about television appearances either. Sarfati has the gift of the gab, TV is his world, he can do it all on his own, he isn't afraid of anyone; but in press conferences, and in meetings too, they're counting very much on my presence; and frankly that's getting on my nerves a bit. In the end they don't really know what they want, and we talked about that a lot, I've got a meeting with a woman tomorrow, a kind of coach . . .'

'Solène Signal?'

'You know her?'

'Not personally, no, but she runs Confluences, one of the best political consultancies on the market, she's been looking after Sarfati since the beginning.'

'Well, I assume she's good . . . In the end that's where we are. It'll take four or five months at the most. Now we've got to look at my diary; we'll have to cut back a huge amount, there's work to be done. No travel until after the election, just campaign travel; we keep the professional meetings that are already fixed, but don't take on any new ones, we'll have to send out a memo to that effect to the advisers. We can get started on that, we could go to my office if you like? In fact . . .' He studied the open Caprice des Dieux on the low table. 'You found something eat, is that OK? If you want something else we can order it for this evening. Do you want to watch Sarfati's declaration on TV?'

'No, Sarfati's fine either way, but I wanted to talk to you about food, you've really got to change your way of life. That's enough pizza and sandwiches. You need to eat green vegetables.'

'*Green vegetables?*' He repeated the words in a baffled voice, as if hearing them for the first time.

'Yes, green vegetables. And fish; and the odd bit of meat as well. Hold off on the cheese and charcuteries. Pasta and slow-release carbs, otherwise you're not going to make it. A presidential campaign is tough, well, I've never done one, but that's what everyone says. Talk to the Signal girl, I'm sure she'll tell you the same.'

Then they walked towards Bruno's office. Their journey took them down the ministry corridors for at least ten minutes, but they didn't bump into anyone. '*Green vegetables* . . .' Bruno said in an undertone. He sounded aghast.

5

The dates of the forthcoming presidential election were announced two days later, after the meeting of the council of ministers, and all that remained was for them to be validated by the constitutional council: they would be held on Sundays 16 and 30 May. These dates were quite late, and there would be just enough time to organize the assembly elections at the same time. It would therefore be quite a long campaign. In the opinion of most of the commentators, this was a surprising tactical choice. The candidate from the National Rally was a relative unknown, all that was known about him was that he was twenty-seven and a graduate of the HEC business school, a city councillor in Orange, and that he was good-looking; that was more or less it. Of course Marine would be present, she would support him in his meetings, but he did suffer from a genuine fame deficit. The president's party should have stifled him from the get-go without giving him time to settle in the political landscape, or at least that was what most observers thought. The only explanation for this choice – mean, and not at the level of what was at stake, but no other option was apparent – was that the president had not the slightest desire to leave his post, and would extend his five-year term to the limit. Bruno had groaned a little; he was in a hurry to get it over with as soon as possible. Sarfati, on the other hand, had taken it well, given that he was on a slow-wisdom trip; Solène Signal had dug him out a Peruvian shaman, and every morning when he woke up, he worked on his slow wisdom, spending two hours on it, and it was almost a month since he had made a joke. In any case it was the president's choice that won out in the end, as usual.

Paul was present for the first meeting between Bruno and Solène Signal, which was held in Bruno's office. She arrived at midday on the dot, with a young man of about twenty-five in an impeccable grey suit, white shirt, claret tie, and clutching a worn, brown leather satchel. He could perfectly easily have been a Bercy civil servant. Solène was a woman of about forty, short and plump, hastily made-up, not particularly impressive at first glance. She was wearing a pair of jeans, a grey sweatshirt and a fur coat.

'Hello,' she said, settling herself on the sofa. 'Any chance of a coffee?'

'I'll sort it out,' Bruno said. 'Two espressos?'

'A big pot of black coffee, very strong. And some hard-boiled eggs.'

'You wouldn't prefer some croissants, some pastries? Maybe an orange juice?'

'Hard-boiled eggs.'

Bruno passed on the order.

'What number do we need to call if we want something?' Solène Signal asked. 'I say that because we're going to be coming back a few times, I reckon.'

'You call twenty-seven for the kitchen, and if you need housekeeping it's thirty-one.' The assistant immediately noted this down in a notebook that he'd just taken out of his briefcase. 'Although next time it might be better if we used my work apartment, it'll be more comfortable.'

'Oh, you live here too? That's great, it's very practical.'

She nodded with satisfaction, then set out four vapes on the low table in front of her. These cigarettes, she would later explain, had four different flavours: mango, apple, menthol and dark tobacco. They were necessary for her to function, and she was convinced that she needed to function if everything else was going to run smoothly.

After spending a few seconds looking at Paul, she said casually, 'So you're the personal assistant. The confidant . . .' She had lowered her voice a little on that last word, and Paul smiled to show that he wasn't annoyed by the term; he was the *confidant*, in fact.

'Fine fine fine, our candidate . . .' She turned her head slowly towards Bruno and this time she studied him at length, for over a minute, before concluding, in a very low voice: 'I expected worse . . .'; then she bit her lips, that had slipped out.

'Well obviously,' she added immediately. 'I've seen you as a minister, but we're going to have to change gear, and we don't have an infinite amount of time in front of us. I've got a girl here who's been working with us for a year, Raksaneh. I think I'll put her on to you.' The assistant immediately jotted down: 'Raksaneh'.

'If there's a problem,' she went on, 'if things don't work out in interpersonal terms, tell me straight away. She's never done a presidential, obviously, but she has worked on big elections . . .' She thought for a few more seconds. 'No, definitely, I have a good feeling about our case. Anyway, we'll debrief every evening, for the first while.

'I thought for a bit last night,' she went on. Paul glanced at her and suddenly realized what it was that had struck him as strange about her and her assistant since the beginning: their features were drawn, and their movements curiously slow, with the occasional nervous twitch; it looked very much as if neither of them had slept the night before.

'We're not going to make you appear together, or not much, or at least not at the start. Mutually self-congratulatory interviews always make a crap impression, so that's not how we're going to do it. Benjamin will say good things about you, obviously, he's always going to be praising what you do. And you will say good things about him too, but later, you've got to get up to speed, that'll be Raksaneh's job, and I don't plan to have you make any appearances before early February.' Bruno noted with a little start that she had switched to addressing him using the familiar *tu*, probably involuntarily, and at that moment he had become her thing, her project, and he was now really committed to this campaign. 'For now, Benjamin is in the front line. We've prepared some reports for him . . .' At a nod of her head, the assistant took a file from his satchel. Bruno flicked through it with surprise for a moment before passing it to Paul. There were about fifty brown A4 envelopes; the first titles he saw were 'The car industry', 'Nuclear power', 'Foreign trade' and 'Balancing the budget'.

'These are for validation,' she said, turning towards Paul. 'You'll probably think they're a bit simplistic, but I don't think we've said anything too stupid. What I'm asking you to do more than anything is to update the figures, they're not the latest ones. Benjamin's not going to have to line up the figures particularly, that's not his role; but if he throws one out from time to time when it seems appropriate it's always dumb to get caught out over numbers. As for us,' she continued for Bruno's benefit, 'we're going to give you a briefing about Benjamin, we'll get on it straight away, but of course it won't be the same, more of a video, I think, about two hours long. Of course, you can zip through the first part of his career. Although . . . We've checked everything, you know, since the first broadcast, we've been working on him for years. He's never the one who comes out with the really low blows, the below-the-belt stuff, it's always an assistant reporter who does that. He's level, he's calm, he's good as gold, there's not even any swearing, it's as if he was warned in advance . . .' She paused thoughtfully for a moment, this time with an involuntary expression of admiration. 'Still,' she went on, 'we're going to insist on what happens next. With politicians, veiled women, mainstream intellectuals, of course there's no problem; but when things get tough, as you'll see, he's pretty incredible: with Badiou he's perfect, impeccable with Greta Thunberg, and frankly majestic with Zemmour. And obviously we're going to go to the max on humanitarianism, migrants, Stéphane Bern . . .'

The assistant, who was jotting things down at full speed, gave a little jerk of surprise on hearing 'Stéphane Bern.'

'Yeah, don't nitpick . . .' she turned to him impatiently, 'humanitarian, heritage, you get it.' He didn't look as if he got it entirely, in fact, but he wrote it down anyway.

The butler knocked at the door and came in holding a tray. She poured herself a mug of coffee and swallowed two hard-boiled eggs one after the other before going on.

'There's one other point, Bruno, which we should really address straight away. Your marriage situation . . .'

He stiffened noticeably. She had expected it, and started again gently:

'Yes, I know, it's embarrassing. It's embarrassing for me too. But there are two questions I need to ask you, it's my duty to ask them, let's do it now, once and for all, and never mention it again. First of all: are divorce proceedings under way?'

'No.'

'And does your wife plan to do that, or anything else that might become public before the election?

'Again, no.'

'Fine . . . That's all amazing. And is there, forgive me that's three questions, and the answer seems obvious: there's no hatred, no particular acrimony between you? She isn't suddenly going to start giving statements to the press?'

'No, I don't think so.' He moved his head oddly and thought again for a few seconds before finishing:

'In fact I'm sure she won't.'

'Good good good good good, that's all excellent, it's amazing. I'm not going to bore on at you about your relationships, it's none of my business, it's not my problem.' Paul sensed that she was lying a bit, she was bound to have done some digging and she knew that Bruno had no romantic relationships at the moment, otherwise she would have taken an interest; but it was a nice, civilized, kind lie in a way. Paul got up on the pretext of pouring himself some more coffee, he had always been good at reading upside down, it was a little trick that he had used in his exams, and he could read that the assistant had written in his notebook, underlining it, 'His arse is clean.'

'I feel that we're going to work well,' Solène Signal went on, 'I'm feeling that more and more this election. We're not going to change the concept, at any rate he's at the net and you're at the back of the court, that's how we're going to play it. But still, we're going to win you a few points in terms of closeness and empathy. If I can't win you some points in terms of closeness and empathy, it's really because I'm rubbish!' She cheerfully raised her hands in the air as if to stress the absurdity of the proposition, perhaps waiting for her assistant to burst out laughing at the incongruous idea, but he merely waited, ballpoint pen in hand.

'And otherwise, do you cook?'

'Erm, no . . .' Bruno thought for a few seconds. 'But I like pizzas,' he added as a gesture of goodwill. The assistant immediately jotted 'pizzas' in his notebook, in spite of Solène's apparent lack of enthusiasm.

'And in terms of your origins, where are you from? Geographic origins, I mean.'

'Paris.'

'Paris-Paris? Both of your parents come from Paris?'

'My mother did, yes – well, my parents are both dead. My father grew up in the Oise.'

'The Oise . . . That's not bad, the Oise, has a good ring to it. Where exactly?'

'Méricourt.'

'And do you still have a house, anything in the area?'

'Well . . . I hadn't thought about it, but yes, in fact, my father kept a house in Méricourt. I inherited it; I thought of selling it, but I haven't had time to deal with it.'

'Is it still furnished? Do you think we might be able to do a shoot there?'

'Yes, probably.'

'Amazing, truly amazing! And also, as far as I can see, it's bang in the middle of Front territory.'

The assistant, tapping on his laptop with his left hand as he went on making notes at top speed with his right, confirmed a few seconds later: 'Sure enough. Totally, in fact. What's funny, on the other hand, is that they have a communist mayor.'

'A communist mayor . . .' She smiled with delight, life is definitely full of wonders, she seemed to be writing. 'Right, well listen . . .' She turned back towards her assistant. 'Can you get that organized for me quite quickly?' He nodded and took another note.

'Right, I think we've done a good job there . . .' she concluded, getting to her feet, visibly satisfied. 'Can I send you Raksaneh this afternoon?'

'You have a meeting with the CEO of Chrysler at three,' Paul cut in.

She turned towards him. 'The CEO of Chrysler, right . . . When do you think that'll be done?'

'It's quite a complicated meeting. Let's say five.'

'Raksaneh will be there at five. It's just to get to know each other, you won't really start until tomorrow. In fact . . .' she addressed Paul again, 'will you deal with those reports for Benjamin?'

'I'll have them for you in two or three days.'

'I need them tomorrow morning.' She didn't speak brutally, but with the certainty that she would be obeyed. 'Well, as much as you can. We have a few interviews during the day.'

'The problem is that I tend to work at home in the morning,' Paul said, reflecting that 'work' wasn't perhaps the exact term at the moment.

'No problem, I'll send a courier round to yours. Eight o'clock?' she asked, extending a hand.

'Eight o'clock,' he replied with resignation.

6

The courier arrived exactly when she said she would the following morning; he had had time to correct about fifteen files. 'You're getting up at dawn now?' Prudence said with astonishment as she came across him in the living room. His heart tightened at the sight of her, tiny in her child's pyjamas, with little rabbits embroidered on the chest. It wasn't that, he said to himself despairingly, it wasn't that at all. Luckily she didn't seem to think about those things. Luckily or unluckily, whichever.

'So that's it now?' she asked. 'You're really embroiled in politics?' In spite of himself, he was filled by a new wave of painful compassion as he remembered Nero's tirade in Racine's *Britannicus*:

> *Beautiful and unadorned, in the simple garb*
> *Of beauty newly torn from sleep.*

Well no, he wasn't really embroiled in politics, in fact it was rather the opposite, his job was to free Bruno up from everything that wasn't directly political; he would have a number of meetings with the cabinet's technical advisers and try to pass the minister's instructions on to them over the months to come; they would link up with the staff directorates.

'And then,' he added, 'I'll see how Bruno's getting on, whether he needs me.'

'He'll need you, I'm sure. This whole media circus is new to him, he's going to have moments of doubt, he'll need you more than ever.' She paused for a few seconds before asking him gently:

'You really like him, don't you?'

'Yes . . .' he agreed after a brief moment of embarrassment. 'Yes, I really do.'

'That's great. Do you want a coffee?'

'I'd love one.'

They moved into the kitchenette, and she made two espressos with her new machine; the sun was rising over the Parc de Bercy.

'I'm not sure he will actually have moments of doubt,' Paul said. 'I've never seen him have any. Moments of pure physical fatigue, yes; but doubt? I'm not sure he's familiar with it. What about you? What about your work?'

'Oh, me . . . Corrective project for finance law, that kind of thing, it hasn't changed that much. I need to get ready,' she said after finishing her coffee, 'I have a meeting this morning at nine.'

'I have to go to Bercy too, I need to consult some statistics for last year. We could go together, if you want.'

They crossed the Parc de Bercy;, the air was cold and dry but the sky was grey and overcast, and it was probably going to stay like that all day. It had been years, Paul thought, since they had set off together like that, for work. When they reached the Yitzhak Rabin Garden she slipped her arm under his. He had a little shock, as if his heart had missed a beat or two; then he recovered and gripped Prudence's arm tightly.

The next two weeks were a strange period for him. He was resuming contact with the cogwheels of the administration that he had rather lost sight of; for the first time in at least a year he left the minister's floor for meetings with directors. In reality, he had been playing a part as chief secretary for all this time, he'd been in charge of Bruno's diary and all his movements. But the real chief secretary, the one he was seeing for the first time since mid-November, didn't hold it against him; he didn't much enjoy those organizational tasks, which in his eyes were barely an inch above secretarial work, and more importantly it had allowed him to spent time on his real passion: fiscal legislation.

More and more often now he set off for work with Prudence in the morning. She linked arms with him at the beginning of the journey, they kissed each other's cheeks before parting ways in the entrance hall of the ministry, but they didn't try to go any further. She had told him that contrary to what he believed, the Wicca meetings in which she was involved did not involve local people but staff members from Bercy – at almost every level, from secretary to duty manager. So the civil servants who were steering the economy had allowed themselves to be seduced by white magic; it was odd.

The evening was different, he rarely came back before midnight, he was now working a lot more than she was; the number of cases that Bruno was able to pursue in person was terrifying. One evening he did a kind of tally and concluded that three full-time finance inspectors would be necessary between now and the presidential election to cover the gap. His own capacity for work was more or less unaltered, since the time, already remote, of his studies. He was able to confirm this without enjoying it, and without feeling particularly bad about it either, whether he worked a lot or not very much was a matter of indifference to him. He was manifestly going through a kind of stasis on every level of his life, in that sense working a lot was probably better, it effectively banished thought of all kinds – about Prudence, about his father, about Cécile. At about two or three in the morning he watched some documentaries on the Animals channel. Prudence had been asleep for a long time; she had probably nodded off over her Anita Brookner.

On the evening of his first meeting with the chief secretary, he watched a television documentary devoted to exotic pets, which paid special attention to the mygalomorph. A large spider of warm regions, highly venomous, the mygalomorph does not tolerate the company of any other animal, and systematically attacks any living creature introduced into its cage, including other mygalomorphs, even including its owner, and even when the owner has been feeding it for years, it continues to attack, any sense of attachment being entirely alien to it. In short, as the documentary's commentator concluded, the mygalomorph 'does not like living creatures'.

7

Paul didn't see Bruno again until two weeks later, on 20 January; he had a meeting with him at midday. He knocked on the door, and thought he heard someone singing in the work apartment. A girl wearing a mauve body-stocking immediately opened the door. 'Are you Paul? I'm Raksaneh – it's an Iranian name. I'm aware that I have to let you have him this afternoon.' She might have been twenty-five, her olive-skinned face topped by a thick bush of black curly hair, and she emanated an extraordinary degree of vitality; it looked as if she could at any moment throw herself into a series of perilous leaps and somersaults just to let off her excess physical energy. He pricked up his ears: someone was actually singing in the dining room; he found it hard to believe, but it really did seem to be Bruno's voice.

> *One fine day, or maybe one night*
> *By a lake, I had fallen asleep*
> *When all of a sudden, darkening the sky,*
> *Wings beating, a black eagle appeared.*

He broke off as he saw them entering the room, came towards Paul and shook his hand. Wearing a T-shirt, jogging pants and trainers, he too was bursting with energy, Paul had never seen him like that. A treadmill was set up in one corner of the room, a dressing table in the other.

'I didn't mean to interrupt . . .' Paul said.

'Yes, yes,' Raksaneh cut in, 'you have things to do together, I know, I'll leave you in five minutes. He's good, isn't he? Obviously we're not going to make a singer out of him, we just do that at the start of the session to warm him up. The important thing is diction.'

'Diction?'

'Yes, personally I like to use Corneille. The imprecations of Camille?' she went on, with a little nod for the benefit of Bruno, who immediately got going, in a strong, firm voice:

> *Rome, sole object of my resentment!*
> *Rome, where your arm comes to immolate my lover!*
> *Rome, whose birth you witnessed, and which your heart*
> *   adores!*
> *Rome, finally, that I hate because it honours you!*

'That's what she says to her brother after he's killed Curiace, is that right?' Paul asked.

'Exactly, and just before he kills her. Afterwards, obviously, we replace it with the political economy of France; but in my view if you can do Corneille you can do anything. A bit more?' she asked Bruno in a teasing, almost tender tone. He complied immediately, good-humouredly.

> *May all her neighbours summoned all together*
> *Undermine her unsteady foundation!*
> *And if the whole of Italy is not enough,*
> *Let East unite with West against her;*
> *Let a hundred people united from the ends of the*
> *   universe*
> *Pass to destroy her with all her mountains and seas!*
> *Let Rome herself throw down her walls,*

And with her own hands rip out her entrails!
Let the fury of heaven lit up by my desires
Engulf her in a fiery deluge!
Let me see with my own eyes the flash of lightning,
See her houses in ash, and her laurel tress in dust,
See the last Roman take his last sigh,
I alone being the cause, and die of pleasure!

'He has an incredible memory . . .' Raksaneh observed, 'he reads something once and he knows it right off, I've never seen that. OK, I told you I was going to leave you, you have work to do.' Six inches shorter than Bruno, she stood up on tiptoes to kiss him on the cheeks – involuntarily, Paul glanced at her little round buttocks in their tight body-stocking. She picked up a handbag and a fur coat from a chair – it seemed to be a kind of uniform among the female members of staff at Confluences – before disappearing.

'It's . . . surprising,' Paul remarked, sitting down at the dining table, 'but it seems to be working for you.'

'Yes, it's true, perhaps it doesn't need to go on for years, but for now I'm fine with it. We can have lunch if you like. Will you tell me how things are going your end?'

'I wrote you a memo,' replied Paul, taking about ten pages out of his folder. 'Well, you'll see, but in my view it's all pretty much in place.'

Bruno read the pages quickly but attentively. Paul was sure that he was memorizing them as he went along; it was nice, in the end, to be working with a prodigy. When he had nearly finished the butler came in and set their plates down on the table.

'Cod and green beans,' Bruno said, 'I listened to you. Right, then, do you see anything that needs urgently sorting out?'

'Just the director of the STDR, it's on the last page.'

'The tax regulation unit? What do they want?'

214

'There are some big returns, Mercoeur in particular. They want to claim back their unpaid taxes, and I'm not sure it's a good idea.'

'Mercoeur's the guy who set up a chain of French bakeries in Vietnam?'

'Thailand too, and particularly in India. It's a big chain in India, eight hundred sales points I think.'

'Wait . . . Wait, I don't understand. You've got a guy who's set up a thousand croissant shops in Asia, he wants to come back and pay his taxes in France and we're demanding his unpaid taxes . . .? I don't suppose they want to slap a late penalty charge on him while they're about it? Obviously we give him an amnesty, I'll call them this afternoon. Don't you agree?' He attacked his cod steak with enthusiasm.

'Absolutely, I haven't said anything, you decide. But I've never seen you so vigorous, so dynamic, this electoral campaign's doing you good . . ., in fact . . .' Paul started eating, although more slowly. 'I have a sense that your second term is going to be even more active than the first one . . .'

'Second, if you like, it's the first one in a sense, I've never been exactly given free rein by the president.'

'From that point of view, is Sarfati what you expected? Not a nasty surprise?'

'Listen, we see each other twice a week to take stock. Our first joint press conference is on Monday, it's going to be big, with the whole of the world's financial press. Politically I don't think he has a lot of ideas, but economically I'm sure he hasn't got any at all. It's a detail, but we've never seen each other in Bercy, he's not interested. He prefers the Élysée, Matignon, settings like that. If he doesn't set foot in Bercy throughout the whole of his term I'm fine with that. But haven't you seen him on TV? Haven't you been following the start of the campaign?'

'I haven't had that much time, to tell you the truth.'

'Sure, you have been working a lot.' He picked up Paul's memo

215

again. 'But now things are going to calm down a bit for you, I think we're OK at the moment. You haven't had time to call Martin-Renaud, either, I suppose?'

'Is something up?'

'There's been another attack.'

'Whereabouts? I don't think anyone's mentioned it.'

'That's true, there's been hardly anything; but France isn't worried this time, this time it was a big Danish company, Cryos. It's the world leader in the sperm sales market. It's a case of arson, their premises were completely destroyed. There are no economic repercussions for us, they have no French competitors, and sperm donation is free in France. Although obviously there are some French customers who get round the law and buy it on the internet.

'Yes, I know . . .' He had no wish to think about Indy again.

'They still have no clues, it's the same kind of message, the same weird characters. But there's no video this time, just a still image. Either way, the terrorists have a sense of context: this time they pirated porn sites.'

8

ack at home, Paul clicked on Xvideos, hesitated for a few moments between 'Hungry cock to suck darling' and 'Enchanting succulent beaver', both suggested on the home page, then moved on to page 2. 'Guy receives a zealous circumscription' wasn't much clearer, but in any case the film had only been going for thirty seconds, and the actress had barely had time to take off her G-string, when the message appeared over it. There was the usual arrangement of pentagons and circles, followed by some text written in the usual characters, but this time considerably longer, at least fifty lines or so, and it concluded with two numbers: apparently, then, this language did not have specific characters for figures. Then it moved on to a map, or rather a city plan, probably taken from Google Maps. The street names sounded Scandinavian, perhaps Danish, in fact. The headquarters of Cryos International, the company targeted by the attack, was located between Vester Allé and Nørre Allé, in the middle of a little street called Vesterbro Torv.

He left a message on Martin-Renaud's mobile, and then after a moment's hesitation he called Doutremont. He was in his office, and the switchboard operator put him through straight away. He sounded stressed, and his speech slowed down distinctly as soon as Paul uttered the word 'Denmark'. He did reply, however. Paul was a servant of the state, as he was, and outside of defence secrets, servants of state owe one another mutual support and assistance,

217

a little like the spouses in a marriage, or at least that was his conception of service to the state.

'What I'm asking you isn't too confidential, is it?' Paul said anxiously.

'It could be confidential if we had anything; but for now we're drawing a blank, as we did on the previous occasions. All we can say is that the terrorists are very professional: they used a mixture of napalm and white phosphorus, both substances used by the military. It's almost a miracle that the night watchmen managed to escape in time and there were no casualties.'

'But this time France wasn't involved at all, was it?'

'Apparently not, but there's one weird detail. I imagine you've seen the two numbers at the end of the message. The first, 1039, is a match for the file of a female French client; the second, 5261, is the file for a French donor; and it was the sperm of 5261, if I can put it that way, that was used to fertilize 1039. Our Danish colleagues gave us the names and addresses of our compatriots: a business-school student and an ordinary lesbian who's been part of a couple for five years. They've never met, and they aren't on file, they're unknown to the police, so nothing seems to make any sense. But nothing in this case has seemed to make sense since the outset. After the attacks on the Chinese container ship, we were tempted to suspect an ultra-leftist group, let's say that that was the idea that came to us first; but here, a sperm bank, even though it's also a capitalist enterprise, isn't among the traditional targets of the ultra-left; it sounds more like fundamentalist Catholics, I would say. We have some of them on file; but fundamentalist Catholics have never demonstrated any mastery of the tools of internet piracy; no more than the ultra-left, and rather less, in fact.'

After thanking him quite mechanically for his call, Doutremont hung up; he had really sounded discouraged. Still, it was a strange job that these people did, and that his father did before them, Paul thought to himself. Without really wanting to, and almost involuntarily, he checked: 1039 and 5261 were in fact prime numbers. A little while later, Martin-Renaud called him back. He nearly mentioned the prime numbers but held back just in time, as a rule it's a better idea to tell people what they are more or less prepared to hear; so he settled for general reflections about the DGSI and the difficulty of the work they did. In fact, Martin-Renaud replied, his subordinate was not in an easy situation at the moment. He himself had had one case like that in his career, a case of total blockage, this was Doutremont's first. 'It leaves a mark, you know, you don't forget,' Martin-Renaud added. 'It happened to your father too. Your father was an exceptional person, you know.'

His affection and admiration were clearly sincere, but still he had said 'was', Paul noticed in spite of himself. Martin-Renaud was happy to learn that Édouard had come out of his coma, and that he had been transferred to a competent care unit; they must have known each other better than he had suggested last time. Several of his father's colleagues had visited him in Saint-Joseph, even after he had retired, and they would closet themselves away in his office to talk about subjects more or less closely related to *defence secrets*, or at least that was what he imagined at the time. He had no memory of Martin-Renaud, but then again he hadn't really seen his father either recently.

Before hanging up, Paul reminded him that he was welcome in Beaujolais whenever he liked, if he wanted to pay Édouard a visit. His father would certainly recognize him, he recognized his visitors, that much was certain. At that moment he would have liked to call Martin-Renaud by his first name, but he had forgotten it, or more likely had never known it – was it Gilles? He looked like a Gilles.

In spite of his affable attitude, Paul had never felt entirely at ease with him, and the Animals channel came as welcome relief. This time it was about rats. Rats are social animals that live in colonies; each colony has a leader that intervenes in the sharing of food, acts as a kind of referee in conflicts, and guides the colony towards new territories. Three species can be identified, the relationship between them being established as follows: a black rat (*Rattus rattus*) that enters the territory of a colony of brown rats (*Rattus norvegicus*) is singled out and chased away. If a larger brown rat, on the other hand, enters the territory of a colony of black rats, it is threatened but seldom attacked; finally, no rat shows any hostility to the mouse (*Mus musculus*).

He finally wearied of rats, and spent some time on the Hunting and Fishing channel, then turned off the sound and called Cécile, who picked up almost immediately. Everything was going well, she told him, in fact there had even been a big bit of news, namely that their father could now blink his eyes, and that they were able to communicate with him as a result. They used the simplest communication code, the one most frequently used with patients in this condition: he had to be asked questions to which he could reply yes or no. He blinked to say yes, and remained motionless to say no. It was amazing, she remarked, how far one could go in the conversation using just yes or no. His swallowing was getting better too, the speech therapist was happy, she thought he would be able to feed himself normally in a week or two, and she was looking forward to making meals for him, They weren't seeing Madeleine as often now, she spent the whole week in Belleville, she had really moved in there, she was getting on well with the nurses, well the one she saw most of was Maryse, you remember, the little Black girl, she added, yes he remembered. Aurélien wasn't back yet, he had trouble getting away, but he hoped to be able to come soon, he'd asked to be transferred to a workshop nearby, that would let him stay longer than the weekends.

'What about you? Cécile asked. 'When do you think you'll be able to come? I suspect you don't have much time at the moment, with the presidential election.' Even Cécile was taking note of the presidential election, he was slightly surprised to note, this election really was a media steamroller. 'It should calm down soon,' he said at last, 'soon we'll be on the home straight, and I won't have so much to do.' As he said those words he realized that it was true, the joint press conference with Sarfati next Monday would mark the real start of Bruno's electoral campaign. Of course he would mostly be there as technical support, 'in the background', as Solène Signal put it, but it would still be a real campaign with all the exhaustion and stress that a campaign entails. Sarfati, for his part, was starting to show some timid and moderately progressive convictions, and there was a growing sense that his term would be marked by one or two easy social reforms like the decriminalization of soft drugs, Paul remembered seeing a file on that, French soil lent itself very well to cannabis growing, better than Holland, in the Périgord in particular cannabis could prove an excellent substitute solution to the traditional cultivation of tobacco – which seemed to have become completely unacceptable.

Bruno had never been known for his political convictions; he was the extreme embodiment of the technician who knew his files, and besides, it was the austerity of his image that had kept him from being chosen as candidate by the president; nonetheless, this time, he would be obliged to go out and about, at least every now and again, he would be 'facing the French people', he said to Cécile, and as Paul spoke those words he was filled with a huge and almost limitless doubt about the idea of the *French people*, but he couldn't talk about that to Cécile, or to anyone else for that matter, it was too negative, too discouraging, and at the same time too vague in his mind. He merely sent her kisses, and told her once again that he would come back to Saint-Joseph as soon as possible.

Immediately after hanging up, he realized that his doubt now applied to the whole of the human community. He had always liked the story about Frederick II of Prussia asking to be buried near his dogs so that he did not lie among men, 'that wicked race'. The human world seemed to him to be made up of little balls of

egoistic shit, unconnected and unrelated to one another, and sometimes those balls grew agitated and copulated in their own way,
each in its own register, leading in turn to the existence of tiny
new balls of shit. As sometimes happened to him, he was filled
with sudden disgust for his sister's religion: how could a god have
chosen to be reborn in the form of a ball of shit? To make matters
worse, there were songs celebrating the event. '*Il est né le divin
enfant*', how would you translate that into German? '*Es ist geboren,
das göttliche Kind*', it came back to him all at once, it was nice to
have done some studying, he said to himself, it gives you a certain
class. For some years, it's true, the balls of shit had been copulating
in smaller numbers, they seemed to have learned to reject one
another, they were aware of their mutual stench, and disgustedly
parted company; an extinction of the human race seemed imaginable in the medium term. That left other trash like cockroaches
and bears, but you can't sort everything out at the same time, Paul
said to himself. Basically he didn't object to the destruction of a
sperm bank. The idea of buying sperm, and more generally of
launching oneself into a reproductive project that didn't even have
the excuse of sexual desire, love or a feeling of that kind, even
struck him as frankly revolting.

Neither did he have any real objection, he realized immediately
afterwards, to the destruction of Chinese container vessels. Neither
Chinese industrialists nor maritime transporters aroused the slightest
sympathy in him, they all competed to plunge the majority of the
planet's inhabitants into sordid misery so as to pursue their basely
mercantile aims; there was nothing there to prompt any great
admiration.

He shouldn't pursue that kind of idea, he said to himself immediately afterwards, and turned on the Animals channel again. Some
time had passed, and now the subject had turned to tapirs, chiefly
the tapir of Brazil (*Tapirus terrestris*) and the mountain tapir (*Tapirus
pinchaque*), also with a few mentions of the only Asian tapir, the

Malaysian or saddleback tapir. In each case these were suspicious and solitary animals, living deep in the forest, most of them nocturnal; they had no social life to speak of, and couples formed only to mate. In short, the life of a tapir seemed incredibly boring, and he switched to a sports channel, but the 110 metre hurdles failed to change the course of his thoughts. Since the very beginning he had felt inclined to pay admiring tribute to these unknown terrorists, for their exceptional mastery of digital and military means, and also for the skill with which they had, since the beginning, managed to avoid any damage to humans – whatever Doutremont might have said, he saw no miracle in the absence of casualties in the Danish attack: they must have acted as they had with the Chinese ships, warning the crews just in time for them to be able to flee, while giving them a clue to the seriousness of the threat. He went on the internet again to find out more: in fact that was exactly what had happened. The night guards' office had received a phone call at three o'clock in the morning, warning them to clear the building, while a first group of offices, empty at that time of night, was ravaged by flames. And even though the headquarters of Cryos International was located right in the middle of Aarhus, the fire had been precisely contained within the company's perimeter; these guys were definitely very good.

The worst thing – but why wasn't Prudence back yet? he suddenly wondered, it was almost nine at night, he needed her now, he needed her and their daily conversations, but it wasn't possible like this, he couldn't wait any longer, he needed to go to bed and try to sleep, maybe some ski-jumping on TV would do the trick – the worst thing was that if the terrorists' goal was to annihilate the world as he knew it, to annihilate the modern world, he couldn't entirely blame them.

9

The press conference was held at midday in the lounge of the Intercontinental Hotel on the Avenue Marceau. There were in fact lots of journalists, seven hundred at least; Solène Signal had turned up in advance and seemed tense, spending the next hour dragging on each of her vapes in turn. Raksaneh, beside her, was calmer, she seemed to have every confidence in her protégé, and in fact Bruno came out of it well, or at least that was how it seemed to Paul; he gave relaxed replies to all the questions, moving from air transport to the Central European Bank, from the CEB to fossil fuels without any apparent effort, he managed to make his audience laugh several times, and the man from the *Wall Street Journal* was particularly won over. Sarfati was less convincing, he didn't really answer the questions, he tried to come out with a joke every time, and that didn't always work; he'd fucked it up particularly badly with the *Financial Times*, Paul thought. After the conference he suggested 'going for a pint'; in fact the Intercontinental offered that, among other things.

It was the first time that Paul had seen Bruno and Sarfati together – the first time, in fact, that he had seen Sarfati. 'We're fine . . .' Solène said, slumping onto the banquette before spreading her legs; she looked exhausted. 'Or rather broadly speaking we're fine, we're on course for now, but we've still got three months. The problem is that we're fine, but the others aren't bad either.'

'Are you thinking of the guy from the National Rally?' Sarfati asked.

'Yes obviously, the others don't count. That little guy is good, I confess I'm shocked.'

'Do you know who's looking after him?'

Solène smiled wearily as if there was no point in replying. 'Bérengère de Villecraon,' her assistant said for her. Paul hadn't seen him during the press conference, but he was the guy in a grey suit from last time, the one who looked like a Bercy civil servant.

'Do you know this Bérengère woman?' Sarfati didn't look very familiar with this file either. Solène let out a kind of weird long laugh that started with comic-opera trills before ending with a series of crane-like yelps, before exclaiming, as she attacked her beer: 'Do I know her? I certainly do, the bitch . . .! A good pro, mind you, I wouldn't say anything else; you just have to prove that you're better than she is. For now we're fine, I'll tell you again; if you look at the projections for the second round—' She broke off abruptly and gave her assistant a furious glare.

'I didn't say anything . . .' the young man protested timidly.

'You nearly did, I heard you thinking. I know what you're going to say to me: the figures don't mean a thing three months ahead. You're right, but we're still obliged to look at them, we can't do anything else. So right now we're at 55. 55 is good, I prefer 55 to 52, but it's too close, we have to look as if we're increasing the gap, it's self-fulfilling, if you manage to create the impression that you're increasing the gap you increase it, and that's what's happening now. So while it's true that I don't like it, we're obliged to appeal to the left.'

This time the pseudo-Bercy civil servant looked flummoxed and finally repeated in a faint voice: 'The left . . .'

'Yes, the left . . .! You know the word, maybe it stirs something in your brain, maybe you heard about it at Sciences Po?'

'But which left . . .?' the unfortunate young man finally droned.

'Well, the left, the real left, the old left . . .! Now, for example Laurent Joffrin is going to write me a thing in *L'Obs* next week.'

'Isn't Laurent Joffrin dead?'

'Not at all! He's in great shape, lover-boy, he goes jogging every morning on the beach at Dieppe. I've just read his paper "A fascism all its own", it's all very pretty, all very cute, the kind of thing that he knows how to do. Obviously that isn't going to be enough, we have to do a ton of things like that, some elderly moral leftists, and maybe two or three Jews if we can find them, as part of our duty of remembrance. We keep all that stuff brewing until the election, we take our time, the idea is to get the humanist centrists moving, you know, the big softies of the Duhamel school, and if the big softies make their minds up to shift their fat arses, and say that we ought to be terrified, that's the joke, we're still along the right lines. At the same time . . .' she turned towards Bruno; the beer had plainly done her good, she was firing on all cylinders again, 'it wouldn't be a bad thing if we pinched a few of their economic proposals. Do you fancy going on the LCI channel on Wednesday?'

'That's going to be a bit difficult,' Bruno replied softly.

'And why might that be, if you please?'

'Because they've got exactly the same ones as we have. They completely approve of everything that's been happening economically over the past five years.'

'Ah . . . I hadn't quite spotted that, my bad.' She thought for a moment and gestured to the waiter for another round. 'So listen up!' she exclaimed a moment later. 'In a sense that's even better, it's totally amazing. So you go on the attack along the lines of "There's nothing innovative about your suggestions, and if your idea is just to keep going with the same policies, we're the best placed to do that", and off you go. And it would be true . . .!' she concluded in a paroxysm of satisfaction.

*

226

Destinies pursue one another, only rarely do they cross paths, and their divergences are even more unusual; but those divergences do happen, every now and again. That same afternoon, Aurélien had a meeting with the directorship of the Heritage Department of the Culture Ministry. He turned up at the agreed time and waited for a few minutes in a rather dirty corridor. At least they couldn't be accused of taking advantage of their position to create a pleasant working environment for themselves: the furniture was an impeccably administrative dull green, and the few posters on the walls wouldn't have looked out of place in a youth club in a communist suburb in the last century.

Jean-Michel Drapier, the director general of the Heritage Department, was a perfect match for his environment, and he made no secret of his sadness as he ushered Aurélien in. 'I have some good news for you,' he said in a dull voice, 'or at least I assume it's good news. You were the one who wanted to take up a post in Burgundy for family reasons, isn't that right?' Aurélien agreed.

'Well, I have a mission for you, or a possible mission: the restoration of the tapestries in the Château de Germolles; it's near Chalon-sur Saône.' He picked up a thin file from his desk, glanced at it with surprise before continuing and, referring to it as he went along, he was plainly rediscovering it at the same time.

'The château itself isn't bad, historically speaking, that is: it was bought in 1380 by Philip the Bold, the first Duke of Burgundy. It was subsequently owned by John the Fearless, Philip the Good and Charles the Bold, before passing into the hands of the Royal Crown. In terms of heritage, there is a good collection of sculptures attributed to Claus Sluter, which were restored last year. The mural paintings as well, by Jean de Beaumetz and Arnoult Picornet, were what was restored first, as usual, ten years ago now. And then there are the tapestries . . .' He made a fatalistic gesture. 'I won't lie, they suffered, there was a fire, there was severe weather – you'll see the photographs. At the moment you're on Queen Matilda of Hungary, and that'll soon be finished, is that right?'

'I finish at the end of the week.'

'Good, that's good. Matilda of Hungary is important . . .' He waved his hand graciously, a series of moderate swirls to indicate the importance of Matilda of Hungary in terms of history and heritage. 'I could put you on the Château de Germolles two days a week,' he went on. 'Monday and Tuesday, for example, or maybe Thursday and Friday, up to you, if you want to spend the weekend with your family.'

'Would three days be impossible?'

'I think that's going to be difficult.' He thought for a moment. 'Your other workshop is the Château de Chantilly, isn't it?'

Aurélien agreed. 'Then no,' Drapier replied sadly, 'I won't be able to. Chantilly takes priority. There are more tourists in Chantilly, and you know how priorities are fixed . . .' he concluded apologetically, seeming to sink deeper and deeper into his chair. 'There is one point on which we have to be very clear,' he said, rising to his feet with sudden concern. 'You're taking care of your own lodging and transport, isn't that right? There won't be any extra costs?' Aurélien agreed. 'Because obviously our line of credit at the Château de Germolles . . . Well, let's say that it's not a huge amount, and we're also quite dependent on the goodwill of the regional council. But you're starting to get used to that, aren't you? You've been with us for ten years now?'

It was ten years, in fact, almost to the day. What could Aurélien do if not to agree once more? He agreed. Drapier immediately fell into a grief-stricken silence.

Leaving the Ministry of Culture, Aurélien went into the first café he came across and ordered a bottle of Muscadet. Unused to alcohol, he quickly felt the effects; alcohol might be a solution, he said to himself, a partial solution. An internet search brought him some good news: the Château de Germolles was only ninety kilometres from Villié-Morgon, almost all of it on the A6 motorway, an easy trip. The photographs of the tapestries, on the other hand, were enough to drive any art restorer to suicide; damage limitation was all he would be able to do.

An immediate problem arose: he had no desire to go home, he wanted to be anywhere but home, the feeling wasn't new, but it was getting worse from week to week, and now from day to day. It wasn't normal, he said to himself, to be afraid of seeing his wife again, just afraid, there was no other word for it. She would inevitably shout at him in one way or another, she would unload on him the frustrations of a disappointing day within a journalistic career that matched her hopes less and less, it was never a good idea to marry a failure, he could see that from both points of view, but he didn't consider himself a failure, he loved medieval tapestries, he liked his detailed, solitary work and had never imagined changing it.

If he got home late it would be even worse, she would see an additional reason to start a crisis, she went out almost every evening in the hope of maintaining contacts that proved to be more and more problematic, she would have liked to be *put on a big story*, there were still big stories but they weren't for her, her time was over, that was all, it was over without ever having properly begun, so she went out, she 'had dinner in town', and she insisted that someone was to stay with Godefroy in the evening, which was obviously pointless, however, since his son, or what functioned as Aurélien's son, his male housemate, stayed locked away in his room, probably on social media, and would not have left it for any reason.

He poured himself another glass, reflecting that he had never yet found the courage to confess to his wife, and this was bound to provoke another scene, that the financial hopes that he had placed in the sale of his mother's sculptures were largely exaggerated, and that Suzanne Raison's market value had literally collapsed. He had consulted three art dealers whose opinions converged, and one of her sculptures could now be negotiated at around one to two thousand euros, not more, and it would probably take a very long time to find buyers, perhaps they would never find any, in fact, there was no point going even lower, there was simply no longer any demand. It obviously wasn't his fault, but she would accuse him of being pathetic all over again, and that was all he needed.

Of course Aurélien hadn't immediately realized that he had married a piece of shit, and a venal piece of shit at that, it's a thing you don't realize immediately, it takes a few months at the very least to understand that you're going to live in hell, and that it isn't a simple hell, there are plenty of circles, over the years he had plunged into a sequence of increasingly oppressive layers, each one darker and more stifling than the last, the acrimonious words that they exchanged each evening were filled each time with more and more hatred. She probably wasn't cheating on him, or perhaps just a little, she probably allowed herself to be stoked occasionally by a trainee who lent faith to her aura as a great journalist, who imagined that she was important within the structure of the organization, unsatisfied ambition had devoured many things within her, and what remained was her inexhaustible desire to show that she was a cool, modern and likeable girl, and that she had no shortage of contacts on the scene. For two or three years Aurélien had toyed with the idea of killing her, sometimes by poison, most often by strangling, he imagined her breath dwindling, the cracking of her cervical bones. These were absurd daydreams, he knew nothing about violence, he had never had a fight, or rather he had never defended himself. Quite the contrary – he had for years been regularly humiliated and beaten by older boys. It usually happened very quickly, a desperate run along the school corridors, some vain pleading, then they brought him to their leader, a big, stout Black boy, at least a hundred kilos of fat and muscle, whom they called 'The Monster'. Then they forced him to kneel down, and he could see in his mind the happy, almost cordial smile of The Monster as he opened his fly to piss on his face, he tried to break away, but the others were holding on to him tightly, and he remembered the smell of his bitter piss. That had happened for two years, between the ages of eight and ten, and had constituted his first real contact with human society. Since then he had never been capable of physical violence.

He was aware of the situation with Indy, alcohol was supposed to give you courage, and he was going to need a bit of courage to unleash the hostilities of divorce. She was obviously going to demand half of their assets, and get them; she was going to demand alimony, and she would get that too; the sum remained to be fixed. In divorces, from the little that Aurélien knew, a good lawyer is essential. He knew tapestry weavers, both high and low warp, ironmongers, print-makers and carpenters; he did not know a single lawyer, and had chosen one more or less at random. Indy doubtless knew some formidable lawyers, lawyers and journalists were pretty much the same thing, in fact they both seemed to him to belong in the same slightly disreputable world, in close touch with lies, with no direct contact with matter, reality, or any form of work. He had, there was no point in hiding it, got off to a bad start.

The bottle of wine was almost finished, that stuff went down nicely; he glanced at the café around him, half full and half empty, and was filled with the immediate and absolute certainty that there was absolutely nobody in this café, and there were probably very few people in the world, who could listen to him, sympathize with him, share his woes. It was evening now, Aurélien had finished his bottle, and more than ever, more than at any other moment in his life, he felt he was at a total impasse.

At more or less the same time, in the centre of Lyon, Cécile was ringing at the door of her first customer. She had been sent by Marmilyon.org, the name of the site. It was probably a start-up,

231

or at least that was how she imagined it, there was only one employee, whom she had never seen, and everything had been done on the phone and, mostly, on the internet. They supplied events with four cooks: an Italian, a Moroccan and a Thai – and from today Cécile, doing French cuisine, was their latest innovation for customers who wanted to 'take a trip through the regions', as they put it on their website.

She was welcomed by a blonde woman, quite pretty, in her forties, who had booked her three days before, she was organizing a dinner for twelve people this evening, which left Cécile three hours to prepare the meal, which was what she had planned for, so she wasn't worried.

The apartment was enormous, it must have been what's called a loft, but lofts are usually set up in former workshops, here they seemed to be occupying the whole factory; as they passed through she thought she could see reception areas and games rooms stretching almost to infinity.

The kitchen was also very big, with a huge central island made of lava stone. 'I've set things up according to your instructions . . .' the woman said with a little rictus of horror; she plainly wasn't pleased to have received instructions from Cécile, but she couldn't do anything about it, the set-up wasn't part of the preparation offered by the website. 'I won't show you the equipment, it's just the usual . . .' she went on with an impatient wave of the hand. It was the usual, certainly, but of the best quality, and in any case among the most expensive; the collection of cooking knives was particularly impressive – Haiku Itamae – and there was even a La Cornue stove. None of it seemed to have been used very much, it all looked as if it had come straight out of the catalogue.

Cécile set to work and gradually relaxed; cooking always had that effect on her, and it was lucky, because she was slowly getting the sense that she wasn't going to like this woman, or her guests. Clients were offered two options: either she left once the preparations were finished; or she stayed to provide table service, then to do the washing up and put things away. Unfortunately the client had chosen the second option, and she would probably be staying until at least midnight. Hervé had gone back to Saint-Joseph, and would drop by to pick her up later.

After starting on the blanquette de veau she concentrated on the dessert, which would be the highlight; strawberry gateau wasn't an easy cake and she hadn't made one for years, but she felt good, at ease, and sure of herself. The starters wouldn't pose any problems: an easy celeriac remoulade and asparagus with hollandaise sauce, which she would make last.

Her impression was confirmed when she served the starters and then the blanquette: she definitely didn't like these people. She couldn't remember what the woman did, probably an estate agent or, rather, something like property renovation – quite a lot of properties in Lyon had been renovated over the past few years. At any rate her husband was in finance; he seemed more likeable than his wife, with a moon-face, a bit dim-witted; weirdly he was the one that she had contacted first, and at least he hadn't tried to negotiate the price down. The other guests were from the same circles; some of them seemed to work in culture – the conversation revolved around contemporary art and various exhibitions; she didn't have time to listen and anyway she wasn't interested. She had a sense of being perfectly transparent; nobody seemed to notice that she was there. She had hoped that at least they would say something about the cooking, but it didn't occur to anyone, none of the twelve, when in fact the blanquette had turned out well.

When she came back with the strawberry gateau, the conversation turned to the next presidential election, and was not particularly animated; everyone agreed to support the current majority, there was 'no alternative', in the time-honoured phrase. As she sliced the cake she felt a sudden desire to say something childish and incongruous along the lines of: 'My big brother knows the minister very well!', but she restrained herself, went back to the kitchen and started on the washing up. Well into her forties, she had a sense of discovering the class struggle for the first time; it was a strange feeling, unpleasant and slightly dirty, and she would have preferred not to know it.

Once the washing up had been done and the coffees served, the guests headed for the sitting room – or, rather, one of the sitting rooms. She finished putting things away and was finally able to leave. 'I won't come with you; you know the way,' the mistress of the house said. Hervé was already there, waiting for her on the corner of Cours Lafayette, as they had agreed. Coming down the stairs, she suddenly felt a strong desire to burst into tears. The car wasn't parked very far away, but the fifty-metre walk through icy air was enough to bring her to her senses, and after sitting in the front seat next to Hervé, after he asked how it had gone, she managed to reply perfectly naturally: 'Very well.'

10

On Friday 29 January, Aurélien finished his work on Matilda of Hungary's tapestry; he had only to wait for the material to be brought to the Château de Germolles; it was bound to happen quickly, the services of the Heritage Department were quite efficient in this area.

Every morning, his approaching departure filled him with anticipatory joy; he liked the drive to the Château de Chantilly, well maybe not the beginning so much, neither Bondy nor Aulnay-sous-Bois were especially delightful, but once he was past Roissy Airport he found himself in the middle of the countryside, and immediately past La Chapelle-en-Serval he was in the depths of the forest, with no human habitation until Chantilly. The return journey was less cheerful, and his anxiety grew the closer he got to their house in Montreuil, whose tiny patch of garden Indy always boasted about to her acquaintances, when in fact it wasn't really a garden, it was at best an uncultivated area filled with tall grass and thistles, with a few empty tins rolling about, and in any case she wouldn't have known how to grow a vegetable.

This Friday evening, pushing open the front door, he felt almost elated, and immediately realized that he would have to hide it from Indy, that it was imperative for him to keep their exchanges in the usual tone of hostility and sarcasm; that probably wouldn't be difficult since she would be going out early anyway, she went out every Friday.

Over the course of Saturday, generally the hardest day, he practically didn't see her, and in the evening he phoned Cécile. She had good news, and was delighted to tell him that for three days their father had managed to feed himself normally again. Of course the food had to be blended and reduced to purée; but he had regained the ability to appreciate flavours. 'Even wine?' Aurélien asked. Yes, indeed, even wine, wine was a liquid, it didn't present any particular problem. Aurélien didn't know much about medicine, and when Cécile mentioned the risk of 'false paths', he didn't know what she was alluding to. She looked forward to seeing him soon, he could come whenever he liked. In a week, he said, two at the most. He added that he would be alone; she didn't comment.

The last week of January was a busy one for Paul; Bruno had been a bit too optimistic, the difficulties caused by his absence took longer to resolve. He saw him once a week, and told him of the few litigious points that needed resolving – it was in fact more to set his mind at rest than anything, they were so used to working together that he could have predicted his reaction almost every time. Then the Bercy machine kicked into operation; it was a good administrative machine, powerful and a bit slow to get going, but things were getting easier from week to week.

Solène Signal's strategy hadn't really worked; the leading lights of the 'moral left' had gone completely silent once and for all, even more than she'd expected, and the great humanist softies hadn't moved at all. It would also have to be said that, for the first time, there had been no sign of the Jews; the fact that the candidate wasn't a Le Pen this time had probably played a part in their defection. The old man was close to ninety-nine, but couldn't bring himself to die. He would have had to deliver one of his jokes about the ovens to scupper his party at the last minute; Solène still kept that residual hope alive, but she no longer really believed it: since the candidate no longer bore his name, he seemed to think that he no longer had any real authority. He himself was 'preparing to appear before his saviour', that was all that could be extracted from him in interviews, and the second-round predictions were stuck on 55–45, which hadn't shifted since the start.

Paul was always pleased to see Raksaneh. She was unstintingly dynamic, and had an impressive collection of body-stockings – turquoise, mint, fuchsia, she seemed to like all the colours of the rainbow; they were also equally figure-hugging. She plainly got on very well with Bruno, but they certainly weren't sleeping together, that wasn't possible for Bruno, not yet, not at this stage, and in any case it might have caused ethical problems, although in fact at Confluences they didn't really seem enormously concerned about ethics. But it did Bruno a lot of good to think that she saw him as a real man, he discovered at the same time. Raksaneh had a naturally sexual vision of people, and didn't even think of hiding it, which was incredibly reassuring.

Things weren't getting any better with Prudence, or hardly. They now set off for work together every morning and came home at similar hours. Every evening they talked for a moment in the living room before going to bed in their respective rooms. They didn't take their meals together, but one evening Paul was bowled over to discover two slices of *pâté en croûte* in the fridge that Prudence had bought for him. On the evening of the 2 February, she went to a party organized by her group of initiates to celebrate the Imbolc Sabbath. This sabbath, according to Scott Cunningham, marked the re-establishment of the goddess after giving birth to the god. The warmth fertilized the earth (the goddess, that is), which made the seeds germinate and sprout; that was how the first stirrings of spring manifested themselves. Prudence was clearly trying, she was bravely trying to re-establish contact with things, with nature, with her own nature. It would be a good idea, Paul said to himself, to invite her to go with him to Saint-Joseph as soon as he could go there himself; she was really worried about the state of his father's health, and she had always liked the house; perhaps they could find a new impetus there, a new departure, the start of a new life; at any rate that was what he needed to hope.

Drapier phoned Aurélien on Monday 15 February early in the morning, when he had just got to Chantilly. Everything was ready there, he told him, he would be able to start his work in Germolles from Thursday. As he hung up, Aurélien realized that he was going to leave on Wednesday evening, in two days, he had not anticipated his liberation coming so soon. What was more, Indy would not object to the move – quite the contrary, in fact, since it was also a matter of selling the sculptures. He had finally agreed with a dealer on a sum of one thousand two hundred euros per unit, but he had still not dared to mention it to his wife. Based in an old factory in Romainville, the dealer had enough storage space – and he was willing to cover transport costs.

At midday he invited his colleague, a girl who had recently joined the heritage service and who was working with him on *The Denial of Saint Peter*, to join him for lunch. The restaurant was in the château itself, in the old kitchens of François Vatel, the steward of the Prince de Condé – probably a good cook, but mainly known to posterity for his suicide.

'Do you have something to celebrate?' Félicie asked him; her surprise was understandable, generally speaking at midday he settled for a chicken wrap that he ate in five minutes without leaving his workplace.

'Not really. Well, I think I'm going to be able to get divorced soon.'

'Ah . . .' She made a laudable effort at discretion and waited for the main course to arrive before asking questions. He broached the subject without any real embarrassment, almost candidly, even softening the topic a little. To the question of whether they had any children, he said no. 'Oh, that's good,' she said, 'when there are no children there aren't as many problems . . .' That was what most people would have thought. Félicie thought exactly the same thing as most people; this girl was reassuring in every respect.

He had packed his suitcase the previous evening so as not to have to change in Montreuil and he left Chantilly at four in the afternoon. The ring road was solid, and the motorway wasn't looking good either; by about nine he realized that it would be very late by the time he got to Saint-Joseph, and he was starting to get tired, so it would be better if he stopped off in Chalon. He easily found a room at the Ibis Styles near the exit for Chalon-sur-Saône Nord. The restaurant was still open, but there were only two other customers, eating alone at their tables: a man of about forty, who looked like a sales rep, or at least a sales rep like the ones you see in films, he had never met a sales rep in real life, and a slightly younger woman, who looked like a commercial traveller as well, something in her make-up or her clothes, he wasn't sure, he didn't know any commercial travellers either, his experience of the world was limited. Fleetingly he wondered if those people who spent their lives on the road, in pursuit of an improbable ideal of keeping a faithful set of clients, who slept in rooms in the Mercure or the Ibis Styles, sometimes had one-night stands with each other, if they knew fleeting embraces when stopping off for an evening. Probably not, he thought on reflection; that kind of thing might have happened in his father's day, but the habit had been lost, and it wasn't in tune with the spirit of the times. Neither did he think that those two, once they had gone back to their respective rooms, would apply for internet encounters based on geo-location; in all likelihood what would happen was nothing at all.

His sleep was peaceful and dreamless; he turned up at the door of the Château de Germolles at eight o'clock the next day, knowing that people start work early in the provinces. The caretaker looked rather like those malign valets, more or less degenerate, who take part in black magic ceremonies involving the strangling of chickens and the drawing of cabalistic signs on the floor of the barn, and whom you encounter in fantastical Z-list films; he had been expecting him. The tapestries were in as bad a state as might have been feared; in particular, one of the most beautiful, showing Bathsheba stepping from her bath, had been half devoured by rats. What he had not anticipated was the cold, the rooms of the château were icy; that was a problem, since re-weaving is delicate manual work that is difficult to do with numb fingers. Grumbling slightly, the caretaker went to find an electric heater, which proved to be efficient; he hadn't much to do during the winter months, when there were no visits to the château, and he seemed to spend most of his day feeding his dogs – about ten of them, and of a not very appealing kind, rottweilers or mastiffs. However Aurélien went for a walk in the grounds at midday; the animals looked at him suspiciously, but didn't approach. Then he went for lunch in the restaurant in Mellecey, the village adjacent to the château; it was very peaceful, like being in a *Maigret* story.

He knew that Cécile wouldn't ask him any questions about Indy, that she would wait for him to talk about her himself; but on the first evening he didn't feel brave enough to approach the subject. They would go to the hospital on Saturday, she told him, to pick up Madeleine, who slept at Saint-Joseph every Saturday. They would bring her back on Sunday, and would be able to spend a moment with their father again.

The next day, after dinner, Cécile went back into the kitchen; she made meals for the whole week now, kept in hermetically sealed boxes, which she would give to Madeleine the next day; it took her at least two or three hours. Once Hervé had gone to bed, Aurélien stayed in the dining room on his own; he wasn't really thinking about what he would say, his mind was more or less empty. Then, without planning to do so exactly, he got to his feet and walked to the kitchen, closed the door behind him and sat down at the table. Cécile finished stirring a soup that was simmering in a stew pot, turned round, wiped her hands and sat down opposite him.

The sale of the sculptures was almost settled, he began; it wouldn't take him more than a weekend to carry out the inventory, and the dealer would come and get them the following week, it was already planned for Saturday the 27th, and he would be arriving early in the morning. He was aware that he was speaking in a toneless voice, he didn't really recognize his voice, which was slightly worrying.

He talked a little more about their mother's works, about the time it would take them to sell, about the sum that they could hope to get from them. Cécile waited, without interrupting. At one point she got up to stir her sauce, then sat back down in front of him.

'I'm going to begin divorce proceedings just after that,' he went on in exactly the same tone. 'I have a meeting with a lawyer on 1 March.'

'What about your son? Are you going to have joint custody, with a right to visit at weekends?'

'I don't plan to see my son again.'

She let his words sink in, remained silent for at least a minute, then walked over to him and took his hand in hers before telling him that she understood, at least that she could understand; obviously he wasn't entirely his son, it wasn't the same, things could probably have been different if he hadn't had the misfortune of being sterile.

'I'm not sterile,' Aurélien replied calmly.

This time she looked at him with bafflement that gradually turned to terror as she realized what he had just said. A squeaking door

241

was heard quite far off. They fell silent; it was probably Hervé getting up. A little later, silence returned. Aurélien avoided Cécile's eyes, but at last he managed to continue in the same detached voice:

'I've never been sterile. She made that up. I never understood why she wanted another donor.'

It was only when he saw a tear welling in his sister's eyes that he, too, started crying. He cried for a long time, calmly, the flood seemed inexhaustible, while Cécile rocked him in her arms. He didn't feel much, at any rate no pain, more a kind of slightly abstract self-pity and also, more worryingly, the sense that he was emptying himself. It might be what you feel, he said to himself, when you're the victim of a massive haemorrhage. As his tears began to subside, however, he felt something else, like a general relaxation of the organism, accompanied by intense fatigue. He went off to bed immediately afterwards.

The next morning, shortly after they reached the hospital, they bumped into Maryse in the corridor leading to their father's ward. 'They've gone out,' she said. 'Madeleine took him for a walk in the garden. You're his younger son, isn't that right?' Aurélien nodded. 'She let him know, she told him you were coming. Dr Leroux would have liked to meet you too, but he isn't here this weekend.'

'She's pretty, the nurse,' Aurélien said as they headed towards the garden. 'Ah, you noticed . . .' Cécile replied without commenting further.

Sitting on a bench beside Édouard, who was wrapped up in his blankets, Madeleine saw them in the distance, waved broadly in their direction and got to her feet, pushing the wheelchair towards them. On the way she crossed the paths of two nurses who moved several metres aside to avoid greeting her. Aurélien had a sense that they had given her a hostile glance.

He walked over to his father and took the hand protruding from the blankets in both of his. 'I've come back, Dad,' he said. 'Shall we get you back to your room? Isn't it a bit cold.' Édouard blinked his eyes, slowly, but very perceptibly. 'That means yes,' Cécile said, 'you remember? Maybe we should leave you,' she added when they got back to the ward, 'if you want to be alone to talk to him.'

Cécile and Madeleine left the room; his father's eyes remained fixed on his own, motionless. There could be no expression, Aurélien repeated to himself, there was no way of communicating his feelings; but it took him another two minutes before he began.

'I'll be able to come back several times, Dad,' he said at last. 'I've found a job near Chalon-sur Saône. And then I'm going to sell Mum's sculptures, I've found a dealer in Paris, we'll be able to clear the barn.'

His father blinked his eyes slowly. Aurélien froze, unable to interpret the movement, and also unable to carry on.

'You were right, Dad,' he finally managed to say, 'my wife is a bad woman. I'm going to ask for a divorce.'

His father blinked his eyes again, more distinctly this time, in a more affirmative way.

In fact he didn't have much more to say, but he felt wonderful as he left the hospital, he felt calm and light, and he carried most of the conversation during dinner, telling them that the tapestries he was currently restoring had probably been woven in Arras, that Arras was, in the late Middle Ages, the foremost European centre of production and that the city owed much of its opulence to the industry. 'That opulence has changed . . .' Hervé remarked, topping up his glass.

On Sunday morning he set to work, taking photographs and measurements of the sculptures; he would pass it all on to the dealer by mail, it was an easy task, but the barn was very badly heated as well, and in the evening he realized that he couldn't face the journey again. He would spend the night in Saint-Joseph and phone Félicie to let her know. *The Denial of Saint Peter* could wait a bit longer.

He left at seven the next day. Even though it was early, Cécile had got up, and hugged him for a long time, a very long time, before he got into the car.

11

The following Friday, Paul and Prudence took the train for Mâcon. They weren't going to sleep in the same room, they'd talked about it at the last moment just before leaving, it was difficult, it had been too long; but Prudence said that she would try and join him in his bed towards the end of the night. 'The bed's very small, you know,' Paul pointed out; she suspected as much, but it didn't bother her, quite the contrary. He didn't really understand what it was that made him go to sleep in his teenage bedroom again; he said to himself that there was probably no point working it out. He didn't think that the walls were still decorated with posters of Carrie-Anne Moss; but if they were he thought it would be a good idea to take them down; once again he didn't really know why, but he felt it was better.

Paul also realized, by the way that she hugged him for so long on the platform of the TGV station, that Cécile would do everything possible to ensure that Prudence felt comfortable over the course of the weekend, that she felt welcome in a family once again. She couldn't, however, help feeling a little surprised when she learned that Paul would be occupying his old room again; but she said nothing.

In fact, no image of Carrie-Anne Moss was visible in his bedroom, there was only the inoffensive Nirvana poster. Strangely, he went to sleep without difficulty. He woke up again immediately, however, to the second, when he heard the faint sound of his bedroom door opening, but he didn't move, he made no gesture to welcome Prudence – on the contrary, he curled up and pressed himself against the wall. It was the dead of night, the temperature had not fallen to suggest the approach of dawn; it couldn't have been later than five o'clock on the morning.

First she put a hand level with his waist, then brought it slowly up to his chest. He didn't move. Then she made some vague, somersault-like gestures, and all of a sudden she gripped him with all her strength while making incomprehensible noises. Paul thought she might have been crying. She was still wearing her child's pyjamas, which were slightly plushy to the touch, he couldn't help noticing. She relaxed her grip a little, she was still holding him very tightly but it didn't matter, he was fine.

He lay there like that for a long time without moving, feeling her warmth – she was practically burning and breathing hard, her cardiovascular system must have been working at insane speed.

The room was already broadly filled with daylight by the time he decided to move; he realized as he turned round that he was terribly frightened.

He was wrong to be frightened. Their mouths were a few centimetres apart. Without a second's hesitation Prudence pressed her mouth against his and moved it slowly, entwining their tongues. He felt that this could last for a long time, for ever.

It stopped, however, nothing lasts forever in the sublunar world. They parted, their bodies now about thirty centimetres apart. 'Let's have a coffee,' Paul said.

Once again Cécile couldn't suppress a feeling of surprise when she saw them coming into the kitchen, hand in hand, in their pyjamas. There must have been something necessary involved, she said to herself, a ritual of rediscovery. You can't say anything, you can't do anything about other people's relationship problems, they are a secret place that no one can enter. At most you can wait for them to make their minds up, perhaps, to talk to you about it, knowing that it probably won't be the case. What happens within a couple is particular to them, it is not transferable to other couples, not susceptible to interventions or comments, quite separate from the rest of human existence, different from life in general as it is from the social life shared by many mammals, not even comprehensible by the offspring that the couple might perhaps have produced, in short it's an experience of a different kind, not even an experience as such, more an exploration.

'Aurélien isn't coming with us to the hospital,' Cécile said, 'he's busy wrapping the sculptures, it'll take him all day, and besides I think the transporters have arrived already.'

It took Paul a good minute to understand what she wanted to talk about. In fact Aurélien must have been there, he had forgotten all about him, he hadn't seen him the previous evening – they had arrived very late, after all; and to tell the truth he had forgotten about his mother's sculptures as well.

'Yeah, you know, Mum's sculptures . . .' he said to Prudence, who nodded mechanically, not understanding what he was talking about.

'Are you going to have a shower?' Cécile asked. She seemed to be in a bit of a hurry.

'No, no, we'll go straight away,' Paul replied. Prudence nodded enthusiastically; she had had the same idea: continuing the day like that, without washing. Their bodies hadn't really mingled, that would happen later, but they had touched each other for a long time, and traces, smells, remained; it was part of the body-taming ritual. The same phenomenon was observed in different animal species, particularly geese; he had seen a documentary on it, a long time ago.

The removal van was in fact parked in front of the barn, its two back doors wide open. It was still very vague but there was a feeling that springtime was beginning, the air was mild and there was a smell of vegetation, the leaves were shedding their winter protection with calm immodesty; they were displaying their tender zones, and those young leaves were taking a risk, a sudden frost could annihilate them at any moment. Getting into the passenger seat of Hervé's Dacia, Paul was aware that he would probably never see his mother's sculptures again – and besides that, he was beginning to forget her face.

Once they were at the hospital and in the entrance hall they found themselves face to face with Dr Leroux, immersed in a visibly stormy conversation with a man in the suit of an executive. He broke off with an impatient gesture and came towards them. 'Good, that's great, you've come to see your father . . . Except that he didn't wait for you, he's left with his girlfriend. We don't see them very much any more, by the way, they go for a walk every morning, I don't know where they go. She remembered that the wheelchair has four hours of charge, so she comes back at midday every day to give him something to eat and charge the batteries. He barely needs a nurse any more, and I've asked Aglaé to take care of someone else. That leaves just Maryse, who helps Madeleine to get him out of bed in the morning and put him to bed in the evening, but otherwise Madeleine takes care of everything, she changes his nappies, she washes him, she feeds him.'

'Doesn't that bother you?' Paul asked.

'No, why would it bother me? She does the job of a carer unpaid, you know we're always short-staffed in a hospital, and I think Madeleine's perfect.'

There was clearly a problem that he didn't want to talk about, Paul felt, but didn't dare ask him about it, and they headed towards Édouard's room. Once again he was struck by the photograph of his parents, embracing on the sea front. They looked young and in love, they were literally glowing with desire. Perhaps they should have stayed like that, Paul said to himself, perhaps they shouldn't have had children, since his mother probably wasn't really cut out for motherhood.

After five minutes, Cécile said that she and Hervé would rather wait in the garden; he nodded. Prudence decided to go with them, because she fancied a look around. Once the others had gone, Paul sank into the guest armchair. Looking at the photographs quickly plunged him into a state of gloomy nostalgia, photographs always do that, they make you happy or sad, you can never know in advance. Looking around the room he saw his father's files. He could consult them, Martin-Renaud had said they weren't classified, and in any case he wouldn't understand a word.

The first one he opened was in fact completely cryptic: over ten pages or so, in his small, clear, leaning handwriting, his father had made notes along the lines of 'AyB3n6 – 1282', and it went on like that for hundreds of lines without any discernible repetition or regularity, and without commentary of any kind. He spent a long time on it, without any light of understanding going on in his mind, then closed it again.

Opening the second file he had a shock, and for a few seconds he couldn't believe it. What he had in front of him was the assemblage of pentagons, circles and strange characters that had for months preceded the videos that announced the attacks on the internet. More precisely, he even recognized the message, the second one, the one that accompanied the video of Bruno's decapitation. It had appeared on the internet, he remembered, shortly before his father fell into his coma. He wasn't at all surprised that his father had still followed the news; but the fact that he had been interested in this image in particular was really strange.

four

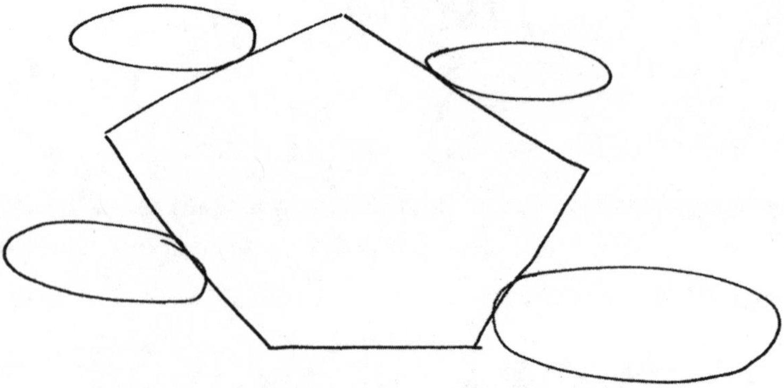

Coʀvmus ,ıCandur gt

Cador qv a q̃ porel am ıvandum

Wc ahqahınzaum

Zac(Yz poɛ γ

(t.bidState=e.bidState,e.bidState===i.b.rendered?
t.timing.renderTime=e.ts:e.ts&&t.timing.setAtTimes.push(e.ts)),t})))
;case"UPDATE_BID_INFO_PROP":return void 0===t[e.slotID]||t[e.slotID].filter((function(t)
{return t.matchesBidCacheId(e.iid)})).length<l?s({},t):s(s({},t),
{},u({},e.slotID,t[e.slotID].map((function(t){return t.matchesBidCacheId(e.iid)&&
(t[e.key]=e.value),t})))));case"UPDATE_SLOT_BIDS":return
s(s({},t),e.bids.reduce((function(e,n){return Object(c.m)(e,n.slotID)?e[n.slotID]=
[].concat(d(e[n.slotID]),[n]):Object(c.m)(t,n.slotID)?e[n.slotID]=[].concat(d(t[n.slotID]),
[n]):e[n.slotID]=[n],e),{}));default:return s({},t)}}(t.slotBids,e),slotIdMap:function(t,e)
{switch(e.type){case"ADD_SLOT_ID":return-1===t.indexOf(e.slotID)?[].concat(d(t),
[e.slotID]):t;default:return t}}(t.slotIdMap,e),sync917:function(t,e){switch(e.type)
{case"SET_SYNC_917":return e.value;default:return t}}
(t.sync917,e),targetingKeys:function(t,e){switch(e.type){case"UPDATE_SLOT_BIDS":return
s(s({},t),e.bids.reduce((function(e,n){return Object(c.m)(t,n.slotID)?e[n.slotID]=
[].concat(d(t[n.slotID]),d((n.bidConfig.targeting?
n.bidConfig.targeting:i.g).filter((function(e){return-
1===t[n.slotID].indexOf(e)})))):e[n.slotID]=n.bidConfig.targeting?
n.bidConfig.targeting:i.g,e),{}));default:return s({},t)}}(t.targetingKeys,e)}}var b=
{getState:function(){return r},dispatch:function(t){r=l(r,t)}};Object(o.d)
("redux")&&Object(c.i)()&&Object(c.m)
(window,"__REDUX_DEVTOOLS_EXTENSION__")&&
(b=window.__REDUX_DEVTOOLS_EXTENSION__(1),b.dispatch({type:"NOOP"})),function(t,e,n){"use
strict";n.d(e,"g",(function(){return c})),n.d(e,"v",(function(){return o})),n.d(e,"b",
(function(){return r})),n.d(e,"f",(function(){return S})),n.d(e,"u",(function(){return
f})),n.d(e,"d",(function(){return l})),n.d(e,"e",(function(){return b})),n.d(e,"c",
(function(){return p})),n.d(e,"n",(function(){return m})),n.d(e,"l",(function(){return
g})),n.d(e,"m",(function(){return a})),n.d(e,"k",(function(){return u})),n.d(e,"t",
(function(){return v})),n.d(e,"h",(function(){return h})),n.d(e,"s",(function(){return
O})),n.d(e,"r",(function(){return S})),n.d(e,"j",(function(){return _})),n.d(e,"q",
(function(){return w})),n.d(e,"i",(function(){return E})),n.d(e,"a",(function(){return
D})),n.d(e,"p",(function(){return T})),n.d(e,"o",(function(){return I})));var r,i,c=
['amznbid','amzniid','amznp'],o=
['amznbid','amzniid','amznp','r_amznbid','r_amzniid','r_amznp'];(i=r=r||
{}).new="NEW",i.exposed="EXPOSED",i.set="SET",i.rendered="RENDERED";var
a,s,u,d="apstagDebug",f=
['redux','fake_bids','verbose','console','console_v2','errors'],l="apstagDebugHeight",b="apst
agDEBUG",p="apstagCfg",m=0,g=0;(s=a=a||
{}).amznbid="testBid",s.amzniid="testImpression",s.amznp="testP",s.crid="testCrid",(u||(u=
{})).video="v";var h,y,O,j,v=['amznbid','amznp'];(y=h=h||
{}).__apsid="ck",y.__aps_id_p="ckp",y.aps_ext_917="st",(j=O=O||
{}).noRequest="0",j.bidInFlight="1",j.noBid="2";var
S="600",_="7.57.00",w="https://",E="function"==typeof XMLHttpRequest&&void 0!==(new
XMLHttpRequest).withCredentials,D="apstagLOADED",T=13,I=1e4},function(t,e,n){"use
strict";n.d(e,"d",(function(){return l})),n.d(e,"c",(function(){return O})),n.d(e,"b",
(function(){return a})),n.d(e,"a",(function(){return S}))),n.d(e,"e",(function(){return
_})));var r=n(3),i=n(2),c=n(5),o=n(0),a=n(1),s=n(7),u=[],d=!1,f=[];function l(t){var e=new
Image;return e.src=t,f.push(e),e}!0===Object(c.c)("exposePixels")&&
(window.apstagPixelQueue=u,window.apstagPixelsSent=f);var b,p={"blockedBidders-fetchBids":
[],"blockedBidders-init":[],adServer:[],appended:[],bidRender:[],bidRenderState:[],bidType:
[],ccpa:[],creativeSize:[],deals:[],fetchBids:[],fifFlow:[],gdpr:[],idRemap:[],iframe:
[],renderFootprint:[],schain:[],simplerGpt:[],slots:[],slotType:[],targeting:[],unusedDeal:
[],useSafeFrames:[]},m=[],g=!1;function h(){g&&(clearTimeout(b),g=!1),Object(o.c)
(m,5).forEach((function(t){v({_type:"featureUsage",p:t,u:Object(s.f)(window)})})),m=
[]}function y(){g||(g=!0,b=setTimeout(h,2e3))}function O(t,e)
{try{return!!i.a.getState().experiments.shouldSampleFeatures&&(void
0!==p[t]&&!Object(o.j)(p[t],e)&&
(p[t].push(e),m.push({cat:t,feat:e}),d&&y(),!0))}catch(t){return Object(a.b)
(t,"sendFeaturePixel"),!1}}function j(t){try{if(d){var e=function(){try{var
t=i.a.getState(),e=t.cfg.PIXEL_PATH,n=t.hosts.DEFAULT_AAX_PIXEL_HOST,o=Object(c.c)
("pixelHost",n);return"".concat(r.q).concat(o).concat(e)}catch(t){return Object(a.b)
(t,"buildPixelBaseUrl"),""}}();return void 0===t.bidId?
e+="p/PH/":e+="".concat(t.bidId,"/"),l(e+=function(t){try{t.__tl="aps-tag";var
e=i.a.getState(),n=null,c="";Object(o.m)(e,"config")&&Object(o.m)
(e.config,"pubID")&&""!==e.config.pubID&&
(n=e.config.isSelfServePub,c=e.config.pubID),null!==n&&(n?
(t.src=r.r,t.pubid=c):t.src=c),t.lv=r.j;var s=JSON.stringify(t);return s=function(t)
{try{return t.replace(/\\.{1}/g,"")}catch(t){return Object(a.b)(t,"escapeJsonForAax"),""}}
(s),s=encodeURIComponent(s)}catch(t){return Object(a.b)(t,"objectToUrlPath"),""}}
(t.payload))}return u.push(t),!1}catch(t){return Object(a.b)(t,"sendPixel"),!1}}function v(t)

1

The second document was quite frightening but more familiar; it looked quite like traditional representations of the devil. The name engraved on the plinth meant something to him as well; he seemed to remember that Eliphas Levi was a nineteenth-century occultist, weirdly a friend of the militant socialist Flora Tristan, herself the grandmother of Gauguin, and in the end none of it still seemed to make much sense. As to the third document, he didn't understand it at all. Either way, his father had spotted a relationship between these three elements, and for ten minutes or so Paul examined them carefully, putting them down next to one another, without seeing a connection. If the relationship was concealed somewhere in the now inaccessible twists and turns of his brain, they weren't close to discovering it; the only thing to do was to inform Martin-Renaud. He left a message, saying only that he had found 'something weird' in his father's files. Martin-Renaud called back ten minutes later and he explained the situation to him.

'Do you want me to mail you the documents?' he suggested.

'Don't do that. You're close to Mâcon, isn't that right?'

'Belleville-en-Beaujolais, exactly.'

'I'll come and get them. I could be there by mid-afternoon, I think.'

Then he hung up, leaving Paul stunned.

*

Madeleine arrived just before noon, as Leroux had said she would, pushing Édouard's wheelchair. Cécile told her that there was some beef bourguignon, some mutton stew, and also some soup, she just needed to heat them up in the microwave, and she had also made some desserts. As soon as she had arrived she had put the dishes in the refrigerator of the common room, where meals were taken, at least for patients who were able to feed themselves without a gastrostomy; there were about ten in all. Paul was impressed by the state of his father, who looked distinctly more healthy, his face was rested, almost tanned, and it even seemed to him that his eyes were brighter. After kissing him on both cheeks, he leaned over to his ear to say, 'We need to talk after lunch, Dad, about a subject to do with your work. One of your old colleagues is going to pay you a visit this afternoon.' Édouard blinked his eyes distinctly, energetically, he thought, but maybe he was imagining things. After the meal they shut themselves away in the room, and he took out the file.

'Do you remember these documents, Dad?' He blinked in the affirmative.

'Did you find them at someone's house?' He didn't move.

'So you printed them out from the internet? All four.' Again he didn't move.

'But did you have a sense, an intuition, that there was a connection between them?' He blinked quickly, twice.

'Do you think you could explain your intuition to your colleague when he comes this evening?' Paul had the strange impression that he was hesitating, that his eyelids were quivering slightly, but at last he was motionless again.

Martin-Renaud arrived shortly after three o'clock, in the back seat of a Citroën DS driven by a soldier.

'I'm surprised you got here so quickly . . .' Paul said to him.

'The airbase at Ambérieu-en-Bugey isn't far, and there are always planes available at Villacoublay.'

'I meant, I think it's surprising that you came in person, that you thought it was an emergency.'

He smiled. 'You're not wrong there, it might be an exaggerated use of state funds . . . It isn't a national emergency, that's true, but this business is starting to exasperate everyone, not only in France. And then there's something else, something much vaguer that I think is a long way from coming to an end. They've been taunting us for six months, doing exactly what they want to; in my view it's not going to stop there.'

With even less reason, Paul thought exactly the same thing. They sat down in two armchairs by the entrance to the clinic, silent and peaceful. After listening carefully, Martin-Renaud shook his head in disbelief. 'Satanists, now . . . Honestly, I feel sorry for Doutre-mont. I'm going to end up on sick leave if it goes on like this.'

'But it's not really serious so far. Well, I mean it's strange, but there hasn't been a disaster.'

'That depends. From the point of view of digital security, it's probably the biggest disaster we've known since the invention of the computer. The only reason people aren't panicking is that there have been no casualties.'

Paul felt that he'd nearly added 'for now' because he too, still for no reason, had just had the same idea. They contemplated this prospect for a while.

'I'm going to pay a visit to Édouard, is that OK?' Martin-Renaud asked at last.

'Are you going to question him? At last, if I can put it that way.'

'No, I have no plan to question him, I just want to say hello. Anyway, I think you've done very well; you've asked exactly the right questions. Perhaps you too should have come and worked for us.'

'I think he'd have liked that.'

'Ah . . .' Martin-Renaud smiled again before getting up from his chair. 'He understands everything you say to him, but he can't reply, is that it?' Paul nodded in agreement. 'He can just blink to say yes when you ask him a question?' He nodded again. Martin-Renaud set off down the corridor.

He got back into his car two hours later, setting off for Ambérieu military base. 'Is that Dad's colleague, or rather his former colleague?' Cécile asked. Paul said it was. 'He's exactly as I imagined,' she remarked. 'Yes, all the same, the television series sometimes get it right. Ah . . .' Hervé concluded.

The meal was animated; the appearance of the secret service had made them all over-excited and expansive. His father's professional life might well have been exciting, Paul said to himself, not at all the irksome life of a civil servant, like his. Well maybe he was overstating his case a little, his life had become more interesting since Bruno entered the political game, but still, economics was a grim discipline, and the ministry a fairly dispiriting place.

Aurélien was informed about events. Things had gone well with the removal firm, he told them in return, everything had been wrapped and would be stored the next day and put on sale early the following week.

They had come together again, Paul said to himself, the brothers and the sister had come together again, for the first time in how long? They parted very late, all of them a little drunk, even Aurélien had apparently joined in, it was the first time that Paul had seen him drink; a few minutes after going to bed, however, he was filled with the most shocking anxiety at the idea that this reunion was an illusion, that it was the last time that they would come together, or almost the last, soon things would resume their course, everything would break down again, dissolve, and all of a sudden he felt a terrible need for Prudence, the warmth of Prudence's body, so much so that he got up and walked in his pyjamas down the glass-walled corridor leading to the main house. Reaching the conservatory he stopped abruptly and his breathing gradually calmed down. The moon was full, and he had a clear view of the vineyards and the hills. No, it wasn't a good idea, he said to himself, he had to let her come, it was up to her to make the journey. At the same time, was he so sure of that? In the Wiccan religion, the god sometimes seemed to have something dominant about him, something virile; he didn't know, he really didn't know. He wouldn't have hesitated with Raksaneh, he suddenly said to himself; not to mention the Ethiopian. They had definitely screwed up, he said to himself, they had collectively screwed up somewhere. What was the point of installing 5G if you simply couldn't make contact with one another any more, and perform the essential gestures, the ones that allow the human species to reproduce, the ones that also, sometimes, allow you to be happy? He was becoming capable of thought once more, his reflections were even taking an almost philosophical turn, he noted with disgust. Unless it all had to do with biology, or nothing at all, he was going to go back to bed at last, it was the only thing to do, his thoughts were condemned to go round in circles, he felt like a beer-can crushed under the feet of a British football hooligan, or like a steak abandoned in the vegetable section of a bottom-of-the-range refrigerator, which is to say that he didn't feel very well. To make matters worse, he was starting to get toothache again; was it all psychosomatic, perhaps?

Strangely, in spite of the persistent agitation in his mind and the piercing pain in his jaw, he went to sleep almost immediately, as soon as his head hit the pillow. Similarly, he woke up as soon as he heard the sound, very faint, of his bedroom door. She had come even earlier than the day before, it must have been the middle of the night, and he felt as if he had been asleep for ten minutes. This time he didn't pretend to go to sleep, he turned over immediately and brought his mouth to hers, which is probably what a god would have done because she reacted well, and once again their tongues mingled. When he put his hand on her buttocks, however, he felt her stiffening; he immediately stopped what he was doing. He would have to be patient, he said to himself over and over again, they would have to take their time, but to tell the truth taking his time was pleasant and even dizzying, because without a doubt they would end up falling into one another's arms, their whole lives were busy turning into a slow-motion tumble, interminable and delicious. Even touching her buttocks was good, they were less scrawny, less bony than he had feared, he had had a feeling that he was getting an erection, or at least that something was happening in that area, but there again he had rather forgotten, for how long exactly? Eight years, ten? It seemed an enormously long time, but in fact it probably was that, sometimes the years pass quickly. He would have to proceed differently, start by going to see a hooker, just to rediscover the sensations and reflexes, that was what hookers were for, to bring you back to life. For now he merely slipped a hand under her pyjama top to stroke her breasts. She reacted well, she had always liked it when he stroked her breasts. Lower down, obviously, it was more complicated.

After Sunday lunch they regrouped, a little like a collection of supplicants, around Aurélien's car, to wave him goodbye, as if he were setting off on the road to Calvary, which in a way he was. He had a meeting in Romainville the following morning, so of course he had to leave, and sleep in the house in Montreuil, that was the best, the reasonable solution. People yield to their fate on the whole, Cécile herself had always done so, and basically she had congratulated herself on it. She said to herself, however, probably for the first time in her life, that in certain cases a rebellious attitude was to be preferred; in Aurélien's place she would have slept anywhere, in an Ibis hotel in Bagnolet or elsewhere, anything rather than go back to Montreuil. She nearly told him that, hesitated, held back; but she regretted it for a long time, once her brother's car had disappeared around the last turning towards Villié-Morgon.

Aurélien hadn't said anything to Cécile, he thought he had already talked to her enough about his worries, but he planned to tell Indy about his intention to divorce this evening; he had a meeting with a lawyer the following day, and the art dealer immediately afterwards, so it wasn't possible to put things off any longer. And then there was the price of the works, he had to tell her about that as well, in short he was expecting an abominable evening in every respect. He had more or less expected traffic jams without thinking about it, but strangely the motorway was deserted, even though they were at the end of the school holidays, or maybe not, he couldn't remember. Godefroy, for example – was he on holiday? He hadn't the faintest idea.

He reached Montreuil a little after eight and had a lot of trouble parking, but in the end how found a space five hundred metres from the house. He had his key. Indy was sitting on the sofa in the living room, watching the end of *It's Politics*, and didn't get up to greet him. A few months previously she was still trying, more or less, to pretend; that time had come and gone. He didn't like television in general, still less the political programmes that she watched assiduously, probably considering them to be part of her job, but he had a special aversion to *It's Politics*, and it invariably plunged him into despair. All those people brought together on screen, the mischievous presenter, the bald historian, the seductive woman investigator all seemed to him like as many malign puppets, he couldn't convince himself that these people lived like he did, breathed like he did, belonged to the same world, the same reality as him. This sinister gang also included a kind of moderator, and she was probably the one that Indy identified with, or tried to identify with; most of the time she must have been getting drunk on humiliation as she witnessed the weekly televisual performance of someone she couldn't even consider as her rival, since this woman was floating at dizzying media heights that would remain forever inaccessible to Indy, reminding her with each passing moment that she was nothing but a failed journalist, and in print journalism, what was more. She was perhaps the worst of all, with her concerned expression, her self-satisfaction, her obvious awareness of belonging on the side of good, her willingness to prostrate herself in front of any VIP of the same camp. Indy shared all of these characteristics, apart from self-satisfaction – inevitably.

He spent some time foraging in the kitchen, trying to make as much noise as possible. In vain: there was nothing to drink, and nothing to eat either, he wasn't hungry, but yes, he did need a bottle of wine. He came back into the sitting room; the guest was a kind of pathetic writer whose name he had forgotten, Indy had turned up the volume almost beyond what was endurable. 'There's nothing to drink!' he yelled. 'I'm not your maid!' she yelled back. 'Not really my wife either . . .' he added in a slightly lower voice; she turned an uncomprehending face in his direction, and repeating his words seemed pointless, at any rate the conversation was over for the evening, their discussion would wait till tomorrow, it seemed insurmountable to him without alcohol, in the end perhaps it was better to see the lawyer beforehand.

As he undressed he found Maryse's mobile phone in one of his jeans pockets. He had asked her for it that same morning, just before leaving the hospital. She had given it to him straight away without asking questions, without comment; no one had noticed, he thought.

2

Seeing the documents that Édouard had put together, Doutremont reacted better than Martin-Renaud had expected. He could see quite clearly what the last one was: it was probably part of a programme for controlling zombie machines; this was a major clue, even if the complete programme would inevitably have involved dozens of pages of analogue instructions. He himself didn't know exactly what the programming language might have been, but he would have no difficulty finding out, it would just take a couple of phone calls. Where could Paul's father have got hold of this page of code? It would have been interesting to know; but judging by what Martin-Renaud had told him, the state of his health made him difficult to question.

The engraving showing a kind of devil, on the other hand, didn't make much sense that he could see; the attack on the sperm bank had knocked him off balance, forcing him to move from a classic ultra-leftist trail to a much more unlikely fundamentalist Catholic one; that image now seemed to send them in the direction of a Satanist track; at this point, that didn't bother him too much, they were still in the same general ballpark.

At the time of the Danish attack he had appealed to Sitbon-Nozières, who was in charge of ideological surveillance in the security service; he realized that they hadn't spoken since. Without really knowing why, he felt ill at ease with this man who was more or less the same age as him, always impeccably dressed in a dark blue suit. He still treated him with perfect courtesy; but in fact there was something fake, something excessive about his curiosity. Essentially he felt in his presence a kind of class inferiority the origin of which he struggled to understand; Sitbon-Nozières had the reputation of being a brilliant mind, an alumnus of the École Normale Supérieure, a history graduate, author of a thesis on the Russian nihilists, but it wasn't his studies that impressed him, he felt no awkwardness, for example, in the presence of a graduate of the École Nationale d'Administration like Paul; admittedly he didn't know any *normaliens*, but in essence that didn't bother him particularly. The thing that struck him about Sitbon-Nozières, and thinking about it he couldn't help reaching this distressing conclusion, was his suits: even though he didn't know much about the subject, he was sure that they must be worth a lot of money, probably thousands of euros. It was largely a reflection of the same kind that had led to the defeat of the right-wing candidate at the last presidential election, and allowed the president to come to power. However full of himself he might have been, there was nothing of the country squire about the president; there was a sense that he owed his dazzling rise solely to his own qualities; and that was what mattered more than anything else in the eyes of the voters.

Martin-Renaud had employed the history graduate two years before to keep an eye on all extremist publications, and other calls for insurrection that might be lying about on different websites, in the most remote corners of the internet. His office was vast, it wasn't on the same floor as the other secret service offices, and it had the particular quality of being connected to the web – none of the others were; after various unsuccessful attempts they had reached the conclusion it was the only way to secure their computers completely, and they did their internet research on shared computers in a dedicated room. Sitbon-Nozières' computer, unlike theirs, contained nothing secret; his job was to access content that was available to everyone, and whose authors, in fact, intended it to reach as many people as possible.

He stared for a few seconds at the demonically inspired engraving before concluding that he couldn't see where it would get them. As far as he knew these people were absolute individualists, and it would have been ridiculous for them to throw themselves into any terrorist or militant action, almost as absurd as giving out voting recommendations.

He wasn't yet certain of anything, but his own research led him in a different direction. Opponents of liberal globalization and artificial reproduction didn't as a rule belong to the same networks, but there was a movement that did bring them both together: that of the anarcho-primitivists. This was an essentially American movement, distantly inspired by the Luddites although much more extreme. The movement's best-known ideologue was John Zerzan. He was also the most radical: he wanted not only to destroy industry, trade and modern technology, but also to abolish agriculture, religions, the arts and even articulated language; his project, in fact, was to bring humanity back to the level of the middle Palaeolithic era. Sitbon-Nozières drew from his bookshelf a thin pamphlet by Zerzan before reading a passage:

'Agriculture enables greatly increased division of labour, establishes the material foundations of social hierarchy, and initiates environmental destruction. Priests, kings, drudgery, sexual inequality, warfare are a few of its fairly immediate specific consequences.'

'It's so simplistic and extremist, I have trouble believing that that might have had an influence . . .' Doutremont objected.

'I don't agree with you on that. There are more extreme voices than his. Some deep ecology ideologues preach the extinction of humanity because they think that the human species is irredeemable and dangerous for the survival of the planet. This applies to movements like the Church of Euthanasia, the Gaia Liberation Front or the Voluntary Human Extinction Movement. Zerzan doesn't want to destroy humanity, but to re-educate it. When he talks about human beings he sees them as sympathetic primates who are good at heart, but who have been going in the wrong direction since the Neolithic. His theses have a lot in common with classic Rousseauism: man is born good, but perverted by society, etc. And people like Rousseau can have a huge influence; you might even say that Rousseau was the sole source of the French Revolution. The myths of primitive Communism, of the golden age, have always had an incredible mobilizing power, and that's even more true today with all the programmes about the wisdom of traditional civilizations, Inuit caribou hunts and so on. Also, what's interesting in the case of Zerzan is that one of his friends acted on it. You remember the Unabomber?'

'No, can't say I do.'

'About thirty years ago. Unabomber is the name the media gave him, he was actually called Theodore Kaczynski. He was a very talented mathematician, I even think he discovered something in algebra, a new demonstration of the Wedderburn theorem, if I remember correctly. He initially taught at Berkeley, before moving to a remote cabin somewhere in Montana. The beginning of *Future Primitive*, Zerzan's first book, is a regular ode to the Unabomber: "He survived like a grizzly or a cougar, lurking in the thick carpet of snow. He emerged from his lair in the spring, explored the forest, walked along the rivers. He hunted, fished, gathered, gleaned. Always alone. Free, but alone." It might make you smile, but believe me, that kind of lyricism has its effect on certain people. Zerzan really has points in common with Rousseau: moderate intelligence, but a real musicality in his sentences; it's a mixture that can turn out to be extremely dangerous. Kaczynski is something else: he's much more rigorous, more structured in his thinking, he's more like Marx, if you like.'

Sitbon-Nozières took two more books from his shelf: *Manifesto: the Future of Industrial Society*, published by Editions du Rocher,

266

and *Industrial Society and its Future* by Editions de l'Encylopédie des Nuisances.

'Take for example the passage in which he talks about nature . . .' He flicked quickly through one of the books before he found the passage: 'It's fragment 184. This is all he finds to say about nature: "Most people agree that nature is beautiful, and it is true that it exerts a great charm." You see, it's not the same style at all. Also he's often very critical about Zerzan. For example Zerzan defends feminist positions, he claims that the patriarchy didn't appear until the Neolithic, and that equality between the sexes prevailed throughout the Palaeolithic; that's an extremely doubtful claim. He's also vegetarian, and claims that what he calls "butchering practices" appeared very late in the history of humanity; there again, archaeologists frankly disagree. Kaczynski accepts natural inequality and predation, and he shows no sympathy for the left, quite the contrary; in a sense he's a more consistent ecologist. The fact remains, however, that in his cabin in Montana he started making hand-crafted bombs, which he sent to various people who he saw as representatives of modern technology, and that he left three people dead and twenty injured before he was arrested by the FBI.'

'What happened to him?'

'Last I heard he was serving a sentence in a penitentiary in Colorado. But he might be dead now, and if he's alive he must be over eighty. In 1996 the Church of Euthanasia, one of the most provocative movements of *deep ecology* – they like to proclaim that the four pillars of their movement are suicide, abortion, cannibalism and sodomy – launched a *Unabomber for President* campaign in the American elections; without consulting him, of course, but that shows that he preserved a certain aura for a long time, a bit like Charles Manson. It's not impossible, either, that he had an underground influence in France. His text was translated twice into French, but not at all into most other languages; and the publishers aren't exactly marginal. One persistent legend is that a young French ethnobiologist joined Kaczynski in his cabin in Montana, just before he was arrested. I've inquired into this ethnobiologist; she's the author of large-scale works on the vocalization of cows, but she doesn't seem to have any connection with Kaczynski; the fact remains, however, that the rumour circulated in alternative fanzines. These are isolated clues, none of which is of any importance in itself, but I've been convinced from the outset that there is a particular connection between these attacks and France. Why choose, in the decapitation video, a French finance minister? It's true that Bruno Juge, more than anyone else, embodies revival through industry, technological modernity, progress; but it's an idea that would never occur to anyone apart from French terrorists.'

'Is Wedderburn's theorem the one that claims that any finite body is necessarily commutative?'

'Yes, something like that.'

Doutremont left his office in a reflective mood, but not completely convinced. There was no room in the *normalien*'s reasoning for the representation of the demonic; that didn't square with the intuition of their paralysed former colleague, and rightly or wrongly Martin-Renaud placed a great deal of importance on his point of view, he had no desire to rule it out it without further examination. Sitbon-Nozières looked for people who acted rationally, according to certain convictions, to attain a specific political objective – he couldn't reason otherwise, it was the result of his training – but the possibility remained that these attacks were linked by something much less rational, that a certain form of madness was involved, or at least that was his impression. Then he thought of someone he had just hired, who had been recommended by one of his old acquaintances, a former hacker – well, he hoped he was former, he wasn't sure by any means in fact, any day he expected to find himself facing him in the dock as a criminal. The new person had been in the building for two weeks, he had just had time to familiarize himself with the services, and he hadn't seen him again since he arrived, he just remembered a very young man, twenty or so; he might have a different opinion on the matter; it was worth asking the question.

Most young contract workers hired by the DGSI for their specialist knowledge of a marginal section of society make a minimal effort to adapt to the dress codes of their new working environment; Doutremont himself had done it some years before. This was not the case with Delano Durand, and Doutremont had a shock when he appeared in his office. With his dirty jogging pants three sizes too big, his little beer belly and his long, dirty, greasy hair, he presented to the world the exact image of the metalhead whose presence has mysteriously persisted in our societies for the past fifty years. Without a word he picked up the documents handed to him by his hierarchical superior. The first, with its strange letters, he knew already, of course, though he knew no more about it than anyone else in the service, and he had already told them as much. As Doutremont expected, he was very quick to reject the last one with this simple comment: 'Don't understand . . .' But he looked for a long time at the second document which he held in his hands, and Doutremont finally asked him:

'Does that remind you of anything?'

'Yeah, sure, it's our old pal Baphomet.'

'Baphomet?'

'Yeah, Baphomet.'

'Can you elaborate?'

'At your service, boss. If you want to be pedantic about it, you could say that the name dates from the Middle Ages, and it's probably a distorted version of Mohamed. We first come across it in a letter from Anselme of Ribemont, companion of Godfrey of

Bouillon, dating from 1098, in which he relates the story of the siege of Antioch. For the Christian knights of the Middle Ages, the Muslims were nothing but devil-worshippers, and you might wonder if they were mistaken . . .' He laughed noisily, noticed that he was the only one laughing, broke off and returned to his disquisition. 'Right, the fact remains that Baphomet was subsequently worshipped by the Templars, which was also one of the main reasons for the destruction of the Order of the Temple, before it was picked up by Scottish-Rite freemasons, and he's now very popular in extreme metal and death metal groups, especially Norwegian ones, he's a real star in those circles. The figure is quite ambiguous, he has the head of a goat, he's bearded, but at the same time he has women's breasts, it's quite curious.'

'And the connection between the two pictures? Do you see one?'

'Well yes of course, obviously: the number five. You've got pentagons in the messages, they've appeared in all of them since the beginning. More precisely regular convex pentagons. You've got a different kind of pentagon on Baphomet's forehead, a regular starry pentagon, or pentagram; that's important, because it's still used a lot in contemporary magic.'

Doutremont gave a start on hearing the words 'contemporary magic', then he thought for a few moments; perhaps this fellow wasn't as pathetic as all that after all, and hiring him might have been a good idea. 'And that gets us where?' he went on. 'I mean in concrete terms?'

'Well I don't know, boss, I'd have to make some inquiries, call some people, you'd need to let me have a bit of time.'

There was obvious irony in the use of the word 'boss', but Doutremont didn't react, he was starting to get old, he said to himself. Had he been as insolent as this boy at his age? He didn't remember very clearly, but he didn't think so. In those days he had undoubtedly had the typical arrogance that nerds have when faced with computing philistines, but that was normal and expected, it was part of their character, and the opposite would almost have been disappointing. Recently he had started to understand a bit better what being the boss implied, and he calmly said goodbye to Delano Durand.

3

Paul had always liked it when the first of the month fell on a Monday, he liked it generally when things coincided, life should have been a sequence of pleasant coincidences, he thought. Ideally. On this Monday 1 March, good weather seemed to have settled in over the Paris region, and even over the whole of France. At about five o'clock he decided to call it a day, he fancied having an aperitif at a pavement café, things he hadn't done for ages, that he had never really done, to tell the truth. Perhaps Prudence was available? It was unlikely but not impossible; few things seemed impossible since their last weekend.

She only picked up after ten rings, and as soon as he heard her saying 'Paul . . .' with relief, in a very small voice, he knew that something serious had happened.

'I'm at home. It would be better if you came home as soon as you could. It's about my parents.'

'What's happening?'

'My mother's died.'

She was sitting on the sofa as she waited for him, her hands resting on her knees, and looked slightly shrunken. She must have been crying before, but now she was calm. He sat down beside her and put his arm around her shoulders. She relaxed and rested her head against his chest; she was incredibly light.

'How did it happen?'

'A car accident. She had bad reflexes, she should have stopped driving a long time ago. She was taken to the hospital in Vannes, they tried to operate but it didn't work. She died on Saturday night. They tried to contact me all weekend, but I'd turned off my phone, well, you know . . .'

Yes, he knew; he had turned off his phone too that last weekend; they were allowed to live.

'In the end their neighbour called me this morning.'

'What about your father?'

'He's under observation, also at the hospital in Vannes. He's not well at all, and he's refusing to talk to anybody. I don't even dare to imagine what state he's in . . .' She started crying again, softly, soundlessly. 'He was ten years older than she was, you know . . . He had never expected to survive her.'

He saw his own father prostrate in the dining-room armchair after his mother's death, then at the psychiatric hospital in Mâcon, dazed with psychotropic drugs, then again in Saint-Joseph; it had taken him months to come out of it, and he would probably never have come out of it without Madeleine. It was strange, his mother had never been an exceptional wife, neither especially tender nor loving, not very attached to her home – come to think of it, she had quite a lot in common with Prudence's mother, apart from the fact that she was more lower middle class in origin. He didn't have a sense, in either instance, that their love had really survived the test of time; and yet they had kept going, they had spent their lives together, brought up children, passed on the baton, and after the death of the wife, the husband had not known how to go on living, he had simply not known how to continue. It was worse in the case of Prudence's father, if he remembered correctly he was just over eighty years old, he had started suffering from Parkinson's, so for him it was really game over.

'You're going there, of course?'

'Yes, I'm taking the TGV for Auray tomorrow.'

He had only gone there once, but he remembered the house in

273

Larmor-Baden very well, the wonderful view from the terrace over the Gulf of Morbihan, l'Île des Moines.

'Were you able to get through to your sister?'

'Yes, Priscilla is supposed to call me back shortly, it's still early in Vancouver. She's coming too, as soon as possible. She really loves Dad, you know, she was always his favourite daughter . . .' She smiled resignedly, without any real sadness; he understood that as well.

'And she's doing well in Canada?' Paul asked, glimpsing the possibility of a less serious subject.

'No, not really, in fact she's getting divorced. I'm not at all surprised, I always knew things wouldn't work out between them.'

This time Paul saw the wedding in his mind, a big wedding in Boulogne, he remembered the garden where the reception was held, he had completely forgotten the husband's face, but weirdly he remembered his profession, he was a Canadian, an English-speaking Canadian who worked in the oil industry. Prudence herself 'had always known that that things wouldn't work out', she had always known and hadn't mentioned it. Communication between sisters, he reflected, isn't always better than it is between brothers; it often is, but not always.

The next morning, he went with her to the Gare Montparnasse, they crossed the Parc de Bercy together, it was almost warm and he undid his coat. 'Yes, it's surprising, isn't it?' Prudence observed, 'I've even brought a swimsuit. Well, maybe I'm deluding myself on that one a bit . . .' Global warming was undeniably a disaster, Paul had no doubt about that, he was entirely prepared to deplore it, or fight against it if necessary; nevertheless it gave life an unpredictable, fantastical aspect that it had been missing before.

They were very early, and had a coffee in one of the bars inside the station. 'Priscilla is arriving the day after tomorrow, just in time for the funeral. I don't imagine you have any great desire to come, you never really liked my mother, did you?' He felt awkward for a moment. 'I won't lie, she was always horrible to you. And to me, when the subject turned to you. I even had a sense, sometimes, that she was jealous.'

Jealous? That was a strange idea, he would never have thought of it, but perhaps she was right. She was definitely right, in fact; he knew practically nothing about mother–daughter relationships, and felt that it was one of the many subjects that it was better for him to remain ignorant about.

'So in the end,' Prudence went on, 'you understood me, I can't say I'm mad with grief. You know, it makes me think about old books, when men used to say of their wives that they deceived all the time: "She's the mother of my children", to show that they respected her in spite of everything; I understood what they meant, it's never struck me as fake, as feelings go. Well now, I'm tempted to say: "She was my father's wife, all the same." The hardest thing, and I hope Priscilla will be able to help me a bit with this, will be to find someone for Dad. Even if he recovers, he won't be able to stay at home on his own, it's unthinkable. And frankly I can't see myself putting him in a care home.'

'Oh no!' Paul had replied with a violence that surprised even him, in a flash he had just seen the house, the little attic rooms, the sunrise over the Gulf of Morbihan. It was a place very different from Saint-Joseph, but it was also a place to live, a place to get old and die, which a care home could never be.

The time for the train was getting closer, and they only had a few minutes. 'You'll be able to come, now . . .' she said. 'It would be good if you came. You've always liked that part of the country, I think? And besides, we have so many things to catch up on.'

Yes, so many things, Paul said to himself. She rose brightly to her feet; she only had a light bag which she carried over her shoulder. 'Right, I've really got to go now, my train's pulled in.' The

TGV for Quimper, stopping at Vannes and Auray, was in fact being announced on Platform 7.

'It's my fault, I know, or at least a lot of it's my fault,' she went on. It was his fault, in fact they were both to blame and anyway it didn't matter any more, he launched into confused explanations, they couldn't stop gazing into each other's eyes, and they had to if she was going to catch her train. 'I know all that, my darling,' she said under her breath, then planted a kiss on his lips, a quick kiss, before turning round and disappearing into the crowd that was heading for the platform.

4

'Characteristics:

1. Put it on and make your lover love you more.

2. Express your sexy charm and fascinate men.

3. Expose your waist and your elegant legs.

4. The best present for your lover.

5. It's a tool for promoting marital relations.

6. Material: 35% polyester, 65% cotton.

7. This teddy will make you very happy and beautiful.'

(Clothing presentation by the brand GDOFKH)

In the famous beginning of *The Girl with Golden Eyes*, in which Balzac depicts human beings as being driven by the quest for pleasure and gold, we might be surprised that he neglected to speak of a third passion, ambition, entirely different in nature, and one to which he himself was particularly prone. Bruno, for example, had never seemed to be inspired by a great appetite for pleasure, even less of lucre; but yes, he was ambitious. Besides, it wasn't very easy to determine whether ambition was a generous or a selfish passion; whether it matched a desire to leave a positive trace in the history of humanity, or simply to the vanity of being numbered among those who have left such a trace. In short, Balzac simplified things somewhat.

Prudence didn't call him until three days later, on Friday evening. Priscilla had arrived, and it was a real relief; her sister was definitely better at organizing things than she was. The funeral had taken place, it had, if one could say such a thing, gone well – which meant, Paul supposed, that a sufficiently large number of people from the village had turned up, and that the priest had performed the rites correctly. Obviously her father wasn't there, and he hadn't even been kept informed about the ceremony. His mind was still wandering in unknown places, and luckily he was sleeping a lot, his medication allowed that at least. The rest of the time he was silent, turning his head disgustedly when anyone came into his room, whether it was a nurse or one of his daughters; even the arrival of Priscilla had not cheered him up. The psychiatrist was very guarded about any possible release date; it would take weeks, perhaps months, before he was stabilized; and a home help, at any rate, was still indispensable.

The rest was more unexpected: Prudence's sister planned to leave Canada for good; her husband raised no objection to giving her custody of their two daughters, he hadn't even shown any desire to see them again, in fact it seemed as if he couldn't have cared less. Priscilla could work more or less anywhere, she did practically everything on the internet, so why not Larmor-Baden? She had always liked the house, and she was sure that the girls would love it.

Paul had never known what Priscilla did for a living, and neither had Prudence; but it seemed to involve logos, emojis, and ideas of different Asian languages. Her job might have been difficult to define for an outsider, but it was still extremely lucrative: it was she, for example, who had designed the new Nike logo, a difficult replacement given the fame of the previous one, and who had chosen the lettering and typography of the slogans printed on Apple T-shirts. From time to time she had to take trips abroad, very brief, never more than a day, all over the world, particularly in the United States and Japan. But to tell the truth those trips were becoming increasingly rare, since almost everything could now be done by video conference, whether in Larmor-Baden or Vancouver.

If she decided to stay, the search for a home help would obviously be carried out under the best possible conditions, and Prudence, after two difficult days (it wasn't easy to find someone, a simple housekeeper was one thing, but once there were medical tasks, a risk of accident, things immediately became more complicated), now felt very optimistic. Apart from that, the weather in Brittany was exceptional, no one had ever seen anything like it in early March, she herself had even gone to the beach that afternoon, she said to Paul, in fact she hadn't actually gone for a swim, but she had been able to put on her swimsuit. 'I noticed that I've got quite a pretty bum,' she added without transition. Why would she tell him something that? She'd never done it before. He should have replied, 'Yes, my darling, you have a magnificent bum' or, even better: 'Yes, my darling, I've always loved your bum', but he couldn't, he hadn't seen her bum for a long time, but he had a perfect memory of it, and the other evening in Saint-Joseph, putting his hand on it, he had felt that it hadn't changed very much, his hands couldn't deceive him on that one. He felt that he was an inch away from getting an erection and he should have said something about that as well. For example, if they had been in a contemporary American thriller, he would have said, 'Stop making me hard!' with a stupid complicit laugh. In fact he settled for a modest chuckle before hanging up; he too had progress to make.

There was another passion that Balzac had forgotten, maternal love, he said to himself immediately after hanging up. He had, strangely, addressed the issue of paternal love, even though it was less widespread, and the Canadian would not have contradicted him on that. His father and Cécile, and Priscilla's father, provided a few examples, albeit less *hardcore* than Old Goriot.

He spent the rest of the night reading, but not Balzac; he

scoured the bookshelf for something philosophical which seemed more appropriate. He didn't have much in the way of philosophy, about fifteen books at most, and they seemed to be quite dim-witted, conciliatory philosophers. He himself had always felt more or less exempt from the different passions that he had just listed, and which had been condemned almost unanimously by the philosophers of the past. He had always imagined the world as a place where he should not have been, but which he was in no hurry to leave, simply because it was the only one he knew. He should perhaps have been a tree, or a tortoise, perhaps, in any case something less agitated than a human being, with an existence subject to fewer variations. No philosopher seemed to suggest a solution of this nature, on the contrary, they seemed to agree that one must accept the human condition 'with its limitations and its splendours', as he had once read in a humanist-inspired publication; some of them even came out with the repulsive idea that one need only discover a certain form of *dignity* in it. As a young person would have said, *lol*.

When he managed to get to sleep at last, dispatching these disappointing philosophers into their void, day was breaking over the Parc de Bercy. In his dream, two Dutch hitch-hikers were waiting by the side of a road in Corsica, which probably led to the Bavella pass, one of the places he and Prudence had visited when they went to the island, and those two young people, even though they were barely more than twenty and both extremely blond, even though in reality they did not resemble them at all, seemed to represent Prudence and him. He then hoped that erotic scenes might follow, indeed that they might get their real faces back, until he had a sense of reliving certain moments, those holidays in Corsica had been fabulously erotic, that was probably the most erotic time of his life. Unfortunately nothing of the kind occurred, and it was decidedly impossible to guide the content of his dreams in a particular direction, or at least it wasn't something he knew how to do.

Instead, a red sports car stopped in front of him, or rather in front of the young Dutch boy representing him, while Prudence had gone to get some water from a nearby fountain. In the car, two Italian twins in their forties, with very black, almost blueish hair and false, hypnotic smiles, turned symmetrically towards him with an ambiguously inviting expression. Unable to help it, he got into the back seat of their car (probably a Ferrari, a convertible, the back seats were tiny, their size at best appropriate for young children), and they set off immediately. At that moment the girl representing Prudence was returning from the fountain, clutching her now full water bottle; she waved her hands madly in his direction; the twins burst into nervous and unpleasant laughter.

Shortly afterwards another car stopped in front of the girl, who climbed in; this time it was almost certainly a Bentley Mulsanne. Even though it was high summer and the heat was sweltering, the interior of the car was cold, almost icy, and lined with Russian furs. While the chauffeur was built like a guerrilla fighter and seemed accustomed to the use of weapons, the man who welcomed her in the back seat was almost an old man, and everything in his appearance suggested a mixture of exhaustion and almost decadent refinement. The pseudo-Prudence then told him what had happened; the decadent old man seemed worried, and convinced of the need to act. 'They're dangerous, aren't they?' he asked his chauffeur. 'Extremely dangerous,' he agreed.

Some distance further along they noticed the red Ferrari parked near a path that snaked to the top of the mountain. The driver immediately parked not far away. To the great surprise of the pseudo-Prudence, the old man got out of the limousine wearing a tight black rubber costume that seemed appropriate for close combat, probably a diving suit; there was a thirty-centimetre dagger, the blade sharp as a razor, attached to his belt.

As they climbed, the pseudo-Prudence was amazed that their path was so steep and difficult, while a few metres away another path, plainly leading to the same place, climbed along a gentle slope with easy bends; a group of schoolchildren was coming down it singing. 'He who seeks difficulty will find it,' the old man replied mysteriously. A little further on, the ascent became so perilous that the pseudo-Prudence nearly fell down the precipice that opened up on the left of the path, where the slope was almost vertical. Demonstrating a surprising agility for his age, the man caught her at the last minute, saving her from crashing a hundred metres below.

At last they reached the end of their climb: a vast, grassy plateau, scattered with rocks, surrounded on all sides by impassable cliffs. A refuge built with the same stones rose in the middle. They stepped inside, but the place was filled only with indifferent tourists chatting noisily while enjoying family feasts, and befuddled and vaguely hostile locals who wandered about silently among them; there was no trace of the twins. Then the old man realized that they had arrived too late, that there was nothing more to be done, and the girl would never see her boyfriend again; in measured terms he acknowledged his defeat. The girl, in other words the pseudo-Prudence, understood in turn that the love of her life was lost for ever.

Paul woke up at around midday, and after making himself a coffee he went on an escort website, made about ten phone calls, left the same number of messages on the girls' answering machines, and settled down to wait. At about 3.00 pm, feeling that his motivation was beginning to drop, he had the idea of watching a bit of porn on the internet, but the result was disappointing and even counterproductive. He should have bought some Viagra or something, but he would probably have needed a prescription.

The first girl who answered – and she would be the only

one – called at around 9.00 pm, yes, she was free at 10.00. Then she asked his age and his ethnic appearance – a white man in his late forties was perfect, that was exactly the type of client that she was looking for; apparently the criteria for escorts were at the opposite end of the value system usually advocated by the centre-left media. Finally the girl reminded him of her rates: 400 euros an hour. She didn't do anal, and of course she required a condom – except for fellatio. She would see him in the sixteenth arrondissement, Rue Spontini – apparently a lot of escorts practised their trade in that wealthy district, less wealthy than Saint-Germain-des-Prés, admittedly, just normally wealthy, which was quite reassuring in the end. She finished the conversation with a rather surprising 'Big kisses'.

In the taxi he re-examined the information file that he had printed out from the website. Mélodie was French, she claimed to be a student and said she was twenty-three: judging by her photographs – which did not show her face, but provided a great deal of information about her body – her age at least seemed plausible. She also declared herself to be 'without boasting, expert at blow jobs', which was extremely reassuring, in case of difficulties he could fall back on a blowy, it was a situation in which one always managed to have an erection, or at least so he remembered.

He called her back as agreed after reaching 4 Rue Spontini. After five minutes he received a reply in the form of a text: '7 Rue Spontini, opposite.' He went to the address he had been given and sent a new message. After a quarter of an hour he received a very short message, '5 mins', which chilled him a little; was she with a client? If he bumped into a client he was far from certain that he would be able to get an erection afterwards. He waited for ten minutes before sending a text of his own, since that seemed to be her mode of communication. He wrote first of all: 'R U avail now?', which he thought sounded suitably like youth-speak, then after a moment's thought, he added 'xx', increasingly inappropriate in the context. She replied immediately this time, with the message: 'B1984. Door C'. After following the directions he found himself in front of a new door, with a new code, like something out of a Kafka short story, but modern – the guardians of the door were automatic. Then he sent the words 'I'm here', which might almost, he reflected in a brief moment of self-pity, have been considered touching. Once again he had to wait for a few minutes, before receiving '11B23, 5th', which appeared to strike the tone of the exchange.

On the landing of the fifth floor, to the rear, a door was half open. The apartment was plunged in darkness, little lights arranged here and there making isolated patches of light. He could barely make out the face of the girl who welcomed him in the door-way, but she was wearing a black miniskirt, suspenders and fishnet tights, a tight, transparent top, also black – fine breasts, he noted mechanically. The lighting was probably supposed to create a seduc-tive and erotic atmosphere – and in fact it worked fairly well; the effect was reinforced by a strong smell of incense, from joss-sticks burning on a coffee table. He handed the four hundred euros to the girl, who quickly counted the sum before putting the notes in her handbag. 'Would you like a drink?' she suggested, address-ing him formally, which he appreciated, it put him at ease, and now he felt that he was really in the position of the client, the actual hand-over of the money had probably clarified matters; he still declined the offer, however, because he would have had to be specific about what he wanted to drink, and he didn't know what she had, it would have been complicated in the end, and he thought it would be better if they avoided speaking.

'So, shall we start?' the girl said.

'Your name is . . . Mélodie, is that right?'

'Yes, although . . .' She waved a hand to dismiss this unimport-ant detail, it was obviously a pseudonym.

'You wrote . . .' he hesitated again, 'that you were an "expert at blow jobs", isn't that right?'

'Aha, someone who reads the ads, that's great . . .!' she said with a smile, all in all this girl seemed quite nice. 'Right, then, sit down,' she added, when he didn't react. He sat down obediently on the sofa, her voice sounded vaguely familiar.

'You can get undressed,' she said after a minute, as he still didn't move. He obeyed, or rather he took off his clothes below the waist, which struck him as enough for now. 'You're not used to this, are you?' He shook his head. 'Don't worry, we'll work it out,' she said; then she knelt between his thighs.

To his great surprise he got an erection, very hard, as soon as she closed her lips over his cock. She did it well, stroking his balls with one hand while with jerking him into her mouth with the other, now slowly, now quickly. Sometimes she looked him straight in the eyes, particularly when she took him very deep in her mouth; sometimes, on the other hand, she kept her eyes closed, concentrating entirely on the movements of her tongue around the glans. He felt better and better, and after two or three minutes he dared to say, 'It's really dark in here. Can I turn the light on?'

She broke off. 'Ah, you like to watch . . .' she said with a smile. She was using the informal *tu* to address him now, but at this stage that didn't bother him. She went on jerking him with her left hand and brought the lamp closer with her right. As the ray of light settled on her face, a shock ran through him and he bent double with horror: Mélodie was Anne-Lise, Cécile's daughter; it was her, absolutely, there was no doubt about it. He had had a fleeting impression, at first, that her face reminded him of someone, but now he was certain that he recognized her. She looked at him with alarm, then recognized him too. She remained prostrate for several seconds before asking, 'You won't tell Dad?'

Why Dad?, Paul wondered; he wasn't very close to Hervé, he

was only his brother-in-law, but yes, there might be a problem with Cécile.

'I think Mum might just about understand,' Anne-Lise went on, as if she had read his mind, 'but it would kill Dad.'

In fact, strangely enough, Cécile would understand; without really analysing, he sensed that she was right. He confirmed that of course he wouldn't say anything, it wouldn't even have occurred to him, and as he said that he had a brief moment of panic, because he didn't want anyone to know either.

'And you'll keep quiet too?'

'Yes, don't worry, let's say that it will stay a secret between us.' She reflected for a moment. 'I don't know what to call you,' she continued. 'I used to call you "unca Paul", but last time I saw you I must have been about twelve, so a bit big for that, I think. Right, let's grab a drink.'

She got back to her feet. 'You'll want something strong, I guess?' He nodded, and managed to readjust himself while she was in the kitchen.

She came back in with a bottle of Jack Daniel's and filled two big glasses. Yes, she'd been an occasional escort for some years, basically since she'd started her studies, the job in the publishing house had always been fake, anyway publishing jobs were shit, she wanted to have a university career, university professors had real status, when she got a post she would stop. This wasn't her place, she lived in a studio flat in the fifth arrondissement; this was a place that she rented with two other girls, two Russians who were a bit stupid but nice enough. With this she set aside ten thousand euros a month, tax free, working a few hours a week. 'Do you want me to give you back your four hundred euros, in fact?' He refused, it really wasn't worth it. 'And besides, I liked your blow job,' he went on without thinking, with an impulse to frankness that embarrassed him, but brought a smile from Anne-Lise.

'Mum makes her living by cooking for people she doesn't like,' she went on, 'while she loves cooking, it's the great passion of her life, is that any better than what I'm doing?'

It sounded like an attempt at self-justification, but apart from the fact that he was in no position to rebuke her it was a difficult question; it was true that in Cécile's mind cooking for someone was normally a demonstration of affection, something intimate, but on the other hand there was also the profession of restaurateur, which was generally seen as honourable. 'Does your mother not get on with her clients?' he asked in the end; it was not something that Cécile had ever mentioned.

'Horrible. She can't bear the Lyonnais bourgeois bohemians, she's going to end up poisoning their food, no I'm joking . . . My clients are nice, well there are some low-lifes, but you can tell by a couple of questions on the telephone. You only get middle-class people, which is insane when you think how much it costs, there really are people from modest backgrounds, they're impressed to come to the sixteenth, they imagine that this is where the very wealthy live, so they're good people, in general. OK, sometimes penetration is a bit awkward, you can really smell the guy's body, his odour, you've got to think about something else and wait. But a lot of people settle for a blow job, and even though they've paid for an hour, it's over after fifteen minutes, sometimes less, it's incredibly embarrassing, so I make a bit of conversation to fill it up to half an hour, so I've got lots of comments on the website, 'pleasant, intelligent girl', 'brilliant social time', 'a treasure, take care of her', so you get the sense that it's the first moment of happiness they've had in years, they're so alone, you could almost feel sorry for them.

'What about you, in fact, what brings you here?' she went on after a pause. 'I know, or rather Mum told me, that you weren't getting on very well with your wife.'

Paul took a long swig of bourbon before replying. There had been problems, in fact, big problems, even, but for some time things had been getting better; and that was exactly why he had come.

She shook her head thoughtfully, a bit surprised, and took a swig of bourbon as well. 'My clients talk to me a lot,' she said, 'almost all of them need to explain themselves. I had never been told that, not exactly, but I think I see what you mean. It's as if you needed a girl to check that it worked, as a sort of intermediary before coming back to normal sex?' Paul nodded. She shook her head again and took another swig of bourbon before concluding: 'Sometimes life's complicated.'

5

A t around the same time, Aurélien was falling asleep in Maryse's arms. He had called her the day before, and she wasn't working this weekend. She had immediately agreed to go out with him that Saturday, she had no car and had never had the opportunity to look around the region since arriving there three months previously.

He had waited for Hervé and Cécile to leave for the hospital and then, a few minutes later, he in turn set off for Belleville. She lived on the edge of the conglomeration, in what was obviously an Islamist district. He had heard a lot about these areas but he had never seen one, or rather he had seen things of the kind in Montreuil, but it was less obvious, there were what seemed to be intermediate zones, and in fact you would have expected more, it was more surprising in Belleville-en-Beaujolais, as far as he knew Islamism was more of a problem associated with the banlieues in the big cities, but basically he didn't know anything about it, it might have spread to medium-sized or smaller provincial towns, he wasn't very well informed about French society. Either way, all the women he bumped into were in niqabs, some with grilles over their eyes, others without, and most of the men had the characteristic Salafist look. There were no low-lifes, on the other hand, had the Salafists driven the low-lifes out of the area? It was hard to tell, it was only ten o'clock in the morning, and low-lifes, like most predators, don't generally go out until nightfall.

Maryse was waiting for him at the bottom of her building, a moderately ugly three-storey block. 'I won't take you up,' she said, 'my place isn't great – when I was hired I took the first place available, and at least it's not expensive. If I stay I'll try to move into something nicer.' She was wearing quite a tight short skirt and a funky T-shirt, and was clearly relieved when Aurélien arrived, she wasn't very comfortable with the looks she was getting since she'd come out of the building. She was also wearing make-up, and big gold hoop-earrings.

He had chosen the Rock of Solutré, it's classic, everyone likes it and he hadn't seen it for ages. In fact as soon as she saw the outline of the limestone mountain standing out on the horizon, with its terraced climb and sharp drop, she was filled with sincere and spontaneous emotion, while he understood that whatever happened next he had been right to suggest the outing.

'Really pretty . . .' she said. 'But wait a second, I think I've seen this place on TV. Isn't that where your former president came from, that old guy?'

'Yes, François Mitterrand.' Aurélien had only the dimmest memory of François Mitterrand, who was up there with the Knights of the Zodiac and Barnaby Bear as far as he was concerned. In his childhood, the entertainment industries had set about recycling vintage goods while at the same time suggesting new products, without clearly distinguishing between them, so that any idea of sequence or historical continuity had gradually been lost. Still, most of the time, he managed to locate François Mitterrand as coming after Charles de Gaulle; but sometimes he wasn't even sure about that.

The climb to Solutré was well tended, with steps and ramps for the few steep passages, it was an easy half-hour's walk under a clear blue sky, with only a few cute little clouds. About halfway up he took her arm; with each step that they took after that, Aurélien felt as if they were falling towards one another as they approached the summit. Was that love? If so, it was a strange and paradoxically easy thing; it was a thing, at any rate, that he had never known before.

Having reached the peak of the rock, they considered the landscape of hills, meadows, forests and vines stretching out at their feet. 'So that's France . . .' she said after a long time. 'Yes,' he replied, 'well, yes, that's pretty much what it's like.' She nodded and didn't say a word. She herself came from Benin, she had told him as they drove there. As he didn't react, she had explained further: 'That's what the French called Dahomey, when they owned the country.' But the word Dahomey didn't mean anything to him either. 'Yes, you preferred history to geography,' Maryse concluded. 'Ancient history in particular,' he added. 'Ancient history . . .' she said softly, detaching the syllables, and looked at him with genuine tenderness, more than desire, a strange look, like a precursor of the look that she might give him much later, when they were very old.

A lot of horse bones had been found at the foot of the rock, he told her. For a long time people had thought it was a hunting technique practised by prehistoric man: they chased the horses to make them plunge from the top of the rock, and then they only had to cut up their carcasses at the bottom. 'That was cruel,' Maryse said indignantly; typical, women always react like that, a tourist guide had told him; women don't like the idea of horses being killed. 'At the same time it was clever,' she agreed a bit later. But it's a legend, Aurélien pointed out, prehistoric man never had that idea, it was invented long afterwards, probably in the nineteenth century. They contemplated the landscape again, the hills and the vines, and he put an arm around her waist. He felt like a man; it was disturbing and new.

For the rest of the day he had planned a trip to Notre-Dame d'Avenas, a very small tourist destination, so small that it barely deserved to be called touristic: the local Romanesque church received maybe a dozen visitors a year. So he didn't expect the intensity of Maryse's reaction when she plunged her fingers into the basin holding the holy water as she entered the building, and crossed herself before walking on. He didn't even know she was Catholic, it was not something he'd anticipated.

The jewel of the church was the altar, a white limestone sculpture showing Christ in glory, surrounded by the twelve apostles. There was nothing to say about it, and they stood in front of it for several minutes, as long as she considered necessary.

'There's another legend about this church,' he said once they had left. 'It was initially planned as a replacement for the old monastery of St Pelagius, destroyed by the barbarians, but after work had begun the workers found that their tools were scattered about every morning, and they said to themselves that this must be the work of the Evil One. The foreman concluded that God didn't want the building to be constructed there. He decided to throw his hammer to find the new location of the church: it landed one thousand two hundred metres further off, near a hawthorn hedge.'

'One thousand two hundred metres is a lot,' she said, 'that's one strong foreman . . .' Yes, in fact, that was one aspect of the question that he hadn't planned for.

'There are a lot of legends in France . . .' he added dreamily, and with a hint of mischief, it was true that France had been a country of legends, but that wasn't seen very often any more, except with Aurélien, because of his position, he didn't even realize that he was seducing her just by treating her like an intelligent person with a potential interest in culture, and not like a little African care assistant – which she was, of course. Maryse had come alone from Benin, she had no family in France, and she was starting to get a bit fed up with it. She had slept with a few men since her arrival, but none of them had treated her like this, ever, none of them was like Aurélien, to be honest she only had a vague image of France, and since arriving in Belleville she had been living in an Arab quarter, which she instinctively hated and feared.

Then they decided to go for a drink in Beaujeu, where a lot of cafés were open, and which deserved more than ever its title as 'historic capital of Beaujolais'. Aurélien had forgotten how charming the village was, it was as if he had deliberately done everything imaginable to draw her into his arms, and yet that wasn't the case, he couldn't have done that, and he mumbled and stammered a lot before suggesting that she come to the house in Saint-Joseph; she accepted immediately, without a second's hesitation.

'You're a shy kind of guy . . .' she observed.

'Yes . . . well, yes, it's true, but my sister's there too, she's maybe a bit strict, she's very Catholic, you see.'

'Your sister, the one I saw . . .?' She seemed surprised. 'And the other one who came once, the older man, is that your brother?'

'Paul? Yes, he's my big brother, in fact he's a lot older than me, I don't know him very well.'

'He seemed a bit strict.'

'Paul . . .?' It was his turn to be surprised now. 'No, Paul isn't strict at all. But he's a serious person.'

'He looks sad.'

'Yes, that's true. He is sad, too.'

French people in general were sad, she had understood that since the beginning, since her arrival, and he knew it too, he even knew it a bit better than she did, but it wasn't the moment to broach the subject. They got to Saint-Joseph at about half past five; the others would be there at about eight o'clock or perhaps a bit earlier, which left them just over two hours.

'Two hours is a lot,' she said firmly. 'After all, I'm Catholic too,' she added. In a sense it was true, that settled the question.

Two hours could in fact be a lot, he understood immediately as

293

soon as he was lying in bed next to her. He had had very few sexual experiences before Indy; when he was thirteen, an elderly homosexual who lived in the building made advances towards him; he had offered this man a modest little hand-job and the poor fellow had looked delighted, but he was worried at the same time that people would find out, so he had made Aurélien promise three times never to mention it, and he had promised, of course, but his homosexual experiences had stopped there. As to girls, of course he had bumped into them at school, but they seemed to live in a noisy, narcissistic universe, in which social status on Facebook and fashion brands played a prominent part, in short it was a universe in which he didn't belong. With Maryse things would be completely different, he understood immediately, after she had taken off her T-shirt and her skirt with evident impatience – almost, one might have said, with relief. He himself didn't dare to undress, he just looked at her; her skin was a deep, warm, almost golden brown, and the bedside lamp brought out magnificent tones in it.

'You're not really black,' he said, 'or rather you are, but not as much as some.'

'Yes, it's true, it's possible that my grandmother strayed with a white settler. Take your clothes off . . .' He obeyed, embarrassed.

'You're blushing!' she exclaimed, 'it's the first time I've seen a man blush, it's cute, you really are shy! And on the other hand you really are white, your ancestors mustn't have strayed.'

'They didn't have the opportunity . . .' Aurélien replied. He had undertaken some genealogical research into his family, to the profound indifference of Paul and Cécile. Their ancestors were chiefly farmers from the Rhône and the Saône-et-Loire, with another line originally from the Nivernais; some wine-growers but mostly animal-breeders, people who were deeply rooted, not the kind to embark on a colonial adventure; people who probably weren't even aware that France had colonies.

Once he was naked, he lay down beside her again; she felt

wonderful to the touch too, and he plunged his head between her breasts. After a minute or two she decided to take things in hand, she kissed his chest and his belly, then took him in her mouth, and after that things unfolded with disconcerting ease, he hadn't known that sex could happen so simply, so gently, it bore no resemblance whatsoever to his old relationship with Indy, or indeed to the few porn films that he had watched on the internet, perhaps to some descriptions that he had read in books but in the end not really that either, it was another world in which he immersed himself completely, and he had forgotten a lot of things, almost everything in fact, when he heard a knock at the door and Cécile's voice telling him that dinner was ready. He immediately got dressed again, his fears had returned, Cécile's voice had been unfamiliar, more distant, it seemed to him, colder, perhaps his unease was down to the fact that he had never made love in this house, he had the sense of it being a kind of desecration, that was obviously absurd, he said to himself, it was a very old house, lots of people had made love there; but still, Cécile's voice had been weird.

6

They went down the stairs and froze by the kitchen door. Standing in the middle of the room, Madeleine was dishevelled, her eyes bright with rage, but as soon as she saw Maryse she burst out sobbing and threw herself into her arms. Cécile stood mute and motionless, she had barely noticed their arrival. As she remained silent, Aurélien finally went over to her and asked her what was happening.

'They've asked Madeleine to leave the hospital. They don't want her looking after Dad any more.'

Some trade union delegates, or rather one in particular, had complained to the management that Madeleine was doing the job of a care assistant without qualifications; they had demanded that she stop. Management had agreed.

'Management? Leroux . . .?'

'No. Leroux is the medical director of the PVS/MCS, but there's an administrative manager who also directs the PEoLC, where there are many more residents, and also a third service, the day-care unit, I think, and he's in charge of all of that. He's someone we've never seen. So that's why they don't want Madeleine to look after Dad, to wash him, to take him for walks, and she's no longer allowed to push the wheelchair herself. They don't want her to sleep there any more, either.'

'They say it breaches the rules on hygiene and safety,' Madeleine broke in. Aurélien looked at her, startled, chiefly because he had never heard her say anything before.

'She's just allowed to go on feeding him – that's the only concession we managed to get from them,' Cécile concluded.

It took Aurélien a good minute to recover and ask Maryse:

'What do you think?'

'I'm not really surprised, that one's been hatching for a long time. I can see very clearly who the trade union delegate is, she's not on the ward, she works at the PEoLC. Essentially the problem is that on the ward there are fifteen nurses and care assistants for forty patients. At the PEoLC there are twenty-five of them for two hundred and ten residents. So it might seem paradoxical for a trade union delegate to try and harm us; but the fact is that they earn the national average wage, and we're the privileged ones. I don't know how Leroux managed to win conditions like that for us, that's basically the only mystery. But since his appointment, the new director is after Leroux's blood, that much is certain.'

'And do you know this guy, this director?' Cécile asked her. Aurélien noticed that she was talking to her warmly, and didn't seem to wonder what she was doing there; it didn't seem to have occurred to her.

'I saw him once, he's a guy in his thirties. Like all care home directors, he went to the School of Public Health in Rennes, it's a college of public administration, more like ENA than medical school, if you like. He doesn't seem like a particularly mean person, but his focus is on profit, so like everybody these days he sticks to the guidelines.'

'When you say he's after Leroux's blood, do you think he's trying to get him sacked?'

Maryse thought, pausing for a long time before answering.

'It's really outside my area of expertise, but I don't think so . . . On the other hand, he could ask to have him moved. There are a hundred and fifty PVS/MCS units in France, which means that people can be moved about; and a complaint from the unions might be enough. As soon as Leroux is gone, he'll be able to distribute us among the other services; I'm not at all sure that I'll still be able to take care of your dad. No . . .' she lowered her eyes, 'no, I won't lie to you, I don't think it's looking good.'

The next day it was even more painful than usual for Aurélien to leave them and go back to Paris. When he finally made his mind up to do so it was after eight o'clock, and almost three in the morning when he reached Montreuil. Indy was in bed, and he set off for Chantilly the next morning without seeing her. In the evening he sat down in a café near the Gare de l'Est, unable to bring himself to go home, and he called Maryse. The situation at the hospital was confused, she said, all the girls were talking about it but no one knew anything; she had bumped into Leroux in the afternoon, but he seemed to be in a very bad mood and she hadn't dared to ask him any questions.

He decided to go home just after eleven, and bumped into his wife, who of course began telling him off for coming back late without warning, he nearly made her miss her meeting. So she had gone out anyway, he said to himself, and replied calmly: 'Go fuck yourself' before going up to bed. She was startled, her mouth wide open, probably less because of the words than the tone; she wasn't used to this unruffled confidence; he was no longer afraid of her, and it was worrying.

Maryse called him back late the following afternoon, when he was getting ready to leave Chantilly. He sensed immediately that the news was going to be bad. She had been talking to a girl who worked in the director's office. Leroux had been called in that morning, and the meeting had plainly gone badly, shouting was heard through the partition and he had come out slamming the door as hard as he could. Early in the afternoon she hadn't been able to contain herself, and had knocked at his office door. He was sitting there doing nothing, contemplating the papers put down in front of him; a cardboard box was open just beside him, but he hadn't yet put anything in it. 'Yes, my dear Maryse, I've been fired,' he said, 'or, rather, I've been moved. I start in Toulon on Monday morning. I don't know how he managed to make it happen so quickly.'

'Officially he can't complain; he isn't going to speak out against his hierarchy,' she went on. 'In fact he's going to say that he was the one who asked to be moved so that he could go back to his own part of the country – and it's true, he comes from there, La Seyne-sur-Mer, I think; but really, I saw that he was completely disheartened. Things are going to get moving now, there's a meeting for the reorganization of the services on Thursday, with officials from the health department. Five of us at most will stay in the unit and the rest will be redistributed around the care home. I would be surprised if I was among the five, they know I was close to Madeleine, and they're going to make me pay for it.'

She fell silent. She was on the brink of tears, and he was lost for an encouraging or even acceptable reply. 'I'll be around tomorrow evening,' he said at last. 'I'll be a bit late but I'll be around.'

'I'm on nights tomorrow, so we won't be able to meet up till Thursday. That's when I have my day off.'

'We could go and see the place where I work – you know, the tapestries . . .' The idea had just occurred to him.

'Oh yeah, I'd love to . . .!' Her voice sounded perkier as she said that, and they exchanged a few relatively meaningless words as lovers do, or parents with their little children, and she sounded almost calm as she said, immediately before hanging up, 'See you Thursday, my love.'

7

Paul expected Prudence to stay in Brittany until her father got out of hospital, or at least until Priscilla took over. There was no professional urgency: all French administrations operated more or less in slow motion, but the Finance Ministry more than most, while they waited for the *verdict of the ballot box*, as they say. Bruno was appearing more and more often on television now; Paul had seen him on various channels and thought he was excellent. What was particularly surprising was the gift for debate that he had developed at the last moment; Raksaneh had done a really good job. Sarfati was looking confident, too, and had broadly shed his playful qualities to give himself the air of a wise old man, quite a young wise old man, in fact, a normal development for a humourist approaching the end of his career, particularly when he is no longer funny. The problem was that the candidate from the National Rally was very good as well, both punchy and unbeatable on the various issues, he generally won the debates in the end with his disarming smile, right now he certainly had the most disarming smile on the French political scene, you would, according to Solène Signal, have had to go all the way back to Ronald Reagan to find such a disarming smile in contemporary political history. He also came out broadly on top in the first round, and the projections for the second round seemed to have solidly stabilized at 55–45, which was satisfactory but nothing more than that. Solène Signal complained, but Bruno seemed not to give a damn, and on the rare occasions when Paul saw him he seemed to be somewhere else entirely – one might have wondered whether he hadn't made a move on Raksaneh, finally.

As he waited for Prudence to come back, Paul tried to find out more about the beliefs of devotees of Wicca. A lot of Wiccans were 'involved in the defence of nature', so they were tree-huggers. There was nothing very new about vaguely mystical tree-huggers, but there was still an innovation compared to New Age, mother earth, the cortex of Gaia and all of those things, which was the importance of the two principles, male and female. Perhaps that was what had drawn her to this new religion, she was trying to wake up her body, Paul said to himself with a surge of emotion. His own body had woken quite easily, all it had taken was Anne-Lise's mouth, he remembered every now and again, and each time he did so he felt a tinge of shame and a hint of anxiety. What were they going to do? How was he going to be able to maintain his composure when he found himself in the presence of Cécile and her daughter? But he reassured himself almost immediately: Anne-Lise was an intelligent and level-headed girl, she would have no trouble coping with the situation.

More unexpectedly, Wiccans seemed to believe in reincarnation. Did Prudence believe in it too? If she did, that was something new. Or at least there was a kind of logic to it, ecology, the basic kinship of all forms of life, reincarnation, it all made sense.

He was pleasantly surprised when Prudence called him the following Saturday, to tell him she was coming back two days later. Her sister had settled into the house at Larmor-Baden with her two daughters, she had organized the move from Canada – and her divorce – with her customary efficiency. He wanted to go and pick her up at the station, but she dissuaded him, she had a surprise for him, she said, and it was better if they met straight away at the house.

Prudence was the surprise: she was tanned, in great shape, and most importantly she was wearing a skirt, a white pleated skirt, just above the knee, that showed off her tanned legs to great advantage.

'Have you been going to the beach a lot?' he asked.

'Since Priscilla got here, every day,' she replied; then she stepped towards him and threw her arms around him. When their tongues made contact he put his hands on her buttocks, and this time she didn't stiffen, on the contrary she pressed herself even harder against him and put her hand on his buttocks as well.

Ten minutes later they were in bed together, and when he entered her she shed a few tears, but she also moaned, several times, and towards the end she almost cried out loud. Then they stayed there for a long time, a very long time, looking into each other's eyes.

8

When they decided to get up, night had almost fallen. They sat down in the living room. Paul poured himself a Jack Daniel's, and Prudence accepted a martini. Was she the same person he had known when they were twenty-five? Essentially yes, it had been almost easy to become one flesh once again, as Saint Paul would have put it. They had lost ten years, but it didn't matter much; there was no point thinking about the past, and there wasn't even much point thinking about the future; it was enough to be alive. He broached a subject that seemed lighter, but one that had intrigued him a little for several weeks: did she really believe in Wicca? Did it have to be taken seriously?

The sabbaths and ceremonies, Prudence said, were of no real importance, it was just a way of punctuating the year and meeting up with other devotees, as with all religions, to tell the truth. The god and the goddess, on the other hand, corresponded to a fundamental reality, that male–female polarity was a crucial element in the structure of the world. It was not, however, the last word of the doctrine: beyond the god and goddess there was the One, the ultimate principle, the organizing cause of the universe; it was sometimes evoked in special celebrations; the god and the goddess were much more present in the majority of ceremonies, and most devotees went no further than that in their spiritual quest.

If there was one thing that she fully believed in, it was

reincarnation. That was still strange, in Paul's eyes, it was a little like renouncing all hope for the current incarnation, and asking for a second chance, a second deal – and yet to him one deal seemed more or less enough to form an opinion on life; but it was the case that this belief was very widespread around the world, half of humanity, or almost, had built whole civilizations on this basis. And even from a Western point of view, many people lived to the end of their days under the illusion that that their lives could branch off, take a radically different turn; considered outside of any religious dimension, reincarnation was only an extreme variation on that idea. What struck him as weird, on the other hand, and even improbable, was the idea that one might be reincarnated as an animal. That was very rare, Prudence told him, in almost every case men were reincarnated as men and animals as animals of the same species. It was only in certain exceptional fates that brought about a climb, or a descent, on the ladder of beings.

The first idea that occurred to Paul was that it was far from idiotic. The second was that for many people today this traditional Hindu version of reincarnation, and the ladder of being, might appear as a *speciesist* idea. The third was that a lot of people today had become very stupid; it was a striking and indisputable contemporary phenomenon.

'Are you hungry, my darling?' he asked a little later. Yes, she was hungry, and she also wanted to go to a restaurant, go out, eat something good, perhaps locally. The *Train Bleu* at the Gare de Lyon, would do, something reassuring and classic, since they were still fragile.

There was hardly anyone else at the *Train Bleu*, they were sat at an isolated table, and immediately after they ordered Prudence asked him if he had any news about his father. He hadn't had any recently, but he imagined that everything was fine.

Cécile had not in fact informed him of the developments in the situation, and without really knowing why she had sensed that the future of her brother's relationship was being played out, and that it wasn't the moment to talk to him about anything else, so she had kept everything to herself, but in fact things were going from bad to worse. The situation had quickly confirmed the gloomy predictions voiced by Maryse, who had been transferred to the PEoLCS the day after the services meeting, when her colleagues had immediately given her to understand that exceptional working conditions were over as far as she was concerned.

When he came back at the end of the following week, Aurélien was struck upon arriving in the ward to see that his father's condition had noticeably declined. Madeleine was in a permanent state of befuddlement, and only came to life when Aurélien visited. As he was leaving he saw that when Madeleine held his father's hand in hers he clung tightly to her fingers to hold her back; so he could move his fingers, he had never noticed it before; but apparently he only did it with Madeleine.

They returned to Saint-Joseph in a state of deep gloom. According to Maryse, the situation was going to get worse over the coming weeks. Taking into account the new staff redistribution it would be impossible to get him out of bed every day, let alone organize his outings in the wheelchair. The frequency of baths would also be reduced, as would that of physiotherapy and speech therapy treatments. There was no point in asking for a meeting with the director, she explained to Cécile; he would only tell her he was applying the national norms, that the economy drives applied to all French establishments.

'The conclusion we will have to draw from that,' Madeleine cut in, breaking her silence, 'is that we have to get him out of here, otherwise they're going to kill him.' Cécile said nothing, unable to contradict her and also unable to come up with a reply.

The next morning, Aurélien went with Maryse to the Château de Germolles. She admired the tapestries, and she particularly admired the way he explained his work to her, the way he intertwined the warp and weft. It was a light-hearted interlude, unexpected and a bit magical too; but when they came back to Saint-Joseph the atmosphere was even grimmer and more discouraging than the previous day.

After dinner they lingered for a while at the table. Hervé had a coffee with his cognac, the only one to do so. After a few pauses, turning the glass around in his fingers, he finally said to Cécile: 'I might know a way of getting your father out of there.'

'How would that be?' She turned towards him.

'There are people . . . people who can intervene in circumstances like these.' As she still looked puzzled, he went on: 'Well, sort of activists . . . Don't get cross, honey-bun,' he added immediately, 'I haven't done anything with them, nothing illegal. I don't even know them, I just know people who do. You remember Nicolas?' Yes, of course she remembered Nicolas; she was still reserved and suspicious. 'Nicolas knows them well,' he went on. 'I phoned him yesterday. They're based in Belgium; you know that euthanasia has grown enormously in Belgium over the past few years, that's where they do most of their work, but I think they also have outposts in France, he hasn't really told me that much about it, but the best thing would be for me to go back to Arras and speak to them there, Nicolas can introduce me, they're more likely to trust us if we make direct contact.' Cécile nodded mechanically, still on the defensive. The truth was that she had suspected for some time that Hervé had started seeing dodgy people again, people on the margins of the law, but she had said nothing, she preferred not to broach the question, she knew that traditional men – and Hervé was certainly one of those – sometimes needed to come back to this kind of thing, that it wasn't possible, or perhaps desirable, to domesticate them entirely.

Hervé set off with Aurélien the next day. At about nine o'clock they stopped for dinner at a Courtepaille grill. Hervé clearly wanted to talk. He thought that society had given him a raw deal, and sometimes missed his militant years; of course with Cécile and the girls it wouldn't have been possible. He automatically moved a bit of chalky camembert around on his plate, next to a greasy slice of gouda. 'Their cheese platter is really disgusting . . .' he said by way of conclusion. There was obviously another topic that he wanted to address, but couldn't. Aurélien said nothing, but went on staring at him attentively.

'And do you love her, that little one, Maryse?' he asked at last. 'Yes . . . I think so. I'm sure of it, in fact.'

He nodded; that was the answer he was expecting, and he added calmly: 'Hang on to her. I think she's OK, that girl.'

9

It was almost two in the morning by the time they got to Paris, and the last train had already left long before. Aurélien dropped Hervé off at an Ibis near the Garde du Nord, and almost wanted to take a room there too, but then he thought better of it and reflected that his wife would probably have gone to bed.

The next morning, when they were starting work on the restoration of a tapestry showing a party leaving for a hunt, which admirably captured the excitement of the crowd, he received a phone call from Jean-Michel Drapier. He wanted to see him very soon, the next day if possible; his voice was even bleaker, deader than usual. 'Is there a problem?' Aurélien said anxiously. Well, yes, in a sense there was a problem, you could put it like that, he would explain tomorrow. Two o'clock? Two o'clock would be perfect, he replied.

This time Aurélien's boss saw him almost immediately, and looked downcast. As he invited him into his office, Jean-Michel Drapier felt a fleeting but painful certainty that he should never have risen through the hierarchy. He didn't like managing staff, managing staff essentially meant making the staff unhappy, and he always found that unpleasant. The idea of karma briefly crossed his mind, and then he invited Aurélien to sit down.

'Right . . .' he said immediately, 'it's boring, I know, but I'm not going to extend your engagement at the Château de Germolles. Another higher-priority project has come up.'

Aurélien's reaction was even worse than he had predicted. It was a disaster for him, was there really no possibility of finding a solution? He had problems at the moment, personal problems, he added, he was in the middle of a divorce. That clearly went beyond the framework that Drapier had planned to give to the discussion, it was becoming embarrassing, and he nodded his head in all kinds of different directions, like a malfunctioning puppet, before managing to reply.

'No, unfortunately, it's really impossible . . .' he managed to say. 'The new project involves a Loire Valley château that suffered from fire damage, I can't remember which one . . .' He glanced vaguely at the files cluttering his desk. 'You know how much the Loire Valley châteaux bring in financially? Do you know how many Chinese tourists visit the Loire Valley châteaux every year?' A vision of horror passed before him, as he thought of those dense crowds of Chinese tourists surging through the portals of the Loire Valley châteaux. 'No, Mr Raison,' he concluded sadly. 'I wish I could be nice to you, you're one of our best restorers, but this time it's not going to be possible, we're facing a real priority.'

'I won't have to leave Germolles straight away, though?' Aurélien pleaded. 'I'll have a bit of time?'

'Of course.' He sat back in his chair, relieved; there it is, he said to himself, we've reached the stage where the victim has accepted his fate and asks only for slight adjustments to be made to the sentence. 'You'll start on the new project in about a month. In the meantime you'll be able to go back to Germolles, which means that you'll be able to protect the workshop, put up tarpaulins, waiting for someone to pick it up again – well, if someone does pick it up one day,' he finished limply, before bending double in a fit of total discouragement.

However, he recovered sufficiently to inform Aurélien about the practical aspects of his new appointment: the Chantilly project would continue until its completion, and he would have to find a hotel to sleep in for two nights a week near the Loire Valley château whose name he would soon discover, he would need to take a look in his files for five minutes, well anyway it was a Loire Valley château. This time his hotel expenses would be covered, and he could even claim for petrol, this restoration was very high up on the minister's agenda, it was a strategic site in terms of international tourism, it wasn't Chambord or Azay-le-Rideau, but on the level just below, and not Chenonceaux either, well the name escaped him for now but it would come back.

It was 2.45 pm, and the meeting was over. Leaving the ministry, Aurélien made for the nearest café, the same one as last time, and once again ordered a bottle of Muscadet. Like last time, not a single human being in the café seemed capable of understanding, much less of sharing, his fate – and at this point in the early afternoon there were even fewer of them. After the third glass, he considered the situation in a less disastrous light. He would be able to go back to Saint-Joseph every weekend, that would pose no problems. It was all still curious, he said to himself, life, love, human beings: only ten or so days ago he had never touched Maryse, and the feel of her skin was entirely outside his realm of experience; and now he was unable to live without that same skin; what explanation was there for that?

In terms of his relationship with Indy, this new project wouldn't change much: he would spend two nights a week in a hotel somewhere in the Loire Valley, and she didn't even need to know about it. At that moment it occurred to him that he could even move out straight away, and find a studio flat in Paris. He had never thought of that before, and he was filled with a feeling of intense joy: leaving the marital home did not constitute an error, he didn't think it would put him at a disadvantage with the family court judge – admittedly it might be better for him to talk to his lawyer, but he was almost sure.

A bit of research on the internet quickly cooled his enthusiasm: property prices in Paris had soared to terrifying levels, and he wasn't sure that he could even afford a studio flat today, so his future as a property owner was close to zero. As regards alimony, Indy had openly laid claim to half of his salary; that was a ridiculous demand, the lawyer had reassured him, an almost insane demand, there was no risk of the judge going along with it; however he should expect a high sum, probably somewhere around a third. He'd been properly screwed by that bitch, he said to himself, he'd been screwed to *fuck*. There were hardly any assets, they had bought nothing together, or nothing important; everything was at play on the alimony.

Alcohol is paradoxical; sometimes it allows you to control your anxieties, to see everything under a falsely optimistic halo, and sometimes, on the contrary, it increases lucidity, and consequently anxiety; the two phenomena can follow on from one another at an interval of several minutes. Finishing his first bottle of Muscadet, Aurélien realized that seeing Maryse once a week, and even a bit less than that because of her shifts at the hospital, was going to seem like very little, it already seemed like very little, and at the same time that a life together was not going to be easy to organize. Normally it would have been a bit early to imagine this kind of thing, but in fact he felt so sure of their feelings, both his and hers, that everything seemed so strangely clear, things were going very quickly, that was clear, but sometimes in life things do go quickly. Having said that, in material terms, the situation was far from obvious: for a low-ranking civil servant, with his income reduced by a third, and a care assistant, living in Paris, or even in one of the inner suburbs, was more or less unthinkable. His restoration projects could potentially take him more or less anywhere in France, and living in Paris wasn't necessary in the end. Where should he live, though? The house in Saint-Joseph would have been ideal in a sense: there was room, they both felt comfortable there, and it didn't cost anything. But Maryse increasingly hated her work at Belleville-en-Beaujolais, and couldn't bear her new working conditions, she had been so much better off in the same hospital, and now there was no going back. Could she resign? She didn't set much store by her own financial independence, that wasn't the question. But could they live on Aurélien's wages alone? It looked difficult.

To see things more clearly, he ordered a second bottle, while saying to himself that he might be better off holding back on the alcohol, it might not have good long-term effects, all testimonies agreed on that.

10

On Wednesday evening, Cécile received a phone call from Hervé. He was at Mons, he said; it was just like home: an opulent Medieval and Renaissance past, then textile and steel industries, all disaster-stricken in recent years; it was just a bit poorer than Arras, but not much. He'd met some of Nicolas's acquaintances, they seemed OK, a bit suspicious but serious. They had a branch in Lyon which they'd contacted, a meeting had been set up for the following Sunday, so in fact things had got moving. The guy from Lyon had asked for Paul to be present; before they planned an operation it was important for them to check that everyone was singing from the same song sheet.

On Friday evening he arrived at Mâcon-Loché on the 6.16 pm train; Cécile was waiting for him at the station. It was the first time they had spent more than two days apart; she had had a lot of trouble sleeping on her own, and she was radiant with obvious joy as she met him on the platform. But as to the purpose of his journey he could see that it was still dubious, and she questioned him as soon as they were sitting in the car. Who were these people, exactly? Did they have a connection with Civitas?

'Ah . . .' Hervé smiled broadly, 'I knew you'd think that, you've got an axe to grind with Civitas. And no, as it happens they have nothing to do with them. The movement was founded by an American businessman from Oregon.'

'A well-known billionaire?'

'No, he's not a media billionaire like Bill Gates or Mark Zuckerburg, and in any case those ones are all progressive. He's a small billionaire, if you like, he made his fortune in forestry, he's not listed in Forbes, but he does have about ten billion dollars; and he's a Protestant, a Baptist, to be precise, like most members of the organization, so you see, it doesn't even have anything to do with the Catholics. Oregon was the first American state to legalize euthanasia, it's a progressive state, they're very right-on where all those subjects are concerned. So Nicolas organized a meeting in Mons for me with the European coordinator. He told me that this American billionaire was originally from Belgium, he still had family there, and that he had been very shocked by some cases that happened there. They set up CLASH, the Committee for Liberation from Assassination in Hospitals, to try and lobby MPs, speak in the media, but nothing came of it. So they decided to dissolve officially, but to continue with more direct action. Later they set up branches in France, and also in Spain, I think. The guy that I met was American, but the one we're going to see in Lyon is French, I spoke to him on the phone and he made a good impression. They're very cautious: they've never attracted police attention, they've never resorted to violence, they haven't even damaged buildings. Most importantly, they're clear that all family members must agree with the action – the husband or wife, the children, the parents if they're still alive; that can make a big difference legally, apparently. That's why he insisted on Paul being there.'

'Yes, that won't be a problem . . .' Cécile said. 'He's arriving tomorrow with his wife.' All of that had reassured her a little, she relaxed in her seat and they were able to discuss less serious subjects, what was happening in Arras again, what Nicolas was like. She had nothing against old-style identitarians, she insisted, or indeed against contemporary identitarians, she just wanted to keep up to date, and talk to him before getting involved with something illegal.

'I haven't done anything illegal, honey-bun . . .' Hervé said softly. 'I just had a beer with an American Baptist.'

The sun was setting over the Beaujolais hills; a few kilometres on she mentioned Civitas again. She couldn't bear them, in fact, they were real extremists, who discredited Catholics as a whole. 'Christian Salafists,' she added, 'if you listened to them you'd end up back in the Middle Ages.'

The Middle Ages weren't so bad from a certain point of view, Hervé observed. Her brother, for example, only really liked being in the Middle Ages.

'Yes, well you know how Aurélien is, he's been like that since he was a child, he was never really in the real world.'

'He's going to have to spend a bit more time it,' Hervé said, 'now that he's got himself a real woman.'

Cécile said nothing; for just over an hour she had managed to forget about Maryse; she had spent almost every night at the house that week, it wasn't going at all well, the PEoLC was even worse than she'd imagined. The residents who weren't able to get out of bed all had terrifying bed sores. She had ten minutes to wash them, which wasn't nearly enough, and lots of them couldn't go to the toilet themselves, she was being called on her mobile all the time, not to mention the patients who were yelling from their rooms for someone to come and tend to them, sometimes when she came back the little old man in question wouldn't have been able to hold it in, he would have shat on himself and on the floor, and she had to clean it all up, it was really horrible with the shit and the dirty sheets, but the worst thing of all was their pleading look when she came to their rooms, and the way they had of saying: 'You're very nice, miss.' Back in Africa such things wouldn't have happened, if that was progress then it wasn't worth it. She'd explained all of that to Cécile the day after Aurélien's visit, she hadn't said much to him, he could see that she was exhausted every night when she came home, but she couldn't imagine telling him that, it was better not to make him face up to reality, she thought; they weren't married yet, Cécile said, but she was already protecting him.

Hervé took the exit for Villié-Morgon. 'That's perfectly normal, honey-bun,' he said at last as they stopped at the toll booth. 'Everybody talks to you. You're the receptacle of all the world's misfortunes; it's your destiny.'

Cécile thought again about Aurélien's confession, about the revelation that he wasn't sterile; who else could he have talked to about it? Certainly not Paul. Yes, Hervé was right, it was her destiny.

Maryse was exhausted, as she was every night, and she and Aurélien went to bed immediately after dinner. Hervé lingered in the kitchen while his wife did the washing up, she could see that he had something else to say, but it took him a long time to get round to it, as usual.

'You remember,' he said at last, 'my unemployment benefit stops in a month. And I can clearly see that you don't like this job you have cooking at people's houses, every time you get back from it you're nervous, you're in a bad mood.'

She turned round, wiped her hands on her apron and sat down opposite him; she had thought that her attempt at concealment was perfect. Women in general live their whole lives in the illusion of being intuitive and with a talent for lying, unlike men. Sometimes it's true, but less often than they think. Hervé had hidden from her the fact that he was meeting up with former identitarian activists – and on top of that 'former activists' was the most favourable hypothesis; she hadn't managed to hide the disgust that she felt in the presence of the middle-class bohemians of Lyon.

'So I talked to Nicolas about that as well, and I think he's got something for me,' Hervé went on. 'I would be an insurance salesman. It's a little insurance brokerage, the boss wants to go into retirement. It's in a good location, less than ten minutes' walk from the house.'

'But you've never done that!'

'No, but I know a bit about law, I know how to read a contract and follow a file. They really like the fact that I'm a former notary.'

He had said 'former notary', Cécile observed in spite of herself. So he had given up that trade of which he had been so proud, he had *done his grieving*, as the books on personal development have it.

'Is he a former Bloc member too, the boss who's retiring?' She knew what the answer was going to be, and had just asked to be clear on the matter.

'Yes, of course,' Hervé replied calmly. 'That's how this works, you know, these days networks and relationships are the only things still working.'

'So we're going home? To Arras?'

'Yes, well whenever you like, really, it doesn't have to be in a week, at any rate he's going to have to stay with me for a bit to explain the files.'

'OK . . .' she said quietly, after a while. 'I'm glad to be going back, in a way. But it was nice staying here, wasn't it? It was a bit of a break for us.'

'Yes, that's right. A break.'

'We haven't had that many breaks in our life . . .' She thought for a few seconds before going on. 'What we need now is to get Dad out of that hospital. Then we'll leave him with Madeleine, which will be better for them. But first we have to get him out of there.'

'Yes, of course, honey-bun. That's exactly what we'll do.'

11

P aul and Prudence arrived the following afternoon. When Cécile told him she'd made up his room he felt embarrassed for a moment, but Prudence replied calmly, 'That's kind of you, but there was no need, Paul and I are sleeping together again.' Cécile nodded and didn't say a word, she had more or less given up understanding what was happening in her family, either emotionally or sexually.

They had arranged to meet the activist from Lyon for Sunday lunch at the Buffalo Grill in Villefranche-sur-Saône. It would be 21 March, the spring solstice, which seemed like a good sign, Cécile said. Prudence could have added that it corresponded to the Ostara Sabbath: waking from her sleep, the goddess spreading her fertility over the earth, while the god walked the greening fields – it was springtime, after all.

They hadn't exactly told each other how they could be recognized, but Hervé had no trouble identifying them. Five men in their twenties were sitting around a table sharing XXL sides of beef and Texan side plates. Four of them, in shirts and ties and navy-blue suits, could easily have belonged to the security services of the National Rally: concerned at all times to present the image of politeness and respectability, but still quite muscular, as one could clearly see under their impeccable blazers. The fifth was very different, with his long curly hair, his torn jeans and his AC/DC T-shirt depicting Angus Young naked to the waist, with his little knees, pressing his Gibson SG against his body and crossing a massive stage while performing his famous *duckwalk*, a move invented by T-Bone Walker and popularized by Chuck Berry, but which had, according to some people, been perfected by Angus Young. The T-shirt also bore the inscriptions '*Let there be rock*' and '*Rio de la Plata*'; the photograph must have been taken during their legendary Argentinian concerts.

It was the long-haired man who got up to come to their table while they were examining the menu. 'You're Hervé, right, the one I spoke to on the phone?' Hervé said yes, not really understanding how the other man had guessed. 'The whole family has come together, I see . . .' he went on, casting an eye at his fellow guests.

'And you must be Madeleine, the one at the heart of this tragedy . . .' he said, turning towards her. She nodded awkwardly. 'Hervé explained the situation to me on the telephone,' he added immediately, 'but I already knew about it, because I happen to know Leroux. OK, let's not beat about the bush: you're right, we have to get your father out of there, and as soon as possible, otherwise his condition is going to get worse very quickly and he won't come out alive. He could already be dead, he was lucky to be transferred to Saint-Luc: a CVA followed by a coma – at his age, in many cases they don't resuscitate. In short, we're ready to help you. Except there are a few things I have to check. First of all, your father isn't the subject of a guardianship measure, right?'

'No, he isn't,' Paul replied bluntly.

The long-haired man turned towards him again. 'You're Paul, the older son? Excuse me, I didn't introduce myself, my name's Brian. So this is the whole family? There are no other brothers and sisters hidden away somewhere?'

'No,' Paul replied again.

'You understand, we're not doing anything illegal, so far, and we don't intend to. In France, there's no duty of care. If I'm in hospital, even an inch away from death, and I demand to leave, they have to let me leave. But if I'm not in a position to communicate my view, that's when the problems start. In practice, the chief consultant has absolute power, at least until legal action is taken to the contrary. If a guardianship order has been imposed, the judge will systematically side with the guardian. Otherwise he tries to gather the opinion of the nearest relatives, and that's why I'm asking you all these questions. In some cases people can be moved abroad, we have some places where they can stay, but in this case it seems obvious to me that it won't be necessary. If I've understood correctly you have a place for him, a house that belongs to him in a hamlet in Villié-Morgon, is that right?'

'Exactly.'

'While we're on the topic, there's one thing that intrigues us, that I wanted to talk to you about. We tried to check, and the house isn't listed anywhere: no electricity bills, local taxes, nothing.'

'You have access to that kind of file?'

'Oh, that's nothing. All the kids do that.'

Maybe not all the kids, Paul said to himself, but some, certainly. He was more and more intrigued by this guy, with his cheesy hard-rock T-shirt. However, he answered the question: 'That's perfectly normal, my father belonged to the DGSI, so when he retired they gave his residence extra security, they took charge of everything administrative to keep him from being identified.'

Brian shook his head, smiling broadly; he hadn't anticipated this. 'So I'm helping to get an old DGSI man out of the medical system . . . That's funny, very funny even.' He looked at Paul again.

'He must have been very high up in the organization to enjoy this kind of treatment.'

'Yes, I suppose so. I never really knew.'

Brian nodded; this time he wasn't surprised. Apparently he knew a lot about the lives of people who worked in the secret service.

Then he asked Paul, almost innocently, but this time he knew the answer in advance: 'Are you with the DGSI too?'

'No, I took a different path. So are you on their files?'

'Oh yeah, I'm sure I've got my own little dossier in there. But my guys haven't, the services don't know them . . .' He looked almost affectionately at his henchmen, who were starting to tuck into their Texan plates and bottles of Morgon: good big peaceful oxen, probably nationalist racists at first, but entirely ready to commit themselves to the cause of Judeo-Christian morality, indeed morality in general, they didn't really make a distinction, and perhaps they were right, Brian said to himself, although he wasn't entirely sure.

'Can I ask another question?' Paul said.

'Yes, of course, if I can answer it.'

'You're the only one who can. I wonder what drives you to get involved in operations of this kind; where your commitment comes from. The founder of your movement, if I've understood correctly, is inspired by religious convictions; but I don't get the impression that that's true of you.'

'No, true enough,' Brian replied calmly. 'I understand why you might be intrigued. I'm not sure I understand myself . . .' he added after a moment. Then he seemed to retreat into himself, to fall into a prolonged meditative silence. Everyone at the table had fallen silent, and all eyes were fixed upon him. It was two or three minutes before he decided to carry on.

'I'm going to have to pick up the story a bit further back . . . The easiest way to explain it is that I became aware very early on of the fact that our society has a problem with old age; that it was a serious problem that could lead to self-destruction. That may have something to do with the fact that I was brought up by my grandparents, that's possible. But I imagine you will agree that collectively we have a problem with old people . . .'

321

Paul nodded.

'The real reason for euthanasia, in fact, is that we can no longer stand old people, we don't even want to know that they exist, and that's why we park them in specialized places away from the eyes of other human beings. Almost all people today see the value of a human being as declining as their age increases; that the life of a young man, and even more of a child, is broadly of greater value than that of a very old person; I imagine you also agree with me on that?'

'Yes, absolutely.'

'Well that is a complete turnaround, a radical anthropological change. Of course, given that the percentage of old people in the population is constantly increasing, this is quite unfortunate. But there's something else that's much more serious . . .' He fell silent again and thought for a minute or two.

'In all previous civilizations,' he said at last, 'the esteem, indeed the admiration, that a man could be given, what allowed people to judge his value, was the way in which he had effectively behaved throughout his life; even bourgeois honours were only granted on the basis of trust, provisionally; one had to earn them through a whole life of honesty. By granting greater value to the life of a child – when we have no idea what he will become, whether he will be intelligent or stupid, a genius, a criminal or a saint – we deny all value to our real actions. Our deeds, whether heroic or generous, all the things that we have managed to accomplish, the things we have made, our works, none of that has the slightest worth in the eyes of the world any longer – and, very soon, even in our own eyes. We thus deprive life of all motivation and meaning; very precisely, this is what may be called nihilism. Devaluing the past and the present in favour of times to come, devaluing the real and preferring a virtual reality located in a vague future, are symptoms of European nihilism more decisive than anything that Nietzsche could have come up with – in fact now we should really speak in terms of Western nihilism, or modern nihilism, and I'm far from sure that the Asian countries have been spared in the medium term. It is true that Nietzsche was unable to identify the phenomenon, which only really manifested itself after his death. So, in a word, no, I'm not Christian; I am even inclined to believe that it all began with Christianity, this tendency to become resigned to the present world, however unbearable it might be, as we wait for a saviour and a hypothetical future; the original sin of Christianity, in my eyes, is hope.'

He stopped talking, and the silence around the table was total. 'Right, sorry, I let myself get a bit carried away . . .' he said, embarrassed. 'Let's get back to our action. My guys are clean, and normally I don't have to do anything apart from drive the van. But we still have to consider the most important thing. But no, first there's one other small thing: at home you're going to need a bit of equipment, at least a medical bed and a wheelchair. That can be done quite quickly, I know the suppliers, and in fact the wheelchair may take a bit longer, they have to be made to measure.'

'Can't we take the one from the hospital?' Hervé asked.

'No. It might seem stupid, but you could be prosecuted just for that, theft of material belonging to the public health service. So we'll have to leave it. Between the bed and the wheelchair that gives us a budget of ten thousand euros. Have you got that?'

'Yes,' Paul said.

'Right, then, that's great, otherwise we could have let you have them in advance – given them to you, basically – but if you've got the money, obviously we'd prefer that. So, let's get to the intervention itself. Essentially it all looks quite simple: the Belleville-en-Beaujolais unit hardly has any protection; it might even be possible to park the van in the courtyard, although I'm not absolutely sure – there is a gate at the entrance, with a security man.' He fell silent and glanced around the table again. 'You're Maryse, aren't you?' he asked her, looking her straight in the eyes.

'The girl who works at the hospital and who's going to be working on site?'

'That's right.'

'You'll be playing the main part in the operation. You've made your mind up – you're sure?'

'Absolutely sure,' Maryse answered calmly.

'Right. The plan's very simple. You push the wheelchair along the corridors, you cross the courtyard very calmly, you push it to the back of the van and we take him on board. If we can't get in we'll park in the corner, there's always room, and I'll come and get you at the entrance on Rue Paulin-Bussières. There'll be a sealed van in the name of the Édouard Herriot hospital in Lyon. My guys will be in nurses' uniforms from the same hospital. Basically that shouldn't matter, but we've got to take all possibilities into account. The idea, if we're stopped, is to say that we're driving to Lyon to pick up a new MRI and a PET scan.'

'Remind me what a PET scan is?'

'Positron emission topography. It's quite a new kind of examination, I'm not exactly sure what it's for. In any case, it would be best if you just came along like that, pushing the chair. So what day would be best for you?'

'Sunday,' Maryse said without hesitation. 'That's when the least staff are working and the most families come, and you often see people pushing a patient in a wheelchair in the courtyard. Also there's no security, and they leave the gate open so that families can park.'

'Ah . . .! I didn't know any of that, that's really good. So yes, no doubt about it, we'll do it on a Sunday when you're on duty, and you'll tell us the best time.'

'Still,' Maryse said, 'I could be spotted by a colleague. I don't think she'd stop me, but she'd be surprised, it's not my normal unit, and it's a patient I'm not supposed to be dealing with.'

He looked concerned for a moment. 'I won't lie to you, that

could be a problem. If your colleague talks, you're going to be questioned by the management, and that could cause you real grief. The only solution would be to say that your colleague was mistaken, that she got muddled with a different day.'

'There's CCTV in the corridors.'

He dismissed the objection with a wave of the hand. 'That's not really a problem. We can deactivate it as we wish via the internet, and resume the recording an hour later. And when I say an hour, that's much too much, I would hope that the whole operation would be signed and sealed in five minutes.'

He fell silent again. 'No, the real problem is if you're questioned by the management in the presence of your colleague. Then it's going to be your word against hers. So . . .' he went on after a few moments, 'are you still willing to do it?'

'Yes.'

'Fine . . .' He looked around at everyone again before continuing. 'I'll take care of the necessary details, and I'll keep you informed via Hervé. It won't take more than two weeks, I would say, then we wait till you're on duty, and we go into action. Don't worry . . .' he added, before going back to his table to join his acolytes. 'We've pulled off much tougher jobs. We'll get him out of there.'

12

The operation, in fact, took a total of four and a half minutes. A few seconds after Maryse got there, two of Brian's men lifted Édouard and settled him on a hospital trolley inside the van; then they took off their nurses' uniforms, which were now useless, and left in separate cars; they hadn't had to say a word, which was lucky, Maryse thought, because they seemed to have a strong potential for violence that would have been difficult to contain. She was already sitting in the front seat of the van as Brian set off along Rue Paulin-Bussières, then Rue de la République, and in five minutes they had left Belleville. Maryse said nothing.

'Did it all go OK?' Brian asked, as she remained silent.

'Not completely, no. I ran into a colleague; to make things worse it was Suzanne, the union delegate, the one who got Madeleine thrown out. She didn't say anything to me, but she gave me a puzzled look; I'm pretty sure that she's going to talk.'

'Shit . . .!' He thumped the dashboard. 'Fuck, shit – it was a perfect operation . . .!' He calmed down a little before continuing: 'She was the only one you ran into?'

'Yes. Just as I was coming into the courtyard, in fact – it's really annoying.'

'The only thing to do is stick to our guns, as we said: you don't know what she's talking about, she must have made a mistake.'

'And you managed to wipe the CCTV OK?'

'Yes, of course, don't worry about that.'

'But are you sure there's no trace of you wiping it? That when they look at the tape they won't realize that part of it has disappeared?'

'Ah, good question . . .' He smiled and looked at her with new consideration. 'So now it's on a hard drive, which I think makes things a little easier, but I'm still going to have to make a quick call.' He stopped on the verge, took out his phone and dialled a number; it was answered immediately.

'Jeremy, it's Brian. Yes, you can turn the recording back on, like we said. But there's something else. Do you think you could download the bit of hard disk and muck around with it a bit so that no one can spot your intervention?'

This time there was a long explanation at the other end. Brian listened carefully without interrupting and concluded: 'Well, right, OK, do it,' before hanging up.

He turned back towards Maryse: 'It's sorted, don't worry: the recording will be just great. Just in case, I'd advise you to ask the director to have a look at it, to prove that you weren't going along the corridor at that moment.'

He set off again. A few kilometres further on, just before they reached Villié-Morgon, Maryse turned Brian to say:

'You're very sure of yourself, aren't you?'

'No, not at all.' He smiled frankly again. 'I'm not at all sure of myself, in fact it's a bit pathetic. But I'm sure of my people.'

Madeleine was the only one waiting for them when he parked the van in the courtyard, but Paul and Hervé came out of the house almost immediately. Paul was pushing a cheap wheelchair that he had bought the previous day while waiting for the made-to-measure model. With Brian's help they had no trouble at all lifting Édouard from his hospital trolley and then putting him in the wheelchair; he had woken up completely. Paul might have been mistaken, but he still had a sense that his father gave a start when he recognized his house; at any rate his eyes were bright, and moved from left to right, carefully exploring the place.

The medical bed had been set up in the dining room; a workman would come the next day to install a stairlift, which would allow Édouard to sleep in his old room.

It was strange, very strange, to see him at home again, amidst his family. What was happening in his mind? Once again, Paul found himself facing that unanswerable question. His expression was calmer, at any rate, and his eyes moved slowly from each of his children to the next, and stopped on Maryse; he must have remembered her working at the hospital, and he must have been surprised to see her in the middle of his family.

Aurélien announced that he had to leave as he absolutely had to be in Chantilly the next day. Under these conditions they really couldn't be happy about that, Cécile said. They would have to celebrate, she added, waving her arms about. In actual fact she still couldn't believe that it had gone so well, without a hitch, without an incident. For want of anything else she opened a bottle of champagne and insisted that Brian accept at least a glass. 'I don't know how to thank you . . .' she said as she held it out to him, 'I'll never forget.' Brian shook his head, also unable to express himself adequately. But it wasn't the first time he had experienced this, the tears of joy, the families, but he still couldn't get used to it.

He left them shortly afterwards, but his troubles weren't entirely over; through the window Paul saw Madeleine dashing towards him before he got back into his van, hugging him violently, gripping his right hand in hers, and at one moment she even knelt down in front of him; it took him at least a minute to break away.

Aurélien didn't manage to hit the road until about five o'clock in the afternoon. 'Don't forget, we're working tomorrow too . . .' Paul observed. Aurélien offered to take them back in his car. 'Will you be able to come back,' Cécile asked, 'so that we can have a proper celebration?' Yes, of course, Prudence replied, they could even stay for a few days.

Aurélien held Maryse tightly in his arms before sitting down at the wheel. He was going to worry, he said, he was really going to worry. She shrugged evasively, she didn't know, she was sure at any rate that her colleague hadn't followed her into the courtyard, they had just crossed paths for a few seconds; but she couldn't really say. 'I'll call you tomorrow,' she said at last before hugging him one last time.

As soon as they were on the motorway he started brooding gloomily again. Maryse risked being fired, and she had done it for them, mostly for him, in fact, he repeated the refrain a dozen times. Sitting beside him, Paul couldn't think of a response.

'You don't think you could intervene at the political level?' Prudence asked all of a sudden. 'Not directly, but by asking Bruno.'

'That's what I've been wondering for a while now . . .'

Aurélien fell suddenly silent; the idea had never occurred to him.

'I don't think Bruno's the right person,' Paul said at last. 'We're already in the middle of an election campaign, and it really isn't the time for him to take risks. I know that if I asked him he would do it anyway; but it's really a long way outside his field of responsibility, and I'm not even sure he's ever spoken to his colleague at the Interior Ministry. On the other hand there is someone; I could easily approach Martin-Renaud.'

They looked at him with surprise. 'It's true, you don't know him . . .' he said to Prudence. 'Neither do you, Aurélien, when I think about it you didn't see him, he only stayed for a few hours, and that was the day when you were wrapping up the sculptures. OK, long story short, he's an old colleague of Dad's, they worked in the same service and apparently they were close, he came to visit him at the hospital. And he's high up in the secret services – very high up, in fact.'

They didn't mention it again until they reached Paris, just before ten at night. Over the last few weeks Aurélien had become more or less accustomed to getting home late enough to be sure that his wife had gone to bed. This time he hadn't dared impose such a late timetable, but as they turned off towards Montreuil he looked so obviously anxious that Prudence asked him, 'Do you want to stay for dinner?' He accepted immediately.

At about one o'clock in the morning he guessed that it would be all right for him to leave. 'You can sleep here, if you like . . .' Prudence suggested. 'You could even stay for a few days, we have a bedroom that we don't even use these days.'

He shook his head resignedly. He was bound to take a studio flat soon, he would find something, but for now he had to talk to his wife, there were certain things they had to agree on. If they only spoke through their lawyers that was obviously going to slow down the divorce; and that was something he wanted to avoid at all costs.

'Will you take care of the important guy in the secret service?' he asked Paul as he stepped out of the door.

'I'll call him tomorrow.'

13

At nine o'clock Paul phoned Martin-Renaud, who had the situation explained to him and arranged to meet at two o'clock at Rue du Bastion. The view they had from his office was truly impressive, Paul said to himself, but the area looked uninhabitable; then it occurred to him that everyone might have thought the same thing when they stepped inside, and the same thing about pretty much any recently built part of the city.

Martin-Renaud offered him an espresso, and took one himself. 'I've looked into your appeal,' he said a moment later. 'For now, no complaints of kidnapping and false imprisonment have been lodged with the High Court in Mâcon. Obviously it's still very early days, it only happened yesterday. We can't intervene directly: the legal system is very sensitive with regard to its independence, and we only try to get round that obstacle in exceptional cases.'

He broke off, seeing that Paul had lowered his eyes with embarrassment.

'I'm not at all used to this,' Paul said at last, looking up. 'It might surprise you, but I've never asked for a favour or special privileges.'

'Yes, it's unusual, for someone who belongs to the political world.'

'I know. Perhaps I don't really belong to the political world; let's say I'm on the edge. At any rate, the person I work for doesn't do that kind of thing. To be perfectly honest, I didn't really have to fight to protect my interests; I suppose I've led what you would call a privileged life. Every time I've got anywhere close to the world of special privileges I've felt a bit ashamed, and preferred to look away. I suppose that until now I've managed to preserve certain illusions about the world. In fact I know they're illusions, but I'm not 100 per cent certain, you know?'

Martin-Renaud didn't reply. 'If a complaint is made,' he went on without comment, 'the public prosecutor will call for an inquiry, and that inquiry will be entrusted to the police – the civil police, in fact, rather than the local gendarmerie. In that case I can definitely make sure that this inquiry is not carried out with great diligence, in fact; I can even guarantee that it will grind to a standstill. That won't trouble my conscience; we've done it in the past to protect colleagues and ex-colleagues. In fact, your father hasn't committed any crime; from a certain point of view, in fact, he could be seen as the victim. So here's what I suggest: we do nothing for now; and if the legal machine starts moving, I'll do what's necessary to slow down the mechanisms of the police – stop them, in fact.'

That suited him perfectly, Paul hurried to reply; he hadn't expected as much, in fact.

'It's strange . . .' Martin-Renaud went on, 'so, you've met these people, the ex-CLASH? What did you think of them?'

'They're good. They're serious, competent, cautious, at no moment did they take any pointless risks.'

'I agree with you. This morning I was going through what we've got on them, and it didn't take long; we've got hardly anything. They don't make any mistakes, ever. We're still trying to glean information from time to time – don't worry, I have no intention of questioning you – but it's more a matter of routine, and they're activists, they aren't terrorists, they've never committed any illegal or violent action. That doesn't mean that they're not extremely disturbing as far as the official ideology is concerned: they force it to turn on itself, to re-examine its own values; and that's what it hates more than anything. What's remarkable is that they always have an inside accomplice, usually a nurse or a care assistant, but sometimes a doctor; and they seem to have them in every hospital in France; I have a sense that the medical fraternity is very divided on the question of euthanasia.'

'And what progress have you made with your internet message?' Paul interrupted, hoping to avoid having to talk to him about their accomplices inside the hospital. His attempt to divert the conversation struck him as quite clumsy, but it worked, clearly Martin-Renaud was more preoccupied with this subject than he was with CLASH. As far as he knew, he replied, the sheets found in his father's file had put them on a new track, but it hadn't yielded much so far. If he wanted to know more he suggested he go and see Doutremont, he was the one following the case.

When Paul stepped into his room, Doutremont was with Delano Durand; he introduced the pair.

'It was your father who had the idea of bringing the two images together, is that right?' Durand asked.

'Yes. Do you think that makes sense?'

'Definitely. The convex pentagon, the one that appears in the messages, represents the beginner, the outsider. The starred pentagon, or pentagram, carved on the forehead of Baphomet, represents the initiate, the one who possesses knowledge. So that's all quite clear; except that to be honest, metalheads don't really resemble initiates. Overall, they're pleasant enough clowns who do it for the look, for fun, nothing more. There are a few Satanists who know more about the magic arts; but there are very few, not nearly as many as we think, and more importantly we don't imagine them in the context of terrorists, any more than the metalheads; it's not the same milieu at all. There are Wiccans too, who use the starred pentagon, but that doesn't get us much further.'

'Wiccans?'

'Why, do you know some?'

'Yes.'

'That doesn't surprise me, there are more and more of them. So for some ceremonies, in fact, they use pentagrams and pentangles; but that's not a reason to call the police, it's one of the most wide-spread magical symbols, since the dawn of time. And most importantly, they're every bit as harmless as metalheads and Satanists – even more so, if that's possible. You can't imagine any of these people getting involved in terrorism, any more than high-level hacking. So apparently that gets us nowhere. And yet I can't shake the idea that there's something . . .'

Doutremont glanced at his young colleague. The job was coming back to him, he reflected with grim satisfaction; he would not have the insolent recklessness of the novice for ever.

'For example,' Delano Durand went on, having warmed to his subject, 'those weird characters that we find in all the internet messages were extremely successful in the world of metal – almost as much as Baphomet. Some metalheads captured the image on the internet, and I've seen the same characters reproduced on T-shirts and flyers; they even appear on the sleeves of the latest records by Nyarlathotep and Sepultura. So yes,' he said in conclusion, turning towards Paul, 'I would like to know what was going through your father's mind.'

14

Aurélien had had a rotten night; when he'd got to the house in Montreuil, Indy was standing waiting for him, even though it was late, and a particularly violent argument had followed, lasting until four o'clock in the morning. Although he didn't know how she had worked it out (a hair clinging to an item of clothing? a hint of perfume?), she had guessed the existence of another woman. Why would she care?, he thought miserably as he tried to endure her yelling, they hadn't fucked for years, they didn't have the slightest intention of starting again, and they were going through a divorce process; why would she care?

The philosopher René Girard is known for his theory of mimetic desire, or triangular desire, according to which one desires what others desire, by imitation. Amusing on paper, the theory is in fact false. People are more or less indifferent to the desires of others, and they are unanimous in desiring the same things and the same beings, just because those are objectively desirable. Likewise, the fact that another woman desired Aurélien did not lead Indy to desire him in turn. Instead she was furious, almost mad with rage, at the idea that Aurélien might desire another woman and not desire her; for a long time, perhaps for ever, the narcissistic stimuli based on competition and hatred had taken over within her from sexual stimuli; and they were, in principle, boundless.

*

He spent a nauseous day in Chantilly, and his first reaction when Maryse's face appeared on the screen of his phone, at about six in the evening, was unease; in the state he was in, he would have a great deal of trouble coping with bad news.

There was no bad news; there was, in fact, no news at all. The atmosphere had been weird all day at the hospital, Maryse told him. People weren't even talking about his father's disappearance, or perhaps implicitly, by way of allusion – but it was probably fear that led her to imagine that, and they probably weren't talking about it at all. She had been given suspicious glances several times; but today everyone seemed to be glancing suspiciously at everyone. The director of the unit hadn't called a meeting of the staff or even the hierarchy; he hadn't done anything at all.

Could things go on like that? Maryse wondered. The director had a reputation for being cautious, and even quite cowardly, and of avoiding making waves where possible; but even so, could a patient disappear like that without leaving the slightest trace?

Well, in fact, perhaps he could; if no one claimed him, if no one was worried that he wasn't there, that did seem possible. The files were recorded, there was a register of admissions; but who would look at them if no complaint was made?

She was so puzzled by this that she had asked Hervé to call Brian, since he was the one with his contact details. According to Brian it happened, and quite often. If a problem came up, several years later, the director could always claim that the patient had left hospital at the request of the family – thus, unwittingly, coinciding with the truth. There were cases when it was in everyone's interest to remain silent; as it happened, they could hope that this was one of those cases.

She hung up sadly; she missed Aurélien terribly, in his current state of confusion. They were living in parallel hells and met up every weekend in their own world, a mini-world that had no real existence, because so far it had no economic viability. She was still as indignant as before about the working conditions in the care home, indignant and startled that such things could exist in France, that old people could, in their twilight years, be subjected to such humiliation.

As for Aurélien, he had been living under the modern illusion that divorces were easy, that they were simple, calm, almost friendly procedures; he was now discovering that it was exactly the opposite, that hatreds warmed over the years until they were white-hot, and reached almost unheard-of proportions when a divorce was involved. He couldn't wait to get it over with; but as his lawyer kept reminding him, in a divorce negotiation, as in a negotiation of any kind, it is the one in the greatest hurry to finish who puts himself in an unfavourable position. So he assumed an attitude of resignation. He held himself back.

They held themselves back, trying to extract as much joy as possible from their brief moments in that mini-world, feeding their daydreams, with no idea whether they were anywhere within reach; they were frozen as they waited for a disaster, or a miracle.

five

1

Two weeks after Édouard's return home, Paul took a week's leave. The electoral campaign was in full swing; a few days before, he had seen Bruno at a huge meeting held in Marseille and shown live on the news channels. A fleeting shot when he was coming back, still sweating from the effort, to rest behind the scenes, revealed Raksaneh, and seeing the look that she gave him, he no longer had any doubt: they were sleeping together.

For once he decided to go by car; he didn't really know why, perhaps because going by car reminded him of going on holiday. They reached Saint-Joseph at about five o'clock in the afternoon. Leaving Prudence with Cécile and Madeleine, he walked along the glass corridor leading to the conservatory. His father spent most of his days there; the room had always been his favourite, even when he was still fit. He turned his eyes towards the door as he came in. Paul kissed him on the cheek and gripped his hand in his; he responded with pressure, faint but unmistakeable. Madeleine had explained to him that she moved the wheelchair around several times a day so that he could see different views of the landscape; at that moment he was facing a clump of beech trees. Paul sat down beside him; he didn't really have anything to say to him, he knew that Cécile had already kept him up to date with developments in his and Aurélien's situations. After a few minutes he, too, lost himself in the same contemplation of the branches, the leaves stirred by the wind. Basically he didn't ask much more of life; it was so completely satisfactory that when Madeleine came to call him for dinner two hours later, he realized that throughout that time he hadn't moved a centimetre, any more than his father had, or uttered a single word.

Paul knew that their Hervé and Cécile's daughters were visiting that weekend, but he no longer felt apprehensive about it, and in fact Anne-Lise got up perfectly naturally to kiss him on the cheek. 'You haven't seen them for a long time – they've grown a lot . . .' Cécile pointed out. Yes, in fact, Deborah was very different from her sister, more spontaneous, more abrupt, but the most striking thing was that she was gorgeous, with a magnificent figure and dazzling blonde hair – in fact she looked very like her mother at the same age. She did not, however, have a boyfriend, even though she didn't share Cécile's religious commitment; it was quite simply the fact that most of the boys she met struck her as 'a bit crap'. Hervé plainly adored her, and that was certainly one of the reasons that made him happy enough in the end to go back to Arras – they were due to leave at the end of the month, and then he would start his new job.

The next morning Paul got up late, and found himself alone facing Anne-Lise over the breakfast table. 'Looks like things worked out with your wife,' she said, breaking the silence. Yes, they had sorted things out nicely, he agreed. 'All the better . . . I'm glad I was able to contribute,' she said softly; it was her first and only allusion to their meeting.

After the girls left, the atmosphere became very calm. He and Prudence took long outings in the car, and he showed her around the region – Solutré, Beaujeu, and once even as far as Cluny. In the late afternoon he dropped by to see his father, and they spent an hour or two together, mostly in silence, they contemplated the sun setting over the vineyards; at those times Madeleine left them alone.

One evening he noticed a book resting on a desk – a Pléiade

342

volume of the *Comédie humaine* – and asked Madeleine. Yes indeed, she confirmed, Édouard could read, with her help. When he had finished a page, he looked at her and blinked; then she turned the page to move on to the next one. That worked with the Pléiade edition, but it was more difficult with normal books, you had to break the spine so that the pages stayed in place. As a rule he preferred reading classics, particularly Balzac, but also a detective novel from time to time; she pointed to a paperback by Malcolm McKay entitled *The Sudden Arrival of Violence*. It was the third volume of the Glasgow trilogy, she explained, he had read the first two. Paul looked at her, surprised that she knew the word 'trilogy'.

'Whenever possible I download the text from the internet, particularly with pamphlets,' Madeleine added. He looked at her with mounting astonishment; she definitely wasn't stupid, in fact she wasn't stupid at all; it was just that she had chosen not to talk, or as little as possible, she must have thought that words were pointless most of the time; and perhaps she was right.

Her level of communication with his father was very high, he realized; they held each other's hands for a long time, their fingers interlaced and gripped one another in various positions. One evening after leaving them, going back up to his room before dinner for a moment, Paul wondered if they still had a sex life. He seemed to remember that tetraplegics had erections, or rather he couldn't remember very clearly, voluntary movements had ceased to exist, but an erection wasn't an entirely voluntary movement. It was dizzying as a thought. If his father could get an erection, if he could read and contemplate the movement of leaves stirred by the wind, Paul said to himself, then he was lacking absolutely nothing in life.

The week passed quickly, as happiness does. Paul phoned Martin-Renaud once, but there was still nothing, no complaint had been lodged. Maryse, for her part, hadn't been troubled at work, at the hospital people were already talking less about Édouard's disappearance, and it seemed that he was being calmly forgotten. Early one Friday afternoon Cécile had a call from Aurélien. The line was very bad, there was hardly any reception, which happened on some days, and her brother seemed to be in a state of great mental confusion, she could barely understand a word he said, except that he was on his way and would arrive soon.

A few minutes later, Aurélien's car crashed violently into the porch after skidding for a distance on the gravel in the courtyard. He got out immediately, holding an open magazine; he appeared to be on the brink of apoplexy. Cécile wondered for a moment if he too wasn't about to have a stroke. He calmed down gradually and managed to say: 'She's taken her revenge. The bitch has taken her revenge.'

Paul took the magazine from his hands. Indy's article, 'Where are the fascists?', spread over six whole pages. She told the story of Édouard's kidnapping by a 'commando unit' that had invaded the hospital at Belleville-sur-Saône, then his 'illegal confinement' in Villié-Morgon. He immediately understood that the article would be skilfully written, that the choice of words would be very harsh, but that it would contain no frankly untruthful or defamatory statements.

It was entirely his fault that she knew about it, Aurélien explained despairingly. They had had a particularly violent argument one evening, she had talked about his father again, calling him a 'vegetable' as she had done before, and he had lost his temper and boasted about getting him out of hospital. He didn't know what had come over him, he had just wanted to show that he was the stronger party, take the upper hand in the conversation, and he should have suspected that she would exploit the information; but he had no idea how she had found out the rest.

The article began with a brief history of the anti-euthanasia movement, set up in the United States 'by evangelical fundamentalists, on the model of anti-abortion groups', and recounted its spread to Belgium, then to France. It wasn't entirely false, and not entirely true, either – there had sometimes been a certain similarity in their ways of operating, but there were no real contacts between the organizations. It went on to discuss the operation in Belleville-en-Beaujolais, led by a 'commando unit of activists from Lyon', with the complicity of a 'ravishingly beautiful care assistant of Caribbean origin'.

'She isn't Caribbean . . .' Aurélien pointed out mechanically, but so far that was the only mistake in the article, and the worst thing was that Maryse was mentioned by name. He himself was depicted as a 'frail-minded outsider who took refuge in Medieval tapestries', another possible description. The MO of the kidnapping was set out perfectly: the van parked in the courtyard, Édouard being transported in his wheelchair . . .

'How come she knows all this?' Cécile said with astonishment.

There was nothing miraculous about it, Paul pointed out. Given the way the place was laid out, it was the most logical way of proceeding; she must have made some enquiries on the spot, that was for sure; and to find out that Maryse was with Aurélien, she had just had to question his colleagues.

'I need to call her,' Aurélien said. 'I need to know what's happened to her.'

'There's very little reception today,' Cécile said. 'You'd be better off using the landline, it's in the hallway.'

A tense silence fell as soon as Aurélien had left the room. When he came back a few minutes later he wore a distraught expression. He immediately announced: 'It's fucked. She was called in by her director two hours ago, and she confessed everything. She had planned to deny it, but when she saw the article she cracked, she went to pieces completely. She's sorry, she apologizes to us all; I

345

told her she had nothing to apologize for, that it was all my fault, and that she was the main victim. What makes it even worse is that the deactivation of the video worked perfectly; but she didn't have the presence of mind to mention it.

'What will happen to her now?' Cécile asked.

'She will certainly be suspended in a day or two. Then there will be a disciplinary inquiry, and she risks being fired, that much is certain, without notice or compensation.'

He stopped talking and silence fell in the room. 'And it's my fault, it's completely my fault . . .' Aurélien repeated a few seconds later, in a plaintive voice. No one replied; there was nothing to say. There was no point making things worse for him, Paul reflected, but in fact he would have been better off holding his tongue. While his brother had been outside, Paul had flicked through the rest of the article, and had understood that he was about to get an earful, and the purpose of the manoeuvre now seemed clear: it was to hurt Bruno. Strangely enough, the press, while it had lost almost all of its readers, had increased its power to do harm over the past few years, it could break lives now, and it didn't hold back from doing so, particularly at election time, legal proceedings were point-less, a simple suspicion was enough to destroy somebody.

'If she loses her job,' Aurélien resumed in an unsteady voice, 'she won't be able to have a residence permit either. I can't marry her, I'm not divorced, and where the divorce is concerned I'm completely in Indy's hands, she's completely capable of dragging it on for years, just to hurt me.' He broke off and for a moment it looked as if he was about to faint, then he slumped onto the sofa before bursting into a fit of sobs. Cécile and Hervé were as if anaesthetized, unable to react, and Cécile herself did nothing to comfort him, since his frailty and weakness had ended up having truly disastrous consequences. 'I don't feel well, I think I'm going to and lie down in my room,' he said a minute later before disappearing upstairs. Two minutes passed, still in total silence, before Paul started reading the article again. In it, Cécile was called a 'fanatical Catholic, close to the ultra-right-wing Civitas movement'. It was really disgusting, she said indignantly, it was a lie pure and simple. Yes, Paul replied calmly, but 'close' was still vague, there was no defamation of her character, and he didn't think they could attack on that basis. It was probably no coincidence, the article went on, that the patient was being illegally held in Villié-Morgon, a village in Beaujolais that served as refuge for the capuchins of Morgon, the fundamentalist Catholic grouping attached to the Civitas movement.

'What's this all about? Were you aware of it?' he asked his sister.

'Not at all.'

'What about you, Madeleine? Did you know about they existed – the capuchins of Morgon?'

'Not a clue.'

'I'm going to call the parish priest for Villié-Morgon,' Cécile said. 'He's a nice guy, and he's bound to know what's happening in his parish.'

When she came back shortly afterwards she seemed disoriented and perplexed. In fact, she told them, it was the capuchin community of traditional observance, which had moved into the convent of Saint Francis. The priest didn't have much to do with them, but he knew them, and knew that they were attached to Civitas. That said, even if he completely disagreed with the political opinions of Civitas, he refused to judge the capuchin community. They lived in poverty, and in the service of the Lord, so as far as he was concerned they were good Christians.

In the rest of the article Indy turned her wrath on Paul, who was described as 'the brain and the financier behind the affair'. The financier, if you like, was the one who had paid for the medical equipment. The brain was more doubtful, that role really fell to Brian, but his sister-in-law's investigations seemed not to have extended that far. He was also described as 'a very influential member of the ministerial cabinet', and that was clearly what she wanted to get at. It was alarming, she stormed, that the most reactionary groupuscules of the Catholic far right could find support at the highest level of the state apparatus. The headline 'Where are the fascists?' now found its true meaning. The article wasn't a bad one, all the same, Paul said to himself. He felt strangely detached and calm, as if all of this concerned him only distantly, but he still had to talk to Bruno. He in turn made for the telephone in the hall.

Bruno replied almost immediately. 'I'm glad you've called me,' he said, 'I didn't want to have to do it first.' His voice was animated, almost cheerful, and he gave no sign of panic. Paul had seen him much more tense during certain business negotiations.

'Right, I expect you've seen the thing . . .' he went on.

'Absolutely everywhere. The first thing I wanted to ask you is extremely simple: are the events as described?'

'Yes. Apart from a few details, it's all true.'

'All right. I rather expected that, to tell you the truth. I won't hide the fact that there's a bit of a panicky mood down at campaign headquarters right now. Solène Signal is in a total state – what's driving her mad is the fact that she can see that the point of the manoeuvre is to hurt me, but she has no idea where it could be coming from. In fact the only one who stands to benefit from this is the candidate for the National Rally, the others are far too low in the polls, but she can't imagine any connection between the National Rally and this magazine, and apart from that the anti-euthanasia movements are more up their street, it's more or less in line with their ideas, in so far as they have any, in short she doesn't know what to think and she wanted to see you straight away. I told her that wasn't possible, that you were with your family, and I managed to calm her down a little, but even so, if we could have a little crisis meeting on Sunday morning that would be great.'

'Yes, Sunday morning is good, I can drive back tomorrow and be there on Sunday whenever you want.'

'OK, I'll call her back, and then I'll give you a call. On this number?'

As he waited for the call from Bruno, Paul first walked along the corridor, then opened the front door and stood for a long time contemplating the sun as it set over the vines. He reflected that he had a number of answers to Solène Signal's questions. There was in fact no political machination, that wasn't where she needed to look, just in the wounded, bruised ego of his sister-in-law, who was prepared to do anything to get herself talked about, and much more if she could hurt them at the same time. It was all perfectly clear in his eyes, but he couldn't explain it to Bruno, not like that, not on the telephone. So, when Bruno called him back a few minutes later and said, 'Eight o'clock tomorrow morning, in my office – is that OK for you?' he replied: 'I'd rather see you a bit before the meeting. Seven thirty?'

Struggling up a rocky slope whose surface is crumbling under his feet, Paul manages to reach a circular outcrop surrounded by puny bushes. In the middle of the outcrop, buried just beneath the surface, is a big coffin of black varnished wood. Men in grey overcoats are lifting the coffin to carry it into town; this is bad luck, because these men are Paul's political adversaries. With its red-brick houses, the town looks like Amiens. Gradually Paul becomes sure that it actually is Amiens. Then he tries to bribe a sixteen-year-old girl on her way to school (probably her first year at lycée, in the science stream) to give him the authentic formulation for a maths problem; if he has the authentic formulation, he knows he will be able to confound his political adversaries. The girl is in the middle of a group of school students, but he addresses her as if she is alone.

The girl agrees to give him an authentic formulation; empowered by this success, Paul is within his rights to order the opening of the coffin in the middle of town; lying inside it is a pale giant wearing a black jacket and top hat; scared at the sight of him, the men in grey overcoats scatter, waving their arms. Resolving the problem contained in the authentic statement, Paul gets a mark of 16. The maths teacher is a young woman in an extremely short pleated miniskirt; she looks like a maths teacher he actually had in final year, and whose thighs he studied for whole hours at a time; he's just surprised that she hasn't aged. Paul knows she is among his political allies, even though she is otherwise on the far left. She and he are now together on a ski-lift with extremely small cabins meant for two people, climbing along the sloping streets of a district that looks like Ménilmontant or Montmartre. The slope gets steeper and steeper, it becomes literally terrifying, almost vertical; and yet little multicoloured birds, almost definitely canaries, are flying fearlessly around the cabin, accompanying its ascent.

Then, without transition, he finds himself in a gloomy cave illuminated by a faint yellowish light; down below are revoltingly filthy basins, probably dump vats, containing nothing but little pools of stagnant water. Immediately afterwards, unexpectedly, a powerful stream engulfs the slope, filling the dump vats again. It carries tiny pigs to a round black opening; intuitively one knows that it leads to an abattoir.

On a television stage, an old man, short, bald and slightly deformed, tries to save a programme by making jokes, but he largely fails and decides to take off his trousers before passing in front of the cameras (we briefly see his genitals, big, soft and pale). Then we find him floating in one of the dump vats. Like the mini-pigs he will be dragged towards the abattoir; he knows it, but he seems to accept the prospect with serenity, indeed with secret jubilation.

*

Paul woke with a start. In the light from the corridor he recognized Cécile, who was shaking his shoulder, urging him in a low voice: 'Come! Come straight away . . .!' Prudence, beside him, moved slightly without waking up.

He joined Cécile in the corridor, closed the bedroom door again and asked her immediately: 'What's happening?'

'Aurélien has killed himself.'

2

Cécile couldn't say anything more until she was sitting in the kitchen, after picking up a bottle of rum that was lying in a cupboard – it was the first time he had seen her drinking spirits. She had woken up in the middle of the night, filled with inexplicable anxiety, knowing only that it had something to do with Aurélien. After knocking in vain on his door, she had gone in and seen that the room was empty. Then she had looked for him without success all over the house, she had gone to their rooms and then to their father's study. Finding no one there either, she had started panicking: had Aurélien gone to the countryside in the middle of the night? It had taken her a long time, too long, to think about the old barn, the one that had been their mother's studio. And as soon as she stepped inside and turned the light on, she saw him hanging five metres above the ground. The worst thing was that his body was still swinging slightly at the end of the rope. It was quite a close thing, a minute might have been enough, if she'd arrived a minute earlier she might have been able to save him. At these words she burst out sobbing.

'You mustn't feel guilty, you had nothing to do with it, it's not your fault . . .' Paul repeated mechanically, tapping her gently on the shoulder, while he couldn't help reflecting that he himself would probably thought of the barn sooner. Aurélien had been close to their mother, he had often visited her while she was working on her absurd sculptures, while basically Cécile had more or less erased their mother from her memory; she got on perfectly well with Madeleine, however, the mother–daughter relationship is never simple, particularly when the daughter is pretty. Obviously he wasn't going to broach that subject, though. Her head was beginning to wobble, clearly she was starting to get a bit drunk; it was quite normal, she wasn't used to drinking, but he felt that he was going to have to deal with everything else, phoning the local police station, etc.

They made their way to the barn without difficulty, it was almost like broad daylight, a harsh light spread from the open door, his mother usually worked at night and she had installed a powerful lighting system. Cécile stopped in the doorway; she didn't feel strong enough to see him again and she sat down on the floor, or rather she dropped like a dead weight before leaning against the door.

It was the first time that Paul had seen a hanged man, or any kind of suicide for that matter, and he had expected worse. His brother's face wasn't swollen or bluish, and his colour was in fact almost normal. He was a bit convulsed, certainly, he was grimacing, but in fact not all that much, his death didn't seem to have been very painful. Less painful, certainly, than his life had been – and at the moment when that thought ran through him Paul was filled with a wave of terrible, crucifying compassion, mixed with guilt because he hadn't done anything to help or support him, he almost collapsed but recovered himself, he needed to make a phone call, he couldn't let himself go now. He clung to certain things: there had been Maryse: he must have had some genuine moments of joy towards the end. And then there were his tapestries, he had loved them with a genuine passion, and that must surely count for something. But even so, his little brother hadn't had much luck in life, the world hadn't exactly welcomed him with open arms.

*

The gendarmes came quickly, less than half an hour later, accompanied by a pathologist and firefighters with an extendable ladder. Once they had got him down they decided to take Aurélien to his old bedroom so that the pathologist could get to work. As they were picking up the body, Prudence appeared in her nightdress at the bottom of the stairs. At first she stood there open-mouthed, then threw herself into Paul's arms. She looked shocked, but not completely stunned, and Paul remembered bitterly that she had warned them, she had told them several times to watch out for Aurélien, she felt he was fragile, far from stable and probably in danger.

The pathologist came back less than ten minute later. He would undertake a complete examination later, but suicide by hanging was of course beyond any doubt the cause.

The lieutenant of the gendarmes turned towards Paul and Cécile. They were his brother and sister, wasn't that correct, they were his closest relations? Paul nodded. Under these circumstances, would they be able to come to the station in Mâcon the following day to give a statement? It would be a short statement, there was no mystery about the case. Paul had to leave for Paris the next day, but in the morning, yes, that was doable.

'Do you know what led him to do this?' the lieutenant asked just before leaving, partly to clear his conscience, as a rule close relatives are caught off guard, they don't understand, they would never have imagined, they had no idea about any of the victim's personal problems, you would have wondered, in fact, about the word *close*.

'No, I really don't know, I'm distraught . . .' Cécile said weakly.

'Yes, we do know,' Paul cut in, irritated. 'We know exactly why he did it. He couldn't bear his guilt towards us, but particularly towards Maryse, the guilt he felt for talking to Indy and for being the source of the article. And also things weren't going to turn out

OK. Maryse was going to lose her job, and he knew it, he had a sense that their life was fucked and that it was his fault.'

'You shouldn't talk to the police about that . . .' Cécile protested feebly.

'Of course we should! Now that it's been written down in that stupid newspaper everybody knows where Dad is, the police would have no trouble finding him if they were looking for him. Our only chance now is to ensure that there's no legal process . . .!'

Turning towards him, Paul caught the startled gaze of the police lieutenant, moving back and forth from one to the other without understanding anything. 'OK, it's quite a complicated business . . .' he concluded with an impatient wave of the hand. 'I'll explain everything to you tomorrow morning.'

When the gendarmes had left with the body a silence fell between them once more.

'I understand, of course I do,' Cécile said after a long pause, 'but at the same time I don't. I don't understand how one could have so little trust in life. It was possible that she was going to be fired, that's true, but even that much wasn't certain. And then he had his own civil servant's salary. Paris was too expensive for them, but they weren't forced to live in Paris, they could have lived here, for example, there's plenty of room. So he had a chance of starting his life over, he was about to get divorced and that girl loved him, that was obvious. Do you think she would have held that article against him? Do you think she'd even have mentioned it again . . .?'

Her voice was entering a dangerously high pitch again. Paul was afraid of a fresh collapse, but he had absolutely no idea what to say to her, except that she was right in every way. He poured himself a glass of rum; that stuff was really disgusting. He set off to find something else in the living room. Rummaging in the sideboard, he was ashamed of himself for behaving like some kind of epicure when his brother had committed suicide less than an hour ago, well, for better or for worse it was done, and he came back into the kitchen clutching a bottle of Armagnac. Cécile seemed to have calmed down a little, she was curled up silently in a ball.

He poured himself a large glass before going on: 'It's hard to say why, but there are people who hang in there and people who don't. We've always known that Aurélien belonged to the second category.' It was a really lousy observation, he immediately berated himself, if that was all he had to say he'd have been better off keeping his trap shut. Besides, Cécile didn't even reply, she acted as if he hadn't said a word. A minute later a sudden thought ran through her mind, an expression of terror appeared on her face and she exclaimed: 'Maryse is on her way here. She's finishing her night shift right now and she'll be here late morning. What am I going to say to her? What am I going to say to her . . .?'

3

I n fact it took a bit longer than planned to provide the statement to the gendarmerie in Mâcon. Paul set out all the facts, neglecting only to mention the identity of the activists who had helped them; on that point he didn't want to say anything before being questioned in the context of the case. In fact he was far from concerned, Bruno had been there early that morning, and Bruno had been very clear. Martin-Renaud's initial plan was in fact no longer applicable since the publication of the article, and trying to influence the judge's decision was still a bad idea, the media were always on the alert for things like that, and they had plenty of contacts within the legal system. It would make more sense to intervene in advance, to avoid a complaint being lodged. The principle was a simple one: hospital managers fell under the direct responsibility of the Ministry of Health; the current health minister wanted to keep his portfolio in the next government; they only needed to talk to him and make him tell his subordinate what attitude to adopt. 'When there is a direct route towards the goal, it's a good idea to take it,' Bruno concluded. Paul couldn't remember if that was Confucius, but it was probably somebody like that. A moment after he hung up, he thought to himself that he should have thought of consulting Bruno first. His unwillingness to exploit his friendly relations with a minister to enjoy favourable treatment was perhaps laudable in principle, but it had cost his brother his life. Either way, all danger had been removed for now, and he felt very much at ease while giving his statement; apart from anything else, he was treated with perfect politeness, the gendarmes seemed flattered to have a member of the cabinet within their walls, and if they had had little cakes to go with the coffee they would doubtless have brought them out.

It was a very mild day and Prudence had got out of the car to wait for him; she was studying the movements of the water, the little whirlpools that formed quickly and then disappeared just as swiftly on the surface of the Saône. 'It's sad, though, isn't it?' she said. 'It's a fine spring morning and he's no longer there to enjoy it, he won't ever be there again for a fine spring morning.' It was sad, that was true, but what else was there to say? It was also a fine spring morning for grubs and maggots, in a few days they would be able to feed on his flesh, they too would celebrate the arrival of the fine weather, that was the first thing that occurred to him. He suddenly remembered that a few years before, Prudence had had long conversations with Aurélien; she too loved the Middle Ages, she was very familiar with medieval paintings but didn't know the tapestries, and she had been very interested in what Aurélien had to say about them. Finding absolutely no comforting words to say, he took Prudence's hand in his own, and that was probably the right attitude, as she suddenly seemed to calm down.

It was even worse when they got to Saint-Joseph, and he parked in the courtyard in front of the house. Maryse was sitting on a little stone bench, just to the right of the porch. In fact she hadn't sat down in the sense that a human being might sit down to rest for a moment. She looked as if she had been plonked there, unable to move or even to conceive of what moving might have involved. Paul froze as well, unable to go any further, to act as if Maryse didn't exist, wasn't plonked beside the front door in what looked like a definitively motionless state. He was surprised to see Prudence break away from his grip and slide towards her, sit down next to her on the bench, rest a hand on her shoulder and stroke it gently.

As if women naturally knew how to do that, as if they were destined by some special knowledge of grief to perform certain gestures. He passed in front of them without stopping, without even giving Prudence another glance. Not only was he incapable of doing that kind of thing, he even struggled to watch it.

They didn't say much on the way back and went to bed early, having a bit of bread and cheese for supper. Paul woke up at dawn the next day, he was ready at half-past six, he knew that this meeting would mark a decisive fork in the road. Just before setting off, he went back to their room. Prudence woke up as well and turned to look at him, even though he was sure he hadn't made a sound. 'Are you going?' she asked. He nodded. She raised herself slightly in bed. He gently kissed her cheeks, then her lips.

As he stepped into the office, he realized that he was glad to see Bruno again. He sat down and told the whole story, from his father's arrival at the hospital in Belleville-sur-Saône to his liberation. He talked about Dr Leroux, his dismissal and the reorganization of the service. Bruno listened to him carefully without interrupting, and only remarked in passing: 'That's Madeleine's a surprising one . . .' Then Paul set out the role played by Maryse, before getting to Indy's article and Aurélien's suicide. After that, he was able to tell Bruno that in his view there was no need to go looking for any hidden hand, any secret political agenda behind the article, that it was inspired only by a bitter and ambitious woman's desire for revenge; if she had been informed about events, it wasn't thanks to any particular sources of information, it was only the carelessness of his unfortunate brother. He had his share of responsibility, he added: he had never concealed from Indy the dislike and contempt that she inspired in him; her revenge had been brutal.

The explanation had taken some time, and they hadn't yet been able to examine the question of the measures that needed to be taken when Solène Signal turned up. She was with her young assistant, every bit as wan and impeccably turned out as ever.

'What worries me isn't the first round,' she launched in immediately without taking the time to say hello, 'we'll lose a few points but we don't care, we'll have made it through to the second one, and that's where a new election begins. The problem is that if the public believes that we have the same positions on a social level as the Assembly, we'll have difficulty taking advantage of the poor position of the greens, or indeed the left, or what remains of it. And that's where things start getting dicey, particularly because the other guy is really excellent. I'd have to admit that Bérengère has done a great job, and she's far from finished, if I ever thought of underestimating her I was making a serious mistake. I don't know if you saw him the other day taking on that ecologist, that little girl, you know the one: "But I like nature too . . .! The song of a lark, in spring, at dawn, there's nothing that I know more beautiful." It was frankly sublime, and when that silly bitch opened her mouth, my God, she hasn't the first notion what a lark even is. Do you know what a lark is?' and she turned round to address her assistant, who shook his head with a certain sadness.

'Right, but you're pretending, and also you're not the green candidate. And after the way he goes off about insecticides, the disappearance of insects, and no insects no larks, that's how it works. So you see, it wasn't just for poetic effect, I know my stuff – no, the kid's really good. In short, where this sort of thing is concerned we've really got to do something, and do it quickly.'

She suddenly fell silent. The silence lasted for about thirty seconds, and then Paul said very calmly: 'I'm resigning.'

She looked at him in alarm, clearly not expecting such a direct statement.

'No,' Bruno broke in firmly, forcefully, almost brutally. 'There's no question of you resigning over this. I'd have done exactly the same thing if my father had been in your father's place. So, no. And in any case, we've got another solution.'

'I'm listening . . .' Solène Signal said.

'You're going to take some time off for personal reasons,' Bruno went on, still talking to Paul. 'Normally that takes a certain amount of time, but if I take care of it we can speed things up and even get it sorted out by tomorrow. In principle that would give you a year.'

'After the elections, I don't give a fuck, you can do what you like . . .' Solène said. 'But tell me: are we going to announce that he's stepped down from his role without going into detail?'

'Yes, civil servants don't need to explain their reasons. Under normal circumstances I wouldn't even be consulted about him taking leave,' Bruno replied.

'Right, then I think that might do it. So I'll go over it again. One, there are several dozen people working in your cabinet, you can't keep tabs on everybody's life. Two, it's a painful family problem that has nothing to do with the professional life of your colleague, with whom you have otherwise always been entirely satisfied. Three, nothing has been clearly established at this point, we have to let justice take its course.'

'Justice hasn't intervened so far,' Paul remarked, 'no complaint has been lodged.'

'What . . .?' she exclaimed, surprised. 'Well listen, that's even better, let justice take its course. I don't see why we should get worked up if no complaint's been brought, I was sure it had been.'

'There won't be,' Bruno stated firmly.

'Right, OK then, if there are no legal implications, who gives a fuck, it's just a little slightly poisonous newspaper article that a second-rate cunt of a journalist wrote to work up a bit of a froth . . . So I'll organize a little press conference, no point today as we wouldn't get anybody, but how about ten o'clock tomorrow?'

'Would I have to do anything?' Paul asked.

'Not at all. You let Bruno take charge of things. You're an anonymous civil servant and that's how you'll stay, much better that way. We were right to come here, though, I'm going to have a better Sunday.'

After they left, calm fell on the office once again. The sun had risen completely now, the sun shed its light on the moving surface of the Seine and the still-deserted embankments.

'I'd really like to thank you for reacting like that,' Paul said.

'Don't mention it.' Bruno shrugged indifferently. 'You heard our expert: it's just a press article, nothing to get worked up about. A legal case would be something else.

'It's really absurd about your brother's suicide,' he went on after a few moments. 'Even as regards his girlfriend, I think it would have been possible to halt her dismissal. A few months away, time for things to settle down, and then she could have come back quite happily.'

Yes, it was absurd, Paul had been convinced of that as soon as he saw Aurélien's body hanging from the beam in the barn, his death had been as absurd as his life; and at the same time he reflected that he could never share that observation with Cécile. As a rule, Christians have trouble with the absurd, it's not really one of their categories. In the Christian vision of the world God takes charge of events; sometimes the world seems to have been temporarily abandoned to the power of Satan, but in any case things have a powerful meaning, and Christianity was conceived for strong characters with a clearly marked will, sometimes oriented towards virtue, sometimes unfortunately towards sin. When God's creatures fall into the clutches of sin, mercy can intervene. He suddenly remembered a line from Claudel that had struck him when he was fifteen: 'I know that where sin abounds, superabounding is your mercy.' The word superabounding was quite ugly, but you would only find words like that in a poem by Claudel, and

362

luckily he picked himself up with the next line: 'We must pray, for the hour of the Prince of the world has come.' But were those words to be understood literally? Was mercy to be considered as a consequence of sin? And had sin not been authorized only to allow the upsurge of grace, starting with mercy?

At any rate there was no place in Christian typology for creatures like Aurélien, whose adherence to life was weak, always cautious, who had tried not so much to participate in the world as to remove himself from it. Perhaps he hadn't even really believed in the existence of Maryse; he had seen her passing by as a happy mirage, the possibility of a life that had been offered to him undeservedly, and which would soon be taken away from him. Sometimes official bodies like the tax office would send letters containing a message that said: 'A mistake has been made in your favour'; what had happened was probably something like that, Aurélien must have thought. There was really nothing surprising about his suicide, it seemed to have been determined by the nature of things; nonetheless, he had been wrong to talk to Cécile in those terms. Determinism is no more of a Christian category than the absurd; besides, the two are connected: a wholly determinist world appears more or less absurd, not only to a Christian, but to a man in general.

When he considered these questions from his youth, God as he imagined him came perfectly to terms with determinism, because he was the one who had created its laws, and in his view it was certainly someone like Isaac Newton who had come closest to the divine nature. Or perhaps David Hilbert, but that was less certain, mathematicians could do without the world entirely in order to exist, so should David Hilbert be considered as a kind of colleague of God? To tell the truth he had never devoted a huge amount of intellectual effort to these questions, even when he was young; in all likelihood he had only given them any thought at all during his last year at school, the only one that included an 'initiation into the great philosophical texts'. That meant that his interest in philosophy had begun at the age of seventeen and three months, coming to an end at the age of eighteen exactly.

The wail of a tugboat siren passing by the office drew him from his thoughts. He raised his head. Bruno was still sitting opposite him, he had respected his silence; quite a long time must have passed, the traffic was a little heavier on the embankments.

'I don't think I could spend all day inactive, I've never done that,' Bruno said calmly. 'I think you would be capable of that.' True enough, Paul said to himself, but he couldn't tell if that was a stroke of good fortune; today, most people would probably say no, but he lived in an age that placed an exceptional importance on work, and on fulfilment in the context of work, while most previous ages would on the contrary have seen leisure as the only suitable way of life for the wise man. Just before he got home, he sat down on a bench in the deserted Parc de Bercy. He was on leave, he said to himself again; he was really very pleased with the phrase.

4

'Occasion: perfect gifts for ladies, friends, fiancées and wives, and New Year's Day, Valentine's Day, Halloween, Thanksgiving, Black Friday, Christmas, Christmas lingerie, Christmas night, wedding night, honeymoon or any romantic and passionate night.'

(Clothing presentation by the GDOFKH brand)

Prudence received the news with unalloyed delight, and also with discreet relief – she had, Paul said to himself, imagined the worst possible hypothesis, that he would be dismissed; at no point, however, had she talked to him about it. They would to be able to go on holiday, she said, she had been waiting for that for a long time. In fact it hadn't been long since they had started acting as husband and wife, since they had been able to imagine going on holiday together; but if she believed it, if she had really managed to banish the years of separation from her memory, then that was fine.

'There's still an awkward matter in financial terms,' he said at last, because it had to be said. 'I wouldn't be able to touch anything in the way of a salary for a year.'

'You've forgotten something, my darling . . .' She looked at him in disbelief for a few seconds before smiling broadly. 'It's incredible, you've really forgotten . . .! While I think about it at least once a week. From next month we stop paying the mortgage on our apartment; next month we really own it, once and for all. And that mortgage accounted for 35 per cent of our salaries; 35 per cent each. So in fact your taking leave doesn't make much of a difference . . .'

Bank holidays weren't at convenient times that year: 1 and 8 May each fell on a Saturday, and Prudence took a few extra days around 1 May to go to Larmor-Baden.

For no particular reason, her sister knew how to steer a sailing-boat. They took long trips in the gulf, passing l'Île aux Moines to get to l'Île d'Arz, or exploring the scattered little islands separating them from Locmariaquer. During her long stay in Canada, Priscilla had developed quite a business-like attitude that contrasted with French ways of doing things, and her behaviour seemed more typical of the United States, but then again she had lived in Vancouver, in the west of Canada, so basically she wasn't far from Seattle, those parts of the world where the future of humanity is drawn up, or at least its technological future, insofar as humanity has a future. She saw the failure of her marriage as that of an entrepreneurial project; her goals had not been achieved, so a line was to be drawn under that attempt before starting again on new foundations, it wasn't the end of the world, almost everyone failed, sometimes several times, before succeeding. Donald Trump himself had suffered several failures.

They didn't really get on with her sister, but they managed to meet over more fundamental values, in which cultural differences were less important, such as the appropriate assessment of the female body, and when they did their shopping together, Priscilla had no hesitation about expressing firm opinions. 'When you have an ass like that, you show it off,' she said quite frankly. 'If I'd had an ass like yours . . .' she would sometimes imagine out loud. Then Prudence wondered if her destiny had been changed, and it probably had been – this kind of thing can determine a person's destiny, today more than ever, it was more or less the contemporary equivalent of Cleopatra's nose, one really was dealing with a destiny, an unjustifiable genetic particularity very much like a decree from the gods. As for herself, she was aware of it, she had done nothing to deserve her ass. Paul was surprised, and quite honestly aroused, the first time Prudence came back in hot pants, and immediately after dinner he took her into the bedroom to fuck, with an enthusiasm the like of which he hadn't known for ages. She didn't dare to do it again in public, but strangely enough he seemed to accept the combination of T-shirt and bikini bottoms, even in the presence of his nieces, proprieties are a curious thing, and two days later she had no hesitation in moving from the ordinary bikini bottom to a string; to sleep, she took off her bikini string to put on a cotton string, and one of the first things Paul did when he woke up was to expose her – she slept on her belly – and contemplating her buttocks was generally enough to make him hard. Now they made love every morning, not immediately, in fact, it took him a few cups of coffee to put his thoughts in a row, but immediately afterwards he was hard again. In erotic terms there wasn't anything very inventive about their unions, it was just a morning ritual of rediscovery; but it made them immensely happy, Prudence was visibly better, physically better. Now he understood the strange notion of 'marital duty', and he didn't find it entirely ridiculous.

Prudence's father spent his days in a wheelchair placed facing the picture window; his sole activity was to observe the back-and-forth of the waves on the shingle, a movement that was peaceful at the moment, sometimes a little more agitated but never extreme, storms in the gulf were much less violent than on the coast directly facing the ocean. His condition was nothing like that of Paul's father, his brain was unaffected, he could have talked if he had wanted to, but he no longer had anything to say. The death of his wife had been an absolute end as far as he was concerned, his life no longer had any reason to continue in his eyes, but one can live without a reason, in fact it's most commonly the case, and he enjoyed the faint stirring of the waves, as well as that caused by the movements of his daughters and granddaughters – all of his descendants were female, curiously enough. He didn't seem to have moved since their last visit, he was still sitting in the same wheelchair, the only difference being that he now had a book placed beside him, on a side table to his right. It was a book by Cesare Beccaria, *On Crimes and Punishments*. Paul fleetingly wondered how one could read such a thing; in fact he didn't read it, the book was open at the same page from one day to the next, it was largely there as a safety net, just in case some kind of intellectual curiosity passed through his mind. Prudence's father had been a judge, first as a magistrate, then a high court judge, and he had finished his career as the first head of the court of appeal in Versailles. Paul had learned all of this during his stay, or rather he probably knew it but had forgotten; he had never been very interested in his father-in-law. The lack of interest was mutual: the old man had recognized Paul, had given him a little nod, and then resumed contemplating the landscape. With a father who was a judge in Versailles, with his main residence in Ville-d'Avray, a holiday home in Brittany, educated at Sainte-Geneviève, then at Sciences Po and ENA, basically there was nothing surprising about Prudence turning out asexual and vegan. It was her current effort to rediscover her inner feminine that was unusual, and Paul was stunned by her hot pants; few women would have done it at the age of fifty – but it was also true that few women of that age could have got away with it.

It was very easy to look after their father, Priscilla explained: he was independent, he could get up on his own, wash and feed himself without assistance. His washing had in fact become perfunctory, he hadn't had a shower or a bath since coming back from hospital; and he barely ate anything now but yoghurts and a few biscuits. Priscilla's American optimism and dynamism had finally yielded to the evidence that her father was waiting for death, and the only thing to do was to go with him as gently as possible, and that was all.

The day before they went back to Paris, the weather was so fine that Prudence and Priscilla managed to go swimming, and Paul fell asleep in the sun. Walking along a path through a pine forest, he emerged opposite a huge lake. It was, he knew, his birthday, so May or June, but he had forgotten the exact date. It was happening in a new country, probably Canada, the air was still a bit cool, but the sky was perfectly clear. The lake seemed to extend into infinity, its water was a surprising, almost turquoise blue that one would have associated more with tropical landscapes. A gentle slope led to the shore of the lake through a meadow scattered with poppies, daisies and jonquils. Paul took off his shoes and trousers before stepping into the water, as he expected it was cold, but absolutely pure, the sandy bed could be seen perfectly clearly, the slope was extremely gentle, twenty or thirty metres from the shore the water still only came halfway up his calves. He had been walking for five minutes and had covered two or three hundred metres when he stopped, with the water reaching halfway up his thighs. Turning back towards the shore, he saw that the landscape had changed completely: the verdant meadows had disappeared, to be replaced by a flat, muddy surface. There was a pathetic deserted bar near the shore, its windows were shattered and several broken parasols lay in the mud. The sky was low now, leaden, the pine forests on the horizon disappeared into scraps of fog, the water of the lake was opaque and brownish. Coming back towards the shore Paul noticed working-class holidaymakers; they were walking slowly around in the fine, sticky mud along the lake with an expression of total resignation. Yes, one of them told him, they were having a horrible holiday, but it was so much cheaper.

When Prudence woke him, the sun was setting over the Gulf

of Morbihan. Swimming in Brittany in June was unusual, and he reflected that she and her sister would talk about it many times over the years to come. He himself had trouble forgetting his dream, and several times in the course of the following weeks he dreamed that the waters of the Gulf of Morbihan had withdrawn during the night, and the villa in Larmor-Baden was now on the edge of an ocean of mud. Basically he had always been a bit afraid of the sea.

The Beaujolais hills did not make him anxious in the same way, and the following Saturday they went to Saint-Joseph, once again by car. This time Prudence had taken three days off; they planned not to go back to Paris until the following Wednesday evening, which would be close to the first round of the presidential elections. Hervé and Cécile had been back in Arras for a week, Madeleine was now alone with his father, and they had settled into habits that would be theirs until the end. His father spent most of his days in the conservatory, contemplating the landscape, and he probably noticed subtle changes from one day to the next that escaped men more engaged in active life. He read sometimes, with Madeleine's help, and that granted him once again an image of the human world that he had largely left. In the evening Madeleine moved his wheelchair to the stairlift, which meant that he could get to his room. To lift him and place him in the medical bed she had the help of a nurse who came twice a day, in the morning and the evening to help her carry out these manoeuvres. If necessary, she could have done it alone, which would have required a degree of effort, but the nurse lived in Villié-Morgon, which was only a few minutes away. At night the medical bed was next to hers, so she could hold Édouard's hand; the movements of his fingers had increased in variety and precision, and they now amounted almost to a language – but a language that could not have been translated into words, one that expressed emotions more than concepts, closer to music than to articulate language.

Paul had a sense that his father was happy, or at least that the logistical arrangements that had been put in place enabled him to have as pleasant a life as possible, and all life, he thought, is more or less the end of life. Of course Madeleine was the key person, without Madeleine everything would have collapsed in an instant, but still, when the moment came, Paul had had no hesitation in coming up with the funding required to buy the equipment; he had proved to be quite a good son in the end, which had been by no means obvious at the beginning.

While Prudence's father studied the movement of the waves, his own father contemplated the movement of the branches stirred by the wind. It was perhaps less rooted in the ancient mental representations of humanity, less connected to its essential myths; but it was also more varied, more subtle and gentler. Paul definitely preferred the peaceful movements that bring a country landscape to life; he definitely felt greater kinship with lakes and rivers than he did with the sea.

Madeleine still didn't talk much, and Édouard, sitting in his wheelchair at the dining table, was himself a constant source of silence, so their meals sometimes finished without a single word having been uttered, but it didn't matter, it was fine.

The day after they got there, Prudence closed herself away in the kitchen; she had decided to make *oeufs en meurette*, and more generally she planned to get involved in cooking – it was probably the presence of Cécile that had led her in that direction. Cécile was quite charismatic when it came to cooking.

It was her first attempt and it was successful: the *oeufs en meurette* were delicious and easy to eat, they melted in the mouth. Paul struggled with the roast, his right molar was definitely moving a lot, and he felt that it could fall out at any moment, and another tooth on the left, probably a premolar, was starting to show signs of weakness.

'Are you still having toothache, darling?' Prudence had paused all of a sudden, her fork halfway to her mouth.

'Yes, it doesn't feel great this evening.'

'You should make an appointment with your dentist, really, that's been dragging on for too long. Call him when we get back to Paris, will you take care of that?' He nodded with resignation; he had decided to find another dentist. Paul still remembered the day when his dentist had announced that he was going to retire. At the time he hadn't yet met Bruno, his relationship with Prudence was non-existent and his loneliness almost absolute. When the old man had told him that he was giving up work, he had been filled with a terrible wave of disproportionate sadness, he had almost burst into tears at the idea that they would die without seeing each other again, when they had never been particularly close, and their relationship had never gone beyond that of a practitioner and his patient, he couldn't even remember them having a real conversation, or talking about anything that wasn't tooth-related. What he couldn't bear, he had realized uneasily, was impermanence; it was the idea that something, anything, could come to an end; what he couldn't bear was simply one of life's fundamental conditions.

5

On Sunday evening Bruno had invited them to the party following the announcement of the first-round results; it was held at campaign headquarters on Avenue de La Motte-Picquet. It would be better, Paul remarked, if Bruno did not appear beside him. It didn't matter much any more, Bruno replied, because the article had been forgotten by now, but it was true that there would be lots of journalists hanging about in the hall, and if they wished to they could go straight to the apartment.

When they arrived, before 8.00 p.m., Solène Signal was already there, accompanied by her assistant and Raksaneh; her face was blank, she tapped away on her phone and barely noticed them, she was plainly receiving bad news. Sarfati and Bruno went round the room, resting a hand on a shoulder here and there, clearly trying to soften the blow, whatever it might have been.

The results that came in at 8.00 p.m. were not good, in fact: the National Rally candidate was at 27%, Sarfati at 20% and the ecologist at 13% – the candidates of the old parties of the right and left shared out the remaining votes in colourful chaos, they were presented in a random order, and most voters, as a recent poll had shown, were unable to quote their names. They still managed – and in the context that was almost a success – to outstrip the Trotskyists and the Animalists; none of them, however, reached the magic figure of 5% required to keep their deposit.

'The projections for the second round aren't going to shift,'

Solène Signal commented immediately. 'For two weeks we've been exactly 50–50, 51–49 at best, not what I expected, I confess, in fact I'm disappointed,' and as she said these words she looked straight into the eyes of Benjamin Sarfati, at whom these rebukes were plainly directed. Bruno had been useful and even often excellent from start to finish, he had done his share of the job more than adequately, but in certain debates Sarfati had shown genuine shortcomings, on a number of occasions he had missed the point of the question completely; the strategy of using reality TV stars might have been reaching its limits that evening.

Prudence and Raksaneh had made for the buffet, which was almost deserted; on the giant video monitors that covered one wall of the hall the audience could be seen gradually thinning out, and there clearly wasn't much in the way of a party atmosphere. Solène Signal left shortly after summoning everybody for a work meeting at 9.30 the following morning. Sarfati briefly gripped Bruno's shoulder before disappearing as well, somewhat embarrassed. Paul found himself on his own with Bruno in the apartment and opened a bottle of whisky. 'Are you disappointed?' he asked him at last, since he remained silent.

Bruno shrugged before replying: 'Not really; but I would think it was a shame if the National Rally were elected, for the sake of France.' Paul looked at him in surprise: was he trying to avoid the question? No, in fact, he realized immediately, Bruno had simply expressed his opinion: he would consider it a shame, for France, if the National Rally were elected. Where did this conviction come from? From reasoning based on a certain form of economic reality? On the basis of an anti-racist, humanist morality that had been dished out to him? Or more simply from his bourgeois origins? All of these explanations might have come together, but at any rate that conviction was his own, and it was the one that had led him to engage in this electoral battle. Bruno wasn't a cynic; he wasn't an idiot, either, and he was starting to wonder about the deeper motivations of the president. Had he not, by advocating the candidacy of a mediocre intellect such as Sarfati, wanted to facilitate the victory of the National Rally? Had he perhaps anticipated that an assumption of power by the National Rally would lead to a series of catastrophes, an immediate economic and social slump, and that the people would soon call for his reinstatement, his re-election in five years would be assured, it was possible that serious events outside the republican legal framework would ensue, and he would not even have to wait for five years. On the contrary, in the event of a modern government pursuing a policy more or less similar to that of the previous government, one that did not fall outside the 'circle of reason', to use the term of various essay-writers from the previous century, there might be an uncomfortable sense of more of the same; in that case his return to business would become problematic.

Was the president's mind twisted enough to come up with such a scenario? Bruno appeared to think so, and after all he knew him better than Paul did, they had rubbed shoulders for years, and there was nothing reassuring about that. There was also something that Bruno wasn't telling him, because he didn't entirely dare as yet to put it into words, but which ran like a thread through his sentiments. He had come out of the shadows over the course of the campaign, he had developed a talent for public speaking, he had taken a growing pleasure in speaking in front of a crowd, in prompting responses of hilarity, sadness or anger. He had even, on a trip to Strasbourg, led a chorus of several thousand people in a rendition of 'The Marseillaise'. That had surprised everyone, starting with himself, and the only person who might have anticipated such a thing was the president. The president was intelligent, not even his bitterest opponents would have thought of disputing that, but he also knew how to use people, he guessed both their unexplored possibilities and their flaws. He had immediately judged Sarfati quite correctly, seeing him only as a clown, who would be satisfied

375

with the trappings of power; but in all likelihood he had also anticipated the change in Bruno, and the possibility that he might, as he gradually gained in self-assurance, have turned his sights upon the Élysée Palace itself; it wasn't Sarfati's ambitions that the president was afraid of, but Bruno's. The president could not imagine – that was the only limit of his reasoning, his blind spot – someone coming so close to the presidential function without being filled with fascination, a dizzying feeling that would lead one to make it the ultimate purpose of one's existence. Spellbound himself, he could not imagine escaping the spell, and in Bruno's case, as in that of almost all other human beings, at least human beings of the male gender – historically, women had been different, even if that was less and less the case – the president was right, Paul reflected with a sigh.

Prudence and Raksaneh came back from the buffet, apparently getting on splendidly, it was curious the way Prudence had immediately recognized Raksaneh as her counterpart, located in a symmetrical position to her own. Bruno had still said nothing about his relationship with her, but it was completely obvious as far as Prudence was concerned. It's hard to know how women reach conclusions such as this so swiftly, it's probably a matter of pheromones turning themselves into olfactory molecules that spread through the atmosphere, it probably all happened in the nasal cavities. Before they left Bruno asked Paul to promise to come back, the next two weeks would be crucial, in fact it was Sarfati in particular who would be thrust into the heart of the reactor, but he too would be under great pressure, and Paul's visits would do him good. 'I've missed you . . .' he said in the doorway, and it was then that he became aware that Bruno had never come to his place, even though they had been very close over the past few years; he invited him to dinner the following week. He already knew that he would like the apartment; it was only out of pure snobbery that Bruno's wife had insisted on going on living in the very heart of

Saint-Germain after his ministerial nomination. She had never liked their little three-room flat on Rue des Saints-Pères, which they rented for a ridiculously high price, and he was relieved to have chosen to live in his ministerial apartment as soon as their separation had become obvious. In spite of everything, living over his place of work, eradicating any distance, was an extreme solution that women as a rule found disagreeable, and the solution chosen by Paul and Prudence, a quarter of an hour's walk from the ministry, was an excellent compromise.

Bruno had warned him that he would 'be accompanied', which was as far as he could go in terms of intimate trust, and of course they were not at all surprised to see Raksaneh turning up; she herself was not embarrassed in the least, and showed an immediate interest in their apartment, so obviously that Prudence suggested giving her a tour, while Paul offered Bruno a drink. The tour was detailed and technical, taking over half an hour, and when the two women came back to the living room as the sun set over the Parc de Bercy, Raksaneh could only say in an undertone: 'Very nice . . . Really very nice . . .'

The second round was now in ten days; it was almost impossible to avoid the subject, and Paul didn't even try to, in any case he was interested in it, he had recorded about ten hours of debates on the hard disk of his TV box, without taking the time to look at them. While Prudence took care of dinner – she was starting to develop a real taste for cookery – they watched one, which put Sarfati up against some kind of guy on the left, Paul knew him but couldn't quite identify him, probably some sort of rebel, but a famous rebel. Bruno quickly lost interest in the spectacle, and topped up his champagne glass three times during the rest of the programme. Raksaneh, on the other hand, immediately got all her professional instincts back: clutching the remote control, playing with slow motion and pauses, she explained to Paul very clearly what it was that made Sarfati's body language absolutely perfect.

Each time he expressed empathy, mockery and rage, underlining the message with facial expressions, changes in posture and hand gestures that were at once precise, convincing and appropriate; there were obviously years of work behind it all. 'The problem with Ben isn't the wrapping, it's the contents,' she said brutally in conclusion before pressing the stop button; they sat down at the table immediately afterwards.

No, she went on in answer to Paul's question, Solène Signal's concern about the election results was not a sham. Victory for the National Rally was inconceivable, but it had been inconceivable for fifty years, and sometime inconceivable things did happen. The gap between the ruling classes and the population had reached unheard-of levels in small provincial towns and the social movements that had arisen over the past few years were, in her view, only a slow start; besides, racial hatred was soaring in Europe, and that wasn't going to be sorted out anytime soon. Solène gave the impression of being nothing but a Parisian who moved in well-informed circles, deeply compromised within the media elite; but she had preserved certain connections with the working class through her family, and she saw the situation as being genuinely alarming. Those polled had also recently discovered a new way of lying to the pollsters; they declared themselves undecided, with no particularly strong opinion either way, when they did in fact have an opinion, and quite a fixed one. And yet they didn't give the impression of lying: who isn't undecided, at least some of the time?

'You don't think I've overdone the cloves in the daube?' Prudence asked. Paul looked at her in disbelief; her indifference to these subjects still surprised him a little; but when, in all honesty, had he heard Prudence express a political opinion of any kind? As far as one could tell, she didn't give a damn about any of it. Raksaneh knew enough about cloves, however, and reassured her: cloves actually were difficult to manage, and as it happened there was a taste of them but not too much, just the right amount, in her opinion. Bruno in turn delivered compliments that were doubtless sincere, but where gastronomy was concerned his experience barely went beyond the four-cheese pizza. The electoral marathon was almost over for him now, Sarfati would be alone at the front right to the end; there would just be a big meeting, three days before the election, the last meeting of the campaign in fact, in which many government ministers would be involved. His own speech would be the longest along with Sarfati's, they had allowed for twenty-five minutes, but yes, he was starting to feel he'd got the hang of it. 'Then . . . if it all goes well, I'll be able to get back to my files.' He had a strange, shy little smile, his eyes met Raksaneh's and they both looked awkwardly away, they had thought the same thing at the same time, he would get back to his files, certainly, but something else had appeared in their lives. Regardless of the extent of their cultural differences, they shared a very old and very strange belief, which has survived the collapse of all the civilizations, and almost all beliefs: when one enjoys the benefit of a lucky chance, an unexpected gift from fate, the important thing is to say nothing, and above all not to be proud about it, for fear that the gods might take umbrage and press their hand. They sat in silence for a moment, heads lowered, then Raksaneh looked up at Bruno. Paul had never noticed that her eyes were such an intense green, an absolute emerald green – their intensity was almost frightening. Bruno slowly raised his head and looked right into her eyes. No one moved, Prudence held her breath, and for a few seconds total silence reigned around the table.

6

Cécile and Hervé never came to Paris, and for their rare visit Paul had planned a typical tourist programme, the kind one reserves for one's family from the provinces: a boat trip on the Seine, visits to museums, dinner in a restaurant on the Île Saint-Louis. It wasn't until Friday afternoon, a few hours before they were due to turn up, that he remembered that Hervé had studied in Paris, like Cécile, that that, in fact, was where they had met, and most importantly that Cécile, like him, had spent most of her childhood in Paris, how had he managed to forget that? Had the others only ever been a faint, ghostly presence for him, which reached his awareness only occasionally? It was probably true in the case of Aurélien; but he regretted it a little about Cécile. To tell the truth, it wasn't only the others that he had trouble remembering; there must have been a school that he went to as a child, a college, a lycée; he had forgotten them completely. Even the apartment where they had lived in Paris evoked only the vaguest images in him, as inconsistent as they were indistinct, which could have come out of a black-and-white film from the 1940s. His memories, his real childhood memories, all brought him back to the house in Saint-Joseph.

It was true that in the case of Cécile it was easy to forget her Parisian past: meeting her, anyone would immediately have been sure that she came from the provinces, more precisely the north – the ch'tis, as they are known. The people of that region were known for their warm and welcoming nature; but even within this context she had shown herself to be highly adaptable.

Like all people of Nord-Pas-de-Calais, Hervé and Cécile defended their region tooth and nail, arguing not only the generally acknowledged hospitality of its inhabitants, but also its beauty, and the architectural splendours testifying to a former prosperity, chiefly connected, in the case of Arras, with the cloth-making industry. Their city thus had two magnificent baroque squares, one overlooked by a belfry that was a UNESCO world heritage site, and it was Arras that had the greatest density of historical monuments in France – which always surprised visitors. At the same time, they never ceased to emphasize the poverty, the unemployment and even the substandard medical health that ravaged the region. What they felt, as most of the inhabitants of the Nord-Pas-de-Calais region did, was an opposition so violent that it sometimes resembled a cognitive dissonance; it could not, however, have been called schizophrenia, because those two aspects included equal shares of reality. In this instance it was the reality that was schizophrenic.

Hervé and Cécile's relationship with Paul's political life was also a bit schizophrenic. They could not have been unaware of his connections with the circles closest to the state apparatus, to the government – the old government, of course, but which would in all likelihood become the government again, the one whose political directions they entirely disapproved of; but that was of no importance in their eyes.

Hervé had seen Nicolas again several times, and his liking for handguns did worry him sometimes, but the fact remained that without him they would never have met Brian, that they could not have acted alone, and that Édouard would probably have been dead by now. He had no intention of immersing himself in militancy again, however; he liked his new job as an insurance salesman. Insurance is an often necessary expense in the eyes of the law, and for the poor, and often very poor, people who constituted his clientele, they made terrible inroads into their budgets. He enjoyed guiding his clients through the swamp of guarantees, helping them not to be swindled excessively by the insurance companies whose greed and cynicism were generally boundless, in short he did his work as well as he could, just as he had done in his work as a notary, his life had a structure and a focus once again – and that too he owed to Nicolas.

Serious and hard-working, Bruno and Hervé loved everyone in their country, but they occupied opposing political camps. Paul knew that his reflections were vain, he had had these thoughts dozens of times without reaching any appreciable result. However the situation did not strike him as particularly symmetrical. He shared Bruno's commitment, he too would vote for Sarfati in both rounds, but he was aware that it was a non-choice, a banal allegiance to current opinion. But the choice was not absurd, the majority choice is sometimes the best, just as in roadside cafés it is usually best to go for the meal of the day, without engaging in passionate debates, and equally, over the weekend, there was nothing passionate about their political conversations. There were some, however, if only because Hervé and Cécile imagined that he had access to information inaccessible to ordinary mortals, and of course they wanted to know what it was. Paul didn't think he had any secrets, but he realized with surprise that he actually did: the mere fact, for example, that the president planned to run for election again in five years, that Sarfati was only a stopgap solution, was quite obvious to him; but of course it had never been publicly announced.

On Sunday morning they had planned to visit Anne-Lise; they returned enchanted. She had a lovely studio flat near the Jardin des Plantes, tastefully furnished. She would be presenting her thesis in less than a month, and thought she would be able to find a job as a junior employee at the end of the summer break. In short, she was coping well and they had no reason to be concerned about her. In fact, Paul reflected, that girl was leading her life with a remarkable degree of intelligence and rationality. He didn't think that in the long term rationality was compatible with happiness, in fact he was almost certain that in every case it led to complete despair; but Anne-Lise was still far from the age where life forces us to make a choice and, if she was still capable of doing so, to bid farewell to reason.

As he accompanied Hervé and Cécile to the Gare du Nord, Paul said to himself that his relationship with his sister was essentially of the same order as the one he had with his father: indestructible and leading nowhere. Nothing would ever be able to interrupt it; but neither could anything make it go beyond a certain degree of intimacy; so in that sense it was exactly the opposite of a marital relationship. Family and marriage: those were the two residual poles around which the lives of the last Westerners were organized in the first half of the twenty-first century. Other solutions had been imagined, in vain, by people who had had the merit of sensing that the old solutions were worn out, even if they could not come up with new ones, and whose role in history had therefore been entirely negative. The liberal doxa persisted in ignoring the problem, in the naive belief that the lure of material gain could be substituted for any other human motivation, and could on its own supply the mental energy necessary for the maintenance of a complex social organization. This was quite plainly false, and it seemed obvious to Paul that the whole system was going to come crashing down, even if one could not at present predict the date or the manner in which this might occur – but the date could be close, and the manner violent. So he found himself in that strange situation in which he was working steadily, and even with a certain devotion towards the maintenance of a social system which he knew was condemned beyond repair, and probably not in the very long term. Those thoughts, however, far from keeping him awake at night, usually plunged him into a state of intellectual fatigue that led him quickly to sleep.

Surprisingly, hidden away inside quite an ugly neo-Gothic church, like those built in the nineteenth century, and which might have been the Basilica of St Clotilde, in the seventh arrondissement of Paris, there was a genuine Carolingian necropolis, guarded by fierce dogs. Paul was called to carry out a mission there, knowing all the while that the dogs would devour him if he was not the elect of God. People leaving the church expressed contradictory opinions on the subject: a first one, in the robes of an archpriest, stressed the severity and intransigence of the dogs; a second, dressed as a tramp, said that in reality the dogs hardly ever ate anyone. However both, mysteriously, were expressing the same point of view.

Finally entering the church that might have been the Basilica of St Clotilde, Paul found the entrance to the necropolis without any difficulty. Huge and silent, the dogs watched suspiciously as he passed, but without making the slightest movement. On the wall, his torch revealed to him, there were geometrical decorations reminiscent of 1970s science fiction. A raised ledge held niches containing mummies in a poor state of conservation. Paul understood at that moment that his mission involved climbing the wall to the ledge. Midway through his climb he felt threatened by danger of some kind, but he managed to grip the end of a firefighter's ladder; extremely flexible, the ladder immediately extended into the air, and Paul found himself on a small platform, about forty metres above street level, which communicated with some scaffolding structures. A seven-year-old child was quickly climbing the ladder after him, holding a butcher's knife; having come level with Paul, he plunged it into his thigh. Blood flowed copiously, but Paul managed to pull out the knife. Crazed with fear at the idea of his response, the child quickly climbed back down several rungs of the ladder, but Paul threw the knife into the street, forty metres below; then the child sat down his heels and studied him contemptuously,

384

before being knocked down and overtaken by two men in their thirties wearing bowler hats, who climbed the ladder at great speed. Coming level with Paul, they introduced themselves to him as a director and his actor. Shortly afterwards, their doppelgangers arrived via the scaffolding, they all clustered together on the platform, which turned out to be wider than expected. Then the four men talked together animatedly, apparently having forgotten Paul's presence, each one showing the others impressive weapons, like retractable razors, with naive wonder.

Driving along the street below, which was in fact a wide boulevard full of people, was a vehicle in the form of a fortress. At the top of the keep, a number of men were unfolding a long, stiff metal wire that cut like a razor across the whole width of the boulevard. Without the slightest difficulty, the wire severed the torsos of the people strolling along the boulevard, leaving heaps of corpses in the vehicle's wake. One of the men beside Paul on the platform spoke of 'Sammy the Butcher' with naive admiration, as if the mere mention of the name might ensure his safety. In that he was wrong, because a metal wire of the same kind was now being unfolded in mid-air from the fortress vehicle, and threatening them dangerously. Immediately afterwards, the conversation took a philosophical, indeed theological turn: in reality, the occupants of the fortress vehicle had nothing to do with Sammy the Butcher, who was merely a popular superstition without any attestable foundation; they were members of a rational cult based on the dispersal of elements that made up living creatures, to allow the creation of new structures, and whose only sacrament was murder. In the middle of the conversation a siren went off at regular intervals, probably summoning the fire engine, which would enable them to escape the danger threatening them at great speed.

Paul was finally woken by the ringing of his mobile phone. He had left it downstairs and could only hear the noise faintly. How long had the phone been ringing for? Prudence was sleeping peacefully beside him.

'Paul?' Bruno said as soon as he picked up. 'I'm sorry, I know it's five o'clock in the morning.'

'I imagine it's serious.'

'Yes. I think it's going to interrupt the presidential campaign.'

Bruno waited for a few seconds before going on. There had been a new attack, announced by a new message on the internet. The message had probably appeared at about four o'clock in the morning, and this time it had been distributed very widely, the video was really everywhere. It would be on the news channels in half an hour at the most.

'What's so serious about it?' Paul said, surprised. 'That's already the fourth attack.'

'The third, if you only count the ones accompanied by an internet message.'

'OK, the third; but still, the novelty's starting to wear off a little.'

'Yes. Except that this time five hundred people are dead.'

7

*'Severe towards himself, the revolutionary must also be
severe towards others. Any tender and soothing sense of
kinship, friendship, love, gratitude and even honour
must be stifled by cold revolutionary passion alone. For
him there is one sole delight, one sole consolation,
reward or satisfaction: the triumph of the revolution.'*

(*Sergey Netchayev*, Catechism of a Revolutionary)

For some years, the boats loaded with African migrants
bound for Europe had stopped reaching Sicily, landing
having been rendered impossible by Italian navy ships. The
people smugglers had therefore regrouped around Oran, in the
area controlled by Algerian jihadists, and were trying to reach
the Spanish coast between Almería and Cartagena. The Spanish
government, now socialist once again after various changeovers,
welcomed them, not least because almost all of them were Fran-
cophone, and their goal was to cross the border as quickly as
possible – the Pyrenees offered many access routes to France which
were impossible to check in reality; those grim and massive mountains, while they might have been able to prevent any large-scale
military invasion, were still vulnerable to clandestine infiltration.
The only danger that the migrants faced came not from the authorities but from local militias armed with baseball bats and knives – it

was not a rare occurrence for an African, venturing out alone from his camp, to have his throat cut or be beaten to death, and as a rule the police showed little eagerness in hunting down the perpetrators, and the Spanish media themselves barely mentioned the event, which had by now become a part of local customs.

The torpedoed boat had been heading on a northeasterly trajectory, and was sunk off the Balearics, more precisely some thirty nautical miles east of the narrow strait separating Ibiza from Formentera. Flat and in a state of disrepair, the boats employed by the people smugglers bore no relation to modern container carriers, and a low-powered, surface-launched torpedo was enough to destroy them – an ordinary rocket launcher, in fact, would have done the job. Cut in two by the impact, the boat had sunk immediately, and most of the passengers – the figure of five hundred was only an approximation – had died within the first few minutes.

The video posted on the internet – there had probably been two cameras located on the front of the boat that had launched the torpedo, one filming in long shot, while the other went close in – went on to show the drowning of the hundred or so people who had survived the initial impact. The shot gave a curious impression of neutrality. It did not dwell excessively on the agony of each of these men and women – the children had died almost immediately – but made no attempt to minimize it. Sometimes one or other of the victims would approach the boat that was filming them. They weren't really asking for help, no cries were heard, the video had no soundtrack save for the bleak and repetitive slap of the waves against the bow, but they mutely held out their hands. Then there was a burst of machine-gun fire, more with a view to keeping them at a distance – but sometimes a bullet would strike them, which took care of their fate.

The sequence as a whole – focusing in sequence on each individual death-throe, the boat moving from one swimmer to the next until the last was submerged – lasted a little over forty minutes, but few web users were likely to reach the end, apart from those who never tired of witnessing the death of African migrants.

Paul could tell immediately that Bruno was not exaggerating when he said that the global impact of these images would be considerable. He came back into the bedroom; Prudence seemed almost awake and he gave her a summary of what had happened. She didn't really react, she blinked weakly before snuggling up again under the blanket and going back to sleep; she probably hadn't heard him.

Reaching his office at six o'clock in the morning, Martin-Renaud had been able only to telephone his subordinates to summon them as quickly as possible, and to suffer the minister's reprimands on the telephone. He had no reply to give, his services had accomplished nothing, in fact, they still had no trail, no valid clue eight months after the start of their inquiry; the only thing he could say in his defence was that the other secret services, all over the world, had done no better.

Doutremont had started the day badly, unkempt and unshaven, he had clearly got dressed very quickly, and he appeared utterly shaken more than anything else. The video had spread across the internet with an unparalleled speed and violence, it had managed for a time to freeze global traffic, they had used means utterly unknown to him, it was unprecedented, he was truly at a loss.

The situation appeared equally incomprehensible to Martin-Renaud from an ideological point of view. After the attack on the container carriers, suspicion might have fallen on an ultra-leftist group; it was surprising that they had the technical means, but it was still a possibility. By contrast the second attack, the one on the sperm bank, suggested a trail leading to fundamentalist Catholics; that is, logistically speaking, more or less nowhere. But in this case, who was one to suspect? The indignation would be universal. White supremacists? Three clueless idiots barely capable of tying their shoelaces, organizing an attack that would resonate around the world, paralysing the internet for almost a quarter of an hour? It didn't make sense.

Sitbon-Nozières was there too, and by contrast he seemed in great form, rested and fresh, his suite impeccable as always; he didn't share the pessimism of his colleagues. Long passages from the writings of Kaczynski, he explained, had been quoted in *2083*, the manifesto of Anders Behring Breivik, the far-right Norwegian killer. There was an eco-fascist movement that saw the human race, as well as other social species, as being made up of naturally hostile tribes, constantly fighting for territorial control. That idea had already been explored by Maximine Portaz, a French intellectual from the mid-twentieth century. Like Theodore Kaczynski, Maximine Portaz had a solid mathematical training; her doctoral thesis was based on the work of Gottlob Frege and Bertrand Russell. A convert to Hinduism, she had married a Brahman and taken the name Savitri Devi, which meant 'sun goddess'. A fervent admirer of Hitler, she also anticipated the theories of deep ecology in her writings.

Viewed from an eco-fascist perspective, Sitbon-Nozières continued enthusiastically, the last two attacks had perfectly complementary goals: artificial reproduction and immigration were the two means used by contemporary societies to make up for the fall in their fertility rates. Modern countries like Japan and Korea inclined towards artificial reproduction, while technically less advanced countries, such as those of western Europe, resorted to immigration. Both instances achieved the goal sought by capitalism: a slow but continuous growth in the world population, which meant that that growth objectives could be fulfilled and investments were guaranteed a suitable yield. The only alternative was an eco-fascist ideology like that of Savitri Devi, or one that was openly primitivist and anti-growth like Kaczynski's, a synthesis between the two being entirely imaginable. These movements could also be considered as being close to nihilism, insofar as they were aimed above all at creating chaos, convinced that the resulting world would inevitably be a better one; and for nihilists, at a given moment, it was necessary to commit truly shocking acts, prompting unanimous disapproval – such as the murder of children – to separate genuine militants from mere sympathizers.

'Quite honestly, I have my doubts . . .' Martin-Renaud objected; he didn't look as if he had fully woken up either. Sitbon-Nozières was a specialist in nihilism so it was no surprise that he should tend to see nihilists everywhere; in fact he was starting to wonder if he had done the right thing in taking on a graduate from the ENS. 'Intellectually that holds together,' he acknowledged, 'but how many people does that mean on a global scale? Ten? Twenty?'

'You don't necessarily need many at this point,' Sitbon-Nozières replied. 'With the internet, a handful of competent and deter- mined people can obtain major results. Breyvik was a man acting on his own, and the attack on Utøya resonated around the world. Today more than ever, power resides in intelligence and knowledge; and these ultra-minority ideologies are the very ones most likely to attract superior minds. If you imagine someone like Kaczynski today, thirty years later, as gifted in computing as Kaczynski was in maths, he could do considerable damage on his own. For some attacks, it's true, a certain amount of finance is required; but it's not impossible to find. The attack on the Danish sperm bank, for example, did a great amount of harm to all the biotechnology companies working on human reproduction; and, in a given market, playing for a fall can bring in just as much as playing for a rise, if not more, it's a classic financial strategy. People who sold their shares in the Danish company in good time probably made a lot of money; that would be tempting to some people.'

Martin-Renaud gave him a worried look; he now seemed quite alert. Biotechnology was one thing; but for people who played for a fall on the Chinese export market, the yield must have been vast;

and in his career he had met financiers who would have had no hesitation in mounting operations of this kind. If his subordinate was correct, the dangers still to come were worse than anything they had been able to imagine.

'So this is how I see it,' Sitbon-Nozières went on. 'A strategic alliance between people who want to cause chaos, and who have the technical know-how to achieve it, and others who stand to benefit from it, and who can supply the finance to make it happen. Furthermore, it's getting easier and easier to disrupt the working of the system. In the near future, for example, companies using container vessels will probably abandon the idea of a human crew except for entering ports. A human crew would in any case be incapable of intervening to avoid a collision, since the inertia of the ships is too great; a satellite guiding system is more efficient and much more economic; as soon as one uses a system of this kind, it becomes possible to pirate it.'

He fell silent, and they pondered this perspective for a moment. Martin-Renaud, lost in anxious contemplation of the futurist landscape of chrome and glass stretching behind the picture window, reflected that his subordinate was right: the means of attack were advancing faster than the means of defence; the order and security of the world were going to become increasingly difficult to guarantee.

By the time Paul got to his office at seven o'clock in the morning, Bruno had already been on the phone to the Ministry of the Interior, the prime minister and the president; they in turn had had conversations with their counterparts abroad. By and large, they were tending towards the idea of a global commemoration, not far from the location of the shipwreck. 'At least it was in the open sea, they won't have those fucking candles . . .' Bruno said with horror; the remark surprised Paul, who had also been repelled at the time of the Islamist attacks by the flood of candles, balloons, poems,

'You won't have my hate', etc. He thought it was entirely legitimate to hate jihadists, to hope that they were killed in large numbers, and to contribute to that where possible, in fact the desire for revenge seemed to him to be an entirely appropriate reaction. He didn't know Bruno at the time; he hadn't yet become a member of the government, he had never had an opportunity to talk to him about it subsequently, and he didn't know that he too had struggled with this outpouring of soothing codswallop.

'In short,' Bruno went on, 'their plan is to dump roses, huge wreaths of roses fixed to buoys, it's easily done by helicopter, the president's office has already done a costing. It's going to happen in the presence of heads of state, they think they can round up a hundred and fifty, or at least a hundred; the biggest ones will be there, the United States, China, India, Russia, the pope of course, he's in, he called back in five minutes, but to hold them all we're going to need an aircraft carrier, only an aircraft carrier provides a big enough surface, in the open sea, so that the TV stations can broadcast the picture. And as luck would have it, France is the only country capable of getting an aircraft carrier there quickly enough, we have one stationed at Toulon, the *Jacques-Chirac*, it could be there tomorrow. To cut a long story short, the president is going to increase his international standing, a week before he is due to leave office; he's really played a blinder, I've talked to Solène Signal, she'll be here at six, she was openly admiring, it's a brilliant communications coup on a global level, it really is.

'After the dumping of the roses there will be singers, also on the platform of the aircraft carrier, and there too they've planned for lots of them, a hundred again, the same number as the heads of state, and all genres all mixed up together: rap, classical, hard rock, international variety; in terms of music they've been thinking of 'Ode to Joy', which might just do it – 'Alle Menschen werden Brüder' always puts everybody in the mood. In short, you see, they've been doing a huge amount of work, since six this morning.'

'And the electoral campaign?'

'Oh that . . .' Bruno gave a mocking smile. 'All I've understood so far is that it was inappropriate to broach the subject. It's more or less the only thing that Solène said to me on the phone, before adding, "Keep your mouth shut apart from anything else, no statement, no declaration, you keep your mouth shut till I get there."'

She actually turned up a few minutes later, very early, but she seemed completely fired up, and for the first time Paul was able to see her unaccompanied by her assistant. However he too arrived shortly afterwards, he looked as if he was doing more or less all right, his tie was just slightly loose. You recover more quickly at twenty-five than you do at fifty, that's for sure. Wasn't it time for Solène Signal to *pass the baton*? Paul thought fleetingly. But to do what? Write her memoirs, given that she had so many secrets? No, that was impossible, communication advisers never do that, they never talk, any more than press attachés do, and that aptitude for keeping secrets is why they are generally women.

'Well, my darlings . . .' She slumped into one of the armchairs, and all of a sudden she really looked like an old woman, thighs spread like that. 'I just had Ben on the phone and he's understood the instructions – grief, caution, silence; anyway we leave the president to do what he wants, that idiot knows what's needed. So the campaign's over, we pack up our bags, we just have to wait till Sunday. The other side are doing the same, we're stopping everything, no meetings, national unity, president on TV. I think they're going to organize their thing on the aircraft carrier the day after tomorrow, even Israel will be there.

'OK, I know what you're going to ask me . . .' she went on after a long silence. 'You're not even going to ask me about it, you know it already, you just want me to confirm it. So yeah, I can confirm that it's going to be good for us, it's likely, it's even definite. Obviously that little kid from the National Rally is going to squeak like a skunk, he's already started this morning on RTL, he was proclaiming his disgust and indignation, I heard it and I thought he was really good, and it's true that he didn't deserve it, but there's nothing he can do about it, he's paying for his party's past, the softie humanists are going to wake up and try and block him, he's just set his sights on another ten points. So yes, we've won,' she said, shaking her head with genuine sadness, it seemed to Paul, it was the first time he thought he had seen her expressing a genuine feeling. 'I'm always happy to win; that's my job, and I was born for it. But I confess that I would rather have won in a different way.'

8

The commemoration ceremony was held on Wednesday, two days later; no head of state had declined to come, and it was rebroadcast by all the news channels. To nobody's surprise, the commentator had decided to centre his speech on dignity, it was some years since dignity had had wind in its sails, but this time everyone agreed that the president was going at full blast, his level of dignity had been quite exceptional. After a few minutes Paul turned the sound off. When people who clearly disagree on all points come together to celebrate certain words, and the word 'dignity' was a perfect example, it means that those words have lost all meaning, Paul said to himself. A dazzling sun was making the surface of the *Jacques-Chirac* gleam; the camera did a slow, curved tracking shot to follow from a constant distance the front row of the heads of state – he recognized the American president and his Chinese counterpart, side by side; the Russian president was a little further behind. The French president, however, was positioned at the very front of the curve, in the foreground in every shot; from a comms point of view it was actually a total success.

The news channels would also be devoted to the attacks on Thursday, the attacks would be the subject of the moment and the news channels can only deal with one subject at a time over a given period, it's one of the limitations of the news channels. There might be a bit of politics on Friday, two days away from the second round, but it wouldn't be long, it all had to break off on Saturday in line with the law. The result was up for grabs, but still the big opinion-makers would be there on Sunday evening, they would be circulating from one platform to another so that everything got done. Psephologists would engage in detailed analyses of the geographical distribution of the votes, which would add nuance to the already outdated analyses of Christophe Guilluy, although without invalidating them. For Paul, the sound of the working of democracy was like a faint murmur.

Prudence came back shortly after five in the afternoon. 'We're going to be able to take a holiday,' she said, once he had informed her of recent developments. Her indifference to any political or indeed historical event continued to startle him; it might have been the result of so many years spent in the head office of the Treasury, Paul said to himself; his own appointment to the cabinet, and then Bruno's deep involvement in the presidential campaign, had by contrast brought him closer to the world of the media, of the show, the elements of language; he was inches away from meeting the big compassionate thinkers, the social justice warriors; at least he had met people who knew them.

'We could go back to Brittany, or go off somewhere, as you wish. It's the last opportunity we'll have, for some time at least.' It was true, the electoral pause was coming to an end, and from the following Monday things would start turning again at the ministry, at an increasing rate.

'To Brittany . . .' he said at last. 'I'd like to go back to Brittany.' He wanted to see Prudence in hot pants again, then drag her into the bedroom, take off her hot pants and fuck her, perhaps he even needed to do that, no, he didn't need to, he just wanted to, Epicurus had definitely been right on that point as on so many others, sex was one of the goods that were 'natural and not necessary', from men's point of view at least, for women it seemed to be more of a need, or at least that was the impression he had. Prudence at any rate looked visibly better since he'd been fucking her every day, her movements were more alert, even her complexion looked more luminous, fresher, Priscilla had even said, on their last stay in Brittany: 'You're ten years younger.'

Brittany was also suitable because he had no desire to discover new places, new landscapes; instead he felt a need to reflect, to take a good look at his life, a sort of inventory. This leave would remain, he knew, a unique moment in his life, soon there would no longer be any reason to extend it, the little scandal unleashed by his sister-in-law was already forgotten, and Aurélien had plainly died for nothing. He hadn't lived for much either, few things would act as testimony of his passage on the earth; Paul had been sad to learn from a phone call to Cécile that Maryse had decided to go back to Benin, without waiting to find out if she was going to face a disciplinary procedure. She was a bit disgusted with France, and that was understandable; it might have been taking it too far to say that France had broken her heart, there were still reserves of love in her heart, but they were inevitably reduced.

'When could we go?' he asked Prudence, and she looked at him with surprise; he was usually the one who decided that kind of thing. 'I'm on leave . . .' he reminded her gently; from now on it was up to her to decide their timetable, his days were completely clear. At that moment he understood, without really sharing it, what it was that had humiliated Hervé during his long period of unemployment. Bruno had been an excellent minister, he had really revived the French economy, its GDP, its balance of trade, but perhaps he hadn't paid enough attention to the issue of unemployment, and that had nearly cost them the election.

'Tomorrow morning,' Prudence said after thinking for a while, 'and we could leave on Thursday morning and stay till Sunday evening.'

'I need to vote, though.'

'Yeah, yeah. It closes at eight, you'll be able to vote,' she replied with an indulgent smile, as if responding to some insignificant childish whim.

He visited Bruno the following morning; the dressing table and the runner had disappeared from his work apartment, but Raksaneh was there, she emerged briefly from the bathroom at one point with a towel tied around her waist, and smiled at him before disappearing into the bedroom. Bruno was already thinking about the composition of the next government, which would be appointed very shortly after the election – always giving the impression of a commando operation, everyone focused and every minute counting for the revival of France, that was a comms trick that hadn't aged. Sarfati had hardly anything to say, in fact he hardly knew anyone on the political staff, it was becoming more and more obvious that Bruno would be the one really in charge, and he listened with his usual concentration to what Paul had come to say to him.

'So unemployment . . .' he replied at last with a long sigh. 'Do you think it's really important? Do you think that's what's boosting the National Rally?'

'There's immigration too, of course. But unemployment plays a part too, yes, I'm worried about it.'

'I think you're right; and it's the worst problem we need to solve. Productivity is going to go on rising in industrial workplaces, it's the only possible outcome, there's no coming back from increased productivity. There's only one solution, which is to create relatively unqualified jobs in services, but not the ones that exist already; cleaners, private tutors, we can't count on those, they'll always be part of the grey economy. We need to create them in administration, and grant massive fiscal advantages to companies that create them. We need delivery men, motor mechanics, craftsmen, people who really help you, people who repair things, who answer the phone; at the same time, we need to put the brakes on robotization and uberization; it's basically another model of society. If we do all that, we can bring down unemployment, but we're going to need a huge amount of money. We also need to make savings, we can't escape budgetary orthodoxy, I don't need to tell you that, given that you've spent ten years in the budget department. We'll need a radical reduction of certain expenses.'

'Got any ideas?'

'National education is probably the biggest budget, we have too many teachers. So it's not easy . . .'

No, it wasn't easy, but Bruno seemed happy to be getting back to work, resuming the normal course of his life; he would be able to get a divorce, and that wasn't negligible either. Paul, for his part, was essentially happy to take a long break, at least that was what he had thought until now. They were silent for a moment, but he was filled with deep sadness at the idea of leaving the room in a few minutes, walking down the corridors of the ministry in the other direction, and crossing the main courtyard towards the exit. He hadn't been very happy in these offices, at least not before meeting Bruno, but it isn't the fact of having been happy in a place that makes the prospect of leaving it painful, it's simply the fact of leaving it, of leaving part of your life behind, however bleak or even unpleasant it might have been, to see it plunging into the void; in other words it's the fact of getting older. As he said good-bye, he had the absurd impression that this was a definitive farewell, that in one way or another he would never see Bruno again, that an unforeseen piece in the configuration of things would oppose it.

'The economic situation is good, which leaves you room for manoeuvre, isn't that right?' he added for no precise reason, mostly to prolong the conversation, when he was filled with a vast and inexpressible weariness.

'Oh yes, it's excellent,' Bruno replied without real joy. 'It has never been better, in fact. I shouldn't say so, but essentially the attacks have been to our advantage. After the first one, exports from the Asian countries dropped, obviously, and our trade balance stabilized. The second one didn't affect us, France stands outside the market for artificial reproduction. As to the third one, it's a horrible thing to say, but immigration is going to come to a halt, and in electoral terms that's entirely in our favour. Economically, I'm not sure that it's good news, or rather it's a complicated calculation that depends on a large number of factors, chiefly demographics and unemployment rates; but electorally it's perfect.'

'Do you really think that's going to dissuade migrants?'

'Of course. I know what people are saying: "They're so poor, they're willing to take any kind of risk", etc. That's wrong. First of all they aren't as poor as all that, most of them are reasonably affluent graduates, the middle classes of their country of origin, trying to emigrate to Europe. And they aren't taking every risk, they calculate their risks. They have a perfect understanding of the way we work, guilt, residual Christianity, etc. They know they'll probably be picked up by a humanitarian boat, and that there will always be a European country to take them in. They take big risks, definitely, shipwrecks aren't infrequent, some of the boats they take are in a wretched state; but they don't take *all* risks. And that's where they're going to have to introduce a new element into their calculations.'

'Violence works, is that what you're getting at?'

'Yes, violence is the engine of history, there's nothing new about that, it's as true now as it was in Hegel's day. Having said that, it works in what way? We still don't know what people want. Destruction for destruction's sake? Unleashing a cataclysm? Do you remember one of the first videos, the one in which I was guillotined?'

'Very clearly, yes. It was from that point that we started taking an interest in the messages.'

'There was something insane, something truly chilling, about the staging of that film. I felt as if I was looking at the madness of someone who has no limits, and that was a shock. Of course there was also the fact that I wasn't very happy to feel as hated as that.'

'We've sorted that one out at least. Right now people like you, I expect you've noticed. What was seen as coldness has turned into seriousness, remoteness has become overarching vision, indifference has made way for level-headedness . . . You're more popular than Sarfati right now.'

Bruno nodded without a word, because there is no reasonable comment to be made about the fluctuations of public opinion. Nothing had been gained, he knew; the free circulation of information tends to introduce entropy into the working of hierarchical guidance systems, and in the end to destroy them. So far he had not made a single mistake; in the end he had opposed the plan for photographic sessions using his father's house in the Oise, and had never appeared in *Paris Match*; nothing had come out about his relationship with his wife, or indeed about the existence of Raksaneh. The anecdote about the abduction of Paul's father, providing neither large-scale financial impropriety nor salacious gossip, short, in other words, of spectacular elements except for a few Catholic fundamentalists 'who no longer gave anyone a hard-on', in the words of Solène Signal, had quickly deflated.

From the next day onwards, the president would utter some sympathetic, humanistic words, which might even be remarkable and poetic, about the European dream and sorrow, about the Mediterranean, where the southern winds blew ashes of shame and remorse; a few days later the second round would be held. The president would disappear, aware of having prepared his return as well as possible; the transfer of power would be accomplished in a relaxed and even a friendly manner. Then the real work would begin; Paul was right, Bruno said to himself, the variable of unemployment would have to be returned to the forefront of his calculations, he had neglected it for too long. The equation was already complex, and was about to become more so; he was far from unhappy at the prospect.

9

It was nearly eight o'clock, and Doutremont was about to leave his office, when he received a call from Delano Durand. He had something, he announced, that he would like to show them. Yes, it could wait until the next day; he would need a room with an overhead projector.

Doutremont left a message for Martin-Renaud, and they met up at nine o'clock the following day in a little meeting room adjacent to his office. When Durand arrived, five minutes late, Doutremont nearly gasped out loud as he observed that his appearance had not improved in the slightest: his running gear was still just as filthy, his hair still as long and greasy. 'Delano Durand, one of our new colleagues, I've just taken him on . . .' he said apologetically to Martin-Renaud.

'A curious first name, were your parents admirers of Roosevelt?' Martin-Renaud didn't seem otherwise surprised by the appearance of his subordinate.

'Yes, my father saw him as the greatest politician of the twentieth century,' Durand replied before setting down a thin file on the desk in front of him. He took out a sheet of paper and put it on the surface of the overhead projector before switching it on; it was the image of Baphomet, which they had found in Édouard Raison's file at the Belleville clinic. 'What we have on Baphomet's forehead,' he began immediately, 'is a starred pentagon, or pentagram. As I explained to you last time,' he said, turning briefly

404

towards Doutremont, 'the shift from the regular pentagon, the one found in the internet messages, to the starred pentagon, symbolizes the shift from the lay stage to the initiate stage.' He took the image of Baphomet off the surface of the projector and replaced it with a map of Europe on which three points were marked in red. 'What we have here is the geographical location of the three attacks spread by internet message: the Chinese container vessel off La Coruña, the Danish sperm bank located at Aarhus, and the migrant boat between Ibiza and Formentera. The first interesting thing to note is that these three points can be connected by a circle . . .' He projected a second sheet with the circle drawn on it.

'Isn't that always the case?' asked Martin-Renaud. Durand looked at him in amazement, stunned by such ignorance. 'No, of course not,' he said at last. 'You can always put a circle around any two points; but that isn't generally the case with groups of three points: only a very few can appear on the circumference of a particular circle with a defined centre.'

'You haven't marked the centre on your diagram . . .' said Martin-Renaud.

'No, that's true.' He studied his map for a moment. 'As it happens it's in France, in the Indre or the Cher, so pretty much at the geographical centre of the country. I must say that it's quite strange . . .' He looked slightly flustered, then continued. 'So, we might deal with the centre in a moment, but that's not what I wanted to talk to you about for now.' He took out another sheet. 'These three points, which correspond to the three attacks, can of course be connected by a triangle; but the important point is that it isn't just any triangle, it's a sacred triangle, the isosceles triangle, the relationship of whose sides equals the golden number; and the sacred triangle is half a pentagram.'

He projected another sheet. 'To obtain this pentagram I add two new points, symmetrical with the previous ones. But we're not dealing with an upright pentagram, with the point at the top, like

405

the one that appears on Baphomet's forehead. For most occultists, the shift from the straight pentagram to the inverted pentagram symbolizes the victory of matter over spirit, chaos over order, and more generally the forces of evil over the forces of good.'

With a conjuror's flourish, he took out one last sheet. 'If I trace a circle around the pentagram, the pentagram becomes a pentangle, which this time symbolizes the shift from theory to practice, from knowledge to power; in concrete terms, the pentangle is the most powerful magical tool that has ever been created, not only in white magic, in black magic as well.'

All of a sudden he stopped talking. There followed about a minute's silence before Martin-Renaud began speaking again.

'If I understand you correctly . . .' he said, looking Delano Durand right in the eyes, 'the two new points that you have drawn on the map . . .'

'The first is situated in north-west Ireland, in County Donegal if I remember correctly. The second is in Croatia, somewhere between Split and Dubrovnik.'

'In principle, these two points should identify the locations of the next two attacks.'

'Yes, that would seem logical.'

Martin-Renaud leapt to his feet. 'I'm going to need this!' he exclaimed, picking up the sheet from the overhead projector. 'Wait, wait, boss . . .' Durand raised a calming hand. 'This was just an approximate dialogue to help you understand. Obviously, I have calculated the precise geographic coordinates of the two points; as I had those of the first attacks, it was a simple matter.' He rummaged for some time in his file, watched by Martin-Renaud, who was seething with impatience. 'There!' he said at last in a cheerful voice, taking out a page scribbled with calculations. 'I have your coordinates. The first is, as I said, in Donegal, somewhere between Gortahork and Dunfanaghy. The second is in fact just off the

Croatian coast; maybe on an island, there are a lot of islands around there, I think.'

'Nine o'clock,' Martin-Renaud butted in, grabbing the sheet. 'We meet up tomorrow morning at nine, in my office. I'm going to have a few calls to make – quite a few, even.'

Doutremont turned up at precisely nine o'clock the following day. Martin-Renaud was already there, along with Sitbon-Nozières, whose appearance was still impeccable. Delano Durand showed up about ten minutes late, as grubby as ever, but Martin-Renaud didn't say anything; on the contrary, when he collapsed into an armchair in front of his desk, he looked at him with a kind of respectful astonishment.

'There's some news,' he began. 'Some important and significant evidence. It hasn't been easy, it took a long time to convince our friends at the NSA, but I had some bargaining chips, some evidence that they were very keen to see. Thanks to you, Durand,' he added.

Durand nodded curtly.

'The first coordinates in Ireland correspond, they told me in the end, to the headquarters of a company called Neutrino, a hi-tech company, the global pioneer in neuronal computing.' He looked for a long time at his subordinates, who stayed motionless, apart from Delano Durand, who nodded again, to the great surprise of Martin-Renaud. Did he know about neuronal computing as well? Where did this guy come from, exactly?

'I didn't quite understand,' he went on, 'if they were integrating human neurons into electronic circuits, or electronic bugs into human brains; I think it's a bit of both, and that their goal in general is to create hybrid beings between computers and humans. It's a company that enjoys considerable funding; it has capital from both Apple and Google. It's also classified as a defence secret, I think its activities have military implications, they're perfecting a new type of fighter which might usefully replace human soldiers, because they would be incapable of empathy and moral scruple. Donegal, where the company is based, is one of the most deserted regions of Ireland; the company's employees are housed on a piece of land far from the surrounding villages, which they never leave, they have their own airfield, so it's a very discreet company.

'Where things get interesting is that their headquarters was completely destroyed three days ago, in an arson attack. Prototypes, plans, computer data, all gone. The crime took place at dead of night, it was caused by napalm and white phosphorus bombs, the same combustibles that were used for the Danish sperm bank. Military methods, once again; the only difference is that they took fewer precautions, and that there were three dead among the night shift. The NSA made sure that nothing was leaked to the media, but obviously when I gave them the precise geographical coordinates they were shocked and agreed to cooperate.

'It was harder,' he continued after a pause, 'to extract information from the second set of coordinates. It's a Croatian island, more of an islet, off the coast of Hvar. It's owned by an American, who bought it about ten years ago to build a summer residence. They eventually told me who this guy is; he turns out to be a kind of legend in Silicon Valley. He's not really a tech bro, in fact he does know a lot about tech stuff but he's more of an investor. He invests only in high-tech companies, and he's known for having exceptional flair: every time he's invested in a start-up it's multiplied its capital within a few years. So obviously he's very rich; but more than that, he's a kind of guru for the new technologies, his opinions are received with some fear and a lot of respect. He's sometimes thought to have political ambitions; I don't know if that's true, but either way the people I've spoken to at the NSA seemed very keen to keep him happy, it went all the way to the defense secretary, and even the president, before they shared information. Every summer he organizes a week-long seminar on his island, to which he invites about fifty leading players from the world of computers and digital technology. It's very informal, there are no lectures, there's no precise schedule, people just have an opportunity to meet and talk about things, which they don't really have time to do the rest of the year. A lot of important decisions have been made during these meetings, a lot of businesses have been set up – for example Neutrino, which I was talking about just now. The next one is due to be held early in July, in just over a month. It would be reasonable to think that an attack has been planned to coincide with this seminar; that was the first thing that occurred to the people I spoke to at the NSA.'

'What are they going to do now?' Doutremont asked.

'They're certainly going to try to collar these people just as they're preparing the attack; I'm far from sure that they'll be able to do it. A file of that kind will be transferred to the CIA; they're good when it comes to operations requiring brute force, but they often lack delicacy; and so far the guys on the other side have been extremely agile. But at least this time they've been prevented from acting; we're ahead of them on this occasion. Obviously they've asked me what our procedure was. I tried to explain to them about the pentangle, but I'm not sure they understood; I'm not absolutely sure I understood myself. Either way, our success is down to you, Durand.'

He turned towards him. Slightly embarrassed, Delano Durand nodded. 'There's also your former colleague, the one who's in hospital . . .' he said by way of deflection. 'The difficult thing was establishing the relationship between the regular pentagon and the star pentagon; everything else flowed from that, more or less.'

'The targets are a match for what a group of anti-tech activists might have chosen . . .' Sitbon-Nozières observed after a brief pause.

'That's true,' Martin-Renaud said, 'it confirms your analyses completely. It's frightening to imagine that totally unknown

411

activists could have engaged in an operation on this scale, but I'm worried that that's not the conclusion we need to come to. The unexpected thing is this desire to connect with a magical tradition; it might correspond to something in a primitivist context. In any case,' he went on resignedly, 'I gave up on looking for rationality in human behaviour a long time ago; we don't need it in our work, we just have to identify structures, and here' – he turned once again towards Delano Durand and looked him straight in the eye – 'there is no doubt that you've identified a structure. The consequence is that you've saved the lives of the most important leading figures on the planet in the field of new technologies; I don't know in the end if you've done the right thing; but that's what you've done.'

10

It was 7.15 p.m. by the time Paul parked in a no-parking space very close to the polling station. 'Are you sure? You don't want to go and vote?' he urged. Prudence shrugged indifferently; he left her with the car keys.

He picked up the two ballot papers on the table by the entrance; there were still quite a lot of people there, and he had to queue up for the booths; a lot of Parisians must have taken advantage of the weekend. When a space became free and he had closed the curtain behind him, he was already holding the Sarfati card in his right hand; as he was about to slip it into the envelope he was filled with a strange and paralysing sensation that froze his hand mid-action. Within a few seconds he realized that he had entered a state of immobility, a kind of psychological equivalent of stasis, of the kind that he had known sometimes, but luckily not very often, since the end of his adolescence. For the next few minutes, or perhaps the next few hours, he would be incapable of making the slightest decision, accomplishing the slightest gesture that deviated even slightly from his daily routine. It was impossible to wait for it to pass; people were waiting behind him, and a few seconds' hesitation was permissible but no more than that. Impulsively he took a felt tip pen out of his pocket, crossed out Sarfati's name and slipped the ballot paper into the envelope.

There was also a queue at the ballot boxes. Paul joined the queue before realizing that he didn't really care very much about taking part in the vote, at any rate he had no interest in being counted among the voided ballots. He left the queue, crumpled the envelope in his hands and threw it into a dustbin before leaving the polling station. 'Was that OK?' Prudence asked him as he sat down at the wheel again. He confirmed with a nod; he preferred not to talk about it. It was the first time since he became an adult that he couldn't vote. Perhaps it was a sign; but a sign of what?

It was already 7.30 p.m. and he just had time to get to the Place de la République. Benjamin Sarfati was scheduled to deliver a short speech just after eight, and then the party had hired a big hall on Boulevard du Temple to hold a reception. The fact that they had announced this a long time in advance, and the absence of the slightest doubt about the verdict from the ballot, had been held by some commentators to be a little arrogant.

Strangely, the VIP car park was on Boulevard de Magenta, on the other side of the square, and it took Paul a long time to get there; the Place de la République seemed pointlessly huge. What was the point of such huge squares? he wondered; so that you could get a view of the pompous statue in the middle, was the only possible response; Republican kitsch was definitely the worst kitsch of all. At 8 p.m., when his doubts about the concept of the Republic were getting louder, he turned on his car radio: Sarfati's vote was at 54.2% as against his adversary's 45.8%. It was a clear victory, less wide a margin than one might have hoped, but clear nonetheless.

The Place de la République was full of people, but it wasn't by any means the same crowd as at previous elections: a lot of young people with a very *banlieue* look. It was then that Paul remembered that Sarfati had won loads of votes in what were still tactfully referred to as *les quartiers*. In Clichy and Montfermeil he got results of 85 or even 90%. The mob had plainly descended on Paris this evening on a scale that one normally only saw at the football World Cup. Joints and packs of Bavarian and Amdsterdamer tobacco had started circulating. Paul noticed as he passed through the crowd that Sarfati was universally known as 'Big Ben', and that the general view of his election was that it would be 'really sick'. They seemed to be in a good mood for now, but he still felt reassured on reaching Boulevard du Temple, when he held out his parking card for the security man. Inside it was entirely VIPs, and within a few minutes he had spotted lots of actors and presenters from French television. More surprisingly, he saw Martin-Renaud the worse for wear and leaning on one end of the enormous bar over a glass of whisky. He walked over to say hello, surprised to see him there. 'Yes, I know, I'm a *man of the shadows . . .*' he said, amused. Then he told Paul about the recent success that their service had achieved; a few hours after the Minister of the Interior, it was the president himself who had called to congratulate him and invite him to this party.

'So you think the attacks are over?'

'Certainly not.' Martin-Renaud shook his head. 'I'd even go so far as to say that the opposite is true; two days after my conference call to the American secret service, there was a new message. A discreet message, this time, which only appeared on ten servers or so, all of them French. A short one, too, only three lines long; and it was followed by an aerial photograph of our offices on Rue du Bastion. It was meant for us, it's a kind of challenge, a way of telling us that they know we know. They've still been knocked of course, though, I think; they're bound to be wondering just how much we know.' He paused and took a sip of whisky. 'So they'll start again; but with a different MO, and taking more precautions. It's just the start of the game; I don't know if I'll see the end of it.'

A huge video screen lit up at the end of the hall; it was basically there to play back Sarfati's speech. Paul noted with surprise that most of the guests weren't interested; many of them carried on their conversations without paying the slightest attention. He also noticed that there was a considerable police presence on the edge of the Place de la République. It was obviously required, given the size of the crowd; an evening that ended with looting and burnt cars would have been a *bad signal* aimed at the middle classes of Neuilly-sur-Seine, who had not been shy in voting for the new president – that was one of the main lessons that observers drew the day after the vote; the Montfermeil–Neuilly axis was in fact quite a novelty.

Bruno's arrival, on the other hand, was quite the event; conversations fell silent all at once, gradually replaced by a hubbub of whispers, since everyone in the hall seemed to have understood that he was the *tough guy* of the next government. Paul had never seen Raksaneh in an evening dress; she was dazzling, and there was an almost barbaric splendour about the silver necklace that she was wearing. There were plenty of journalists and photographers roaming the hall, but Bruno had clearly decided to *go for it*.

A few minutes later, Sarfati and the president arrived, arm in arm. They froze for a moment by the door, long enough to receive the applause of the crowd and to be photographed together, then the president let go of Sarfati's arm and disappeared into the throng, heading for a man that Paul recognized, eventually, as the Minister of the Interior. Sarfati, grinning broadly, waited for the photographers and the cameramen to have done with him before heading for the bar. It was then that Paul noticed Solène Signal. Sitting alone in a corner of the hall, she was watching with great fascination as the president moved from one guest to the next, resting his hand on the shoulder of each one to hold their attention, devoting one or two minutes exclusively to them, each time giving the impression that he was interested only in them, that they were the only reason he was there. He was still a magnificent political animal, she thought with genuine regret. He had never consulted a communication specialist or a spin doctor; since the start of his meteoric rise he had managed on his own. She quickly said hello to Paul without taking her eyes off the president, who had just spotted Martin-Renaud in the hall. 'Who's that guy? I don't know him,' she wondered out loud. For once Paul knew something that she didn't, and he told her of the recent successes of the DGSI. That was an unexpected stroke of luck for the president, she said immediately; while he was sound on the economy, his record on security left a lot to be desired. She still had a few days to exploit this information: it would probably come out in the major press outlets the next day, and he would mention in it in his farewell speech on Wednesday. His re-election in five years really seemed to have got off to a good start – particularly if Sarfati made a few mistakes, which was almost bound to happen, she added with resignation. She herself had nothing to blame herself for, she had done her share of the job, and even more – when she had taken on Benjamin Sarfati as a client some ten years ago, it hadn't been obvious that she would be taking him to the presidency of the Republic; among the five people on his team at that point, she was the only one who believed in him.

They headed for the bar. Solène Signal poured herself a glass of white wine, and Paul asked for a fresh glass of champagne. He had trouble being served, since Sarfati's gang had gathered in front of the bar and snaffled most of the bottles. They were shouting and laughing loudly; most of them were already off their faces, the weed and coke had started doing the rounds. Sarfati had managed to keep them out of sight during the electoral campaign, but after the victory they had come back, it was inevitable, they had all come out of television circles, and some of them had been with him since his first broadcasts. They were the ones who were going to squat at the Élysée, organize parties and throw up on the sofas of the National Furniture Office throughout the five-year term. It was an unpleasant prospect, particularly for the staff of the presidential palace, but it wasn't really serious. The president had been right in his predictions: for him, Sarfati wasn't a threat. It seemed increasingly clear that the next presidential battle would be between him and Bruno; the key to the next five-year term would be a secret struggle, long-distance, between the two men. Solène Signal nodded, having anticipated all this. She wasn't going to offer her services to Bruno straight away, that would happen in due course. And what about his own availability? she wanted to know. She was being really strange this evening, she seemed almost dreamy, it was the first time since Paul had known her that she seemed to be interested in anything apart from her professional goals. Well, he replied, he could have picked up his work again right now, in the present context it seemed to have gone unnoticed; but there wouldn't have been much point, he would sit out the legislative elections, then the summer break, and he would be back for the second half of August, when things really got going. Bruno hadn't entirely had free rein during the previous term, he had had to strike deals with some senior civil servants in Bercy who were protected by the president, including the inspector of finances himself. He wouldn't have that problem with Sarfati.

Solène Signal nodded; she had been listening attentively. Probably, in fact, there would be small-scale dramas, they would start marking the next fault lines, but it would be two or three years before the president really started repositioning himself, marking himself out as different. For some time the legislative elections hadn't been the kind of thing that Solène dealt with; she could have afforded to take a total break over the next few weeks, perhaps take advantage of the opportunity to reorganize her life, to imagine having some kind of private life; but she never mentioned that aspect, not with anyone else, and not even when she was alone.

Paul left shortly afterwards, without even having had time to say hello to Bruno, who had been surrounded by people all evening. Sarfati's gang was getting increasingly noisy, and his gums were painful again, a fetid taste was spreading in his mouth, he really

418

needed to make an appointment for the following morning. This election was good news for the country, he had no doubt about that; in any case it was good news for him; but since just now, since that strange moment of being petrified when he was about to put his ballot paper in the box, he felt hesitant and sad.

six

1

The first time you consult a dentist, a doctor, or any kind of service provider, it's almost always at the recommendation of someone, a relative or a friend; as it happens, though, Paul knew no one who could recommend a dentist for him in Paris. And if he didn't know anyone who could recommend a dentist to him, it was because he didn't know many people at all. Still, his life should have been a bit livelier, he thought with a burst of self-pity that disgusted him immediately. There was Prudence; a few exceptions aside – Bruno, Cécile – he lived with Prudence as if on a desert island in the middle of nothingness.

When you thought about it, that nothingness in terms of human relationships had been part of his life for ever. It was already there when he was at university, and even during his school years, theoretically so promising in terms of establishing human relationships. Only sexual desire had sometimes, rarely, been powerful enough to break down the wall. We always communicate, more or less, within a particular age range; people who belong to a different age range, to whom you are not otherwise connected by a direct family relationship, the billions of people with whom we share the planet, have no real existence in your eyes. As Paul grew older, and sexual encounters naturally became increasingly rare, his loneliness had gradually deepened.

Nonetheless, his toothache was getting worse and worse, particularly on the left side, even moving his tongue had grown difficult, and it was becoming imperative to do something about it. The Doctolib website allowed him to access the list of dentists working in the twelfth arrondissement quite easily. Many of them, judging by the sound of their names, were Jewish – an *idée reçue* that was confirmed, he noted in passing. However, he chose one, Bachar Al Nazri, whose origins were more likely to be Arab. He chose him for no precise reason except that it was more convenient for him to go to Rue de Charenton when he left his home: all you had to do, once past the church of Notre-Dame-de-la-Nativité de Bercy, was go down Rue Proudhon – a street that was really more of a tunnel, dug beneath the railway lines leaving the Gare du Lyon; he must have passed over that street many times by TGV without being aware of it; then you emerged into Rue de Charenton, no distance from Dugommier metro station. He was glad of the opportunity granted to see the church of Notre-Dame-de-la-Nativité de Bercy again; he had a sense of something unfinished in his life with that church – and perhaps with Christianity in general.

'Open wide . . . Open very wide,' Al Nazri repeated patiently once he was sitting, almost lying, in the dentist's chair. He was a young man, brown-skinned and with short hair, probably less than thirty. He didn't look North African, more Syrian or Iraqi, although there was nothing to suggest that he was Islamist, or even Muslim, in every respect he gave the impression of being extremely serious and professional, and of having perfectly absorbed the procedures and customs of rational medical methods. Immigrants were still enjoying some successes in France, Paul reflected, even if they had become rare, and the evidence suggested that Al Nazri was one of them. When he introduced a metal probe into Paul's mouth, he looked concerned. The right-hand side wasn't too bad, but when the metal rod made contact with his molar Paul couldn't help crying out.

'Yes . . .' he immediately withdrew the probe, 'you should have come to see us months ago, as I imagine you're aware. As things stand, we're not going to be able to avoid an extraction. If it's any consolation, still having all your wisdom teeth at your age is unusual, two has more or less become the norm. You tell me you also have difficulty moving your tongue, and sometimes a bad taste in your mouth?'

'Yes, a taste of something rotten, it doesn't last long, but it's very unpleasant.'

He slipped on a pair of latex gloves, and gently ran his fingers over Paul's jaw. 'There's a swelling here,' he said at last, 'haven't you noticed? As a general rule, people notice swellings. Right, I'm going to take an X-ray to check, while you're here.'

Once the X-ray had been taken he raised the chair and then spent a long time looking at the images on a light table before concluding: 'There's no doubt that we need to do the two extractions. I'm also going to give you the address of an ENT doctor, just in case. Could we proceed with the extractions today?'

'Yes, of course, I didn't expect it would be possible to do it so quickly, but I'd rather.'

'It won't hurt at all, you'll see, and you'll feel much better afterwards.'

In fact it was quick and painless, the anaesthetic had worked perfectly, and he immediately had a sensation of lightness and comfort in his mouth the like of which he hadn't known for ages. 'You see,' Al Nazri said, 'you were wrong to delay. I expect you smoke?' Paul nodded. 'We'll have to see each other regularly for scaling, every six months at an absolute minimum. And don't forget to make an appointment with Nakkache, the ENT doctor whose details I gave you. We don't pay attention to our teeth, we think they're of secondary importance, but sometimes it can be serious.' Paul nodded, trying to adopt the requisite gravitas, in the hope of giving the impression of having taken his warning fully into account, of not being one of those people who see dentists as second-class doctors, but still, as he left on to Rue de Charenton, his state of mind was one of joyful abandon, and the first thing he did was phone Prudence to tell her that he had just come out of the dentist's, and that it had all gone well. Most of all, he wanted her to congratulate him for finally taking care of his teeth; one of the traditional roles of women is to encourage their men to take care of themselves, particularly their health, and more generally to connect them with life, since men's friendship with life, even in the best of cases, is always quite precarious.

He had not been back inside the church of Notre-Dame-de-la-Nativité de Bercy since the beginning of January. It was, he remembered, the day after he discovered the Christmas tree decorated by Prudence, and when he had for the first time, without really spelling it out for himself, imagined in a semi-conscious manner that something might happen between them again one day. It was probably in that unformulated hope that he had lit candles at the time – a curious action, given that he was atheist, or rather agnostic, his atheism as a matter of principle was fragile, since it was unable to rely on a consistent ontology. Was the world material? It was a hypothesis, but as far as he knew the world might just as well be made up of spiritual entities; he no longer knew what science actually meant by 'matter', or even if it still used the term, he didn't really have a sense that it did, as far as he remembered it was probably more to do with matrices of probable presences, but his studies were far behind him, at any rate they hadn't been taken very far in this field, a science baccalaureate, nothing more, and he couldn't have found out about such things at Sciences Po. A passage from Pascal returned to him, a not very Christian passage in which the author laments that nature gives him nothing on the question of the existence of a creator 'except matter for doubt and concern'.

Perhaps at the same time Prudence was engaging in Wiccan

426

incantations, it wasn't impossible. Now, according to their calendar, they were close to the Sabbath of Litha, which corresponds to the summer solstice, a period 'particularly propitious to healing and the magic of love', he had read the previous day. Were there, in fact, other kinds of magic? Whether it was the African marabouts who sometimes dropped their advertisements through people's letter-boxes, or Wiccans or Christians, they all asked more or less the same of their respective deities: health and love. Were human beings more disinterested than we commonly supposed? Or, the Anglo-Saxon countries aside, did they consider financial issues too vulgar to trouble their gods with? The candles that he had offered to the Virgin in those first days of January had at any rate been unexpectedly effective, and he placed two new candles in front of the altar.

Back at home, he looked to see what books he could dig out that might give him more information about the existence of a creator. Once again he was obliged to note that his library was poor when it came to philosophy, but in the end he happened upon a large volume among his science books, entitled *Contemporary Philosophy and Physics*, which seemed to provide some enlightenment, or at least some perspectives on the subject, not that the author was really setting out the case for the existence of God, but he did express some doubts about the existence of the world, and more generally prompted questions about the concept of existence in general. Thus, for example, in a rather sibylline phrase, he asserted: 'The word is not made up of what is, but of what happens.' At the end of the book there was a glossary, which included an entry for the verb *to happen*. According to the author, this meant: 'To be attested by an observer, in line with a certain principle of attestation.' Paul turned on the television, interrupting his intellectual quest. The Public Sénat channel was broadcasting the parliamentary session abolishing the function of the prime minister and creating mid-term general elections. The adoption of these measures left no doubt: from this evening, Bruno would in practical terms be the most powerful politician in France. Things were going to get a bit more serious now, the battle for the next presidential election was already prefigured here, however distantly.

It was a very particular kind of man who won the presidency, Paul had known that for a long time; he just hadn't anticipated Bruno being one of them. He did, however, remember an unusual conversation that would have led him to suspect as much. He had been waiting for Bruno in his work apartment, after the president had called Bruno to the Élysée for a work meeting, because he had sensed that this meaning would be tense, and that he would need to talk when he got back. It was midwinter, night had already fallen at rush hour, and as happened to him with increasing frequency, he had felt oppressed by the flood of vehicles travelling at a walking pace along the elevated sections of the metro, by that accumulation of individual destinies, as identical as they were boring. He had ordered a bottle of wine from the butler, a Bordeaux, he had insisted; the butler had brought a Saint-Julien a few minutes later, and had offered to decant it, but Paul had refused, he needed to drink straight away.

Bruno was discouraged, in fact. The president had overruled him, and opted to close about ten nuclear power stations, in the hope of gaining a few green votes that were part of the majority in any case, since no ecologist was ever going to vote for the National Rally, it was ontologically impossible, those closures would allow them to avoid a few abstentions, at best. Bruno wasn't entirely hostile to the ecologists; on his own initiative, for example, he had increased tax reductions for energy savings made by private individuals in their homes, but overall he still saw them as dangerous imbeciles, and in particular he saw the idea of depriving oneself of nuclear power as absurd, it was a point on which he had never

428

budged. Could anyone cite a single point on which the president's convictions had never budged?

'Essentially,' Bruno had said to Paul at last, 'the president has one political conviction, and only one. It is exactly the same as that of all his predecessors, and can be summed up in a phrase: "I am made to be president of the Republic." On everything else, the decisions that need to be taken, the direction of criminal policy, he is willing to do more or less anything at all, as long as it goes along with his own political interests.'

Had this same kind of cynicism taken hold of Bruno too? Paul didn't think so, even though some details might have suggested as much. For some years the general atmosphere had been in favour of protectionism, and Bruno was more and more openly protectionist – but he was completely sincere about it, and for a long time he had seen the free market as a suicidal option for France. Besides, he thought, economic patriotism could be a powerful unifying factor. A war had always been the safest way of bringing a nation together and boosting the popularity of the head of state. In the absence of a military conflict, which was too expensive for a middle-sized country, an economic war could take its place perfectly, and Bruno had no hesitation in pushing in that direction, increasing his provocations with regard to emerging or recently emerged countries. In Bruno's view, one shouldn't worry about engaging in economic warfare, since the only economic wars that one was certain to lose, he had once told Paul, were the ones that one was not brave enough to wage.

Later in the evening, while Paul was working his way through the bottle of Saint-Julien almost entirely on his own, Bruno, who seemed to have been left very depressed by his meeting, had started voicing doubts about the possibility of political action in general. Could a politician really influence the course of things? It seemed questionable. Developments in technology could do that without a doubt; and so, perhaps, to some degree, could economic power relations – even though Bruno still tended to some degree to see the economy as a sub-product of technology. There was also something else, a dark and secret force which might be psychological, sociological or simply biological in nature, it was impossible to know what it was, but it was terribly important because everything else depended on it, both demographics and religious faith, and finally people's desire to stay alive, and the future of their civilizations. The concept of decadence might have been a difficult one to figure out, but it remained a powerful reality; and what was more, perhaps more importantly, politicians were incapable of influencing it. Even such authoritarian and determined figures as General de Gaulle had proved powerless in opposing the direction of history, Europe as a whole had become a distant, ageing, depressive and slightly ludicrous province of the United States of America. In spite of the general's picturesque fanfares, had the fate of France really been any different from that of other parts of western Europe?

Bruno's voice had dropped further and further, as if he was talking to himself, and these were in fact things that he could under no circumstances have expressed in public. Rush hour was over, and the traffic had started flowing again along the Quai de la Rapée, when he finally said, almost in a whisper, that the lack of conviction in a political leader was not necessarily a sign of cynicism, but rather of maturity. Had the kings of France shown up armed with a political programme, a plan of reforms? Never. Nonetheless they had gone down in history as great kings, or on the contrary as appalling kings, for their tendency to fulfil an implicit but precise set of specifications. Not reducing the territory of the kingdom, on the contrary increasing it if possible, either through purchases or more often through wars, while at the same time avoiding increasing the costs of mercenaries to excess, and more generally avoiding any unnecessary fiscal pressure. Avoiding civil wars within the kingdom, in particular religious wars, they had always been the deadliest, which had been achieved by unambiguously designating a single dominant religion; other minor religions could be granted broad religious licence, on condition that they never forgot that they were tolerated at best within the national territory, and that that tolerance would always be at the sovereign's discretion. Perhaps increasing the prestige of the kingdom by erecting monuments and supporting the arts. For some centuries this ideal programme had ensured the prestige of the curious partnership of Richelieu and Louis XIII; no one really knew how it had worked, but the fact remained that it had. The balance sheet for Louis XIV was more mixed; he himself agreed as much on his deathbed, as Saint-Simon and others testified. The 'Sun King' had regretted not so much his ostentatious constructions as his excessive appetite for warfare, for ultimately mediocre financial results, and his deafness to the suffering of his people, which had in fact been extreme, famine included, even though they had been indicated to him by Vauban, La Bruyère and indeed by the best minds of his time. The task of the presidents of the Republic, Bruno said, Paul remembered as he followed with diminishing attention the broadcast of parliament on the Public Sénatchannel, the task of the presidents of the Republic, contrary to what an exaggerated belief in progress, and more generally in the importance of historical changes, might have led one to think, was essentially the same as the task of kings. To a certain degree, but not entirely, economic rivalry had replaced military rivalry, and today it was less a matter of conquering territory than market share; but the question of territory could not be forgotten entirely. The task of the presidents of the Republic, prime ministers or kings, the holders of the highest office, was as it had always been to defend as best they could the interests of the country, whether republic or kingdom, of which they were in charge, rather as it is the job of a company director to defend the interests of his firm against the ever-active interests of its competitors. The task was a difficult one, but in principle it was of the same order, and did not imply the choice of an ideology or of any particular political orientation.

The meeting of the Vienna Congress went without a hitch. One by one, the senators came to the podium and dropped their ballot paper in the box, since this was a secret election; then they would be followed by the deputies; it was repetitive, and its guiding principle was quite conceptual. Around half of the MPs had voted when Paul fell asleep on his sofa. In his dream he had just made the acquaintance of a friend, a tall, thin black man who expressed himself in Portuguese, probably a Brazilian. They met in a part of the city behind the Gare du Nord and the Gare de l'Est; the streets were dark and almost deserted. In principle this was an immigrant quarter where many different communities lived; however, Paul quickly came to understand that these tales of immigration were merely a decoy, and that behind the façades of the buildings pornographic practices were being performed that were as sordid as they were terrifying. Then his Brazilian friend introduced him to one of his own friends, a young North African, and almost immediately they abandoned him in a little square which was almost certainly the Place Franz-Liszt, on the pretext of 'going to get something to eat'. The square was in darkness. Groups of immigrants of various races circulated, looking at him from below. Terrified, Paul began walking at random along poorly lit streets. Some of the immigrants followed him at a distance, but to his great surprise none of them dared to attack him, as if he enjoyed some kind of supernatural protection. Paul came back towards the square which was almost certainly the Place Franz-Liszt. It was then, to his great joy, that his Brazilian friend came back and hugged him tightly by the shoulders. Following close behind, his North African friend was transporting pots full of shellfish and prawns; they planned to have them with some white wine. In the embrace of the Brazilian and his North African friend, Paul climbed the steps of the hotel where they were going to spend the night, gradually he could tell from their conversation that these so-called friends planned to torture and dismember him, while filming the stages of his torment; that was the purpose of their presence, and their supposed friendship; it was only later that they would celebrate the completion of this new film while enjoying the white wine and prawns. The manageress of the hotel was waiting for them; she was a woman in her sixties, stocky and stout, with small eyes and a short chignon of grey hair; she looked a little like the politician Simone Veil, and also the big sand woman. She announced that everything was in place for the shoot. Paul then realized that she was going to take part, and even play an important role; the previous week, positioned on a landing with a camera, she had managed to film a hand, severed at the wrist, falling into the courtyard.

He was awoken by Prudence gently shaking his shoulder; the parliamentary meeting was over, and it was time for the political commentators to get worked up in front of the television screen. 'Has the plan for constitutional reform been adopted?' he asked her. She nodded. He got up groggily, followed her into the bedroom and quickly undressed; then he huddled into her arms and went back to sleep almost immediately.

2

He slept deeply and for a long time, and when he woke up it was nearly eleven o'clock. He was surprised to hear sounds coming from the kitchen, it took him several seconds to realize that it was Saturday and that Prudence wasn't working. He had not been on leave for long, but he was already starting to forget the alternation between weekends and the working week; it's strange how quickly the reflexes of submission disappear.

'It's really difficult to buy you a present . . .' she said when he sat down at the kitchen table. 'Your birthday's in a week, and I still haven't found anything.'

'Don't trouble yourself, darling. I've never really liked celebrating my birthday.'

'We'll do something, even so. Fifty is a special one. We won't have anyone over if you don't want to, but at least I'm going to make a decent meal, because now you can eat normally, it's the least I can do.'

His appointment with Amit Nakkache, the ENT doctor recommended by the dentist, was on 29 June, the same day as his birthday. He had a surgery on Rue Ortolan, a street of modest length that connected Place Monge and Rue Mouffetard. Paul was glad of the opportunity to come back to this district, a part of town that he liked in principle; at least when a conversation about this district arose, which was rare, he claimed to like it, to some degree it was his *official position* about the district. He wasn't sure that he could actually *like* a district today, the word seemed excessive, for example it wasn't something he felt for his own district, even though it was generally agreed to be a good one among people who shared his education and his social standing, but it was a classic subject of conversation that allowed most people to express authentic feelings without involving any overstated passion, which meant it was a good subject.

Climbing the stairs leading to the doctor's surgery, he suddenly became aware that he had just turned fifty. How strange it was! How quickly life had gone by . . .! And the second half, he could tell, would go even faster, it would vanish in a flash, it would pass like a breath of wind, life really didn't amount to very much. Besides, talking about the second half was probably excessively optimistic, although even that wasn't certain, lots of people lived to be a hundred these days, living to be a hundred was increasingly becoming the norm, except among people who had done hard manual work, which was obviously not true of him.

The ENT doctor was a man in his forties, quite rotund, with a benevolent yet anxious appearance. He asked Paul to sit down and asked him some basic questions – identity, address, profession, family situation – warm-up questions, of a kind. Meanwhile Paul attempted to reconcile his two first impressions of the ENT doctor, and he did so more and more successfully: a state of worried benevolence is in fact entirely suitable for a doctor, it's even effect-ively the definition of his professional attitude. After these initial questions Paul handed him Al Nazri's letter. 'Yes, in fact, my col-league did call me about this,' he said, but he still ran quickly through it before saying that he was going to give him some com-plementary examinations, and asking him to sit on a wide, padded, reclining chair with elbow rests, precisely reminiscent of the dentist's. Paul felt reassured by the idea that they were staying in the same general area, dental and nothing more, with perhaps a few minor

435

complications. At first, in fact, it all went smoothly, he too asked Paul to open wide, then very delicately palpated his gums before introducing a wide spatula of light-coloured wood; the instrument was neither metallic nor pointed, and was entirely harmless compared to the ones a dentist would have. Then he palpated his neck for a long time, pressing harder in different places, which was weird but not painful. Finally he picked up a long, thin cannula, supple and transparent, lowered the back of the chair until Paul was practically horizontal, before gently bringing the plastic tube to his nostrils. Paul was starting to be frightened for the first few moments, but after five seconds he felt a terrible, searing pain, he couldn't help but scream, he had the feeling that the plastic tube was boring its way into the middle of his brain. The doctor immediately withdrew the tube and looked at him with concern.

'I'm sorry,' he said hesitantly, 'your nostrils seem to be very sensitive.'

'Yes, that was really terrible.' Paul was very embarrassed to notice that he was starting to cry uncontrollably.

'The trouble is that I need to examine the other nostril.'

'No, not that!' The plea had slipped out.

'Listen, I'm going to do this as gently as possible, and I won't go as deeply, but unfortunately it's a necessary examination.'

He then introduced the canula into the right nostril, very slowly; it was less violent, but even worse in a sense, the pain grew and grew and he started crying out again when Nakkache pulled out the cannula and he was shaken by a second convulsive fit of weeping.

'Right, I've finished the examination.'

'It's really over? You're not going to start again?'

'No, I shouldn't have to do that again. I'm very sorry it was painful, but it wasn't pointless. At least I know now that there are no complications involving your nasal passages.'

'What sort of complications?' Paul asked the question automatically, still unable to stop himself weeping. Nakkache hesitated: this was the difficult moment. 'You have probably noticed . . .' he began very gently, 'you have a strange swelling on your gum. At this stage, of course,' he continued very quickly, 'we don't yet know the nature of the lesion, we're going to have to do a biopsy.' He took out a long syringe ending in a needle. 'I'm still going to have to give you a bit of a prick,' he added with playful haste, adopting a tone of feigned menace to hide the fact that he was changing the subject. Paul didn't react. 'Swelling' and 'lesion', generally speaking, sounded better than 'tumour', but still, at this stage, people started asking questions, while he wasn't asking any at all, Nakkache observed with surprise, he was still weeping with relief at the idea that they weren't going to touch his nostrils again, and he opened his mouth mechanically, without protest; a small incision was nothing in comparison. In fact it happened very quickly, just a slight pricking sensation. Nakkache injected the contents of the sample into a glass container filled with a translucent liquid, then started writing out prescriptions while going on talking. As well as the biopsy, Paul was going to have to have an MRI of his jaw and a PET scan, the word fleetingly reminded him of something, he thought he had already heard it in the context of his father. Then he arranged a new appointment for him in exactly a week, same day, same time. It might be a good idea, Paul remarked, to do all of the tests. He wasn't to worry, Nakkache replied, he had written down the names of the doctors who would take charge of things, he would call them himself, and they would always be able to free up a place if necessary. Before leaving the surgery, Paul felt a little embarrassed, his tears had finally stopped, and he apologized for making a spectacle of himself. Nakkache told him it didn't matter, gave him a friendly squeeze of the shoulder and left him with a comforting 'Good luck'. The consultation was over.

*

It was only after going down the stairs, going back up Rue Ortolan and sitting down on a bench on Place Monge while the memory of the pain faded, that Paul started wondering about the nature of his illness. A lesion could be serious, and it was also surprising that the doctor had set about finding appointments for him so quickly, he had said 'if necessary', but that might have been a euphemism for 'in an emergency', and the sympathetic way in which he had gripped his shoulder while wishing him good luck was worrying in itself. He turned on his mobile phone and did some internet searches which immediately confirmed his suspicions. Nakkache probably suspected mouth cancer. It was eleven o'clock in the morning, it was market day on Place Monge, there were cheesemongers, charcutiers, displays of spring fruit and vegetables. He would have liked to be able to do the shopping, know enough to choose his vegetables and his fruits, to spot an interesting catch at the fishmongers; it was too late now, he said to himself as he became aware that he was going to die, that his fiftieth birthday was probably the last, that he no longer occupied the same reality as the women of various ages moving around among the displays, pulling their shopping trolleys behind them with wise expressions. Then everything turned upside down, he felt once again that he belonged to the same world, perhaps he wasn't going to die straight away, everything would depend on the result of the tests, it was lucky that he was available, he wasn't going to mention it to Prudence, if everything went well she wouldn't even be aware of the incident. He stepped onto the escalator; he had always loved the huge, dizzying escalator at Monge metro station, which went down very quickly, very deeply under the ground and never broke down, unlike all the other escalators on the Paris metro, he'd known it for thirty years and he'd never known it to break down, this time, though, plunging into the subterranean darkness felt oppressive, as he reached the bottom he turned round and noticed, very high above him, a corner of sky, sunlit branches. He immediately took the up

438

escalator, he was angry with himself for his reaction, but still wanted to find himself back where the fresh air was stronger. He would go back by taxi, shared transport wasn't appropriate, there was an underlying sense of having been *set apart*, which could come back at any moment. He emerged just in front of the pharmacy and kitchenware shop on Rue Monge, which he had also known for almost thirty years. He walked around the alleyways of the market again, studied the displays of Italian charcuterie, of *saucisson du terroir*, was he really going to give up all that? Obviously it was possible, in fact it's the most likely way for things to come to an end, you say 'He had a beautiful life', then the funeral happens, sometimes it's more or less true, in fact, a life is never beautiful if you bear in mind the ending, as Pascal put it with his customary brutality: 'The final act is bloody, however beautiful the comedy of all the rest: in the end dirt is thrown on your head and that's it for ever.' Suddenly the world struck him as limited and sad, almost infinitely sad.

The taxi turned out not to have been such a good idea in the end; the journey back took him past the hospital of La Pitié-Salpêtrière and he was gripped by the sudden certainty that he was going to end his life in a state of suffering; the hospital looked gigantic, a monstrous citadel in the heart of Paris, entirely dedicated to pain, sickness and death. The impression faded as soon as they reached the Parc de Bercy; he asked the driver to stop and finished the last stretch on foot, he absolutely needed to calm the oscillations of his mind, or at least to reduce their amplitude, before seeing Prudence again. At least his father had managed to escape from hospital, he was ending his life at home, in the setting that he loved. He had managed to achieve that result for his father, but could he do the same for himself? He wasn't sure of it, and wondered if Prudence would manage to defend that point of view. She was inclined to obey the authorities, to trust competent people – doctors in this instance – and it would take an enormous effort on her part to impose the rights conferred upon her by law as his wife. He himself, in fact, had not had to do the same thing in the case of his father, he had stood up against an administrative authority whose stupidity was generally acknowledged, but not against the power of medicine, represented in this instance by Leroux. When one really had to oppose the power of medicine, the only solution was to have in one's pocket a sufficiently swashbuckling doctor, at the very least the former intern of a hospital with a good reputation, but a former clinical director would be better, a professorial title was always a good thing too, the value system that applied in medical circles showed almost as much imagination as that of the court of Louis XIV, Prudence would immediately be swept aside. As for himself, he needed to toughen up and prepare for confrontation.

Back home, he poured himself a big glass of Jack Daniel's and slowly calmed down, then arranged the prescriptions in a desk drawer in his old bedroom, which had become a spare room and also an office, to the extent that he needed an office at all, he hardly ever went in there and Prudence never did so there was no risk.

She came back from work a little after six and immediately started cooking; she had decided to make a creamy risotto with scallops, accompanied by a saffron sauce, you can't assume that a risotto is going to turn out fine, it calls for a certain amount of concentration. Sipping on a glass of Sauternes while he listened to the sounds coming from the kitchen, Paul said to himself that in the end he had managed to attain a certain form of happiness, and that it was a shame to die now; then, with renewed determination, he tried to banish the thought. As he expected, Prudence had paid no attention to his appointment with the ENT doctor, she even seemed to have forgotten it, so for now there was nothing to fear. Over dinner she talked about the holidays, she would have liked to go Sardinia, she'd wanted to discover Sardinia for a long time, she added. It was the first time she'd mentioned it; she honestly imagines, Paul said to himself with a burst of emotion, she doesn't realize that she's trying to repeat the miracle of our holiday in Corsica twenty years ago. Unfortunately it was already the end of June and much too late to book anything in August. They might be able to take their holidays in September, or at least part of them; a high degree of conformity was the rule at the ministry where summer holidays were concerned, they would probably have to take at least two weeks in August, and planning a trip to wherever, even to a less popular destination than Sardinia, would be impossible. That left Saint-Joseph and Larmor-Baden, which one did he prefer? Saint-Joseph, Paul replied without hesitation. Choosing between Saint-Joseph and Larmor-Baden in a sense meant choosing between two people in their death throes, and he had a sense that he hadn't quite finished with his father, that there were still some things to be cleared up where his father was concerned, while Prudence seemed entirely calm about her own father. 'So we'll forget the hot pants . . .' she said with a little smile. Not at all, Paul replied, she could go cycling perfectly well in hot pants, there were some lovely bike-rides in the area. He could certainly take her into a grove to fuck her, he remembered reading in a magazine, probably a women's magazine, that making love in forests was a fantasy for 100% of the women questioned, there must have been something about the vegetation that stimulated their hormone production, it was odd. Yes, he said to himself, it could be a very good holiday; still it was most likely, he thought a moment later, that his summer holidays would play out in the Pitié-Salpêtrière.

3

As Nakkache had said, it was easy for him to make appointments for the scanner and the PET scan, it was coming back to him now, it was the nurse in Lyon who had talked to him about it first, the one who was nice and full-figured, and Brian had also talked to him about it, its full name was a 'positron emission tomography scan'. The phrase was impressive and so was the machine, massive and curved, in white metal with a hint of cream that was immediately reminiscent of spectacular science-fiction films; it looked as if it consumed half the working budget of the hospital all by itself.

At ten o'clock the following Tuesday he went back to the ENT doctor's surgery. Nakkache held on to his hand for a long time before asking him to sit down, then seemed to sink into an extended personal meditation. Paul wondered whether the idea of this bit of theatre was to plunge him into a state of anxiety appropriate to the seriousness of what he was about to say; if that was the case, he had achieved his objective.

'There's good news and bad news,' he said at last. 'The bad news is that the biopsy has confirmed the malignant nature of the tumour on your gum.'

'Malignant, meaning cancerous?'

Nakkache darted a reproachful glance: no, that was exactly what he didn't want to say; but yes, in fact, if we got down to it, it was a cancer. The good news, he went on quickly, was that the cancer was at an early stage. So, the lymph nodes in the neck had been affected, but that was almost routine, at any rate the next course of action would be a lymphadenectomy; sometimes, when the lymph nodes were affected, one might worry that a cancer of the larynx was associated with cancer of the mouth; but that wasn't the case. 'And most importantly,' he went on, 'the PET scan revealed no metastasis. Your cancer is absolutely not becoming general, and that really is good news. So we have a tumour, a serious tumour, and we are going to do whatever we can to get rid of it for you.' He had assumed a martial tone, Vietnam-style, he was highly skilled at human relationships, Paul said to himself, he himself would have been incapable of doing the same.

'In the absence of metastases, then,' he went on, 'surgery should be more or less enough, with a bit of chemotherapy and radiotherapy, but very little, really, I think. The less good news is that the tumour has reached a certain extension; that's a shame, if you'd consulted us only two or three months ago, we could have avoided that, so we're going to have to engage in a serious surgical intervention.'

'Meaning?'

'I would prefer to let the surgeon talk to you about that himself. If I've understood correctly, you're not working at the moment, your days are more or less free?'

'Yes, you could say that.'

'I've taken the liberty of making you an appointment on Friday morning, so that you can meet him. I'll come with you, of course.'

'Where will that be?'

'At the Pitié-Salpêtrière Hospital.'

After taking what seemed to Paul an interminably long walk along pale green corridors endlessly following other pale green corridors, they finally found themselves outside room B132. Nakkache knocked on the frosted glass that made up the upper part of the door. They stepped into a little room with white walls furnished only with a table, which was also white. Two men were sitting there with files set down on front of them. They were both almost entirely bald, wearing hospital coats, and had black moustaches – they looked a bit like Dupont and Dupond in *Tintin*, the detectives known to English readers as Thompson and Thomson, except that their moustaches were less full and they looked less identical, one of them slightly stouter and apparently older than the other, but they both managed to look slightly dour and benevolent at the same time, as if patients were beings from whom one should not expect too much, but who still needed, when push came to shove, to be helped. It was all quite reassuring, as was the fact that they had already consulted his file – Paul recognized the letterhead of one of the laboratories – and he wondered which one was the surgeon.

'I'm Dr Lesage,' the older one said. 'I'm one of the duty chemotherapists.'

'And I'm Dr Lebon, radiotherapist,' the other one announced.

'You'll see Dr Martial a bit later,' Nakkache explained, 'he will be your surgeon.'

The surgeon in question arrived five minutes later. He was very different from the other two, handsome, early thirties, quite long, curly hair, very much a surgeon from the Harlequin collection, or an American series. He distinguished himself from George Clooney, however, by affecting a much cooler style, with John B. King trainers, named after a young American basketball player, the highest paid sportsman in the world, whose salary had just outstripped Real Madrid's striker; the sole was at least five centimetres thick, Paul had never seen shoes with such thick soles, except once in a documentary about Swinging London, in which the girl wore both an extremely short miniskirt – it was practically a belt – and shoes with extremely high soles, filled with water and with goldfish swimming inside them. In such conditions the fish died within a few days, and those shoes had quickly been banned after action from an animal protection charity. He didn't know why he was thinking about all that again, he was struggling to listen to the surgeon, who was now speaking to him, he had called him 'Monsieur Raison', but the rest of his words were incomprehensible, he was talking about mandibulectomy, glossectomy, resection, none of which meant anything to him. His brain had started working slowly since he had entered the room, as if he had been affected by something in between anaesthetic and a magic spell, but he managed in the end to formulate a question.

'So, there's not just surgery . . .' he said, addressing Dupond and Dupont, 'there's also radiotherapy and chemotherapy.'

They wriggled on their chairs with modesty, like chimpanzees who want to show their best side during an interview for the circus.

'That's right,' the radiotherapist finally said in a languid voice, 'unfortunately surgery can't do everything.' He glanced suavely at Martial, who shivered slightly but didn't reply. 'Dr Lesage will intervene pre-op,' he went on, 'to reduce the size of the tumour, if possible, or at least to stabilize it; I will intervene post-op, to eliminate the persistent cancer cells close to the tumour.'

'But I thought there were no metastases . . .'

Lesage looked at him seriously, opened his mouth and closed it again several times before speaking again. The PET scan had not, it was true, revealed any metastases; but this was in fact a surprising result. These cancers of the jaw are often very invasive, particularly when they touch the lymph nodes. In that case cancer cells can move into the lymph, which irrigates all areas of the organism. In short, it would have been more realistic to say that there were no metastases *for now*. Apart from that, sometimes the PET scan failed to detect certain metastases, he said sadly; there were plenty of reasons to be sad, in fact, Paul said to himself, if that apparatus that looked like it cost the price of an Airbus was incapable of fulfilling its function.

'The PET scan still represents enormous progress,' observed the younger of the two doctors whose name Paul had already forgotten; he had already decided to call him Dupond to himself – there was something unworldly about him that corresponded well with the final 'd', while the older one, earthier and more rooted in day-to-day reality, would make a perfect Dupont. As to the surgeon, he was going to call him King, to keep things simple. He returned his attention to him and confessed that he had not understood a word of his previous explanation of the operation that needed to be performed. In fact, King agreed, there were certain technical terms that he could have explained. Resection was simply the removal of the tumour. Segmentary mandibulectomy consisted in removing part of the lower jaw; if necessary, they would proceed to the removal of the entire horizontal branch of the left jaw, as well as the central symphysis – in other words, the chin. As to the glossectomy, that was the removal of the tongue; unfortunately, in his case, it would apply to the whole of the moving part.

Complete silence fell in the room. Paul did not react, which worried the surgeon. At this stage, some patients collapse in a state of despair; others become angry, energetically refusing the prospect given to them, even sometimes insulting the doctor; still others try to bargain as if, by resorting to a cunning ploy, they could negotiate a somewhat less severe surgical intervention; but he had never known anyone to accept the operation immediately, and willingly; or indeed anyone who, like Paul, remained absolutely inert, as if they had not understood the diagnosis. It was so unusual that he finally asked: 'You have understood what I was saying, haven't you, Monsieur Raison?' Paul nodded, still in silence.

'Will I have to spend a long time in hospital?' he asked at last, breaking an increasingly heavy silence. The surgeon flinched slightly; it's a question that patients always ask at some point or other; but it's hardly ever the one that they ask first. 'In the absence of complications, we assume a minimum stay of three weeks,' he replied. 'It is still a serious operation, you're going to be spending a certain amount of time under the knife, as they say.'

'How long?' This was better, the surgeon said to himself, he was starting to ask normal questions. 'Between ten and twelve hours. There may be one or two complementary interventions to be taken into account, an hour or two, no more than that. The first intervention is the most important: I will proceed to the resection, then to the reconstruction, which means that you won't be disfigured in the meantime. The solution of classic reconstruction consists in using the bone from the shoulder-blade to reconstitute a jaw, and part of the large dorsal muscle, with the adjacent skin, for the tongue. But the use of a titanium artificial jaw, made with a 3D printer, might be possible in your case, I would need to consult a colleague; in that case the intervention would be slightly shorter.'

They should also point out, the surgeon went on, that the newly grafted tongue would not be entirely functional, it was chiefly intended to fill the mouth. It would not have taste buds or muscles, when a normal human tongue has seventeen muscles. If he managed to move it, it would only be thanks to the remaining muscles on the base of the tongue, which could not be removed without leading to the necrosis of the whole. It was only at the end of a lengthy period of rehabilitation, probably lasting at least three months, that he would be able to speak and eat more or less normally again. At the beginning he would have to be fed by catheter, and he would also need a tracheotomy to breathe, at least for the first week.

Nakkache looked uneasily at Paul, who still wasn't reacting; it was almost as if he was only half there, and not really concerned. After another long silence, he did speak again to ask if the operation was urgent. Unfortunately so, the surgeon replied: the longer they waited, the more time they allowed the tumour to develop. They had to think in terms of an intervention before the end of the month, in early August at the latest. And to tell the truth, when they thought about it, that would very probably rule out the solution of a titanium artificial jaw; at the moment they were made only in the USA, and it would take too long for it to be delivered. Paul shook his head in silence; there were no other questions.

Still accompanied by Nakkache, he walked down the interminable pale green corridors in the other direction. A dozen or so taxis were waiting in front of the main entrance to the hospital, but he decided to go home on foot, it was only a fifteen-minute walk, twenty minutes at the most. Nakkache took a taxi. He turned towards him again, hesitated and tried to find his words. 'It's a shock for you, an operation happening so quickly, I understand . . .' he said at last with difficulty. Paul gave him a look of indifference before answering calmly: 'Having an operation like that is out of the question. Radiotherapy and chemotherapy, fine; surgery, it's a no.'

'No, wait, wait one minute!' Nakkache exclaimed in a panic. 'You can't react like that! What you have is a serious cancer. The prognosis when the bone is affected is not good, compared to other ENT cancers: a five-year survival rate of 25%. If you refuse surgery that'll get even lower.'

'You mean,' Paul broke in, 'that I'm supposed to have my jaw removed and my tongue cut out if I'm to have a chance in four of surviving?'

Nakkache fell abruptly silent; that was how it was, Paul understood. The ENT doctor was embarrassed, he hadn't planned to leak the information like that, but that was how it was. 'We'll have to discuss it again . . .' Nakkache replied hastily. 'I don't have my appointment book to hand, but call me tomorrow and I'll find you a spot.' Paul nodded in silence, having resolved to do nothing. He had made his decision.

He froze in the middle of the Pont de Bercy. On the left he was facing the Finance Ministry, and beyond it he could make out the clock of the Gare de Lyon; the Parc de Bercy stretched out to his right. His life had definitely unfolded within a limited space, he reflected, and it would carry on like that until the end, because behind him lay the Pitié-Salpêtrière Hospital, where in all likelihood it would come to an end. How strange it was, all the same! It was infinitely strange. Less than three weeks ago he was a normal person, he could feel carnal desires, plan holidays, imagine a long and possibly happy life, in fact he could imagine that more than ever, since he had come back together with Prudence, he had always loved her, and she had always loved him, that much was obvious now. And then, in the space of a few medical appointments, everything had collapsed, the trap had closed on him, and the trap was not about to open, quite the contrary, he would feel its grip more and more cruelly, the tumour would go on devouring his flesh until his annihilation. He had been rushed into a kind of incomprehensible slide whose only outcome was death. How much time did he have left? A month? Three months? A year? He would have to ask the doctors. Then there would be nothingness, a radical and definitive nothingness. He would never see anything, hear anything, touch anything, feel anything, ever again. His consciousness would disappear completely, and it would be as if he had never existed, his flesh would rot in the ground – unless he chose the more radical destruction of incineration. The world would go on, human beings would pair off, feel desires, pursue goals, feed dreams; but it would all happen without him. He would leave a faint trace in people's memory; then that trace would fade too. All of a sudden he felt a real surge of hatred for Cécile and her stupid beliefs. Pascal was right, as usual: 'In the end dirt is thrown on your head, and that's it for ever.'

For now, though, he was going to have to talk to Prudence, it couldn't be put off any longer. Luckily it was Friday, he couldn't imagine making such an announcement on a weekday, knowing that she would have to go back to work the next day; neither could he imagine talking to her about it on a Saturday, to tell the truth, he couldn't imagine talking to her about it at all. But he had to.

4

In fact he didn't get to talk to her until late on Sunday morning, after they had made love for longer than usual, and he had given her, he was sure of it, more pleasure than usual, but of course there was more at stake than that, what was needed was an absolute, telluric orgasm, an orgasm that was enough on its own to justify a life, in fact it would have taken something that didn't exist except perhaps in the novels of Hemingway, he remembered a particularly idiotic passage in *For Whom the Bell Tolls*.

He talked at length, in some detail, for over ten minutes, not hiding anything from her and not even trying to lie to her. She listened to him, curled up in bed, propped up on two pillows, without saying a word. She didn't burst into tears, indeed she barely showed any real reaction, from time to time she made a kind of punching gesture with her right hand, punching the void, and from time to time her breathing became heavier. After it was over, she fell silent, for a minute or two, before turning back towards him and saying very crisply, almost with hostility:

'You'll need to get a second opinion. An opinion from another doctor.'

'What doctor?'

'I don't know. Call Bruno.'

'Why him? Bruno knows nothing about medicine.'

'He intervened with the Health Ministry over your father; they know each other, they have a good relationship. The other man must know who the best doctor is in this field; at least, I should imagine that a health minister knows a few things about health.'

'Yes, you may be right.'

'Call him now.'

'It's Sunday.'

'I know it's Sunday. Call him now.'

He had more or less forgotten Bruno's working rhythm; he reminded him of it straight away. He listened without a word, and then concluded: 'I have some calls to make, I also have to wait for the replies. Can I get back to you in two or three hours?'

They waited for his call while watching the retransmission of *Sunday Morning* on Arte. Jacques Martin, one of the *lords* of French television during the second half of the twentieth century, was on his way to becoming a national treasure, as Michel Drucker was too, even more quickly, in the first few weeks after his death.

Bruno called back exactly two hours later. 'You have an appointment at 10 o'clock tomorrow morning with Professor Bokobza; he's the best European specialist in mouth cancer surgery. He's at the Gustave Roussy Institute, in Villejuif. Dr Nakkache – he's the ENT doctor you saw, isn't he? – will mail him your file this afternoon.'

Paul came off the A6 motorway at Avenue du Président-Allende, then took Rue Marcel-Grosménil, before turning down Rue Édouard-Vaillant, where the institute was located.

The son of Hippolyte Grosménil and Julienne Fruit, Marcel Grosménil, after obtaining his university diploma, had a three-year apprenticeship before doing his military service in the cavalry in Provins. A lathe operator, on 31 October 1924 he married Marie Mathurine Cadoret. The couple had one son, Bernard. The family lived at 10 Rue de Gentilly, in Villejuif, where the wife had a shop. A lathe operator for Hispano Suiza in Paris, in the fourteenth arrondissement, he joined the Gnome et Rhône engineering company in 1935, and was elected municipal councillor in Villejuif in May of the same year, as one of the Communist candidates put forward by Paul Vaillant-Couturier. The council of the prefecture stripped him of his mandate on 29 February 1940 for membership of the Communist Party. Marked as 'in exile' by his employer on 30 June 1940, he was reinstated on 23 April 1941. Arrested with his friend Raymond Pezart when he was about to join the Free French Forces in Algeria, he was imprisoned in Bordeaux, then interned in Compiègne before being deported to Germany, to the camp in Oranienburg, where he died in the course of April 1945. He was recognized as having 'died for France' on 14 December 1948.

Villejuif more generally, run uninterruptedly by Communist mayors from 1925 until 2014, had for a long time been an iconic example of the 'red suburbs', before more recent population movements influenced the course of things. There were no longer, to start with, many Jews, and the borough had instead become known for various Islamist attacks, or planned attacks. In January 2015, Amedy Coulibaly, who would later take part in the hostage-taking at the Hypercacher minimarket at Porte de Vincennes, where he would murder four people, had blown up a car in Villejuif. In April 2015 an Algerian student, Sid Ahmed Ghlam, had been arrested when he was planning an armed attack to coincide with Sunday mass, in the two churches in Villejuif. On 13 November 2015, the town hall was burned down as a sign of homage to the massacre which, a little earlier that evening, had cost the lives of 129 people in Paris. Driving back up Rue Édouard-Vaillant towards the hospital, Paul passed by the regional park of Hautes-Bruyères, where in January 2020 a mentally disturbed individual who had just converted to Islam attacked walkers with a knife, leaving one person dead and two seriously injured. He was beginning to wonder if it wouldn't have been better to come by metro; he was pleasantly surprised to discover that there was a car park in the courtyard of the hospital. Its façade, brightened by touches of vivid colour, reminded him a little of the one at the Saint-Luc hospital in Lyon. After the PET scan, the prospect of a tracheotomy and a catheter, that façade . . . Definitely, he said to himself with an ambiguous mixture of feelings, he was following more and more in his father's footsteps.

Wearing an impeccable light-grey three-piece suit under his white doctor's coat, Professor Bokobza was the spitting image of the *big medical director* as popularized by various films and television series, which Paul found very reassuring; it's always better in the end for things to correspond to their image. His austere expression, his wire-framed glasses – everything about him, in fact, was reassuring to the highest degree; the surgeon at the Pitié-Salpêtrière might have had slightly longer hair and, most importantly, trainers whose soles were too thick. Paul didn't know if he was being conformist or if he was *old school*, but he apparently became so as soon as questions of life and death were broached, and everyone must be more or less so in that circumstance, he suspected.

'So, you're a friend of our minister . . .' Bokobza said with a little smile once he was sitting opposite him.

'Not exactly,' Paul replied, 'more a friend of one of his colleagues.'

'I know that people speak ill of nepotism, of privilege, of advantages . . . Obviously it's justified, but everyone uses the contacts they have, even people situated at the bottom of the social ladder, and we must acknowledge that it sometimes allows us to unblock situations rendered insoluble by excessive regulation; we would also have to say, in your particular case, that your cancer is a serious affair, and of course you have the right to the best possible treatment. There is already one thing that I need to point out to you: there's nothing unusual, in a situation such as yours, about feeling the need for a second medical opinion; but it's still not an anodyne

454

procedure. Is it possible, in one way or another, that you are prompted to do so by a lack of trust in your current surgeon?'

'I don't know,' Paul said after thinking for quite a long time. 'First of all, it was my wife who wanted me to do it. Otherwise, I would have to say that I don't like the idea of this operation at all; but I really don't know if it's the surgeon that I don't like, or the operation itself; a bit of both, I think.'

'I hear that you have a doubt,' Bokobza said almost immediately. 'In my eyes that's enough. If you don't have absolute trust in the surgeon who is going to be operating on you – even if it's irrational, even if it's unjustifiable – you don't have to be operated on by him. Have you read *Disturbance* by Philippe Lançon?'

'No, I've heard of it, though, he was a journalist with *Charlie Hebdo*, isn't that right? One of the victims of the Islamists?'

'Exactly. He took a burst of fire from a Kalashnikov full in the face, which led to a situation of reconstruction quite close to your own once the jaw has been removed. I mention it because reading him one understands the importance of a relation of trust with one's surgeon; also, much of it takes place in the Pitié-Salpêtrière. So I'm recommending it to you because it's a good book, but I would have to admit that it isn't necessarily very encouraging for patients. The author goes through I don't remember how many surgical interventions, ten or fifteen, you lose count of the exact number; over all, he spends two years in hospital. You would have to say to yourself that it's unusual, that you won't be in the same situation. The book came out a bit more than ten years ago, and some progress has been made since then; the graft is always a delicate operation, and it can often end in failure; but 3D imaging technology and artificial jaws have really brought us a lot.'

'The surgeon at the Pitié thinks it isn't applicable in my case; the operation is urgent, the prosthesis has to be manufactured in the USA and there isn't time.'

'Well, on this point I would have to say that I disagree with my colleague; your cancer is aggressive, but it isn't very invasive. With a good course of chemotherapy your tumour can be reduced, or at least its progress can be halted for a few months, long enough to make the prosthesis; and Lesage is an excellent chemotherapist, I have every confidence in him. If you were my patient, I would launch the manufacturing process straight away, and would plan for an intervention in late October. It's perfectly possible to operate on you here, and to carry out the chemo and radiotherapy at the Pitié-Salpêtrière; I would even advise you to do that, in fact, these are tiring processes, and you would be well advised to keep your movements to a minimum. I don't want to exaggerate my importance as a surgeon, the decision is up to you, of course; I would advise you to think about it calmly, and also to have another word with Nakkache, he's a good doctor, you're lucky.'

He particularly wanted to talk to Prudence about it, in fact; after all, who was concerned, really concerned by his death apart from her? To a certain extent, he was; to a lesser degree, it seemed to him, our own death is of relatively little concern to us, Epicurus was right as usual. Still, he wasn't going to get back into that, not for now.

'According to Nakkache, the chances of survival ore more or less one in four,' he went on in a curiously detached tone; he didn't know where it came from.

'Yes,' Bokobza replied calmly. 'In cases where the bone is attacked, those are the figures more or less. Having said that, in your case, in the absence of any metastasis, the relatively non-invasive character of the cancer, that could rise to one in two, I would say.'

'One chance in two: it's a bit like being in a film, isn't it?'

'You're right to respond with humour,' the surgeon replied with a hint of sadness. 'Coming from me obviously, it would be inappropriate; but you have the right to be humorous about your own survival; it's one of the rights of man, to some degree.'

'I have another question. Replacing bone with a titanium artificial jaw doesn't bother me that much, quite the contrary, in fact, I've had so much trouble with my teeth that it would almost come as a relief. On the other hand it seems to me, after what the other surgeon said that at the moment there is no good solution for the tongue.'

Bokobza lowered his head, and this time he sighed wearily before answering:

'Quite. That's true, we haven't fully got there in that field. Food won't taste the same, and it will be difficult for you to speak. More generally, the mobility of the tongue will be reduced.'

'Would it not be possible to limit the operation to the jaw, and not intervene on the tongue?'

The surgeon smiled involuntarily. 'You know what you're doing? You're trying to bargain. I have some more reading matter to recommend to you: Elisabeth Kübler-Ross. She's the author of the theory on the five phases of grief. That can be applied to one's own death or that of a loved one, but more generally to any form of grief, it could be a divorce or an amputation.' He became serious again and shook his head sadly. 'To come back to your question, unfortunately the answer is negative. There would be no point in partially removing the tumour, it could even encourage the spread of the cancer.'

'And what if I refuse any form of surgery? If we keep it to chemo and radiotherapy?'

'Then your chances of survival are much lower; having said that, you can never be sure, a perfect prognosis is impossible. Chemotherapy alone doesn't effect a cure; but sometimes, although we don't know why, radiotherapy leads to the stabilization and then the shrinkage of the tumour, until it is completely reabsorbed. It's rare, but it does happen.'

'And if we do nothing at all, how much time do I have?'

'About a month.'

Paul burst out laughing for a moment, then fell abruptly silent. Bokobza lowered his head in embarrassment, raised it a few seconds later, and was even more embarrassed to see tears flowing gently, silently, down Paul's cheeks.

'I have no more questions, Doctor,' he said at last in a perfectly calm voice.

'I would rather you agreed to the surgery, of course,' Bokobza said as he walked him to the door. Just before he stepped into the corridor, he took him by the sleeve and looked him right in the eyes before adding: 'One last thing. If radio and chemotherapy were to fail, it would still be possible to come back to surgery. It's more difficult, the tissue is weakened, the graft has a greater risk of being rejected, but it's not impossible. I have sometimes attempted that operation – and succeeded.'

5

Before going home, Paul stopped at the FNAC in Bercy Village, on the Cour Saint-Émilion, where he easily found Philippe Lançon's book. He also bought a paperback of *La mort, porte de la vie*, by Elisabeth Kübler-Ross; he found the title very unconvincing, since at first sight it was more or less the opposite of what seemed to him to be the truth. After thinking for a while he added *La mort est un nouveau soleil*, another stupid title, but one that reminded him of something, he didn't know what. He complemented his purchases with a little book by one David Servan-Schreiber, apparently consisting of psychological advice for people with cancer. It wasn't a very good choice, he realized almost immediately; filled with positive thinking, the author insisted on the need to maintain a series of pleasant moments, good little meals among friends, accompanied by local wines drunk in moderation and punctuated by hearty laugher – he even went so far as to praise Belgian jokes; it all made him want to go to bed and die, particularly the hearty laughter, to tell the truth it hadn't been long since praise of local wines and hearty laughter had been coming out of his ears, so it wasn't a book for him. Elisabeth Kübler-Ross was hardly any better; he was far from convinced by her theory of the five stages of grief. The first two, denial and anger, didn't seem to have happened at all in his case; the third, bargaining, barely; as to the fifth, acceptance, in his view it was a joke pure and simple; in the end only the fourth stage, depression, struck him as real;

her theory was nothing but smoke and mirrors, and he very quickly gave up on *La mort, porte de la vie*. Opening *La mort est un nouveau soleil*, he immediately remembered what the title reminded him of; the stupid comparison made by La Rochefoucauld, in which he claimed that neither could be stared at, which was trivially false in the case of the sun, as you can confirm every morning when it rises, and quite often when it sets. In spite of its stupid title, the second book was considerably more interesting than the first; the Swiss doctor had been a pioneer in the description of 'near-death experiences', which he remembered vaguely from an American romantic comedy whose name he had completely forgotten. He immediately went back to FNAC to buy a book by the other precursor, Raymond Moody, and that was immediately exciting, probably more than the film. First of all there was disembodiment, when you left the physical body and floated several metres away from it, in the hospital ward or near the crashed car. Then the shrill ring of a bell like the one at school summoning pupils back to class, and being sucked into a dark tunnel, which you then hurtled down at dizzying speed. Then the tunnel threw you out somewhere, in a new space, one that was unknown and almost abstract. When that happened, some people saw their whole lives in a sequence of several hundred very brief images. Then came the beings of light. First the loved ones who had gone before, and who had reassembled for your benefit, not least to teach you the course of the subsequent stages; you recognized them all, your grandparents and your old friends, individually, you recognized each one. Last of all, you saw the primal light, which had temporarily agreed to assume visible form; then you understood that it would always be there, but that for now it preferred to entrust your loved ones with the task of guiding you.

These testimonies were beautiful and convincing, all the more so in that they came from simple people with limited vocabulary, who seemed incapable of inventing stories of this kind. The experience of disembodiment was certainly the most crucial; Paul found it impossible to imagine life outside of the physical body, it was inconceivable to him; and yet that was exactly what people remembered when they woke up, and that memory, unlike the ones filled with light and serenity that marked the rest of the journey, was not particularly pleasant, or indeed unpleasant, most people felt only a relative indifference towards their physical body, sometimes, however with a desire to return to it, simply because they were used to it, but their predominant feeling was one of deep uncertainty, as in the testimony of this Walmart cashier: 'I thought I was dead, and I wasn't sorry that I was dead, but I just couldn't figure out where I was supposed to go. My thoughts and my consciousness were just like they are in life, but I just couldn't figure all this out. I kept thinking, "Where am I going to go? What am I going to do?" and "My God, I'm dead! I can't believe it!" Because you never really believe, I don't think, fully that you're going to die. It's always something that's going to happen to the other person, and although you know it you really never believe it deep down . . . And so I decided I was just going to wait until all the excitement died down and they carried my body away, and try to see if I could figure out where to go from there.' The fact that she waited for further instructions was touching, she must have been an excellent cashier in her lifetime, and one could certainly not have suspected these narratives of being connected to an excessive production of endorphins, there was nothing ecstatic about them, they were simply radically strange; at any rate for all of those revenants, those moments were at the bottom of a crucial change in their idea of what life should be like. Probably, Paul said to himself, if he had had an experience of this kind, he would have had no difficulty in accepting death. The mere fact of being able to remember one's own death, the actual state of death, would have been a source of great comfort to humanity, as one realized while going through the testimonies of those who had escaped clinical death. For example that of a farmer in Arizona: 'All I felt was warmth and the most extreme comfort I have ever experienced. I remember thinking, "I must be dead."' Or a metalworker in Connecticut: 'I felt absolutely nothing except peace, comfort, well-being and calm. I felt like all my troubles had stopped, and I said to myself, "How gentle this is, how peaceful, I don't hurt anywhere anymore." A great attitude of relief. There was no pain, and I've never felt so relaxed. I was at ease and it was all good.' Plain and actual in most cases, the testimonies attained the sublime when they tried to describe the primordial light. Had he been lucky enough to experience something like this, there was no doubt that Paul would have waited for death without fear of any kind; that was not the case, however; he had always seen death as absolute destruction, like a terrifying plunge into nothingness. No description, however moving it might have been, seemed capable of replacing lived experience. However he continued his reading all afternoon, captivated, and it suddenly occurred to him that if Prudence happened upon the book she would immediately conclude that he was preparing for death; he would have to hide it in his office and read it when she wasn't there. Finally only the Lançon remained; but as he flicked through it he quickly realized that the situation was different, since 3D printing was still a futuristic dream at the time; and most importantly, even though the journalist's jaw had been pulverized, his tongue had not been affected, so their cases ultimately had nothing to do with one another. So it was without any aids that he set about cobbling together an acceptable version for Prudence; she would question him straight away, almost as soon as he got home, but he didn't think she would talk to him on the telephone first, it was too important a subject and they would have to be physical together; he had a bit of time to refine his account.

The ideal lie consists in the juxtaposition of different truthful elements, with certain ellipses left between them; in essence it consists of omissions, sometimes carefully blended with a number

462

of slight exaggerations. Professor Bokobza struck him as a remarkable doctor, Paul trusted him completely, more than the doctor from the Pitié-Salpêtrière; he could say all of that, it was true, and Prudence believed him without any problem, she trusted Bruno's recommendations implicitly. There were two possible paths of treatment, one involving surgery, the other radio- and chemotherapy; that was true too, he just neglected to mention that the two paths weren't incompatible, that they didn't promise equal chances of success, and that Professor Bokobza had clearly recommended the first. He immediately tried to forget this awkward piece of information: a good lie is a lie that you believe yourself, and as he developed his explanation Paul sensed that he was lying well, that Prudence's mistrust was gradually fading, and that he himself would soon forget reality, at least for a while.

An excessively reassuring story would not have been credible – they were dealing with cancer after all – so troubling and painful aspects also had to be introduced; radio- and chemotherapy would do the trick, accompanied as they were by a stream of amply documented secondary effects: extreme fatigue; vomiting; loss of appetite; sudden loss of red blood cells, white blood cells and platelets; sometimes hair loss. This particular cancer, of the oral cavity, had the additionally distressing quality of being fetid; a pestilential odour would gradually emerge from his mouth, Paul had learned; chemotherapy would help to reduce the phenomenon, without getting rid of it entirely. Their conversation lasted just over two hours, and Paul maintained the same attitude until the end, with increasing difficulty and some moments of doubt, he did not utter a lie in the strict sense, but the temptation returned more and more powerfully to tell her the whole truth. He resisted doing so, and he knew that he was right, of course he was fucked and she would realize that sooner or later, and probably within the very near future, but she needed to understand it herself, in her own time. It would be hard for her, perhaps they should have had children after all, that would have been something in spite of it all, replacement love. He had had this idea several times in his life, before rejecting it as absurd. Various magazine articles in his youth had popularized the ideas of American sociobiologists about the 'selfish gene'; American sociobiologists saw procreation as a kind of primitive scream from the gene, ready for anything to ensure its own survival, even to the detriment of the most elementary interests of the host individuals, via an audacious deception that by reproducing they would win the game against death, while of course the opposite was true, in all animals reproduction was a crucial step towards death, when it did not actually cause it, and that partial genetic survival would in any case have been nothing but a derisory parody of authentic survival. Nothing in the memory that he had of his father corresponded to that pattern; having devoted his life to French military success, his father saw himself everywhere, he knew, as one of the guardians of the order and security of his country, and perhaps of the Western world more generally; disappointed by Paul's attitude towards the DGSI, he had been even more disappointed by Aurélien's, seeing it as a rejection of the principles that had governed his life, so the bulk of his affection had been transferred to Cécile, and later to her husband, there was nothing genetic in any of it, this was cultural transmission in the purest state.

This stupidly reductionist conception on the part of the sociobiologists strangely lent support to an already well-established American conception of childhood, to which the contemporary American novel continued to bear witness; in it, professional, friendly and romantic relationships were depicted with the most repellent cynicism, while relationships with children appeared as a kind of enchanted space, a magical little island in an ocean of selfishness; that might have been entirely understandable in the context of the baby, who can send you in a few seconds from paradise, when its flesh huddles against your shoulder, to the hell of

464

unmotivated cries of rage, in which it already manifests its tyrannical and domineering nature. The eight-year-old child, sanctified as a partner in a game of baseball and as a mischievous little chap, still has his charm; but things go sour very quickly, as everyone knows. Parents' love of their children is well attested, it's a kind of natural phenomenon, particularly in women; but children never respond to that love and are never worthy of it, children's love of their parents is absolutely against nature. If by some misfortune they had had a child, Paul reflected there would never have been a chance of getting back together with Prudence. As soon as the child reaches the shores of adolescence, the first task assumed by the child is to destroy the couple formed by its parents, and in particular to destroy it in sexual terms; the child cannot under any circumstances bear its parents engaging in sexual activity, particularly with each other, it logically considers that from the moment of its birth that activity has no longer any reason to continue, and is henceforth only a disgusting old people's vice. This is not exactly what Freud taught; but Freud didn't understand much about it in any case. After destroying its parents as a couple, the child sets about destroying them individually, its chief preoccupation being to wait for their death so that it can inherit its legacy, as clearly established in the French realist literature of the nineteenth century. One can consider oneself lucky that they do not set about hastening the settlement date, as they do in Maupassant, who didn't invent anything, and who knew Norman peasants better than anyone. So that is how things happen, generally speaking, with children.

They could perhaps have had a dog, but they hadn't, and now they only had each other, and that would have to do them until the end. The entity made up by a couple, and more precisely by a heterosexual couple, remains the main practical possibility for the manifestation of love, and Prudence would lose that for ever within a few months, perhaps a few weeks. Then she in turn would have to die, she would do it quickly, but her last moments would be difficult, not because of her own death, she didn't care about that at all, women identify easily with their function and easily come to understand that when their function is at an end their life itself is over – men are in a more delicate position, for different historical reasons they have sometimes been able to define their function in relation to their being, or at least that is what they have believed, so of course they have ended up granting a special importance to that being in question, and are entirely flummoxed when that too comes to an end. Prudence's last moments would be difficult simply because they would be lonely and absurd: what was the point? to what end?

She fell asleep in his arms, apparently reassured; when someone, especially a woman, passionately desires something, it's never very hard to persuade her that the thing is going to happen. It would be less easy with Bruno; he knew that Bokobza was a surgeon, and he had probably even had an opportunity to talk to him; Paul would have to call him the next day.

Essentially it was quite recently that the codes of politeness that applied in Paul's circles had come to include the obligation to conceal one's own impending death. First of all it was illness in general that had become obscene, the phenomenon had spread in the West in the 1950s, first of all in the English-speaking countries; every illness, in a sense, was now a shameful illness, and fatal illnesses were of course the most shameful of all. As to death, it was the supreme indecency. Funeral ceremonies became shorter – the technical innovation of cremation meant that the process could be considerably accelerated, and from the 1980s onwards things were pretty much over. Much more recently, in the most enlightened and progressive strata of society, attempts had been made to sweep aside the last days as well. It had become inevitable, people who were dying had disappointed the hope that was placed in them, they had often been reluctant to envisage their own passing as opportunity for a huge party, and unpleasant episodes had ensued. In those conditions, the most enlightened and progressive strata of society had agreed to pass over hospitalization in silence, since the mission of partners or, in the absence of those, of the closest relatives was to present it as a kind of holiday. If the hospitalization became prolonged, the already risky fiction of a year's sabbatical had sometimes been used by some, but that was barely credible outside of university circles, and in any case it was only rarely necessary since prolonged hospitalization had become the exception, the decision in favour of euthanasia was generally taken within several weeks, or indeed several days. The ashes were scattered anonymously, by a family member if there was one available, or by a young clerk from the solicitor's office. That lonely death, lonelier than it has ever been since the beginnings of human history, had recently been celebrated by the authors of different books on personal development, the same ones who had praised the Dalai Lama some years previously, and who had more recently adopted a fundamentalist line on ecological matters. They saw it as the welcome return of a kind of animal wisdom. It was not only birds who hid to die, according to the French title of a famous best-seller by an Australian author, which had also led to an even more famous and more lucrative television series; the great majority of animals, even those that belonged to highly social species, such as wolves or elephants, felt the need to remove themselves from the group when they felt death approaching; so the voice of nature spoke in its immemorial wisdom, the authors of various works on personal development stressed.

Bruno, he knew, was not in any way a supporter of these new civilized codes that applied among the cultured middle classes; he was more inclined to approach things head-on, calling a spade a spade, without making any effort to conceal reality. He was in fact the one who called first, and Paul had not quite had time to refine his presentation of things. However, he had managed reasonably well, or at least so it seemed to him. His first decision was to refuse surgery, which, as he openly admitted, reduced his chances of survival; but it would be possible to come back to it later, if radiotherapy proved unsuccessful. He refrained from mentioning that in that case the operation would have a much smaller chance of success. Two truths, followed by an omission; the same lying tactic that he had used with Prudence, and it seemed to work equally well with Bruno; he would catch up with him regularly, he concluded before hanging up.

The next day he had a meeting with Dupond and Dupont, this time in the office of the chemotherapist, a cosy little space, the walls covered with green velvet; it was very surprising to find that in a hospital. Paul sat down on a little sofa in the right-hand side of the room. Dupont was sitting in a revolving chair behind his desk, Dupond in a Voltaire armchair opposite him. Dupond turned towards Paul and looked at him for a long time before saying: 'Of course we will do everything we can,' and his resigned tone already seemed to indicate that he considered failure a likely option. 'Bokobza has described the situation to you quite clearly, I imagine,' Dupont went on; everyone seemed to have huge respect for Bokobza, Bruno himself had never enjoyed such complete unanimity among his peers and colleagues, and Paul reproached himself, having only spent a few minutes in Bokobza's presence, for not having paid more attention to this man, a specialist, an eminent technologist in his field, one of those – a few thousand or indeed a few hundred, certainly not more – who are at the base of the edifice, who make it possible for the social machine to work.

Dupont could by no means guarantee his survival, no one could do that, except God, perhaps, or the rulers of different societies located more in the future, of which South Korea might supply a vague approximation; he could guarantee only that as much as possible would be done within the social context that applied in his country. France was in decline, certainly, but it still offered better technical opportunities than Venezuela or Niger.

The therapists then launched into an animated duet the foundations of which were doubtless common to all patients, while the details were improvised for each, and the goal of which was to accustom them to the idea that it wasn't going to be easy, and that it might even be frankly distressing – particularly in his case, since renouncing surgery meant that a direct attack would have to be launched on the tumour, with massive doses of radiation. Fatigue, vomiting and nausea would be inevitable. He was very likely to lose a great deal of weight, since cancer cells consumed a huge amount of energy, much more than healthy ones. Yes, it was ironic, Dupont agreed sadly, ironic and cruel, that cancer cells were such greedy consumers of energy, and that they could grab anything that reached the organism; cancer really was a bunch of crap, no doubt about it.

6

The following Monday, just before midday, Paul went to the hospital for his first sessions. It was 19 July, the city's residents were already starting to leave for the summer vacation, and the moment of greatest peace would arrive in two weeks; under normal circumstances it was a time when he loved being in Paris.

He had some difficulty finding the place where his first appointment was meant to be: it was a huge prefab building, all on one floor, isolated within an internal courtyard. About a dozen patients were waiting in a glass-walled corridor. When he sat down in the midst of them after presenting himself to the nurse at reception, they looked up and glanced at him briefly before turning away again. No one spoke, no one was reading; their solitude was complete. Every now and again they looked at each other 'with pain and without hope', as Pascal says, before plunging back inside themselves. Indisputably, this was 'the image of the human condition', as Pascal also says, and this was the best example of it, that of an old civilized society; there were plenty of places in the world where human beings had spent their days in death's waiting room hurling themselves enthusiastically into the intoxication of a massacre; there were plenty of places in the world where the departure of a peer, a *colleague*, for his place of execution, might have been received not with indifference but with an explosion of fierce joy.

Paul had brought the book by Philippe Lançon, but he was surprised to realize that he didn't want to open it. He should have bought it some weeks before, when he was worried by the idea of joining the camp of seriously afflicted patients; but it was too late now. Philippe Lançon had been seriously, even definitively afflicted, he would always prompt revulsion in his fellows, in fact in a sense he would probably never have fellows ever again; but he himself, since he had been mortally afflicted, had gone past the stage when one can actually go looking for one's fellows; he was in the midst of the damned, the incurable, in a community that would never be one, a mute community of beings gradually dissolving around one, he was walking 'in the valley of the shadow of death', to use the expression that came to him, for the first time, with all its force; he was discovering a strange and residual form of life, completely apart from the rest, where the stakes were completely different from those that preoccupied the living.

He didn't have to wait long before he was summoned to one of the rooms on the left-hand side of the corridor. Standing in the middle of the room was a huge apparatus, made of the same creamy white metal as the PET scanner, and which, like it, looked like something straight out of *Star Wars*. Accompanied by a nurse, Dupond seemed to be a kind of servant of the machine; he laid Paul down on the couchette, between the lines drawn on the felt, before taking out a stiff resin mask. 'I'm going to have to put this on your head,' he said, 'you have to remain perfectly motionless during the treatment, to avoid irradiating the healthy areas'; then he clipped the mask to the couchette. Paul was aware of giving a start in spite of himself, but his face and shoulders were held firmly in place. 'Don't worry,' the doctor said gently. 'I know it's unpleasant to be wedged in like that, but it won't be very long, and it won't be painful in any way.' Paul closed his eyes.

After the session Dupond helped him back to his feet; his head was spinning a little, that was normal, he said to himself, the best thing would be for him to rest on a nearby bed before setting off again. He had a meeting for the chemotherapy session at 1.00 p.m., so he had time to grab a bite to eat if he wanted, the hospital cafeteria was excellent in his view, although probably he wouldn't be very hungry. As soon as he was lying down Paul felt a violent wave of nausea and dashed to the toilets, but only threw up a bit of acrid bile.

The chemotherapy took place in another part of the hospital, which he also didn't know; the hospital was really vast. He found himself in a high-ceilinged room, with long rows of identical beds arranged a few metres apart, and which looked old. In fact, Dupont confirmed, it dated from 1910, almost all eras from the past century, the past two, even, were represented in the hospital; obviously the patients preferred the more modern wards, but in fact that didn't matter in the slightest, the equipment was, of course, the same in all of them, but it was true that the atmosphere of a public health service hospice was quite depressing, no one would have wanted to sleep there, and the place was only ever used as a day hospital. As to the chemotherapy itself, 'I've made you up a little cocktail,' he said with an attempt at a mischievous grimace, but it wasn't very successful, his face wasn't made for malicious grimaces. 'This should help reduce the most unpleasant aspects,' he went on more seriously. 'The smell?' Paul asked. 'Yes, the smell in particular,' he shook his head sadly. 'Your tumour is really starting to stink. I know how horrible it must be to see your dear ones avoiding you, there's nothing you can do about it, you know, sometimes it's really pestilential; but right now I can guarantee that we're going to avoid that.' The treatment was administered by drip, a nurse would be coming at any moment to put the drip bag in place, the drip itself would take approximately six hours, and he would come back in an hour or two to check that everything was going well. Paul was astonished; he hadn't anticipated being on a drip for six hours. Yes,

472

Dupont agreed, it was restricting, but it was the most effective method; later, perhaps, if it all went well, they could attempt oral administration; but the drip was required for now. The nurse was already approaching, pushing the drip bag stand on its rollers. 'Your wife is coming to get you in a moment, isn't that right?' the doctor asked. He nodded. That was better, Dupont said; normally the undesirable effects would only be felt later in the evening; but still, he thought it was best.

After the doctor left, Paul looked around. The ward was almost empty, there were only ten or so patients there, very far apart, like randomly scattered stars. Most of them were lying down like him, others were sitting in armchairs beside their drips. A ray of sunlight from a high window played through the dust; the silence was total. Six hours on a drip per day, five days a week, struck him as a huge amount. He was going to need books to get through it, but which ones? In the end it was his survival that was at stake, and he needed books to match. Maybe Pascal, quite simply. Or else something completely different, escapist novels or adventures, like Buchan or Conan Doyle.

Dupont came back a little after seven, just before it was time to liberate him; he had called by for the first time at three, he said, but Paul had been asleep. Before he left, he gave him a sheet of paper listing the undesirable secondary effects, which repeated in greater detail what had been explained to him already. A blood sample would be taken at the end of the week; sometimes a drop in blood cells took some time to appear.

Prudence was waiting for him by the main entrance to the hospital; she gave him a worried look and put an arm around his waist before leading him towards a taxi. He wasn't too bad, he argued; but in fact, as soon as he arrived at the apartment, he felt a need to lie down, and later he only managed to gulp down a few mouthfuls of soup before being filled with an irrepressible desire to vomit. Poor Prudence, he thought, she had blended the vegetables and everything. He was still going to need to eat a little, she said; the hospital information sheet recommended potatoes, pasta and starches. It was the beginning that was particularly difficult, he replied, they'd promised him that things would sort themselves out within a few days. They hadn't promised him anything of the kind, and as he said the words he was aware that Prudence didn't believe it, not only because she wanted to believe any kind of good news, but more deeply because she was incapable of lying, or even of conceiving of a lie, it wasn't in her nature.

He easily found the complete Sherlock Holmes on his bookshelf, published in two volumes in the *Bouquins* series, but he was still surprised, the following afternoon, that he could detach himself so quickly from his own existence, to lose himself in the deductions of the brilliant detective and the dark manoeuvres of Professor Moriarty; what else but a book could have produced such an effect? Not a film, a piece of music even less so, music was intended for the healthy. But even philosophy wouldn't have been suitable, and neither would poetry, poetry wasn't made for the dying either; he absolutely needed a work of fiction; he needed the narration of lives other than his own. And essentially, he said to himself, those other lives didn't even need to be captivating, it didn't even require the exceptional imagination and talent of Arthur Conan Doyle, it wouldn't have mattered if the lives related had been just as bleak and uninteresting as his own; they just had to be *other*. They also, for more mysterious reasons, needed to be invented; neither a biography nor an autobiography would have done the job. 'What a novel my life is!' Napoleon had exclaimed; he had been wrong. The account of his life in *The Memorial of St Helena*, was just as pernickety a read as that of a postal worker, real life really wasn't up to it. Lives like Napoleon's might have been occasionally interesting – one might imagine, for example, that he had *shone* at

Wagram or Austerlitz; but going from there to naming metro stations after them was quite a jump.

Mediocre and narrow lives, transfigured by the author's gifts or genius or whatever term one might choose, might also have had the advantage of making him aware that his own life hadn't been as pathetic as all that. His holidays in Corsica with Prudence were on the level of a decent pornographic film, in particular the sequences on the beach at Moriani, that was definitely the name of the beach, it was coming back to him now; some conversations he had had with Bruno wouldn't have been out of place in a political thriller. In short, he had lived.

On Friday afternoon he had just dived into *The Valley of Fear*, or more precisely the scene where McMurdo, with remarkable courage, endures the initiation ceremony of the Scowrers, when a nurse came to tell him that his sister was asking to see him. 'My sister?' he repeated stupidly. 'You do have a sister?' the nurse said, worried, she couldn't let just anyone in, she was in a position of responsibility. Yes, in fact, he did have a sister, Paul said slowly; he was having a terrible struggle dragging himself out of his book.

As soon as Cécile was three metres away from his bed he realized that this was not going to go well, that she wasn't going to be able to contain her anger. 'Your operation . . .!' she began, before falling silent, choking with indignation, unable to carry on. 'There's no point trying to pull the wool over my eyes, I went to see your ENT doctor.' Surprised, he stammered something about medical secrets.

'He absolutely didn't betray any medical secrets. I told him I knew you'd decided not to have an operation; I was sure you'd do something like that, I've read all about your cancer on the internet, and I'm getting to know you. I told him I'd come to ask him to make you change your mind. He said he would have loved to try, but that you didn't even call him back to make an appointment, you arranged things directly with the hospital.'

'Anyway, it's too late . . .' Paul said feebly.

'Yes, I know, he told me that too. From where we are now, it would be better for you to pursue your course of radiotherapy, it's going to last for seven weeks and then they'll take another look at the situation.

'Why seven weeks?'

'You didn't even ask the question!' she yelled furiously, apparently on the brink of exploding once again. 'With five sessions a week, that's seven weeks to reach 70 grays, the maximum dose of radiation that a human being can bear; radiotherapy isn't harmless, there's collateral damage, as your doctor told me. But as for you, apparently, as soon as you can avoid surgery you don't care. I don't understand, Paul. He told me that the best surgeon in Europe had agreed to operate on you. I know men are cowards, but to take it that far . . . I'm also sure that you've lied to your wife.'

'No, not really.'

'Oh yeah? You've refrained from telling her certain things, then?'

'Closer to that, yes.'

'I see. You don't even have to courage to tell a real lie. Don't worry about it . . .' she went on after catching his anxious expression, 'I won't say anything, I won't get mixed up in your private life. And in any case it's too late to change your treatment, there's no point making her suffer for nothing. But I really wonder how long you're going to wait before telling her the truth . . .'

Paul said nothing; in fact he had been wondering the same thing. Cécile also fell silent; she seemed to be starting to calm down, her anger was turning gradually into sadness.

'We've already had Aurélien dying this year, so the numbers are growing,' she said at last. 'Do you think it's amusing to me to have two brothers committing suicide?'

'That's not it . . .! I'm not committing suicide, I'm choosing one treatment rather than another. There are cases of cure by radiotherapy, you can ask the doctors, they'll confirm it.'

She pulled a broadly dubious, almost contemptuous face; Nak-kache clearly hadn't sung the praises of radiotherapy.

'It's a difficult case, but I can heal like that,' Paul insisted. 'And besides, you can pray for me, if you like.'

'Stop it!' She leapt to her feet, all her anger coming back all of a sudden. 'Stop that this minute!' What had he said that was wrong? He really didn't understand anything about her religion. 'There's no point praying in your case,' she shouted, 'it would almost be blasphemy, prayer can't have any effect on you because basically you don't want to live. Life is a gift from God, and God will help you if you help yourself, but if you refuse the gift from God there's nothing he can do for you, and basically you don't even have the right to refuse it, you might imagine that your life belongs to you but that's wrong, your life belongs to the people who love you, you belong to Prudence first and foremost, but also a bit to me, and maybe to other people that I didn't know, you belong to other people, even if you don't know it.'

She sat down again, embarrassed, before gradually calming herself, her breathing was becoming normal again, but it took her a good minute to recover herself and continue: 'OK, I'm useless, there you are with your drip and I come and tell you off . . . But I'm really annoyed. I was shocked that you refused to have the operation. I don't want you to die, Paul.'

In a faint, almost inaudible voice, he replied: 'I don't want them to cut out my tongue.'

She sighed for a long time and stood up. 'Forgive me. Everything I've said to you was completely stupid, I'm going to go now, I've got to collect myself and think a little. But there's one thing I want you to know.' She looked him straight in the eyes, her face loving and clear again, she was recovering herself, moral indignation really wasn't her register. 'Whatever happens, you can always call me, I'll drop everything come to your bedside, it'll only take me a few hours. You can call me even if it's at the very last minute and you didn't call me beforehand, if you didn't keep me up to date with anything. I'll be there.'

As she headed towards the exit of the shared ward, she turned around several times to give him little waves, and for no apparent reason her outline was increasingly blurred; perhaps he had a problem with his eyesight, on top of everything else.

seven

1

As she passed through the door of the ward, Paul had a very clear sense, a certainty even, that he would never see Cécile again – or indeed Hervé, or even less Anne-Lise. He would never again see people on this earth, and each time he would do everything he could to avoid giving the impression of a final farewell, at no point would he abandon a reasonably optimistic and even humorous attitude, he would act like everybody else, he would conceal his own agony. However much one might despise, or even hate, one's generation and one's era, one belongs to it whether one wants to or not, and acts in line with one's views; only an exceptional moral strength allows one to escape it, and he had never had that strength. Probably for the last time, some days before, he had talked to Bruno on the phone, and as usual Bruno had shown himself to be competent, devoted and efficient. He had seen Cécile again, and as usual Cécile had been affectionate, bad-tempered and emotional. He was going to see his father again, he didn't yet know exactly when, but he needed this last meeting, and now that would be even simpler, taking his condition into account his father was bound to be impenetrable, enigmatic and silent, as he had always been. In the end, relationships between human beings don't change very much in the course of a lifetime, they follow established patterns from the very start of the relationship, and perhaps from the start of everything.

At last he found himself alone with Prudence, until the end, more alone than they had ever been. Prudence was the only one upon whom he had the right to impose the ordeal of his wasting body, to make her go with him as he weakened and suffered, she was responsible for his body, that was, it seemed to him, the meaning of marriage, he had put his body in Prudence's hands and in the end he had done the right thing, she would know how to take care of it until the end. He was filled with a strange sense of recklessness that was not fully of this world, and he plunged with a light heart into the adventures of McMurdo, Scanlan and McGinty. He remained immersed in Sherlock Holmes's investigations all week, which allowed him to endure the six daily hours on the drip without any difficulty. Dupont dropped by to see him every day in the middle of the afternoon; he used a tongue depressor to examine his palate, sometimes moved on to examine the tumour and seemed satisfied, it wasn't progressing, it might even have regressed slightly, in short he didn't want to give him false hope, it could start growing again at any moment, it was still unpredictable.

For her part, Prudence had finally discovered some things that he was able to digest, which it was possible for him to eat without immediately feeling a desire to vomit; essentially these were boiled potatoes, pasta without sauce and flavourless cheeses along the lines of the brand Vache qui Rit; in gastronomic terms, there was nothing remarkable about the end of his life.

The situation regarding sex was less clear. He was very much weakened, and his movements within the apartment were gradually limited to the space between bed and armchair, as in the Jacques Brel song, but he hadn't yet reached the final stage, 'from bed to bed'. He was able to get up, but he could only walk a few metres before his legs gave in spite of his efforts and he had to sit down; merely turning round in bed required a huge effort. Under those conditions, making love didn't seem very much of a possibility. And yet he did get hard, in an almost normal way, his cock apparently paid little attention to his state of health, it claimed its due, and seemed to lead a life completely independently of the rest of his body. To tell the truth, much the same was true of his brain; he had no trouble reading, he could easily understand the author's quips and allusions, he appreciated his stylistic effects; but it was all still strangely organized.

The Sabbath of Lughnasadh fell on 1 August; this was a moment when, according to Scott Cunningham, 'the God loses His strength as the Sun rises farther in the South each day and the nights grow longer. The Goddess watches in sorrow and joy as She realizes that the God is divine, and yet lives on inside Her as Her child.' That Sunday 1 August, it was around 6 p.m. and Paul, sitting in the marital bed, propped up by two pillows, had just finished 'The Adventure of the Blanched Soldier', that admirable short story that ends with a kind of medical miracle, and was saying to himself that he would have fewer and fewer misgivings in asking for a miracle from the Lord, the gods of paganism, or any entity at all, when Prudence came over to the bed, naked to the waist, wearing only a short T-shirt, to ask him if he wanted a blow job. She had been very hesitant about doing that over the past few days, because suggesting a blow job was in a way lending credence to the idea that he would never again be able to fuck, to ensure actual penetration, but in the middle of the afternoon she had realized in a moment's insight that he was really tired, and that they were going to have to adapt if they wanted to go on having a sex life, they had to take the reality into account, and in any case she had always had a gift for a blowie, she had the instinct for it.

It was a very long, dreamy blow job – starting just after 6 p.m., it finished at around nine – and it brought him huge pleasure, one of the greatest pleasures he had ever felt in his life. During one of the breaks that she allowed herself to get her breath back, he set about licking her; while he might not have been as talented as she was, he wasn't bad at oral sex, and he tried to be ironic about the

consequences that the removal of his tongue might have for their
life as a couple; but he immediately realized that the subject was
not very suited to irony.

They were about to enter the two calmest weeks, the first fortnight
in August, when the whole of Paris started to feel like a hospital,
although without the worrying quality, perhaps more of a rest home.
On Tuesday 3 August, at the beginning of the afternoon, shortly
after the nurse had set up his drip, he started reading *His Last Bow*,
or more precisely the eponymous short story, the last one in the
collection. Immediately before the outbreak of the First World War,
Sherlock Holmes came out of his beekeeping retirement to serve his
country and help to capture the German spy von Bork. Paul med-
itated for a long time about the last page, which could not be seen as
Conan Doyle's final testimony – he had gone on to write many other
things – but perhaps as that of his most illustrious character.

> *'There's an East wind coming, Watson.'*
> *'I think not, Holmes, it is very warm.'*
> *'Good old Watson! You are the one fixed point in a*
> *changing age. There's an East wind coming all the same,*
> *such a wind as never blew on England yet. It will be*
> *cold and bitter, Watson, and a good many of us may*
> *wither before its blast. But it's God's own wind none the*
> *less, and a cleaner, better, stronger land will lie in the*
> *sunshine when the storm has cleared. Start her up,*
> *Watson, for it's time that we were on our way.'*

Paul did not believe for a second that England, any more than
any other European nation, had emerged strengthened from the
First World War; quite the contrary, it seemed obvious to him that
this stupid carnage lay at the origin of the terminal phase of Europe's
decline; but if Conan Doyle had managed to convince himself that

England would come out of it regenerated, that was good; after reading two volumes of Sherlock Holmes, he felt filled with affectionate gratitude towards Arthur Conan Doyle, who had, for two weeks, really allowed him to forget his drip, his cancer and all the rest. The fifteen volumes of the complete Agatha Christie, which he had just bought, would be broadly enough for his radio- and chemotherapy – there was a little under six weeks to go, from what Cécile had told him.

One problem quickly made its appearance felt, which was that Agatha Christie was a good author, but not on the same level as Conan Doyle. Her books were less captivating, their effect less radical, and he very quickly began thinking about his drip again, about that needle stuck in his arm, and feeling the desire to tear it out. Ideally he would have gone to sleep, but he had never managed to sleep on his back. That position reminded him of the prostrate figures in church tombs, the French kings fixed in a hieratic attitude for the centuries to come, hands joined in prayer; it wasn't his idea of a good night's sleep. Sleeping on his belly was hardly any better, it wasn't really comfortable after too generous a meal, and in fact it recalled the dull-witted sleep of an exhausted animal. What he preferred, essentially, and had always preferred, was sleeping on his side. It was also the only way in which, curled up, one could return to the foetal position that awakens within us, until the end of our days, an irreparable nostalgia.

Not only did he prefer to sleep on his side, but he had always preferred to make love on his side, particularly with Prudence. In Paul's eyes there was little difference between the missionary position and doggy style, in both cases it was the man who controlled the rhythm and brutality of the embrace. In both cases the woman – either by parting her thighs or lifting her bottom – placed herself in a position of submission, which was an argument strongly in favour of those positions but also, by virtue of the fact that they borrowed directly from the animal world, constituted their limit, even more so in the case of doggy style. The position in which the woman is on top of the man, on the other hand, struck him as too solemn, it placed the woman in the position of a female divinity engaging in a sort of ceremony of devotion to the phallus; neither he nor his phallus seemed to him to justify such grandiloquence. Most importantly the position lying on his side was the one that allowed him, while penetrating Prudence, to hold her in his arms, to caress her, and most particularly to caress her breasts, which she had always liked; of all the sexual positions, for Paul it was the most loving and emotional, the most human.

In many circumstances in his life, he had felt more comfortable on his side. Even when engaged in a less essential activity such as swimming, he had always favoured swimming on his side, also known as 'Indian swimming', that had always been his favourite. It let you keep your nose and mouth out of the water, and consequently allowed the swimmer to breathe entirely at his own rhythm, independent of the speed of his movements; the only way, then, that turned swimming into a harmless and banal activity. Swimming on one's back, it was true, could also have matched these criteria, but because it left one unable to control one's direction precisely, it contradicted the essential principle of swimming – which is, like walking, a means of locomotion from one place to another – and by that very fact it remained a pointless and artificial exercise. One might, in summary, say of Paul that he had tried, most of the time, to live on his side.

2

On Friday 6 August he reached a considerable state of irritation with his drip that the books of Agatha Christie no longer helped to dispel, certain Poirots aside, and he decided to broach the problem with Dupont, since it was the day of his weekly visit. The doctor listened to him without surprise, even with a degree of resignation, before taking a folder from his briefcase. 'You have managed for three weeks without complaining,' he observed, 'that's pretty much the average. Hardly anybody can bear the drips to the end. Sometimes that's a shame, in some cases it might have offered a hope of a cure, but in yours, it's true, we're stabilizing your condition at best.' In his case, on the other hand, perhaps there was a new possibility for treatment, something completely different, he wasn't absolutely sure, he needed to take a sample of some of the cancer cells and carry out a molecular analysis before making a prognosis; he could take the sample today. Paul nodded. If it wasn't too much of a bother, Dupont went on, they could even keep going with the drip for an extra week, they would decide on that later. He nodded again.

Dupont didn't come back until the following week; it was Friday 13 August, late in the afternoon. Paul wasn't really thinking about his drip, he was immersed in *Appointment with Death*, quite a good Poirot, the character of the tyrannical Lady Boynton was done brilliantly. She was depicted as a real monster, her children trembled with fear in her presence, and ended up imagining her death as their only chance of liberation. The molecular analysis had taken a certain amount of time, Dupont said, and then he had groped around for a while, it was important to understand that this was an innovative treatment that had not yet really been tested. 'As far as I'm concerned right now,' Paul remarked, 'I think you can do experiments . . .' The doctor couldn't help smiling. 'In fact' he said, 'I would have preferred things to be otherwise, but that's not wrong.' What he was going to suggest for him was a mixture of light chemotherapy – applied orally – and immunotherapy, which was based on a completely different principle: it wasn't a matter of attacking the tumour directly, but of directing the immune system to recognize and destroy cancer cells. In practical terms, there would also be drips, but they wouldn't take as long, they could be applied at home, and more importantly they would be less frequent, one injection every two weeks would be enough.

'But that's nothing . . .!' Paul exclaimed. 'That's completely different.'

'In a sense that's right, but you've got to understand that we're not very far ahead with immunotherapy, there haven't been many clinical trials, so the result is far from guaranteed and there might even be secondary effects that we're not aware of.'

'And when could we start?' Paul asked, having barely listened to the warning.

'Next Monday.'

It was nearly 7 o'clock by the time Dupont left, Prudence was going to call by in a few minutes and he felt a genuine surge of joy as he realized that, for the first time, he wouldn't have to lie to her. He could even stress the innovative character of the treatment, without putting too much emphasis on the dangerous aspect. At any rate, from the following Monday, he could be home by one o'clock in the afternoon, and the radiotherapy would also come to an end three weeks later, so by early September he would no longer have to come back to the hospital, and they could even imagine leaving Paris.

He waited for them to be home before talking to her about it. She couldn't receive such news without being filled with a wave of hope and enthusiasm, without having the certainty that this time this was it, that the healing process had well and truly begun; Paul couldn't remember ever seeing her so happy, and he lacked the courage to temper her optimism; he knew, however, that the situation could develop in a very different way. Unlike Nakkache, Dupond and Dupont never tried to present things in an unnecessarily favourable light, on the contrary they tried to warn him against being over-optimistic, they had even been almost excessive in their honesty, most doctors wouldn't have behaved like that. They hadn't concealed from him, for example, the fact that a tumour that appeared to be completely reabsorbed on an MRI or a scanner might in fact have become microscopic and undetectable, and would resume its progress a little later; also, sometimes, a chemotherapy that had been initially effective could suddenly cease to function when the tumour had managed to adapt to it. Paul took mental notes about all this information; most of the time he thought rationally and said to himself that he was in fact in all likelihood totally fucked, but most of the time he succeeded in not fully accepting the fact, since essentially he found it impossible to imagine his own death.

That did sometimes happen, however, in a flash of terrible awareness, always when he was surrounded by other people, never when he was alone. He came gradually to fear crowds and even little groups, because the first feeling that crept over him, and the most horrible, was a puff of pure jealousy at the sight of all those people around him who tomorrow, the day after tomorrow, for decades perhaps, would go on living in the middle of things and living creatures, to feel their fleshly presence, while for him there would no longer be anything, he imagined himself being buried in icy mud in the middle of an endless night, the cold invaded his being and he went on trembling for an hour or two, sometimes taking a whole day to recover. Sometimes, on the other hand, he was filled immediately afterwards by a burst of delirious optimism: he was going to get better, immunotherapy was a miraculous discovery and Dr Dupont was a genius – but that never lasted for long, no more than a few minutes.

They were sitting in the living room, and the sun was setting over the Parc de Bercy. To all appearances, Prudence had begun to believe in his recovery as soon as he had talked to her about immunotherapy, to believe in it with all her might, and after all it wasn't impossible, there can be real progress in medicine, it happens sometimes. He himself was filled with a wave of optimism, and he started drinking quite a lot. It was still a bit foggy the next morning when he felt Prudence taking him in her mouth, she did it often before he had really woken up. The day seemed broadly to have broken, but the curtains were drawn, he couldn't see much, and it seemed to him that she was moving in a strange way, she had got up and was jerking him off with her right hand, suddenly he worked out that she was bringing herself off with her left hand, which was quite unusual, all of a sudden he understood when she moved her leg over him before grabbing his cock and plunging it into her, she was very wet and took him in easily. Then she began contracting rhythmically, gently at first, then faster and faster, once she had reached the root of his prick she started rising, her movements became slower and gentler when she reached the glans, then she came back down again, pumping him harder and harder, she was really controlling her pussy brilliantly, the rising pleasure was irresistible and he came inside her without ever considering the possibility of controlling himself. Then she slumped on top of him and wrapped an arm around his neck as she gradually got her breath back. 'It's weird, we've never done it like that, I don't understand why . . .' Paul said, still thinking in spite of himself that he had definitely chosen a very bad moment to die. 'I don't understand either,' she replied, before continuing, a bit later: 'Maybe deep down it's more natural for me to be passive, in fact I've never thought of changing, so your illness will have achieved that at least.' She was still projecting herself into the future, resolutely convinced that he was going to live, which made him uneasy for a moment but he set about convincing himself of the same thing, it was a kind of training, a knock that he had to take, and he succeeded in doing so. Most of the time. But this time the thought of death came back very quickly, with the violence of a punch to the stomach, and he lost his breath for a few seconds. The problem was that Prudence had understood everything now, she reacted immediately, and a frisson of impotent sadness passed across her face. He felt that soon, very soon, he was going to abandon any trace of privacy, of modesty in her presence; then they would be truly together, more so than they had ever been, the two of them would be constantly as they were now when having sex, they would walk the valley of the shadow of death together. There would be physical love to the end, she would come to terms with it. In one way or another she would come to terms with it. And even if his tumour really began to stink, she would blink slightly, concentrate on sending her sense of smell to sleep and manage to love him, some very loving women had done the same with the stench of shit rising from their husbands' ruined entrails making their breath stink; it was true that the tumour gave off a smell that was even worse than shit; it was the smell of corpses, of decomposing flesh – that's how nature goes about its business, it's Mother Nature, that's it's style, but they weren't going to get there anyway. Dupont had promised him that chemotherapy would considerably reduce the smell, and Dupont did not seem like a joker or a clown; if Dupont had made him a promise, it would be kept.

Weirdly, Paul's thoughts sometimes took a political turn these

491

days. It was normally too late to think about these things, but he had spent years of his life in the political world without thinking about it, without really talking about it, whatever it might be. His opinions had never been very important, and now they weren't important at all, the only thing that mattered was the uncertain battle taking place in his flesh between the cancer cells and the immune cells, on which his survival depended. Even so, that didn't mean he was incapable of forming certain ideas, not many, his intellectual needs had always been modest; every now and again it floated to the edge of his consciousness. In that he was like most men, he couldn't keep himself from thinking about these general questions completely, even though he knew he would never be able to resolve any of them.

Paul had known men who could never have imagined going back on their word, there was no need to resort to the formality of delivering a sermon to them. It was surprising that such men existed in the present day, and they weren't even extremely rare. Bokobza was probably one such, but he was more familiar with Dupont, and particularly with Bruno. For about a century, other men had appeared in growing numbers; they were jovial and slimy, they lacked even the relative innocence of monkeys, they were carried along by their infernal mission to gnaw away and corrode any bond, to annihilate everything that was necessary and human. Unfortunately, in the end, they had reached the public at large, the people. For a long time the cultured public had fallen prey to the principle of decadence, under the influence of thinkers that it would be otiose to list, but that didn't matter very much, the wider public was of the essence, it was now, since the Beatles and perhaps since Elvis Presley, the norm of all validation, a role that the cultivated class, having failed both in both ethical and aesthetic terms, and also being seriously compromised on the intellectual level, was no longer qualified to hold. Since the wider public had thus acquired the status of a source of universal validation, its programmed debasement was a bad idea, Paul reflected, and could only lead to a sad and violent end.

During the first week, Dupont came to visit him every day during his resting time, immediately after his radiotherapy session. He subjected him to a clinical examination, always with his tongue depressor, and took a blood sample; he seemed absorbed in dark reflections. Paul, meanwhile, at his mirror, avoided looking at his tumour, the thing was pretty disgusting, but at least it didn't smell too bad. He still couldn't imagine kissing Prudence on the mouth again, but the smell was still bearable.

On Friday 20 August, at the end of the first week, Dupont told him that he was reacting well to the immunotherapy, at least there hadn't been any obvious secondary effects, and in his view they could continue. He had reached the end of his explanation when his colleague Dupond came into the room and also took a seat next to his bed; he thought it was a better idea to bring the radiotherapy to an end a week before the planned date, to avoid irreversible necroses. There was nothing unusual or alarming about that, the resistance of patients to irradiation varied, and in his case 60 grays might be more appropriate than 70. Paul then wanted to know if the treatment had taken effect, and if he was satisfied by the results. But that, essentially the crucial question, he couldn't tell him; the tumour often underwent an involution. He would have to wait for at least a month, meaning the start of October, while of course pursuing chemo- and immunotherapy, before having another complete health check: scanner, MRI, PET scan, thorough clinical examination. He doubted that an extra week of radiotherapy would change the situation; but at the same time it wasn't completely out of the question; on the other hand he was sure that his system wouldn't be able to bear a dose of 70 grays without suffering irreversible damage; that kind of dilemma was posed constantly, in oncology. They could go for something in the middle, Paul suggested. Yes, that was a possibility, Dupond replied. He picked up his folders and did some swift calculations. The 65-gray dose, which really seemed to be the maximum, would be reached if they stopped the treatment on 31 August.

3

So, that 31 August he went to the Pitié-Salpêtrière Hospital for his last session with Dupond. It was perhaps the last time that he would see Dupond, and also perhaps the last time that he would see the Pitié-Salpêtrière; if he had to die in hospital, it would probably be in Villejuif; every time he did something now it felt like a farewell. Sometimes, in spite of himself, he found Sherlock Holmes's final sentence coming into his head in spite of himself: '*Start her up, Watson, for it's time that we were on our way*', and each time it did so he was on the brink of tears. He had no desire to leave this world, no desire; and yet he had to.

In his book, Philippe Lançon mentions various sites within the walls of the Pitié-Salpêtrière that are remarkable for their beauty or their historical character; he hadn't seen any. It was true that Lançon had stayed there for two years, and had had time to do a bit of tourism; given Paul's condition, all he could imagine doing was internet tourism. On the website *www.paris-promeneurs.com*, he happened on an article devoted to the old prison of La Petite Force, located within the hospital walls, and which, after welcoming all those who were 'cancerous, scabrous, weary, truculent and epileptic', in other words the incurables of the time, was now home to the psychiatric service, after being used under the Ancien Régime as a prison for prostitutes awaiting transfer to the new colonies, which they were intended to help populate. During the Revolution, the prison had been the stage of one of the September massacres.

Lançon didn't mention that in his book, he had probably not visited the place; it would have to be said that in the photographs displayed he was ugly and even frankly sinister – as sinister as the events that had played out there; those dark little courtyards, surrounded by grey buildings, that the sun never seemed able to reach, were the ideal place for a massacre.

In September 1792 the Petite Force prison had been, like others, invaded by a crowd of sans-culottes, acting spontaneously according to historians, in search of aristocrats to exterminate. As in other prisons, some prisoners had been arbitrarily freed while others had had their throats slit before being literally cut into pieces. Continuing with his reading, Paul came upon a letter from the Marquis de Sade, who had been in prison during those days and related the events like this: 'Ten thousand prisoners died during the day of 3 September. The Princesse de Lamballe was among the victims; her head, carried on a pike, was presented to the eyes of the king and queen, and her unfortunate body dragged through the streets, after being soiled, it is said, by all the outrages of the wildest debauchery.' Gilbert Lély, his biographer, saw fit to add, in a story that must have fired the imagination: 'Her breasts and her vulva were cut off. One executioner made himself a moustache of that delightful organ, to the great hilarity of the "patriots", and he cried: "The whore! No one's going to be threading that needle from now on!"'

It's probably normal for old people to take an interest in history, which contextualizes their own passing by retracing the fates of important, illustrious and sometimes even all-powerful people who had nonetheless returned to dust. And Paul was a very old person, if we consider that real age is not measured in the years that one has lived already, but those that one has yet to live. It's probably what brought him close to Joseph de Maistre, having recently discovered that his father had been an assiduous reader of his. He bought a volume of his major works, which he could read in alternation with Agatha Christie, which struck him as a good *mix*. He quickly grasped the main theory of the Savoyard author: the French Revolution was, from start to finish, satanically inspired, and the philosophers of the Enlightenment who were its source had, like Luther and a few centuries after him, received instructions directly from the Prince of Darkness. It had to be acknowledged that that interpretation, if one assumed the inevitably unusual point of view of a royalist Catholic, was not without a certain coherence.

He had never realized that he had been so exhausted by radiotherapy, the fatigue had taken root very progressively, but he was struck by how quickly his strength had returned after 1 September. The effect was already apparent after a week, and became completely obvious after two. Not only was he walking more easily, he could imagine quite long strolls in the Parc de Bercy, but he was managing to fuck Prudence on his side. Doggy style and the missionary position were still out of the question, and would probably remain so for ever, but the return of the side position was enough of a delight on its own, he fell asleep after ejaculating but went on holding her in his arms, he slept for maybe an hour or two, then woke up, got hard again and penetrated her immediately, then they fell asleep again and they resumed after an hour or two; she was almost permanently wet. It was an ideal and perfect way of life that didn't cost very much. Now they had finished paying off their apartment, Prudence having a part-time job would broadly have covered it.

At the end of the second week, when he was starting to feel better and better, he suggested that they go away to Saint-Joseph for a few days; she accepted immediately. He needed to see his father again, she knew without knowing why, even less, of course, than he understood himself. If they left the following Saturday, and spent three days there, they could be back on the evening of the 21st, it would be the first day of autumn, the ideal date to come back under any circumstances. Paul had always liked 'Signe', the poem by Apollinaire, in particular the first line, 'I am subject to the Head of the Sign of Autumn'; every time, he felt as if he were passing through the porch of a sumptuous mystery. The last line, on the other hand, 'The doves tonight are taking their final flight.' The doves? What doves? *What's up with the fucking doves?*

Even if he was feeling better he didn't really feel quite up to driving, and Prudence took the wheel, early afternoon on Saturday the 19th. As soon as they reached the first forests he understood that the trip was an excellent idea, and that they were going to spend those few days being very happy, perhaps for the last time; it was certainly, in any case, their last trip. Prudence drove well, she was calm and confident at the wheel. They didn't talk much, but it wasn't necessary; the landscape, very beautiful as soon as they entered Burgundy, was magnificent just past Mâcon, as soon as they arrived in Beaujolais proper. The vines were lit with scarlet and gold, more, it seemed to him, than they had ever been, but perhaps it was just because he was about to die, that he would never again see this landscape that he had loved since childhood.

Prudence had given Madeleine a watered-down version of the situation: in fact he was ill, it was cancer, after all, but the treatment was under way and they were hopeful. Bourgeois decency was beyond Madeleine's capacity, and as soon as she saw Paul in the doorway – the light on the vines was overwhelming, terrible in its beauty – she couldn't help exclaiming: 'How thin you've got!'

Of course he had got thin, the cells of his tumour were consuming the energy ration of two ordinary adults all by themselves, and he had always had a great deal of trouble feeding himself. It wasn't bourgeois decency alone that led Prudence to attempt to come up with an optimistic version, but more the fact that she had started believing her own story; Madeleine worked out within a few seconds, and just as she realized that she had made a mistake, she lowered her head before Prudence's glittering gaze and only regained her equilibrium by clinging to her old functions as a servant. 'Your room is ready,' she said, 'you can go and rest, you must need to.' Not that much, in fact, after four easy hours' drive on the motorway, but she had to say something. Paul wasn't going to have anything to eat this evening, Prudence said, he was actually tired, he wouldn't see his father until the next day; but a bowl of vegetable soup would be good, and perhaps some mashed potato.

In fact he went to sleep almost immediately, about ten minutes after lying down, without really understanding what had happened between the two women; it was an unusual situation that Madeleine was going to have to get used to, sons don't die before their fathers as a rule, and this time it was the older son. Prudence woke Paul so that he could eat the light supper that she had brought up for him, he had been less nauseous since the end of the radiotherapy, now it was a bit as if he was her young son having fallen victim to a childhood illness, or her old father suffering from some partial disability, at the same time she loved his cock more than ever, but none of that bothered her, he could be her son, her father and her lover all at once, the symbolism that came into play was a matter of complete indifference to her, the important thing was that he was there.

The next morning, Paul wanted to spend a few hours in his old room. Prudence nodded gently; like all women in love she was moved to think of those few years when she had not yet met Paul, even though he was almost an adult already; those few years, both empty and full of enormous potential, when both of them, independently, for good or ill, were abandoning adolescence, when they were getting used to shouldering the burden of adult life.

In fact Paul realized immediately, as soon as he opened the door of his bedroom, that he was done once and for all with Kurt Cobain. Perhaps less obviously so with Keanu Reeves. He had certainly not finished with Carrie-Anne Moss, quite the opposite, and he understood immediately that he was going to have to destroy those posters, now or never, and in reality it was more like now.

After lunch, which had gone quite well – he had managed to eat a little more than usual, but had once again felt the need to lie down in the middle of the meal – Madeleine told him that his father was in the conservatory; she didn't add that he was waiting for him, but that was the clear message. He still had a bit of trouble getting to his feet, but wasn't particularly alarmed, there would be incidents of that kind for some time to come, the radiotherapist had warned him, and they didn't have any particular significance. Prudence helped him down the stairs, then went and looked for his father's old wheelchair, the ordinary model.

As Prudence turned into the glass-framed walled corridor, pushing the wheelchair, he had another shock at the sight of the landscape of forests and vines; that juxtaposition of green, scarlet and gold was one of the images that he wanted to keep till the end, to the very last seconds. Then they reached the conservatory; his father was sitting at a little round table, with his wheelchair in the reclining position. Prudence straightened him up and put Paul on the other side of table, directly opposite him, so that they could see each other clearly.

'What time would you like me to come and get you?' she asked before leaving again.

'Just before dinner, I think.'

'You want to stay as long as that? All afternoon?'

'What I have to say isn't simple.'

When she came back, a little after seven, Paul was sitting beside his father, facing the picture window. They were contemplating the landscape which was now, in the rays of the setting sun, supernaturally beautiful; she froze at the sight. Her initial intention had been to tell Édouard that she was going to take Paul away, that it would soon be dinner time, and that Madeleine would come and get him immediately afterwards; she was going to do it, of course, but not immediately, dinner could wait a little, and the idea of interrupting their contemplation of the sunset was unthinkable. In some of his paintings, Claude Gellée, known as 'Claude Lorrain', had sometimes done as well as that, or worse, placing within the hearts of men the intoxicating temptation to leave for a more beautiful world when our joys would be complete. That departure usually happened at sunset, but it was only a symbol, its true moment was death. The sunset was not a farewell, the night would be brief and would lead to an absolute dawn, the first absolute dawn in the history of the world, that was what one might be led to imagine, Paul thought, by contemplating the paintings of Claude Gellée, known as 'Claude Lorrain', and also by contemplating the sun going down on the hills of Beaujolais.

It didn't take long, a quarter of an hour at most, for the darkness to become total, and for Prudence to decide to take him back towards the dining room. As he was still silent, she finally asked him, just before they got there and met up with Madeleine:

'How did things go with your father?'

'I didn't say anything to him.'

'What, nothing?'

'Nothing in particular, nothing more than before. That I was ill, that I had cancer but was being well looked after, that we were hopeful.'

It wasn't a complete lie, but it was a very simplified version. 'I thought there were more things you wanted to say to him . . .' Prudence said after a while.

'I thought so too; but in the end, no.'

4

Mid-morning the next day they went off for a long drive. Paul wanted to take the little winding secondary road that falls from the Col du Fût-d'Avenas towards Beaujeu, the one that he had taken, alone at the time, when he had gone to see his father at the hospital in Belleville-en-Beaujolais for the first time. He didn't know that Aurélien had taken the same route with Maryse, and that it had been the start of their love, the only joy in his pitiful existence. That moment had happened, he couldn't have done without it. Moments happen or don't happen, people's lives are altered and sometimes destroyed by them, and what can one say? What can one do? Apparently nothing.

Prudence folded away the wheelchair before putting it in the car boot, in case he wanted to stop somewhere. A thought occurred to him, quite a comical one, about hot pants, she had brought three pairs, but apparently she wouldn't be able to use them, not for now.

In fact Paul asked her to stop halfway to Beaujeu, in exactly the same place as he had stopped some months earlier. She unfolded the wheelchair, and he sat facing the landscape; she sat down cross-legged beside him. The huge forest that stretched in front of them was not still, a light breeze stirred the leaves, and that very light movement was even more soothing than complete stillness would have been, the forest seemed animated by a calm breath, infinitely calmer than any animal breath, beyond any agi-

502

tation or any emotion, but unlike anything purely mineral, more fragile and more tender, a possible intermediary between matter and man, it was life in its essence, the peaceful life, unaware of strife or pain. It did not conjure eternity, that wasn't the question, but when one was lost in contemplation of it life seemed much less important.

They stayed like that for a little over two hours, allowing themselves to be filled by a deep sense of peace, before getting back in the car. 'We'll leave tomorrow, as planned,' Paul said before Prudence set off again. 'Unless you want to stay a bit longer.' We can come back, Prudence said. He said they could, but she had developed a terrible sensitivity to his slightest intonation, and something about his reply gripped her heart, she felt that he didn't entirely believe that they would be back, that he had a sense of doing all of this for the last time, like a kind of commemoration, and that in a sense he was already far from her, very far; but at the same time he needed her presence beside him more than ever.

They stopped for a drink in Beaujeu, and there again, without knowing, Paul chose the same café as Aurélien had done some months before, when he had stopped for a drink with Maryse, the Retinton.

Their stay had been a short one, he said to Prudence, but in essence it was a perfect match for his expectations. He had been struck once more by the solidity, the seemingly indestructible nature of his father's will to live, which contrasted so starkly with the feebleness of his own, not to mention his unfortunate brother's. Then he began to generalize, men's original sin, they like to generalize; it's also in a sense, if you like, their greatness, where would we be without generalizations, without theories of some kind? Just as the waiter brought their beers, he remembered a conversation with Bruno, one of their first long conversations, shortly after they came back from Addis Ababa, in fact Bruno did almost all the talking, to broach what was, as he would soon discover, one of his chief obsessions. The *baby-boomers* were a very surprising phenomenon, he had told him at the time, like the *baby-boom* itself. Wars were generally followed by a fall in the birth rate, accompanied by a psychological collapse; shedding light on the absurdity of the human condition, they had a powerfully demoralizing effect. That was very particularly true in the case of the First World War, which had risen to an unprecedented level of absurdity, and which had also been, if one compared, as one could not help doing, the suffering of the private soldiers in the trenches and the profits of the ones who had stayed behind, quite stunningly immoral. So, quite logically, it had been followed by a mediocre, cynical and spineless generation – and above all a generation that was small in number; beginning in 1935, in France, the birth rate had even fallen below the death rate. The exact opposite had happened in the 1950s, and even in fact in the 1940s, while the war was still raging, and that could only be explained, Bruno had said, as Paul remembered, by the ideological, political and moral character of the Second World War: however bloody it might have been, the fight against Nazism had not been limited to the possession of territories, it had not been an absurd fight, and the generation that had triumphed over Hitler had done so with the clear conscience of fighting in the camp of Good. The Second World War had thus been not only the usual kind of foreign war, but also in a sense a civil war, in which one was fighting not for ordinary patriotic interests, but in the name of a certain vision of the moral law. It could thus be compared to revolutions, in particular to the mother of all of them, the French Revolution, of which the Napoleonic wars had been merely a stupid extension. Nazism had been a revolutionary movement in its way, aiming at replacing the existing system of values, and had attacked all the other European countries not only to invade them, but also to regenerate their system of values; and, like the French Revolution according to de Maistre, there was no doubt

504

about its satanic origin. Thus the baby-boom generation, the one that had triumphed over Nazism, could in many respects be compared to the Romantic generation, the one that triumphed over the Revolution, Bruno thought, Paul remembered. It also corresponded to that very particular moment when, for the first time in world history, popular cultural production had proved to be aesthetically superior to the cultural production of the elite. Genre fiction, whether thrillers or sci-fi, was broadly superior, at that time, to the mainstream novel; the comic-book outclassed by far the creations of the official representatives of the visual arts; and most particularly, popular music made a mockery of subsidized attempts at 'experimental' music. In spite of everything, it had to be agreed that rock, that generation's greatest artistic phenomenon, did not quite attain the beauty of romantic poetry; but it shared its creativity, its energy, and also a kind of naivety. By defending God and the king against revolutionary atrocities, and appealing for a Catholic and royal restoration, by trying to restore the spirit of chivalry and the Middle Ages, the first Romantics, like the opponents of Nazism, were sure that they were in the camp of the Good. That was nowhere so clearly apparent, Bruno asserted, as in 'Rolla', a long narrative poem relating the suicide of a young man of nineteen, after a night of debauchery in the company of a fifteen-year-old prostitute, albeit one who was also good, almost saintly, and indeed *super good*, Musset was not the kind to play down such a thing, but the young man's despair was so intense that she was unable to bring him back to life, the poem was truly impressive, Bruno claimed, in similar scenes Dostoyevsky had done nothing better, and that despair was caused, Musset did more than suggest, by the destructive atheism of the previous generation.

Paul had then been completely stunned to see Bruno rising from his desk – it was already past midnight and the ministry was deserted – to declaim 'Rolla'. He had already been surprised by Bruno's interest in historical reflections, but he was flabbergasted to discover that he knew Musset's poems by heart; it wasn't part of the training of a *polytechnicien* or indeed an ENA alumnus; some politicians came out of Rue d'Ulm having studied literature, which might have explained the anomaly; but this was not true of Bruno.

> *I do not believe, O Christ, in your holy word.*
> *I arrived too late in too young a world.*
> *A century without hope gives birth to a century*
>   *without fear,*
> *The comets of our own have unpeopled the heavens.*

Later, in the last section of the poem, Musset raged directly at those he held to be responsible, and even in his eyes the main person responsible for that disaster of civilization. Like everyone else, he felt a certain indulgence for Rousseau; Bruno did not agree with him on that, in his eyes Rousseau was responsible for the Revolution, and even more than all the others, in his eyes Rousseau was *the last idiot* and *the worst bastard*, but either way Musset raged at the other *Enlightenment philosopher* in these words that had remained famous:

> *Do you sleep happily, Voltaire, does your hideous smile*
> *Still float above your fleshless bones?*
> *Your century was, they say, too young to read you;*
> *Ours should please you, and your men are born.*

After declaiming this verse Bruno had fallen silent, embarrassed, realizing that Paul was no longer really listening; during the months that followed he spoke only to address technical issues. However he did go on reading Raine, Renan, Toynbee and Spengler, although he had gradually become resigned to the idea that there would probably never be anyone that he could talk to about these questions. It was perhaps at that moment, Paul said, that Bruno had begun, without being fully aware of it, to entertain presidential ambitions. Save when one is dealing with a pure opportunistic demagogue like Jacques Chirac, or other local personalities on a lesser intellectual scale, who sometimes won certain elections by virtue of their popularity among the very stupid, and who thus saw themselves as being elevated much higher than their normal level via a regrettable fate, traditionally in France people expect a president of the Republic to have the bare minimum of a historical vision, to have thought a little bit about history, or at least about the history of France, and that was true of Bruno, something in him was already driving him, Paul continued, to become more than a minister. Prudence listened to him benevolently, relieved that he was thinking about something other than his illness, and something other than his last encounter with his father, which had, she sensed, contrary to what he himself said, slightly disappointed him. Dusk was gradually falling on the Place de la Liberté, and the waiters of the Retinton were starting to set up tables for dinner. In this establishment, the 'Beaujonomically inspired' cuisine was guided by the seasons and their ideas, taking flavours and quality as references; consequently, the prospectus stressed, the establishment was as suited to a meal between work colleagues as it was to a *girly* party or a romantic evening. They decided, however, to go straight back to Saint-Joseph to make love, this time once again as Aurélien and Maryse had done some months earlier. Contrary to all expectations, while he still felt very tired in the morning, Paul was now finding it almost easy to move. The bedside light cast a halo of warm and muted light. It was slow and progressive, sometimes with long tender and pornographic caresses. 'It's good to have done it here, I think,' Prudence said just before they went down to dinner.

At about nine o'clock the next day Paul was already sitting in the front of the car when he announced that he wanted to go and see his father again one last time; Prudence turned off the engine.

When he came back about ten minutes later he said nothing, and just sat down. She glanced at him, intrigued, but remained silent and only asked him about it later, just before they reached the motorway. He replied that no, he hadn't said anything else; he had merely settled for looking at him in silence.

5

All of his medical imagery tests were clustered together during the last week of September. The tests were carried out in the same laboratories as last time, early in the summer, but whether it was during the MRI or the PET scan, he had a sense that the doctors, the nurses and even the receptionist were treating him with a particular gravity and even a kind of pity, of unction, as if they were constantly aware that this time it was his survival that was at stake, as if he already carried death on his face. It was probably more than an impression, Paul said to himself – except in the case of the receptionist, maybe he was overstating things where she was concerned. Either way, the medical imagery tests proceeded in the planned order. That ended with an appointment on 1 October at the Gustave Roussy Institute, where Professor Bokobza would, under general anaesthetic, undertake a search for additional tumours – he would take advantage of the moment to carry out biopsies.

He came out of anaesthetic a little after 5 p.m., Prudence had said she was coming to get him at six and Professor Bokobza saw him for a few minutes; Paul just wanted to know what was going to happen next.

Quite a few things, in fact; there were plans to hold a multi-disciplinary consultation meeting, bringing together, aside from Bokobza himself, Drs Lebon and Lesage, whom he already knew – after a brief hesitation, he translated them into Dupond and

Dupont – along with Dr Nakkache as the attending physician, and other specialists: an anatomopathologist to decode the biopsies, a nuclear medic to help read the PET scan. Several interdisciplinary meetings of this kind would probably be necessary to draw up a proposal for treatment. In short, Western technological society was mobilizing all its resources – which were far from negligible, they remained the most significant in the non-Asiatic world – to ensure his survival.

'Then,' Bokobza concluded, 'we will come together once again to consider the prospects; that could be some time around 15 October. Where that's concerned, I wanted to ask you: you've come alone to your medical appointments, since the beginning?' He nodded.

'Forgive me for being indiscreet, but I think you have a partner, isn't that right, the one who's coming to pick you up shortly?' He nodded again.

'Obviously it's none of my business, but mightn't it be time to let her know? I mean really let her know? I understand your desire to protect her; but even so, at a certain stage, it's better to be completely transparent, don't you think?'

'It would be pretty hard for me to hide my death from her,' Paul muttered, and immediately afterwards, seeing Bokobza's face contorting with displeasure, he regretted his words; Bokobza was a decent guy, and the best European surgeon for cancer of the jaw, he was doing his best. He would come with Prudence, yes, he replied at last.

A light rain was falling on the morning of 15 October, and the traffic was light on the A6 motorway towards Villejuif. They found the meeting room quite easily, at the end of a long, bright corridor. Nakkache gave him a friendly grimace, Dupond and Dupont merely nodded mechanically; their faces were blank, but Nakkache by contrast seemed to want to talk, it was hard to interpret.

Prudence sat down beside Paul and have him a panicked glance – he had forgotten to tell her there would be so many doctors; he gripped her hand tightly. A few seconds later Bokobza made his entrance into the room, a large file under his arm, which he set down brusquely before sitting down – he seemed to be in a bad mood, as if he had been summoned against his will to a boring weekly meeting – then he cast a quick glance around the room before getting down to it. The results of the tests and analyses were surprising, he began, because they were contradictory. The radiotherapy had been outstandingly effective where the jaw was concerned, the tumour seemed to have been eradicated, so much so that surgical intervention now seemed almost pointless. Sadly the same could not be said of the tongue, on the contrary, the tumour had extended towards the base, so much so that as things stood it was difficult to see how it could be eradicated without total amputation. Paul understood at that moment, and a faint shiver ran through him; Dupond and Dupont understood as well and abruptly shrank in on themselves with perfect synchronization. What was more, Bokobza went on, the examinations had revealed an invasion of the supra-palatal zone. His glance swept around the table once again; this time no one seemed to have grasped the importance of the information. It was up to him to draw conclusions, in any case; that was his role. He breathed slowly, several times, before continuing: 'Under these conditions I don't see the possibility of a surgical option, the consequences of which would be extremely disfiguring, and would inevitably lead to an impaired way of life; it also seems unlikely that the patient, given his state of general exhaustion, could bear such a severe intervention.' This time Prudence understood, and she began to weep silently; the tears started flowing and she didn't even think of wiping them away, it was the first time that she had cracked, Paul said to himself, the first time since the beginning. He tried to take her hand again, but she huddled defensively in on herself. Over a minute's silence followed, everyone stared embarrassed at the table, not knowing how to resume, until Prudence raised her head, her crying having stopped. 'If I've understood correctly,' she said before turning towards Dupond, who stiffened as if she had slapped him, 'we're not planning on a new course of radiotherapy.' Looking beaten, he nodded before lowering his head again. Then she turned towards Bokobza, who humbly raised his head as well. 'A surgical intervention doesn't seem possible either,' she went on. He hesitated, unable to bear her gaze, seemed to want to say something, then pulled a face in agreement before lowering his head in turn. 'So,' Prudence turned gently towards Dupont, 'we're left with you.' He sat there silently, shrunk in on himself, for about thirty seconds, before replying in a low voice: 'That is the case, madam.' That wasn't everything, he was aware of that, but it took him another thirty seconds before he went on: 'Chemotherapy, as I pointed out to Monsieur Raison, will bring him relief, but under no circumstances will it cure him. As to immunotherapy, to be honest, we know nothing, or very little. Surprising remissions have been observed in certain cancers, of the lung in particular; but unfortunately as things stand never in the case of ENT cancers like your husband's.' His eyes remained fixed on Prudence, decent and regretful; then she started weeping again, even more gently.

It was time to conclude, Paul said to himself, and he rose pointedly to his feet, it was his meeting after all, he was to some degree its *master of ceremonies*; Bokobza got up too and hurried towards him, he must have intended to talk to him, but stopped short and instead gripped his arm tightly. That's strange, Paul said to himself, he must have been in this situation dozens of times and he still can't bring himself to do it. Even more surprisingly, the surgeon turned towards Prudence to ask if she had come by car, if she felt able to drive back, otherwise it would be very easy to arrange for her to be driven. Typical male, Paul said to himself; men need to exercise technical competence, to assume some kind of technical control over a situation that is defeating them. But after some hesitation Prudence replied that she did feel able to drive back, in fact it would do her good.

Once they got home they didn't talk about it at all, and Paul felt quite good after two glasses of Grand Marnier, he didn't have the strength to move but it was nice to see Prudence coming and going, between the depths of the bedroom and the bathroom, wearing a short T-shirt and hot pants, she really looked like Trinity, he said to himself, but Trinity in hot pants, Trinity in a different film. Either way, he hadn't been mistaken, she had shown courage; Trinity had also shown courage when Neo was dying, but that hadn't taken as long.

6

When he woke up the next day he was pleased to see that she had thought of putting on a G-string, and was lying flat on her belly across the blanket. He tried to reach out towards her bottom, but could barely raise his arm a few centimetres, his limbs felt terribly heavy, and he fell back on the bed with a sigh. She woke up and rested an arm on his chest.

'Not feeling great? Are you tired this morning? Will you be able to get up?'

'I'll be OK, I think.'

Sure enough, he got up half an hour later and walked without difficulty, he managed to get downstairs unaided, these abrupt variations were really disconcerting. Still, it would be best to bring the bed down into the living room. Two removal men came that same evening and set it up downstairs, by the picture window.

It was strange to be living in the same room, which was likely to remind them of the years of their youth, their first shared home on Rue des Feuillantines. It was Prudence's studio flat, which was nicer than his. Her taste had always been better, she was also the one who had found their apartment, the one where he was now going to die, the view over the Parc de Bercy was still pretty even with winter on the way. Now and again he made the effort to get out of bed to sit on the sofa, he was still a bit worried about bedsores, while he also knew that he probably wouldn't have time to develop them. But most often he remained calm, and sat back on a pile of pillows. Sometimes Prudence went upstairs, or went out to do the shopping, but as a rule she was there, he could watch after her when she went in and out of the kitchen corner or the bathroom. Sometimes she was wearing only a G-string, she would be happy to the end to show her breasts and her bottom, proud to the end to make him hard. He himself was startled that he was still getting hard, it was unexpected and even absurd, senseless, grotesque, in a sense even unworthy, it didn't correspond in any way to his idea of dying, it was clearly an instance of the species pursuing its own goals, quite independent of those of individuals; but it also allowed them a little tenderness, perhaps it even encouraged it, which meant that from another angle sexual pleasure could come to seem like a simple extension of tenderness. What was now entirely unimportant, on the other hand, was language: they spent whole days without exchanging a word.

Early the next morning he went for one last appointment with Dupont. He hadn't been back to his office since the start of his treatment, almost three months before. This time he sat down in the Voltaire armchair opposite his desk; the place was even more charming than he remembered, he had forgotten that the window looked out on a little garden. Admittedly it would be difficult to die in springtime, but that wasn't going to happen to him, he wasn't even sure that he could hold out till winter, it was a question worth asking.

Moments of intense exhaustion, then; Dupont looked surprised. He did not have anaemia, though; it was one of the classic secondary effects, but no, not in his case, his blood levels were almost normal. 'You realize you've lost even more weight?' he asked him at last. His tumour was using a lot of energy, and it was going to consume more and more, he would have to force himself to eat more. His attacks of nausea had also calmed down, hadn't they?

Paul said they had. 'Well there we are,' Dupont said, 'you eat more and things should get better, you won't get those waves of exhaustion any more.' Paul was already eating a lot, he objected, and high-calorie foodstuffs at that: whole platefuls of mashed potato drenched in melted butter, fatty cheeses like Brillat-Savarin and mascarpone; and yet, as the scales confirmed, he had lost another two kilos since the last visit.

Dupont called an internal number within the hospital, and asked for a scan to be taken immediately. Coming back from the examination room Paul waited for a few minutes, Dupont had received another patient in the meantime; then Dupont brought him in and asked him to take a seat, glanced at the scan and set it back down. It was probably time, he said at last, to ask his wife to stay with him at all times. He was going to give him the number of a nursing service, one that could be on-site in two minutes.

He picked up his file again and sighed, he looked tired and visibly forced himself to concentrate on certain pages before continuing in a confident voice: 'In terms of treatment I'm not going to change anything as regards immunology and chemo; except it's possible that the tumour will become more painful in the weeks to come; I'm going to put you on morphine. To be taken orally, a mixture of Sevredol and Skenan should be enough; normally we shouldn't expect the pain to be too violent. I don't think we need to install a morphine pump at home; but obviously if I'm wrong, if it doesn't work, you're to call me immediately. Also, your wife loves you.' He fell silent all of a sudden, his face froze and he blushed, it was worrying and almost disturbing, this austere, bald man in his fifties starting to blush.

'I'm really sorry,' he stammered, 'I didn't mean to say that, obviously your private life has nothing at all to do with me.'

'No, go on,' Paul said very gently, 'tell me, I'm not particularly attached to having a private life.'

'Well . . .' Dupont hesitated for another few seconds before going on. 'Unfortunately, I've had the opportunity to acquire a certain amount of experience in this area. The people we put on morphine, the ones who come through, that is, are very enthusiastic about it. Not only has morphine allowed them to conquer their pain, it has introduced them to a universe of harmony, peace and happiness. Generally speaking, when radiotherapy has failed, and surgery has been deemed impossible, or worse, when it has produced bad results, and they're in a very miserable state, they are put on palliative care, because it's simply impossible to keep them at home. There is a lot of talk of solidarity and family members, but you know that most of the time old people die alone. They're divorced, or they've never been married; they never had children, or they've lost touch with them. Getting old on your own really isn't much fun; but dying alone is worse than anything. 'There is one exception, however; rich people who are able to afford a nurse at home. From that moment I don't see the point of putting them in palliative care, they would prescribe the same things as me, and everyone prefers to die at home, it's a universal desire. In such cases I am the last medical point of contact. I can say that I've seen a lot of rich people die, and believe me, at those times, being rich doesn't count for much. Personally I never hesitate to prescribe a morphine pump; when they want it, they just have to press a button to inject themselves with a dose of morphine and find themselves at peace with the world again, enveloped in a halo of sweetness, it's like a shot of artificial love that they can take at will.

'And then,' he continued after hesitating once again, 'there are people who are loved to their very last days, the ones who have had a happy marriage, for example. That's a long way from the norm, believe me. In that case, I think the morphine pump is surplus to requirements – love is sufficient; I also think I remember that you don't like injections that much.'

Paul nodded. There were a few framed photographs on Dupont's desk. Even though he couldn't see them, he was suddenly certain that they were family photographs, and that Dupont himself had a happy family life.

He had one last question, and it was his turn to hesitate slightly. Still, he wanted to know. 'In your view,' he asked finally, 'how long have I got?'

'Ah . . . I could reply that I have no idea, but it wouldn't be completely true; I do have an approximate idea, however. It might be a few weeks, or a few months; keeping to the statistics, I would say between one and two months.

'So I should die towards the end of the autumn? Before the days start getting longer again?'

'Probably, yes.'

Before Paul left his office, Dupont said again that they wouldn't abandon immunotherapy, that there was still one last hope; Paul nodded indifferently, aware that they each believed it pretty much to the same degree. Then Dupont ushered him out with an expression of vague rancour on his face; he shook his hand before closing his office door.

7

Paul had always liked the time of year when the days really did get shorter, that sense of a blanket rising gradually over your face to enfold you in its darkness. Prudence waited by the entrance to the hospital; he just told her that they were going to put him on morphine. She shivered slightly, but didn't react more than that. She knew what it meant; she had been expecting it.

They bought the Sevredol and the Skenan on the way home. Paul started taking them the following morning, and the pain eased immediately. The most striking thing over the course of the following two weeks was the absence of change. Death would soon come, however, there could no longer be any doubt about it; but he had a sense that he still couldn't approach it, not beyond a certain limit. It was as if he was constantly walking on the brink of a precipice, and losing his balance from time to time. At first he dreaded the horribly drawn-out nature of the fall, the terror that took his breath away the closer he came to the crash. Then he had a sense of experiencing the impact, his internal organs exploding, his shattered bones piercing his skin, his skull transformed into a puddle of brain and blood; but none of that was death, it was the anticipation of the suffering that would, it seemed to him, inevitably precede it. Death in itself might be the following stage, the one when the migratory birds peck and devour one's flesh, starting with the eyeballs and finishing with the marrow from the broken bones; but it never went as far as that, he recovered at the last minute and started walking along the precipice again.

Prudence got better and better and recognizing those phases, down to the change in his breathing, without his even needing to mention it. Her first thought was to take him in her arms, but it always took him some time to calm down. One afternoon, when he seemed particularly anxious, she ran her mouth all the way down his belly, unbuttoning his pyjamas. It probably wouldn't work, he said to her; she pouted doubtfully and undid the last button. To his great surprise he got hard almost immediately, and in less than five minutes his thoughts of death had evaporated; it was unlikely, obscene and absurd, but that was how it was. They even went on making love, only in the position with Prudence on top; the side position had become too difficult. Sometimes she stayed facing him, looking him straight in the eyes, and blew him with love, and also with despair; sometimes she turned round to show him the movements of her bottom; both positions brought them the same degree of pleasure.

In a week it would be 31 October, the day of the Sabbath of Samhain according to the Wiccan calendar, but Prudence didn't seem to be thinking about that at all. That day, however, was intended to commemorate the year just past, indeed the whole of his life, and to prepare for his death. It was a bit disappointing, Paul reflected, that her religion wasn't more of a help to her on these issues; normally that was what a religion was for. Added to that, most of the time, was a variable amount of waffle about various subjects, sometimes introducing risible limitations or commandments, but still, the true subject of every religion was death, one's own and that of other people, and it was regrettable, Paul thought to himself, that Wicca wasn't more help to her.

It did help her, though, more than he suspected, but he didn't realize that until the 31st, the day of Samhain itself, or All Hallows' Eve according to the Catholic calendar. It was a Sunday, and late that morning Prudence suggested that they go for a stroll in the forest. They had lunch at the Bistrot du Château, in Compiègne, and surprisingly they were able to sit on the terrace, since it was very mild for the season; then they made for the nearby national forest. It was huge, and everything in it was huge, starting with the trees, oaks or beech, he couldn't remember, but their splendid, widely spaced trunks, several metres thick, rose to the sky.

Broad, perfectly straight avenues crossed at right angles and stretched to infinity, covered with scarlet and golden leaves, which naturally conjured death, but this time it was a peaceful death, the kind one associates with a long sleep. For Christians, the elect would awaken into the dazzling light of the new Jerusalem, but essentially Paul had no desire to gaze upon the glory of the Eternal, what he really wanted to do was sleep, perhaps sometimes with moments of being half-awake, a few seconds, not more, long enough to rest his hand on the beloved body lying next to his. They could perfectly easily have got lost that day, all the more so since the forest was deserted, which was even surprising for a Sunday after-noon. They walked for a long time, and he didn't feel tired in the slightest. The autumn leaves were strewn in increasingly dense, increasingly beautiful layers on the avenues, and at last the couple stopped to sit down under a tree. It wasn't yet quite the season of death, Paul said to himself, the colours around them were too warm, too dazzling, they would have to wait for the leaves to grow dull and mix with mud, and also for it to get colder, so that early in the morning they would begin to feel, in the atmosphere, the first hints of the long winter freeze, but that would all happen in a few weeks, a few days, and that would really be the moment for farewells. His thoughts had taken him far beyond the present real-ity, and without thinking he asked Prudence: 'Will you be ready, my darling?'

Without showing any surprise she turned towards him, nodded and smiled; it was a strange smile, and Paul felt a wave of dizziness when she went on, in a gentle voice, 'Don't worry, my love; you won't have to wait very long for me.' He wondered for a moment if she wasn't delirious, then all of a sudden he understood. It had been a long time since they had talked about reincarnation, but she must still have believed in it, and even believed in it more than ever. He perfectly remembered the fundamental idea as Prudence had summed it up to him: at the moment of death, his soul would float for a while in an undefined space before joining a new body. His life had been free of either particularly distinctive merits or demerits, he had had few opportunities to do either a great deal of good or a great deal of harm, and in spiritual terms his position hadn't changed much; he would probably be reborn with the features of a human being, and the foetus would in all likelihood be masculine. Some time after that the same thing would happen to Prudence, except that she would be reborn as a woman, since the laws of karma in general took into account the division of the universe between the two principles. Then they would find each other again; this new incarnation would not only be a new chance for their individual spiritual development, but also for that of their love. They would recognize one another at a deep level, and they would love each other again, although they would not remember their previous lives; only a minority of sannyâsin, according to certain authors, managed to remember their previous incarnations, and Prudence even doubted that. If, however, their incarnation brought them together again, one autumn day, in the national forest of Compiègne, they would probably feel that strange frisson known as *déjà-vu*.

That would be repeated over successive incarnations, perhaps dozens of them, before they could leave the cycle of samsaric existence to pass to the other shore, that of illumination, of timeless fusion with the soul of the world, of nirvana. A path so long and arduous that it was in fact preferable to travel it as a couple. Prudence had rested her head against his and seemed to be dreaming, no longer thinking about anything, in any case; night would be falling soon, and it was starting to get a bit cold. She huddled against him, then asked him or said to him, he wasn't sure if it was a question: 'We weren't really made for living, were we?' It was a sad thought, and he felt that she was ready to cry. Perhaps the world definitely existed in reality, Paul said to himself, perhaps there was no place for them in a reality that they had only passed through with frightened incomprehension. But they had been lucky, very lucky. For most people that journey, from start to finish, was a lonely one.

'I don't think it was in our power to change things,' he said at last. There was an icy gust of wind and he drew her more tightly to him.

'No, my darling.' She looked him in the eyes, half-smiling, but some tears glittered on her face. 'We would have needed wonderful lies.'

Acknowledgements

I f some facts are incorrect, that is not down only to possible mistakes on my part, but more particularly to deliberate distortions of reality. After all, this is a novel, reality is only the raw material. One also needs be somewhat familiar with it, which is why I have tried to do some research, particularly in the medical field.

First of all I should like to thank Professor Xavier Ducrocq, head of the neurology service at CHR Metz-Thionville. It is worrying that the human brain is so difficult to understand, that we are so alien to ourselves; at any rate, if my knowledge in this field has advanced at all, it is down to him.

He then introduced me to people who were more directly involved in caring for people with disabilities. First Dr Bernard Jeanblanc, who ran (I imagine he has now retired) a PVS/MCS near Strasbourg; in my story, the equivalent character would be Dr Leroux.

If I write that Astrid Nielsen is brave in looking after her husband, she isn't going to be happy; so I won't write that, but I should like to take the opportunity to tell her something else, which I didn't dare to say to her out loud: it was when coming back at night, to Thionville station, after the day I had spent with her, that I felt for the first time, whatever happened, that I had to finish this novel.

Later in the novel, a lot of information was supplied to me by Maître Julien Lauter, notary; information and words; certain terms used by Hervé in his 'turn as a notary' are included, I acknowledge, not least for fun.

The ending of the book introduces another pathology that led me towards other specialists. My thanks first of all to the dentist Fanny Henry; the medical journey described in this book should begin in the surgery of just such a conscientious dentist.

Among the physicians that I consult regularly, the ENT doctor Alain Corré is certainly the one who has inherited the heaviest responsibilities; given the life I've lived, an ENT cancer would arguably have served me right. Aside from some precious medical information, it is to him that I owe the 'Vietnam-style' expression used by Dr Nakkache; thanks for that.

As my character's condition deteriorates, it was Dr Corré who sent me to Dr Sylvain Benzakin, ENT surgeon, head of oncology at the Rothschild Foundation Hospital in Paris. Rereading our email exchange, I am startled by the precision of his replies, and more particularly by the time he must have devoted to them, even though he had many other things to be doing.

Essentially, French writers should be less reluctant to gather information; many people love their work, and enjoy explaining it to the uninitiated. By chance I have reached a positive conclusion; it's time for me to stop.

Credits

A NOTE ABOUT THE AUTHOR

Michel Houellebecq is a French novelist, poet, and literary critic. His novels include the international bestsellers *Serotonin, Submission, The Elementary Particles,* and *The Map and the Territory,* which won the 2010 Prix Goncourt. He lives in France.

A NOTE ABOUT THE TRANSLATOR

Shaun Whiteside is a Northern Irish translator of French, Dutch, German, and Italian literature. He has translated many works of nonfiction and novels, including *Manituana* and *Altai,* by Wu Ming; *The Weekend,* by Bernhard Schlink; *Serotonin,* by Michel Houellebecq; and *Magdalena the Sinner,* by Lilian Faschinger, which won the Schlegel-Tieck Prize for German translation in 1997.